A HERO'S HEART

Books by Mellyora Ashley:

**A LADY IN DISGUISE
A HERO'S HEART**

Georgian Sister Series:

**FORBIDDEN ARABELLE, Book 1
PURSUING GENEVIEVE, Book 2**

**THE ROGUE AND THE ROSE
THE INSTANT HEIRESS**

A HERO'S HEART

By Mellyora Ashley

A Regency Romance Novel

England, 1815

Coachman
Publications

All characters in this book are purely fictional and have no existence outside the imagination of the author except for the following historical characters portrayed or mentioned:

Beau Brummell
Lord Alvanley
Countess Lieven
Mrs. Drummond Burrell
King George III
Jane Bell

These hymns are sung in part:

"Come, Thou Long-Expected Jesus" by Charles Wesley, 1745

"O God, Our Help in Ages Past" by Isaac Watts, 1719

Dedication

I dedicate this book to you, **Tricia** and **Derek,** with thanks galore for special research material, and for the wonderful times we've shared, first as pen friends, and now as true friends.

Acknowledgements

Thank you, **Margaret**, for sending me fascinating facts about Robin Hood's Bay before I had the joy of exploring it myself.

Thank you ever so much, **Robert**, for taking us there.

As always, **Glen**, thank you for everything you do for me with love.

Author's Note

Before I went to Robin Hood's Bay in Yorkshire, an English pen friend sent me research material about that historic smuggling town. When I finally stood there gazing at the red-roofed cluster that tumbles down to the sea, I felt a thrill of recognition. The ancient Robin Hood's Bay Hotel room that we slept in was the one I had given the Duke of Rowan in this story, so it meant a lot to me to actually stay there.

Was I ever surprised to wake in the night to the sound of rushing waves! I leapt up, dashed to the window, and in the moonlight I saw that the tide had risen so high that there was no beach left. I felt like I was on the bow of a ship. Fast white waves came whooshing, whooshing, and slamming the wall of the hotel with force, straight below me! It was the perfect setting for Rowan as he investigated the evil doings of the smugglers, all within a stone's throw of this dramatic old bedchamber.

This is a wholesome love story—adventurous, humorous, mysterious, and romantic. It accords respect toward God, and is free of offensive words.

Our hero and heroine fight the villains and villainesses with hearty courage, high morals, and imagination. It is my pleasure to lead you through their great troubles and on to their joyful victory.

Mellyora Ashley

Chapters

A HERO'S HEART

By Mellyora Ashley

England, 1815

CHAPTER 1

Escape

The Duke of Rowan drove his coach around a bend in the York road, fuming over his naïveté. He still marveled in disbelief that such a new widow had pursued him, and so blatantly. "She actually tried to trap me!" he shouted. "And it's only been a week since her husband's funeral!"

At his outburst, the white ears of his four horses pricked with interest, so he called, "Don't ever be too nice and sympathetic to a female. She's liable to spring a trap on you!"

As birds chirped their dawn chorus in the golden summer light, Rowan drove more slowly, enjoying the smell of plowed earth one minute, and freshly-scythed hay the next. Sheep lay in clusters, munching grass within dry-stone walls. Rowan relaxed the reins and left the road to his lead horse. He took a deep breath and let his eyes follow the fields undulating away like a crazy quilt.

His vehicle suddenly careened and jerked as his horses halted. He was startled to see a flash of corn silk hair as a boy made a flying leap from a stone wall right into the horses' path. Rowan yanked the reins to a full stop just in time.

The long-legged scamp didn't even pause at the

near collision, but hurtled over a stile and landed in a field of harvested hay. He ran and dove into the pyramid base of a large hayrick in such a twinkling that Rowan would have been hard-pressed to prove that there had been a boy at all but for the bits of chaff that fluttered to the ground.

The Duke removed the black top hat which had shifted to the bridge of his nose. This was revolting. His perfectly-fitted hats never moved from his head. Staring at the oily inside band with revulsion, he spat, "Whose is this?"

It had been four in the morning when he slipped out of Lady Flitcroft's country house. By the weak flickering of the hall sconce, he had seen this hat silhouetted on the table and assumed it was his. Was he not the only male guest there? Or had Her Ladyship lured another fool into her lair? His mind filled with disgust, most of it directed at himself. He had never felt so ridiculous as when he had had to lock his chamber door in self-defense.

He jabbed his fingers through his dark hair, sending it rippling like waves full of life. He couldn't properly drive without a hat so he crammed the surrogate back on.

Lincoln Minster in the distance appeared in dark magnificence against the blinding sun, and in the opposite direction, tangerine light bathed Belvoir Castle's round and square towers, giving its windows a liquid sheen.

While thus distracted by the views, he gave his team office to walk on, but almost instantly his vehicle lurched to a stop so violently that he landed with an elbow on the tufted seat. "What next!" he expelled. He shoved the hat up off his eyebrows.

A burly farmer had plunged over the stone wall, and dodged Rowan's rearing leader. With eyes bulging to and fro, the man bellowed into cupped hands, "You won't get away with it, you ruttin' swine!" He waved a hairy fist in the direction of the hay field.

Watching this ludicrous performance, Rowan grabbed his coach horn and blasted the notes for *Clear the Road!*

The rustic jumped in alarm and stared wildly at him.

The Duke strove for patience. "Can you not see a team on the road and keep yourself out of harm's way? My horses could have trampled you."

The heavily-breathing farmer sat onto a stone of the stile, popped up, rubbed his backside, and gaped at the impressive gentleman whose dark brows formed such a scowl. After noting the crest on the carriage door, he tugged his forelock. Turning away, his complexion turned purple with renewed venom as he roared, "That wily cracker! Which way'd 'ee go?"

Rowan replaced each leather ribbon between the fingers of his driving hand and dropped the man a look from under bored eyelids.

This produced a clumsy bow. "Sir! Did ye happen to see where that scoundrel made off to?"

"A scoundrel, is it?" Rowan threw a pointed look toward the hillock of oaks a good hike beyond the hay field.

Following this glance, light dawned on the farmer. He muttered a form of gratitude and clambered his bulging rear over the stile. Rowan watched his dirty cap until it disappeared into a thick plantation of trees.

A volcanic commotion erupted at the base of the nearby hayrick. The blond youth emerged through flying chaff and bounded toward the Duke's carriage.

Seeing the terrified eyes, Rowan, for the third time in a few yards, halted his team.

The lad darted into the shade of his carriage. With a suspicion of tears and a smear of dirt, his face was earnest as he fixed large blue-gray eyes on the Duke. "Oh, thank you, Sir! You were prime! So clever to send him wrong without actually lying." The voice flowed out in a cultured stream and created a strange combination with the ill-cut hair and tattered coat.

Rowan saw alertness in every line of the youth's body, from the long, tightly-clasped fingers to the awestruck face. "You find it remarkable that a stranger should aid you?" he inquired.

"It's remarkable in the extreme, Sir. Why did you do such a thing for me?"

"That is a question I am hard-put to answer." Rowan smiled, realizing it was sympathy for the pursued which had prompted him. He had just left a similar situation. "Suppose you regale me with an explanation of your, ah, evasion."

"I would like to explain after what you did, Sir, but it would take too long, and," he shot a worried glance toward the woods, "I haven't the time. I must escape while I can. I am obliged to you forever and ever, though. Oh! Could you please whip up these fabulous horses so I can run in your shade up the hill, just until I'm past that gibbet? If Ramsbottom sees me, he'll hang me with the remains of that grave robber."

With the ghost of a grin, Rowan gave an acquiescent nod and swiveled his reins. His wheels and their long shadows spiraled up the slope, concealing the thin form in the floppy gray pantaloons.

Rowan saw determination in the smudged face beneath the pale hair which cut a silky swath across the smooth forehead. He wondered how the sensitive-looking lad came to be called a *ruttin' swine* by that ham-fisted farmer. How incongruous. With a friendly grin, the Duke said, "You seem awfully young to be pursued by such raging accusations. How old are you?"

"Er, sixteen, Sir."

* * *

Beneath the ill-fitting tweedy coat, her heart pumped guiltily. She had just told a lie. She was not sixteen; she was eighteen. Warily, she glanced up at him.

The smile he flashed at her was rather shy, yet showed such kind camaraderie that she felt a rush of warmth toward him. Though desperate to make her dash, Patricia Ravenscar marveled. A stranger was doing a great kindness for her. What a Godsend! As she jogged up the hill beside the whirling silver spokes, she ventured another look at him. Her heart skipped. She had never seen such a magnificently handsome man in her life, or in her dreams.

At the crest of the wold, the sunrise lit with clarity the gruesome gibbet. Its latest victim dangled there, chains clanking, rags a-flutter. A nauseating stench seared into their nostrils. Tricia covered her nose with her hands and made a gagging sound. The gentleman groped inside his dark coat and pulled out a handkerchief.

"Come," he commanded, leaning down and thrusting his handkerchief at her, "up with me, Vagabond, away from that grisly sight. Shall we make our escape together?"

Above the fresh-smelling linen of the handkerchief, Tricia's eyes widened in surprise on her benefactor. "You astodish me!" she said with her nose pinched inside the pristine linen. "I am so grateful for your offer, Sir. Even a mile's ride will help me immensely."

"Quickly, then!" Rowan lifted his whip and moved aside.

She vaulted up to the driving box in a boyish manner and took the seat next to him.

From the spinney came a roar. Swiveling their heads, they saw Farmer Ramsbottom advancing on them in fury, head leading, limbs pumping, fists redoubled.

"He's seen me up here, and he's horn-mad!" cried Tricia.

The Duke's lips curved with a smile for the challenge. With a harmless sing of the whip, he urged his snowy team of grays up Gunnerby Hill.

"How far do you wish to remove?" he shouted.

"To the end of the earth!" she returned with feeling.

"Ha! Likewise. But aren't you that man's relation?" The Duke observed her face, then gave a short laugh. "Surely not."

Tricia shook her head and wished he wouldn't look at her too closely. She tried to make her hair fall more over her eyes. She resumed a more masculine attitude, legs and elbows apart, bracing herself against the jolts.

With manes slapping, the frenzied team pounded the road to Grantham, rattling them over every stone and pit without compunction. The Duke slackened their pace eventually and said, "Now we can hear each other talk without bellowing. Tell me, does that farmer employ you? Do you have to return when his wrath has cooled?"

Words poured out of Tricia. "I *was* in his employ, but for a fortnight only, amen! He is harsh and mean and accusatory. Were I to forfeit a month's wages, nothing would induce me to return."

"Indeed?" The gentleman's dark eyebrows lifted as he considered this.

"He'd likely track me down in Grantham, so you can let me off on Witham Common, Sir. The Black Bull Inn is there. I heard that coaches go through constantly as it's the border of the counties so maybe I could—"

"Excuse me." He tapped her forearm. "I thought you wanted to remove as far as possible from that embodiment of tyranny." He motioned backward.

Startled by his touch, she gobbled out, "Oh, I do, I do."

"Well, if you don't find a ride in my conveyance too lowering or my company too agèd," he grinned disarmingly, showing nice teeth, "why not ride farther with me?"

"Could I ride to Stamford, perhaps?"

"Why, yes; but why not to London? There your taskmaster would have a rare task to find you. You could acquire a more suitable post. Pages, for instance, are in great demand with the Little Season upon us."

"Pages?" Tricia let go her grip as they swung around an S in the road. Teetering off balance, she snatched for the nearest stationary object, which was the stranger's arm encased in a coat of midnight blue wool with black corduroy cuffs.

"Is there pardon for me?" she wailed as she righted herself. "Let me clean your sleeve at the first stop. You took me aback about pages, Sir."

* * *

The lad's pathetic reaction touched Rowan. "Did you aspire to a more exalted position, then? You appear a bit young to be a first or even a second footman. My opinion, of course; my steward hires them."

"No," said his passenger, "quite the opposite. I was but the scullery boy for Farmer Ramsbottom. He engaged me to pluck the hens and dress them, water the sheep and swine, empty the slops—oh, pardons by the thousands—I mean, throw out the—you know—and carry hot water to his daughter's chamber."

Just as he reached the verge of laughter, Rowan saw that the boy looked uncomfortable.

"That's how I came into Ramsbottom's bad graces."

Rowan shouted with glee. "It's beyond my capability to envision Ramsbottom with graces of any description!"

The lad dimpled and picked hay out of his waistcoat. "You see, his daughter, Matilda, is his prize pullet. I was to set the water bucket in the hall, rap on her door, and skedaddle. This morning, her door hung ajar. I thought she had sneaked out to see her flame behind the grove again, so I put the water inside. Otherwise, if Ramsbottom came by and saw the water untouched, he'd storm in, bellow at her for lying abed, and discover she wasn't even in. He would be furious to know she meets the ostler on the sly."

"So what happened?"

"Miss Matilda wasn't out. She was in."

"And?"

The words dragged from the lad's lips. "She was making her toilette."

"You don't say! At what stage was she?"

"Hardly a scrap on."

"Zounds! Were you thrilled?" His eyes danced teasingly over the youth.

In the driest manner possible, he returned, "Utterly thrilled, I assure you."

"Did she screech in mock horror?" Rowan warmed to the subject. "Did she accuse you of vile designs upon her person?"

"Some such garble. How did you know?"

Rowan tightened his jaw. A flood of memories deluged him, ruining his light-hearted mood. "Though she often has no virtue to speak of," he said woodenly, "the woman of our day makes a great show of modesty. It is modesty that goes no deeper than her sweetest expression." He glanced at the listening boy. "If you had professed admiration for the ruffled Matilda, you would have found in her an astonishing reversal of character, my lad."

"Sir! That is ridiculous. *Me* professing admiration for Matilda!"

"Granted, you are rather young. But the day will come."

Rowan guided his horses carefully through a flock of sheep that streamed across the road, their varied bleats creating a chorus, from lamb sopranos to the grumpy bass protests of an old ram.

* * *

Tricia was grateful for the diversion. Goodness, but her story had been embarrassing. Glancing at the powerfully-built gentleman driving the slowing white horses so skillfully, she wanted to know more about him. She did not want to talk any more about herself, for it was difficult to continue in what she hoped was a boyish manner. She took a breath of courage and said, "You seem to know a great deal about women. Would it be experience, Sir?"

A cynical expression flickered over the handsome face. "Yes."

Tricia's heart sank. He looked so kind and strong and appealing. He *was* those things. He had to be. She could not bear to think of him having tangled with women who were not good for him.

He said confidingly, "I told you that I, too, am escaping."

That surprised her. "From what, Sir?"

"Black gloves. She is a widow. A very showy one, whose late husband was a friend of mine. I thought his bereft spouse needed advice about her estate when she begged me to come to Yorkshire. When I got to her country place, lo and behold, she displayed the same licentious tendencies I have found lodging in the hearts of every woman I have known save my mother."

"You mean she tried to—"

He frowned and nodded. "Seduce me, of all things. I could not believe that a lady could be so callous a se'nnight after her husband's funeral. And he was so honorable."

Tricia could find no words of optimism to offer.

He continued, "I don't know any women who are truly caring or giving unless it suits them to appear so; and then it is likely done in order to snap up a man for his wealth or his title. They are then far too possessive when they think they've hooked you. They are free to be yours every moment you have, and every moment you haven't."

Tricia's pulses pounded. Was this really what well-born women were like? She must hear more. "Can you explain that to me, who am not a gentleman and never likely to be one, Sir?"

"The women in my social sphere fling their virtue at a man so that he—" Reigning his horses to a walk, he abandoned that sentence in seeming frustration, then plunged on with a slight flush, "so that I, at least, have no pleasure in their company. It's all I can do to avoid the whole lot."

"Is that so difficult?" asked Tricia, understanding with all her heart why women would fling themselves at him.

He looked at her skeptically. "The trouble is, if I do avoid all eligible women, I will never fulfill my duty."

"Which is?"

"To find a wife. I owe this country an heir. I've been told that it is past time." He turned his face away.

Tricia gripped the iron side bar. How she hated the thought of his finding a woman and fulfilling his goal. "Too bad!" was all she could emit from her whirling mind.

They clattered over a bridge. "Yes, and I cannot forever poke my nose into perfumed drawing rooms, looking over new crops of debutantes," he muttered. "I hate it most of the time. I am not a social person, and young schoolroom misses do not interest me in the least."

Tricia ventured, "You certainly deserve a good wife who will love you and make you happy." In a careful way, she added, "*If* such a lady exists. Have you . . . prayed about it, Sir?"

Between the thick lashes, his eyes held a sad smile. "Believe me, I have."

Feeling a bit choked by this tale of woe, Tricia crossed her arms and sat with her legs apart like a boy, and said with a tremor in her voice, "I will pray for you, too." She wanted, with all her being, to help him.

It was terrible. He was obviously someone of rank, though if he did not introduce himself to one as lowly as she pretended to be, she would never know who he was. Not that it mattered, she mused depressingly. She would soon be out of his life forever. But she would carry with her the memory of a wonderful, noble man who had cared enough to save her, even while he anguished over this quandary of his own.

As they jounced over cobblestones behind the clopping horses, he said with a regretful smile, "Now, my lad, I will not allow you to tax your mind over my problems."

Tricia protested, "But Sir, the telling of your dilemma cast my own terror right out of my mind!"

"Well, that does give me a certain satisfaction." He smiled sidewise at her.

Ten minutes later, he veered his team toward a medieval inn in Grantham. "Want something to eat? I will stop for a half hour and then push on."

"Pardon me, Sir, but who *are* you?" asked Tricia, bursting with curiosity. Etiquette or not, she had to know.

"I am sorry! I was born Lucas Beaufort." He reached out and shook Tricia's slim hand with genial warmth. "However," he added wryly as he jumped down from the driver's seat of his coach, "I am known first and foremost by Society's daughters as the Duke of Rowan." He looked at her from under long eyelashes. "It's as though there are trumpets and a banner proclaiming *Duke, Duke!* wherever I go."

Tricia laughed. Then, jolted by the news, she tugged her coat into some semblance of order. "Your Grace!" she breathed reverently. In confusion, she stood on the driving box and managed a jerky bow to the Duke down on the cobbles.

"See what I mean? Halt such ridiculous posturing

and hop down here. What is your name?"

Self-consciously, Tricia smoothed her slippery hair and found a hay stalk behind her ear. "Patrick Raven, Your Grace."

"It's a pleasure to know you, Master Raven," the Duke said, and smiled. "Let's see what the Angel Inn has in store for hungering travelers."

Joy coursed through Tricia as she followed the Duke into the beautiful old inn. She would be cared for and taken all the way to London! –by a Duke of the Realm! This was astounding indeed.

But the whole thing was extremely risky. She feared that at any moment he would see through her guise.

She eyed his well-cut dark blue coat as she followed him. Catching up to him and clearing her throat for attention, she offered to clean the sleeve she had grabbed with her dirty hands. He laughingly waved her off.

They passed through a stone arch into a cobbled courtyard swarming with yapping hounds and mounted hunters about to depart across the fields. The Duke's sweating horses were half unhitched and the empty coach was already receiving deluges of water from ostlers with buckets and rags.

Tricia asked the Duke, "Do you always travel alone? Don't you employ a groom or a driver?"

Rowan grinned over his shoulder as they climbed a staircase into an aroma of roasting ham and baked apples. "I left them all in the clutches of the widow," he said behind his glove. "It was more vital that I depart without a disturbance than to take my servants."

Tricia grinned at him with great approval. "That

was extremely wise, Your Grace!"

He raised his black eyebrows at her and grinned. As they rounded a landing hung with hunting scenes, he continued, "At the first village, I sent a message to my men to follow, and to see that my six tired teams get the best of care along the way to London. I had no choice but to slip out when I did if I wanted body and soul intact." He leaned toward Tricia. "Between you and me and that stout door, Lady Flitcroft planned to have me for breakfast in her boudoir, I believe."

Tricia rolled her eyes in horror, and then clapped a hand to her mouth in a boyish guffaw.

They entered a populated dining room with an uneven oak floor and white walls crisscrossed by brown half-timbering. The Duke pointed his whip at a linen-covered table to which a maid promptly ushered them.

Tricia, aware of her dirt, begged to be excused, and asked the maid where the privy was, and where she could wash. When she had streaked away from the water spout in as clean a state as she could achieve in two minutes, a steaming hunk of ham had arrived on the Duke's table. It was surrounded by dishes of kippers, sausages, apple tarts, a blue pitcher of milk, and a flowered pot of tea. Feeling a growl of starvation, she stood uncertainly in the archway, eyeing the basket of golden buns the maid added to the table.

Rowan beckoned her, so Tricia hesitantly approached him. "That's better," he said, looking approvingly at her clean face. She wished she could have stayed dirty, for she had looked much more like a boy then. But she had wet her hair down so it was plastered low across her brow, hiding one of her graceful eyebrows. How she hoped she could pull off her disguise and get to London. He would never take her with him if he knew she was a female.

The Duke motioned to the seat opposite.

"Oh no, Your Grace, that would not be right."

"What's not right?"

"Me, at table with you, a Duke."

Rowan gave an exasperated scowl which made him look fiercely attractive. "Do you think I like doing everything alone? Sit there! You'll be grateful bye-and-bye for some sustenance. We'll travel at a clipping pace. We won't stop at every other town for food and drink, old boy; just what we can procure while changing horses."

"Your Grace, I did not expect to." Tricia gratefully bit into a delicious-smelling hot-cross bun dripping with melted butter. Someone had poured her a hot cup of tea already. She added milk and sugar, and sighed. How long had it been since she had drunk such strong and tasty tea? Not since she had been forced to leave Soaring Gables, her home on the cliff top.

The Duke of Rowan laid his well-shaped hand on the table, catching her attention. He whispered, brown eyes earnest, "I will not allow Lady Flitcroft to catch up with me, so we must eat quickly and fly. And we don't want that gentle farmer to get his hulking fists on you by any means."

"Oh no, Your Grace," Tricia returned with jocularity, eyes brimming with laughter.

Rowan wiped the curving corner of his mouth with his napkin and said, "A priority when we reach

London will be to procure a new suit of clothes for you. That coat is slightly ... inelegant."

Tricia giggled. "I know I could use much better clothes than this, but *you* must not think of it, Your Grace. Thank you for your goodness in taking me to London, but beyond that I cannot take from you."

"But," Rowan objected, fork and knife lifted helplessly, "I need a page. I had hoped—"

Tricia sat up ramrod stiff. This was unbelievable. No! "That *I* might be your page?"

The Duke lounged back in his seat. She noted the dignity in every angle of his form as he cocked his head and asked, "Well, Master Raven? What are your qualifications?"

Despite the giddy way her heart jumped, Tricia's mind exploded with possibilities. He was offering her a chance to serve *him*, of all people. Surely he would be kind to her, would live in a nice house, and would feed her. He would keep her far away from not only Ramsbottom but more importantly, her lecherous guardian, Lord Kilver. Though qualms over her gender disguise niggled at her, she knew she had nowhere else to go.

"Qualifications?" she repeated, sitting up straight. This was worth her best effort. "Well, I read and write, do mathematics, know geography and history and all the usual subjects. And I ... well, I notice things." She felt silly as she blurted out even dafter words. "I can open and close doors without a sound." She glanced at her listener to see how she was doing.

The Duke cut his kipper with no change of expression, his dark lashes lowered. "Do continue."

What else would a page do? "I can dash up and down hills without tiring—for messages, you know—and I can shine boots and blanch a shirt and starch a cravat should your valet be indisposed. I can follow directions to the letter," she added brightly, "because I remember things." She could not think of anything else she dared to add. If she rabbited on about needlework and playing the pianoforte, that would be fatal.

The Duke was staring. "You starch cravats? How does that go with hauling water and plucking hens? Never tell me Farmer What's-His-Bottom ever dons a starched cravat!"

Tricia laughed. "Ramsbottom? Never! It was for my brother that I . . . starched them."

The Duke looked curious. "Who is your brother?"

Tricia squirmed at her unwise disclosure but said simply, "My brother, David, was my hero."

Rowan forked his apple tart and asked, "He was? What did he do?"

She had to be cautious. Her chance to go on with the Duke of Rowan could dissolve if she told too much. "David worked in a Customs Office until he could buy himself a commission in the Army. Then he went to war against Napoleon."

"So that's why he's your hero?"

She nodded. "He came home from the Peninsula once. When he walked through the door, I was amazed at how impressive he had grown. He was very confident, and strong besides. It was during that furlough that he taught me the correct method of caring for his uniform. I gladly acted his servant. As I said, he was my hero, and he meant so much to me." She dropped her eyelids over her prickling eyes. Oh no, she better not cry.

"Was?" repeated Rowan gently.

"David has gone to his eternal glory. It was at Toulouse where he died, on Easter Sunday 1814."

"That is too bad! Did you know that eight thousand were killed in that battle, counting both sides? Wellington described it as *a very severe affair*. Is that why you wear David's trousers?"

Tricia fingered the gray pantaloons striped down the sides in red. "Yes. He was a gunner in the Horse Artillery."

"Be proud of what he did."

"I am proud of him. I know he was a good soldier. I'm glad to know that *death hath no victory*. Jesus won that final victory for him, and for us, too. That calms me every time I miss David."

The Duke's eyes misted. "Yes," he said. "That's good. He never has to worry about anything again."

When he rose abruptly, Tricia perceived the emotion in him. The courageous set of his manly shoulders as he strolled toward the alcove told her that his struggles were great. Hastily, she wiped her lips on a napkin and followed him.

They stood in an oriel overhanging the front of the inn. Rowan said, looking down at the street through the diamond-paned window, "My coach has not yet appeared." He pulled out an ivory pipe and measured a sweet, pungent tobacco into it.

"Where," asked Patrick, sniffing, "did you get that tobacco? My father had some of that exact aroma."

"He did?" Rowan looked surprised as he clicked the box shut. "This was a gift from the woman whose tentacles I narrowly escaped. The box is made in Turkey, and it makes me wonder." He thrust the oval of red and blue enamel at her.

"It could have slipped in duty-free," whispered Tricia so others wouldn't hear. "Smuggling is common in Robin Hood's Bay, for example."

"How do you know?"

"I lived there."

"Oh? With whom?"

"My father and my mother." Too late, she knew she should have halted her flow of reckless information.

"Tell me about your parents." They both looked down through the window at the crimson and black hunters' coats as they streamed out on clattering horses to the cacophony of hunting horns and baying dogs.

Not wanting to comply, Tricia hedged. "Your Grace, why would you be interested in my parents?"

He disengaged the pipe from his lips. "Since you are to become a member of my household, I should know something about you. Well, Patrick? Shouldn't I?"

"Yes, you're right." She leaned a shoulder against the stone wall and let her stressful gaze follow the intricate molding which curved to a rotunda inside the oriel. "You see, they died, too."

The Duke made sounds of concern. "How did that happen?"

"They were rowed out in a fisher coble to board a ship in Robin Hood's Bay. A gale blew up before they got there." Tricia turned to the curtain and said wanly, her throat tight, "That was eight months ago."

"My word! You *are* bereft. Do you have anyone else?"

Defiantly she crossed her arms over her chest. "No! I do not."

"*No* relations or friends?"

"None worth speaking of." She lifted her chin and looked out between the wavy leaded panes.

"You do now," Rowan said kindly, touching her shoulder. "Come on, let's be off."

Tricia stiffened and pointed through the glass, her heart seized with terror. "He's here!"

"Who?"

"Riding the neighbor's horse! It's Farmer Ramsbottom! Oh, where can I hide?"

"Wait!" The Duke pushed her behind his shoulder. Peeking around him, she watched as Ramsbottom dismounted heavily, shouting queries at every ostler in sight. Rowan cracked open a pane and they heard, "—'ee kidnapped me servant, and I intend to snatch that rascal back! Have you seen 'im, have you seen 'im, I say? Get back here and answer me, or I'll 'ave yer hide!"

The Duke gave a nice whistle to their maid, who had glided toward a table of passengers just in off the *Stamford Regent*. She colored prettily and curtseyed to him.

"Miss, please run and order the Rowan coach and team parked under this oriel right now. Have a ladder on it. Tell ostlers to set the ladder to this window as if to make a repair and to hold it *very steady*." He gave her a silver crown. "The important thing is speed, miss."

The maid rushed off, saying, "Yes, Sir!"

To Tricia, he said, "Pull that long curtain around you. We don't want Ramsbottom to catch sight of you and spoil everyone's breakfast."

Surrounded by the dusty-smelling velvet, Tricia felt her pulses pounding in her temples. Inching her eye closer, she watched the magenta-faced Ramsbottom stalk through the arch below, heading for the courtyard.

The seconds ticked dangerously by as the Duke returned with his whip and gloves, thrusting them into his waistcoat. He pushed wide the window and swung his boot over the sill. "Well done, isn't it?" He flicked her curtain apart and grinned at her. "My horses appear below me. Ah yes, I behold my coach and a ladder. Patrick, follow me as soon as I am down. I'll whistle when I'm ready for you." He lowered himself until nothing remained but his whitened fingernails.

Tricia moved out of her hiding place and cast a nervous look back. People had suspended their eating, their eyes glued to the spectacle of a slap-up gentleman taking his leave from the oriel window.

The stairs creaked heavily. The bulbous nose of Farmer Ramsbottom appeared in profile in the doorway.

Tricia gasped. Scrambling in terror, she flung a leg over the windowsill.

With a roar of triumph, Ramsbottom lunged after her, weaving between the tables and the outraged people.

Tricia's legs dangled in air as she desperately tried to connect with the ladder. She found it with such a hard kick that it toppled and crashed to the ground. Her arms began to shake as she hung in mid-air, and she knew she would fall.

She heard a whistle. "Let go!" shouted Rowan from below. "*Now*, Patrick!"

Ramsbottom, mad as fire, grabbed for her.

She fell in a blur and landed with a *woof* into the Duke's arms.

"Thank you, lads!" Rowan thrust her down into the seat and flung coins at the grinning ostlers. Grabbing the reins, he sent his fresh horses leaping forward. The clatter of their ringing horseshoes drowned out in part the rampage of threats issuing from the lungs of Ramsbottom.

Tricia slid a palm across her damp forehead and cast an ashen look back. "Whew! Was that ever close! I could smell his breath!" She gripped the side iron and turned to the Duke. "How can I *ever* thank you?"

The Duke's eyes twinkled mysteriously. "You'll see," he said.

CHAPTER 2

A Page in the Duke's Life

Their pace was nothing less than hair-raising. Rowan drove his horses with enthusiasm through half-a-dozen villages and towns where the first hue-and-cry would be sounded, and people would, compelled by the law, take up the chase.

The Duke passed every coach on the road and fast tandems and curricles as well, with his clarion *Clear the Road* trumpet calls. He only slowed to pay turnpike charges and to take fresh horses that waited for him in snug inns every twenty miles or so.

He asked Patrick questions about his life with the irate farmer. Tricia kept her explanations short and truthful, telling only that she had been forced to find work after her parents died. Focusing on speed, the Duke did not press for details.

Tricia felt dazed by her good fortune. Her elation, however, was marred by stabs of unease, especially as they passed Alconbury and the intersecting dykes, yawners, and gullies which sent forth evil, steaming vapors. What potential quandaries lay ahead of her?

The Duke drove in comparative silence, only speaking when the noise of carriage wheels and horses' hoofs diminished. Their air of companionship remained. Once, he asked, "Have you been ill or starved of late, or are you just naturally thin?"

Tricia grinned. "I am naturally a beanpole."

"Ah well, your muscles will come into their own before long. I will see to it that you are stuffed with good food. You'll need to be hardy and hale in order to keep up with my demanding life." He lifted a forefinger sagely. "Not that I doubt your quickness of foot or mind, for it was those talents which brought about our meeting."

Smiling at him despite her unease, Tricia's heart swelled toward this generous nobleman. She sent thanks to God, who had so interestingly provided deliverance.

But fear redoubled when they rolled into the streets of Huntingdon and the Duke pointed. "Here is our inn for the night."

The George Inn was a thatched, balconied establishment with a painted sign of the white-wigged first King George of a century ago. Rowan drove his third relay of horses through the arch, and relinquished them to ostlers who ran from various doors around the courtyard.

"Come," said Rowan to Tricia as he lowered himself from the coach with a relieved and weary air. "It's a good time to claim a room while the sun is still high. The next few hours will, no doubt, bring hoards of travelers."

Tricia's mouth went dry. Evading his eyes, she said, "Your Grace, I can sleep in the stable."

"You will not sleep anywhere of the sort. You are my page now, remember? I need you with me, especially since I've left all my other servants behind."

She panicked. Trying to keep up with his long-legged stride, she said, "But you are a Duke and I am only a—"

He smiled, lifting a delaying finger to the eager landlord ready to serve him at the counter. "Patrick, I won't have any more of such lowering talk," he said quietly to her. "And don't call me Duke," he whispered, "for I am going to register under another name so the likes of our pursuers won't know we're here."

"Oh, I'm sorry," she said, and dropped her lashes.

Her heart thumped with new alarm as he told the innkeeper, "I'll take your best room, with an extra bed for my man, if you please."

Extra bed? For her, his *man?* She stood rooted to the spot, powerless to stop the proceedings unless she blurted out that she was a female. Though she was on tenterhooks, she simply could not do that. He had asked her to be his page. She had accepted, for she had never in her life wanted anything so much as to stay near and serve him. True, she needed to get far away from Robin Hood's Bay, Lord Kilver, and Ramsbottom, but those reasons had diminished in importance now.

Of course, she could just dash away into the town. She backed out of the door and eyed the end of the stable yard for an exit.

Rowan finished signing the register, cleared his throat, and lifted a quizzical eyebrow at her.

Running her eyes over his manly figure in the shapely coat and slightly dusty top boots, her heart melted. The quick, white smile that told her he had secured a room took her breath away. Tricia knew she was a goner. There was no way that she could leave him. After spending only hours with this Duke, she knew that he needed someone. It had to be someone he could talk to, someone who would support him. He had a distasteful goal, but a goal born of duty. His moral convictions were difficult to adhere to in his high position in Society, she could see that. The Duke of Rowan needed someone to encourage him to hold to the parameters he clung to by his conscience.

Perhaps he had no one at all. It sounded as though he had been treated disgracefully by more than one woman. Thinking this over and blinking back the threat of tears prickling her eyes, Tricia knew that she could never abandon him without knowing that he was in good hands for life.

When they entered the room at the end of the first floor corridor, she looked around in dismay. Though she searched the bathing room, the water closet, and the dressing room, there was only the one grand tester bed.

The two men were discussing meal arrangements when Tricia caught the Duke's attention. She made a querying look, pointed at herself, and made a mime of sleeping with her head on her flat, praying hands. She was, indeed, praying that she would not be told to lie with him since there was no other bed.

Rowan turned to the innkeeper. "The extra cot for my page is where?"

The rotund man gestured at the grand Hepplewhite bed with its valance and counterpane of red and white roses and green leaves.

The man leaned down and pulled a carved wood panel. Out from under the bed rolled a trundle bed on squeaky wheels.

Tricia laid her hand on her heart.

The Duke saw her do it. After the man left, he said, "You were afraid you would have to sleep on the floor?"

"No, I wasn't, Your Grace. I said I could sleep in the stable, so the floor would have been warmer, but a bed is the best of all. I am grateful."

He grinned accusingly. "Aw, I bet you were terrified you would have to sleep with me."

Tricia flushed. "Aw, Your Grace. It's because I—" She thought quickly. "I kick. I am not worthy to sleep with you, anyway—never! But if I had to, I would surely give you bruises."

"I see." The Duke was chuckling as he added, "Come on, old bruiser, why don't you roll that trundle bed to wherever you'd like it?"

In the dressing room, she brushed her corn silk hair into its boyish style some minutes later and stared fearfully at her large eyes in the mirror. This chamber was surely the best at The George, and she was grateful it had this separate dressing room where she could at least undress in private, but how on earth would she handle staying with the Duke all night?

She couldn't possibly undress. This blue and gray tweed coat would have to do to keep her disguised. She undid the buttons, and, turning her face to the corner while keeping her foot firmly against the bottom of the door, she loosened the cotton band under her shirt. She retied it snugger below her breasts to give herself a flatter-looking chest, and did the same to the bosom bandeau. She buttoned the coat and then cleaned the dust from her shoes.

Peering critically into the spotted looking glass, she practiced her masculine attitude. When she lifted her chin, she could lower her eyelids a bit and they didn't look so innocent. The charcoal she had lightly stroked under her eyebrows to lessen their arch needed replenishing, certainly by morning. She would have to search for some in the fireplace. She must remember not to relax her mouth, or its feminine curves could give her away. After all, she would be face-to-face with the Duke all evening, she supposed.

With a resolve to remember her male mannerisms, she forced herself to open the door.

"Ah. Patrick. Do you mind helping me out of these?" Lounged in the depths of a red brocade chair, the Duke gestured to his Wellington boots.

She gladly knelt before his outstretched legs and gripped the leather of his heel and toe. She pulled and strained, and pulled again, grinning, while Rowan eased his foot out from his end. With a determined tug on her part, the boot came loose and propelled her backward onto her bottom. A set of brass fire irons clattered out of their stand and toppled onto her. Feeling utterly gawky, she warded them off with an elbow while keeping Rowan's boot away from the dirty poker.

Rowan was laughing silently. Tricia met his eyes and thought perhaps it was good she had bungled it. She looked more convincing as the gangly youth. My, but he was breathtakingly handsome laughing.

Standing in one stocking foot, the Duke picked up the coal shovel, the poker, and the broom from various parts of her person. "You do put effort into your job, I must say."

She felt embarrassed, but grinned up at him. "I'm sorry, Your Grace. I'll try to be more refined in the future."

"Nonsense. You are doing fine. Let's get this other boot off. It's new, and it's killing me."

Looking behind her, she made sure a hassock would stop her backward momentum, and with a laughing tug-of-war between them, the deed was done. Hefting the tall boots, she said, "I'll clean them right away," and made a beeline for the dressing room.

"Patrick, I did not hire you for such menial tasks, thank you just the same. Put them outside the door for the boot boy."

She did so, almost reluctant to relinquish the new-smelling leather with the white tops which had molded to Rowan's long legs. But what were her duties to be, then? She clicked the door shut, apprehensively crossed the carpet, and looked at him.

He was unbuttoning his black double-breasted waistcoat. Still wearing his coat, he lifted his arms and said, "It seems easiest if I shed both of these at once. My valet would be horrified. Give a tug to this cuff, will you?"

Trying to steady her skipping heart, Tricia gripped the black corduroy cuff and eased the well-tailored coat off the Duke's right shoulder. She helped him pull the waistcoat off of his white wrinkled shirt sleeve. She moved behind him to remove the garments from his other arm. Her heart was racing. She had never undressed a man before, and he was powerful and warm, and she found that touching his clothes made her unable to think straight.

When she gathered up the fine wool and silk waistcoat, she made her way hastily into the dressing room. She hung the garments side by side on two pegs. Irrepressibly, she buried her nose into the coat again, surrounding herself with the wonder of how good he was to her. Catching sight of her enraptured face in the mirror, she immediately felt foolish, and pulled herself into order.

Emerging, Tricia saw that he looked despondent, sitting in a chair, just gazing at the evening sky outside the glinting leaded window.

She asked, "Is that woman well behind you now, Your Grace?"

He did not look disgruntled by her question. "She had better be. What an unfortunate entanglement." He leaned and looked at the brightening sunset above the inn's chimneys. "Sometimes I miss my mother. She passed on to Heaven, as yours did; but for twenty years, she taught me in such a good way. She brought me up *in the nurture and admonition of the Lord,* as the Bible says. So did my father, who died two years before she did, leaving me with the reins of the family when I was eighteen."

"That's young, Your Grace."

"Yes." Rowan fingered his jaw. "Mother told me something on her deathbed that my heart says is important, but I find very difficult to manifest in my situation."

Tricia, listening intently, asked, "What is that, Your Grace?"

"Fetch my Bible, will you please? It's in that shaving case I smuggled along with me this morning."

Tricia unstrapped it, and found the soft leather Bible wrapped in a clean shirt.

* * *

When Rowan had flicked pages, he said, "Here it is, Second Corinthians." He read, "Be ye not unequally yoked together with unbelievers, for what fellowship hath righteousness with unrighteousness? And what communion hath light with darkness? That is what she quoted to me."

"Was she was warning you not to marry an unbelieving woman?"

"Not only that, but also to avoid them completely so I wouldn't be tempted."

"Haven't you been able to avoid them, Your Grace?" The youth looked so concerned.

Rowan lifted his hands helplessly. "They're forever around."

With an irrepressible smile, Patrick quipped, "I can see why they'd follow you like filings to a magnet."

"Oh, get out of here!" Rowan said, amused.

"But I believe you're stronger than that, Your Grace," asserted his page. "You have the Word to back you up. But if you want it to be one of *my* duties," he offered, "I will shoo away any scheming women who try to accost you."

The Duke mirthfully retorted, "That would be something to see." The sudden freedom to talk compelled Rowan to continue his cleansing tirade. "What I have found is that every pleasant or attractive woman I've known still lacks something. Faith, spirit, belief in the same God I do, not the god of mammon or greed, or whatever it may be. There's *got* to be a woman out there who's beautiful both inside and out, wouldn't you think?" In frustration, he passed a hand through his hair. "He said it is not good for man to be alone. I pray God has created the right woman just for me."

"I hope so, too, Your Grace."

* * *

She prayed to God about it.

Respectfully, she returned his Bible to his satchel. She lifted out his clean shirt and laid it out for morning, spreading out the wide gathered sleeves across a chair back, and smoothing out the wrinkles in front as best she could.

From across the room, she heard low humming. Rowan was strolling around in stocking feet, buff-colored pantaloons, and his creased white shirt. He was unwinding his cravat, around and around, from beneath his high collar. When he got it loose, he tossed it to her.

"Since my trunk got left behind, will you find the laundress and discover if that cravat can be pressed by morning?"

"I can press it," Tricia said quickly, needing to escape the room before he asked her to strip him of his nether garments.

"I know you said you are *able*," he said, locking brown eyes with her indulgently, "but this place has a good laundry, and you need rest as well as I do. On your way back up, will you tell the innkeeper that we are ready for dinner? We will have it here since we're in hiding."

"Yes, Your Grace." As she left, he was kneading his shoulders and wincing. It looked as if he was sore from driving so long.

After they had sat companionably at the trestle table in front of the hearth to partake of their dinner, Tricia's safer duties progressed to uncertain challenges.

Rowan stretched and said, "Ho boy, I think I'll have an early night. Will you assist me?"

"Certainly, but how, Your Grace?"

Rowan took out his shirt buttons and dropped them, one by one, onto her palm. When she held seven jet buttons, the Duke pulled his shirt over his head and threw it on the bed. He shed his undervest next.

She didn't know where to look, and tried to keep her face impassive even though blood was thumping through her temples. It was nearly impossible when her eyelashes flickered and she saw his bare arms and chest, well muscled and smooth.

There came a knock on the door. She literally ran to open it, dizzy with relief. She glanced back. "Your Grace?" she said, her eyes feasting on his broad shoulders and narrow waist silhouetted against the lace-covered window. "I'll just peek in case it's someone pursuing us. In fact, I think I should go down to the carriage house and make sure the crests on your coach doors are covered up so that if our pursuers come, they won't see them." With the need to leave the room, Tricia thought this was a brilliant excuse.

"What a good plan. But don't go if you see Ramsbottom, and don't be long. Give me four knocks, will you?" He stepped around the corner into the bath and out of sight from the door.

Tricia opened it to admit a roly-poly maid who barged past her, nearly knocking her aside. The girl looked around the room eagerly, didn't see the Duke, so she grabbed napkins and clanked dishes until she rumbled the cart out across the carpet and down the uneven gallery to the dumbwaiter with petulant force.

Tricia slipped down the black walnut stairs, scanned carefully the noisy public room, and avoided it. She sped to the courtyard, walking in the shadows and averting her face. She found the Duke's carriage at the far end of the mews.

When she had explained to an ostler that she needed a tarpaulin to keep the dust off the coach, he produced one. Together they covered it up. She gave it extra tugs to make sure the ducal crest was hidden.

Tricia slid her hand along the smooth, old banister on her way up the outside stairwell of the inn. What else could she do to absent herself from the bedchamber until the Duke was asleep? She could think of nothing, but delayed awhile until she heard voices approaching.

She dashed to their chamber door. There was no answer to her four knocks, even after the second time, so she went in. She heard water sluicing in the bathroom.

Towels! Earlier, the laundress had given her a stack of fresh ones just off the line. She had folded them and stowed them in the dressing room. She retrieved the two largest ones and waited nervously outside the bathroom door.

The splashing stopped. "Patrick?" The lever moved and Rowan's wet head emerged, comically coming almost nose to nose with her. "A towel?"

She lifted them up to shoulder level and turned her head away.

"Thank you. I rejoice to have acquired a page with foresight."

Tricia grinned roguishly, eyed his wet black hair and eyelashes, and snapped the door shut. When he came out, he wore long, skin-hugging drawers and a long nightshirt.

Not knowing what to do, she queried, "What else do you require, Your Grace?"

Walking by, smelling of slightly aromatic soap, he smiled down at her a bit sheepishly. "Could you knead the tight muscles in my neck and shoulders, by any chance?"

Tricia gulped.

"I often need a massage after hours of driving. You see, I tend to roll my shoulders forward, keeping my horses in line, and end up in pain after a long trip. Who can sit up straight on a driving seat, anyway?"

She took a deep breath. "Who, indeed?"

He quipped, "I would rather ask you than that rigorous maid who brought my hot water."

Tricia giggled, picturing with what relish that damsel would attack him.

"If you don't mind?" the Duke asked courteously.

Taking resolve, Tricia replied as Patrick, "Of course I'll do it, Your Grace, if you would find my poor services adequate."

"Thank you. Anything will help."

Rowan threw aside the red and white counterpane to reveal the snowy sheets underneath. When he relaxed his bare chest onto a pillow, he looked up at her sidewise. I've thought of another portion in Proverbs."

"Oh?"

"I should read it. If you'll light that candle and hand me my Bible again, I'll see if I can find it."

That delayed her immediate quandary of how to massage him and where. She lit the bedside taper with the one already burning on the candelabrum, and brought his Bible into his outstretched hand.

"Thanks."

As he rose onto his elbows and flipped pages, Tricia waited, looking over his shoulder.

"Hmm," he said, searching. *"To deliver thee from the way of the evil man."* There's a different part I was looking for . . ."

Tricia suddenly felt joyful that she was here, helping this wonderful Duke whom God had sent to deliver *her* from the ways of two evil men.

The Duke said slowly, "Here it is: *To deliver from the strange woman, even from the stranger which flattereth with her words."* Rowan laid down the book and closed his eyes. "That's what she does."

Tricia said nothing. Her heart was pleading with God to deliver this dear man from each and every strange woman who *dared* to flatter him for her own gain.

The Duke pulled off his nightshirt. "You may begin any time, Patrick. I would appreciate it."

Her heart was catapulting, and she hoped he didn't notice anything odd in her behavior. "Yes, Your Grace." She hesitantly put a knee on the bed next to him and dropped her palms onto his warm shoulders. A tremor went through her. Noting his waiting attitude, she knew she had to be bold. He needed her help because he was in pain from his mad dash through all those miles, as much on her account as for his own. She needed to help him the very best she could. She asked conversationally, "How many miles do you suppose you drove today?"

"Well, we're fifty-eight miles from London here at Huntingdon, so that makes it well over sixty that I covered today. I have never pushed it that far before, but I've never had such motivation, either."

As she continued to massage him, he gave a glad groan. She gained a little confidence when he told her she had found the afflicted spot in his left side, resultant from his driving arm's concentrated effort all day. She gave his smooth, splendid back a good working over, and then stopped.

In a relaxed voice, he asked, "Are you tired?"

"No, just resting. I think you might need your neck rubbed, too, Your Grace."

"Yes," he sighed.

She moved her hands gently inward from his shoulders to the base of his neck. His short waves of dark brown hair were so tempting to touch. She had never had such an impossible task playing Patrick as now when her feminine fingers worked his smooth skin and eased his aches away.

As she worked gently up his neck, Tricia saw his dark lashes close. "That will do. Thank you so much."

* * *

The massage was so wonderful that he could have enjoyed it for an hour. It was odd, though, and somewhat alarming to Rowan when Patrick moved up his neck at his request. The slim thumbs making small circles up both sides of his spine and into his hairline sent chills and thrills coursing through him.

Unaccustomed to sharing his most private thoughts, the Duke nevertheless felt that this sprite-like, conscientious boy was a great comfort to have near. He was an attentive listener, filled with willingness to help. He even made him laugh.

What was the difference between his valet's massages and this youth's? He didn't know exactly, but there was a vast difference. It felt like young Patrick's hands were powered by caring consideration and a selfless wish to help. He thanked him, and knew no more.

* * *

Tricia moved carefully off the bed. Gradually his breathing became even, and he slept.

Dear Lord, she prayed, please watch over him. Bless him well for what he has done for me. In Jesus' name, amen.

After covering his shoulders softly with the sheet, she tiptoed to her own little bed across the room.

CHAPTER 3

Kicking Against the Pricks

Tricia woke first, gripping an unfamiliar quilt. Her disoriented mind whirled. Had Lord Kilver locked her in another chamber? Blinking herself awake, she recalled in great relief that she had escaped from him. Farmer Ramsbottom's bellow jumped to her mind. Was she late to water the sheep and swine? She sat up so fast that her bed moved. It was on wheels.

At sight of the curtained bed across the room, with its white and red roses on the bedclothes, it all came back to her. Her heart swelled in more joy than she had felt upon rising for many months.

She stood and peeked at the dark head lying on the pillow. He lay exactly as she had left him last night. He must have had a peaceful rest.

* * *

The Duke and his page bowled over the arches of Huntingdon Bridge at half past six. As Tricia watched the horses' dark tails swishing across their shiny black rumps, Rowan asked, "By the way, I've been meaning to ask you: what was your father's occupation?"

"He . . . worked around ships," was all she dared to say.

The Duke waited for more, but she craned to see the ducks on the river.

In a kind voice, he asked, "You aren't destitute, are you?"

A flame kindled in her as she thought of Lord Kilver. "I may as well be. My aunt's husband took over all my possessions!"

The Duke looked askance at her. "You have an uncle?"

"No. He's *not* my uncle. He is married to my aunt. He kept me locked in his house, so there was nothing I could do but sneak away one night." She had never been able to tell anyone this.

The whites of Rowan's eyes widened in alarm.

Tricia lifted her chin and said, "I found work on my own."

"You did. But life can be frightful for a youth alone in a merciless world."

"Yes. But God has shown mercy to me. He saw me through two squalid weeks with Ramsbottom, which fed me and kept me alive, but now that servitude is over."

As the breeze strengthened, Rowan shoved his ill-fitting hat down over his thick, wavy hair again and asked, "Shouldn't I write your aunt's husband to let him know that you're with me?"

"No! Never! Please!" Tricia breathed deeply several times to control her emotion. "He does not care for my good, so there is absolutely no reason to contact him. I never, *ever* want to see that man again! I do not want him to know where I am, or that I'm even alive."

The Duke gave her quite a look and said, "Well! That's that, then." He slowed to traverse a village green full of people, who stared curiously at them. Tricia and the Duke were again on the look-out for anyone pursuing them

The day brought them little chance for any more probing dialogue. Tricia relaxed a little, and focused on the various views, the animals in the meadows, the groves of trees and fields being harvested, and the houses, shops, and market squares in the towns and villages.

The jolting miles blurred into evening. Stars dotted the sky by the thousands when she covered her first yawn and blinked her damp eyes. She saw the faint lights of a sprawling metropolis ahead.

"That's too long of a trip for two days," said the Duke, kneading the back of his neck, "but you have persevered, old boy." He slapped Patrick's knee. "As my page, you will do well, I have no doubt."

Tricia thanked him, and coaxed dried mud out of her stockings. "I want to be the best page you've ever had," she said humbly.

"That's easy." Rowan grinned. "I've never had one before." Tricia was touched that he had created a position just for her, thinking she was a lad leading a wretched, low life.

As they rolled down off the plains of Hampstead Heath and approached the smokestacks and chimneys of north London, Rowan slowed his coach to a crawl in the endless stream of lit and unlit carriages, carts, wagons, and men on horseback. Patrick had never seen so much activity, especially after nightfall. Rarely had there been wheeled traffic in Robin Hood's Bay, for the streets were too steep. Here horseshoes clopped, wheels rumbled, and people with different accents shouted from every direction.

By lantern light, Rowan's eyes showed his fatigue, although he kept his sixth team of horses well in control. At last he drew into a street of gracious houses on the left which faced an expanse of trees and grass rolling away to the right. "Here's Park Lane and home, Patrick. You look ready to meet the dustman."

She gazed in awe at the curvy-fronted white mansion before which they halted. "Is this your home?"

"Yes."

An immense white neoclassical façade soared upward, gracing a curved bow window rising three stories. Massive columns bore Corinthian capitals carved with acanthus leaves. Suspended delicate ironwork lanterns lit their fluting in scalloped elegance. Through the long windows, gilt frames gleamed on colorful paintings and silver fringe sparkled down the edges of the curtains. Tricia sighed. "To think that you spend your days in such a magnificent house, Your Grace!"

The Duke smiled as he jumped down. "I'm glad you like it. Come on in."

When her shabby shoes struck the pavement, her heart sank in dismay. "Your Grace, I am too filthy to step foot on those marble steps. Please, is there a back door?"

"Come on, Patrick, it doesn't matter tonight."

The long white doors swung inward, and people appeared within. Tricia heard running footsteps behind a tall, middle-aged man who presented his balding head in a bow. "Welcome home, Your Grace."

Rowan flashed him a tired smile as he walked across the threshold. "Thanks, Aldwin." Removing the hat from his head, Rowan tossed it to the first of four tall footmen who stood resplendent in dark teal and silver livery. He said, "Burn that, Stefan."

Tricia, following, saw him thrust his riding whip and gloves at the second footman, and if that were not enough to raise her awe, the Duke spread out his arms and two more footmen grasped his cuffs and whisked off the travel-worn coat simultaneously, with practiced ease.

Tricia was impressed. Now *this* was a fairy-tale existence. What a privilege it was to stand in this hall of chandeliers to witness such service rendered to her Duke. Then she felt jealousy. She would rather be the one taking care of him.

His Grace had crossed the spacious hall to the foot of a circular white staircase with black balustrades. He turned back to Aldwin, the butler. "Will you ask Mrs. Pollard to take Patrick Raven under her wing right away? We've driven fast and hard for two days, so have her feed him and introduce him to a pillow."

"Right away, Your Grace."

From their various positions, all four footmen turned to stare at Tricia.

"Good night, Patrick." The Duke gave Tricia a little salute as he ascended.

"Good night, Your Grace. And *thank* you," she breathed soulfully as she watched her Duke disappear at the top of the stairs.

It felt strange to see him in his own realm. She

felt alien now, and so far from home. But what did it matter if she were far from home? Where *was* home anymore? If this mansion and this mighty Peer were to be her sanctuary and salvation from worldly evils, she would take it as a great blessing for which she could only give thanks to God on high.

She was left standing tentatively on the expanse of white marble as Aldwin disappeared importantly down a corridor. The footmen, all over six feet, gave the new page dubious glances, making her feel intimidated.

The good-looking, dark one stowed the Duke's whip in a cabinet and threw the driving gloves to another, large-nosed footman. He passed them, as well as Rowan's coat, to a maid and said, "Clean these."

Tricia cleared her throat and asked, "Can we exchange names now?"

The first footman, ignoring her, held the top hat aloft and examined it. "Did he say to burn this?"

"Why don't you keep it, Stefan?" ventured a pale, freckled, blond footman. "You have a big enough head." To Tricia, he said, "I'm Theodore."

Stefan set the top hat on his flame-red hair and posed with his chin cocked before a mirror. "Right you are, Theodore. It's just my size."

Tricia could not believe his effrontery. "Excuse me, but you heard what the Duke said."

Stefan whirled. "Who do you think you are?"

As the four footmen closed in around her, she asserted bravely, "I am Patrick Raven." She turned to the dark-haired, handsome footman. "What is your name?"

"I'm Lionel, and the Nose, over there, is Rupert." He indicated the brown curly-haired man, the tallest of the lot.

Rupert said, "How do you do? And *what* do you do?"

Standing as tall as she could, Tricia declared, "I am the Duke's page."

"The Duke's page?" queried freckled Theodore, obviously ridiculing the idea. "He needs no page. He has us."

Lionel grasped Tricia's hand, shook it once, and then lifted it high, eyeing her critically as he tried to turn her around for further examination. He crowed, "Where did he find *you?*"

Tricia yanked her arm down. They were none of them serious, these footmen. "In Yorkshire," she replied.

There were jeers and titters. "Oho, he's from the North!"

Stefan pointed at her and sneered, "What was it you said to me?"

"I only repeated that you must burn that hat. The Duke took the wrong one from a country house, and he doesn't take a shine to that one. Apparently it's nasty."

Lionel's eyes danced. "Visiting Lady Flitcroft and he got the wrong hat?" he whispered to the others.

Theodore whistled. "It passes everything!"

Stefan perused the scuffed black beaver. "Well, well, whose could this be?"

Theodore sniffed the inside. "Euw!" He passed it to the fourth footman, who possessed the grand nose. "What is it, Rupert?"

Rupert promptly deduced, "The owner wears

Macassar oil. Whom does Lady Flitcroft know who wants to increase the growth of his hair?" They sniggered, and some names were mentioned.

Tricia said indignantly, "Do not speculate over our Duke's acquaintances like that."

"O-ho!" Stefan pointed straight at her. "How do *you* dare to tell *us* what to do, you little shab-rag?"

She felt woefully small as they regarded her menacingly down their noses. But she had gone too far in His Grace's defense to back down now. "Because it's a despicable way for you to behave to your employer, and it's none of your affair!"

"No, it's *his* affair," crowed Theodore. "Ha, ha, ha!" His laugh ended with a snort.

Stefan said to Tricia between his teeth, "Take a damper, you ridiculous infant, or I'll burn those pillowcases you're wearing."

Lightning forked through Tricia's heart. "You'll what?"

Stefan tipped his head to examine the red military stripes down the gray wool trousers. "Think you're for the Army, do you? Or did you beg those off some old soldier so you could play dress-up?" He nudged Rupert and they grinned.

In overflowing emotion, Tricia cried, "These were my *brother's!*"

Stefan splayed his hands over his chest and made a mocking half-bow. "His brother's! Ooh, Blimey!"

That did it. Tricia, infused with blind rage, kicked him in the shin for emphasis as she yelled, "He *died* for this country—and for *your freedom!*"

Stefan, hopping on one leg, appeared not to hear, so murderous were his squinted eyes as he lunged at her. "You worthless sprig! I'll squash you!"

Though Tricia sprinted, the other footmen deftly caught her and threw her back. She scuffled with all her might, but her tormentor knew something about wrestling and her shoulder blades hit the floor before she knew what had happened.

She was in trouble now. She struggled ferociously.

With vengeful breaths, Stefan clamped her head with a vise-like arm and put painful pressure on her neck. The chandelier whirled in her vision.

When her cheek was flat against the cold marble, footsteps clattered down the corridor and vibrated in her ear. The butler loomed. Aldwin looked twenty feet tall. Fiercely, he hissed, "What could *possibly* be the cause of this brangle! *Get up at once!*"

Tricia was yanked up, hauled to her feet, and presented to Mr. Aldwin by a grip on her collar.

"What have you done?" demanded the butler. He cast an uneasy eye back up the staircase.

"I kicked him in the shin, Sir." Tricia pointed at the red-faced Stefan, whose cravat was every-which-way.

"What for?" asked Mr. Aldwin.

"This little page is a hot-headed scapegrace!" spat Rupert, clamping her arm hard behind her back.

"No, don't pummel him, Stefan," Lionel said surprisingly, for the red-haired footman's ire still boiled by the look of him. "The Duke might discharge you as he'll discharge this . . . object."

"You're . . . choking me!" Tricia eked out as she was hefted higher by the collar.

"Let go of him!" commanded Aldwin.

The teal and silver coats parted suddenly, for they all heard a quick footfall from the corridor.

Tricia felt herself instantly freed.

It was a sweet-faced little woman in a lace cap whom they greeted with "Good evening, Mrs. Pollard."

"For mercy's sake, stand still! What on earth has occurred here?" The looks she cast each footman in turn jerked them into respectful posture. "I hear His Grace has got himself a page at last," she continued, sounding breathy and pleased. "Tell me all about him." She smiled at Tricia.

They told what had just transpired, and very politely made Patrick Raven sound like the vilest pest.

CHAPTER 4

In Hot Pursuit

Last evening had been a disaster for Tricia. It was bad enough that she had deceived a Duke of the Realm for two days, but why, oh why had she caused such havoc with his footmen?

She slipped out of bed and walked barefooted to the bedchamber window. There were carriages in the street and a rider cantering by on the bridle path in the park across the street.

There came a knock at the door, which made her jump. Mrs. Pollard, the housekeeper, called, "Good morning, Patrick! May I come in?"

"Yes."

She entered, smiling, and said she had rummaged through the house and found some clothing for him. She bade him follow her.

In her huge nightshirt, Tricia looked both ways in the corridor, fearful lest those footmen see her feminine feet and ankles. In a wash room, a housemaid ran steaming water into a tub from one tap, while cold water poured from another. Tricia had heard of this luxury in great houses, but had never seen it before.

Eyeing the door, and Mrs. Pollard whisking in and out with articles of clothing and shoes, Tricia, in her most boyish tone, asked, "Is there a key for that door?"

"Are you afraid Stefan will try some revenge on you? Here's a key, but don't fret, they're all busy. The Duke does business and sees callers in the mornings, which keeps them occupied taking calling cards and serving refreshments and running letters across town."

In turmoil at the very idea of Stefan stalking her with vengeance, Tricia made her bath a speedy one. She scrubbed her hair, dipped it for a rinse, and wrapped a towel around it. At the creak of the floorboards, she yanked it off. What boy would sit in a tub with a towel on his head? As she crossed her arms over her chest, her heart thumped convulsively. The key was pushed from the outside, and it fell with a clink to the floor. Someone was trying to open the door!

She grabbed a towel to her chest, which slopped halfway into the water. She covered herself and called, "Who's there?"

"It is I, your lord and master," boomed Stefan. "Open up. I need a cake of soap from that cupboard."

"Wait!" Tricia splashed out of the water, clamped the wet towel around her feminine form with one arm. With the other, she yanked on masculine drawers. It took nervous effort, and much jerking, for they stuck to her damp legs.

The door vibrated with rapping. "Speed it up! Why did you lock the door anyway?"

Why indeed. Her mouth dry with fear, she grabbed a long, narrow cloth bundle, tied it across her chest, and desperately pulled on the undervest.

She heard voices and the jingling of keys. She was plunging her arms into a shirt with her back turned when a new key turned and Stefan strode in.

Not looking at him, Tricia pulled on breeches, worrying that she would look nothing like a boy. It was crucial that she be a lad of sixteen, even half-dressed. Scared, she lifted her jaw as she buttoned her breeches flap and gave her intruder an offensive squint.

"If you keep me waiting like this again, I'll—" The vindictive Stefan grabbed her arm and jerked her. "I had to beg this key from Mrs. Pollard because you took so long!"

Tricia's eyes flared a warning at him, and she said, "Stop it! I'm good at kicks when you least expect it."

"Stefan!" Mrs. Pollard whisked in and snapped a towel at his thigh. "How do you dare to man-handle our newcomer? Get out! You've just lost your next day off. I would not have believed this of you, our first footman! How would you like to be fourth?"

At that, Stefan said, "I'm sorry, Mrs. Pollard."

"Are you going to say you're sorry to him?"

Stefan's face grew red with indignation, but he mumbled an apology in Tricia's direction under the housekeeper's watchful eye, and left without the soap.

Mrs. Pollard lifted her hands in wonder. "What seraph stands before me? My, my, what a handsome young man you are!"

Tricia affected embarrassment. After submitting to a hair trim in the back, she donned a silver-buttoned teal coat and knee breeches. She heard herself called "bang up to the echo" by Mrs. Pollard, who proudly escorted her transformed page to luncheon in the Lower Five's dining hall.

She explained that she was head of the women servants and third only to the steward and the butler in what was termed the Upper Ten. After her came Eldred, the Duke's valet. Theirs was a more exalted realm than that to which a page, or even footmen, belonged.

"I thought you were highest of all," said Tricia, remembering the way Stefan and the others fell into line at her appearance.

Mrs. Pollard chuckled. "That is because of my manner. I never tolerate slip-ups in any quarter, and they all know it. Do not repeat this to a soul, but I have found that whatever you do and say with conviction, people will believe. If you totter, you lose their confidence. I hold firm and speak my mind, but never out of line, mind you, and always as fairly as I can. There, I've told you my secret. It can be yours, too."

Tricia made a respectful bow and a flourish, saying, "What wisdom you impart to one as lowly as I."

They laughed together. Tricia decided she liked the woman very much. She felt encouraged that a respected servant with power in this house showed such kindness toward her.

* * *

As she sat at the bottom of the Lower Five's table, Tricia felt thankful to be separated from the footmen. The laundresses and scullery maids chatted to the new page, trying to discover where the Duke had found him. Tricia said as little as possible, but took in every aspect of the servants' life that she could. This was now her world.

Rupert left the room and reentered shortly with a tray held high. "Attention! We have ice cream from Mrs. Pollard in honor of our new little colleague, Patrick Raven."

The maids exclaimed in pleasure, and smiled at Tricia.

With heat creeping up her cheeks, she accepted with thanks the first dish of ivory ice cream from Stefan, who had leaped up to serve it. She had tasted ice cream once when her father bought her one in Whitby after they had checked the building of his ship. But this—this tasted bland and greasy! She spat it onto her spoon and cried, "Butter!"

The footmen roared with laughter.

Tricia's face flamed as she scrubbed her tongue with her napkin.

Stefan slapped his thigh in great glee. "Wasn't that a treat? It was certainly a treat for me!"

Tricia endured her abasement with a boyish grin. She cast a bright, level look at him to acknowledge that he had won himself a point.

How she hoped this was the end of their stupid war.

* * *

As the clock of jousting knights in the hall chimed and clanked seven in the evening, Tricia finally saw her Duke. His imposing presence beamed like a ray of sunshine into her heart. He was speaking with Mr. Aldwin in the dining room beneath a portrait of his dark-haired mother. Tricia saw the resemblance through the wide-set eyes. She was beautiful, and the wise mother who had taught him right from wrong. She had warned him not to link himself with worldly women.

Mrs. Pollard said, "Here is Patrick Raven, Your Grace." Dressed in black silk with a lace jabot and cuffs, Tricia walked toward him in the flat velvet pumps and white clocked stockings she had been given.

The Duke looked startled. "Pollard! What a wonder you have wrought."

"Well, Your Grace, it was a snap with the raw material you brought me." The woman winked at Tricia, curtseyed slightly to the Duke, and left.

Leery lest he had been apprised of her brash behavior toward Stefan, Tricia made the Duke a deep bow.

He laughingly rebuked her. "Enough of that."

Aldwin cleared his throat and announced that dinner was served.

Tricia pulled His Grace's chair out as Mrs. Pollard had instructed, but it was extremely heavy, so she helped lift it with her knee. She stood aside for the Duke to sit at the head of the table.

In the soft light of a dozen lighted candles, the expression on the Duke's serious face touched her heart when he dropped his eyelids and thanked God for his blessings. How fabulously handsome he was; how well-attired, with pearl buttons in his white linen shirt, and his neck encased in a black silk cravat. His wine-colored coat became him exceedingly.

He looked up and caught her staring.

Tricia flicked her lashes down and backed herself into the corner, out of his line of sight.

When Stefan and Lionel glided in and offered him dishes from under crystal domes, and the silver clinked against the fine porcelain, she felt qualms about her aspiration to serve a Duke. He was a nobleman of weighty importance. She wished she could serve the same Duke who had rescued her from Farmer Ramsbottom, not this sophisticated Peer of the Realm who was so at ease amidst the trappings of wealth and grandeur.

Rowan turned and beckoned her. He said he wished to instruct her in various aspects of performance as his page. "In other houses," he said, "I will leave you positioned where I can see you. When I need something, I will summon you thus." He cocked a dark eyebrow at her.

"Yes, Your Grace," breathed Tricia, a thrill streaking up her spine. She could daydream a long time over a look like that. "Do I bow when I approach you?"

"Come to my side and lean close so my orders will be private. That will be bowing enough. If I'm seated, place your ear convenient to my whispers."

She nodded in anticipation.

"If you don't understand, ask me quietly what you need to know." He smiled and gestured over her fine costume. "Look at you. You'll be an asset to me wherever I go."

Flushing, Tricia felt the eyes of all in the room. In the mirror, beyond the glowing candelabra, she glimpsed what they saw: a slim boy with corn floss hair swept in a smooth curve across the brow, dark-fringed large eyes, and a much too sensitive mouth. Drat! She must tighten her lips and keep a male attitude in every move she made.

Without preamble, the door to the entry hall opened wide. There, with a black lace shawl slithering from her shoulder to the floor, posed the most startling woman. Her full red lips formed a pout, a purple turban set off her auburn curls, and a black-gloved hand clutched a rope of pearls. Her eyes sought the Duke's. She seemed to be awaiting his exclamation of pleasure.

She achieved an exclamation. "Lady Flitcroft!" His glass halted in mid-air as his face drained white. "What a . . . surprise to see *you* here." His goblet hit the table with a bang and he stood, tipping his heavy chair into Stefan's middle. He clicked his fingers at the two footmen. Reluctantly, they filed out of the room.

Tricia looked at the Duke, who gestured her to stay.

Lady Flitcroft advanced in a high-waisted purple silk gown. "Lucas, I could not let you leave me in such a manner, knowing you misunderstood me so."

"I misunderstood nothing," returned the Duke in a level tone as he crossed his arms and looked sidewise at her down his nose.

Tricia thought he looked far too attractive. A pang assailed her as she watched Lady Flitcroft admire him and purse her lips. The Duke must stand his ground! The woman looked older than forty, and definitely a female to be reckoned with.

She undulated toward him, grasped his elbow,

and eyed him from under russet curls which mingled with her eyelashes. "You left so early! Did sleep elude you as it did me? Next time, you will see how wonderfully we can get on together, Lucas. I'll not embarrass you with any more gifts. You're so shy; I will just have to behave myself. In fact, I will let you do the chasing from now on. Promise?"

Rowan replied, "I can assure you, Lady Flitcroft, that I do not feel impelled to pursue a lady in return for contraband treasures, as freely as they are offered." He looked at her with a stern reprimand.

Her laugh tinkled. "But I can nevermore be considered a smuggled treasure. I have a husband no longer," she pouted, endeavoring to look sad.

"I am very sorry that he died; very sad indeed. Now," the Duke added in a harried way, "if you will be so good as to excuse me, Lady Flitcroft, I should finish my dinner meeting." He indicated Tricia. "My new page needs dinnertime instruction."

Lady Flitcroft gave Tricia a supercilious look before she turned back to Rowan. "Then I will await you in your sitting room, Lucas. I am sure I can find it with the help of those able footmen. Don't be long." She twirled her rope of pearls and winked at him over her shoulder.

"Await me—if you must—in the drawing room!" said Rowan between his teeth.

"Let's not be boring, Lucas," she reprimanded, and left.

Looking extremely harassed, the Duke swiped a hand through his hair.

Tricia felt like intervening. She had to stop that outrageous woman from getting her vile way. She pummeled her brain. What could she do? She knew she had to wait and see what the Duke would do.

He spied the black silk shawl in the doorway and scooped it up. It looked European. Tricia had seen similar lace when her father brought in a shipment from Chantilly. Rowan flung the shawl at the surprised Aldwin in the hall, and shut the doors together. He strode back to the table and grabbed his glass. To his page, he said, "I suppose you're wondering what that was all about."

"Oh no, it was quite apparent," was Tricia's quick reply. "Why did she come here? And seemingly without an escort!"

"She feels free of constraints as the widow of a respectable Peer," he said tightly. "Nadine Vavasour, Lady Flitcroft, makes her debut as Lady Consolable."

"Is she ever on the catch for you!" spat Tricia.

"Why is it that I find it almost amusing through your eyes? I said *almost* amusing."

Tricia felt that the Duke was much more objective now. He had only to throw the woman out.

"Well, Patrick," he said with a long look, "I expect your presence will do me good. My world is so wearisome at times that I need a loyal confidant to aid me with the occasional social . . . hitch. Those footmen live only to gossip with servants from other houses, but I know you will be the soul of discretion."

"I will, Your Grace." Tricia's heart felt ready to spill over. He needed her! A pang of guilt made her hate the deception she was playing on him because he trusted her.

Rowan resumed his seat, finished his apricots in brandy, and let out a stressful sigh. "Ho boy, I have yet to learn that women are not worth a ruffle in a man's mind."

"Not that kind of woman, anyway," Tricia murmured. She straightened a taper in the candelabrum. "Be strong; no matter what she does, Your Grace."

He pierced a look at her, and then laughed. He strolled out and headed for his drawing room, trying to loosen his collar without use of his hands.

* * *

Tricia felt frantic, for Lionel had told her behind his white glove that Lady Flitcroft was still in the house.

She hurried up the central staircase. What could a mere page do? She realized with dread that, should the Duke ever discover that she, his trusted confidante in matters such as women, was a young woman herself, then that would be the end of the page . . . the end of the story.

A quarter hour later, she could not sleep, although Mrs. Pollard had dismissed her for the night. Tricia's eyelids kept jumping open. Exasperated, she threw off the sheet and went to the window. All looked peaceful along Park Lane, with an occasional lighted carriage or knot of people passing through Hyde Park opposite.

She worried about what the Duke and That Woman were doing together downstairs. Why did it irk her to such a flaming degree? The Duke was well acquainted with the wiles of grasping women, especially that one.

Unable to remain in ignorance an instant longer, she opened her door and tiptoed to the balustrade. She heard Rowan say, "You absolutely cannot stay here. No! It's unthinkable. I will escort you out."

Tricia peeked down at the spiral ebony staircase rail which descended dizzily to the ground floor. Sconces lit the stairs at intervals. She caught her breath at what she saw.

There was a feminine hand on the rail, sliding slowly downward. Soon the top of Lady Flitcroft's russet coiffure, minus turban, appeared as she leaned over the banister, her hair tumbling. "Oh Lucas," she crooned, grabbing him forcibly, "I will convince you yet!" She pulled the Duke's dark head toward hers.

Sounds of kissing carried to Tricia's ears. It was Lady Flitcroft doing the kissing along Rowan's jaw and then onto his mouth.

"*Stop this*, Nadine!"

So much for the Duke's power to resist passion-driven women, thought Tricia with horror, watching Lady Flitcroft retain a two-handed grip on his head.

Anger boiled over within Tricia. Scornfully, desperately, she looked around her. The plant on the landing would have to do. She denuded a stem savagely and positioned herself above the couple. She dropped her handful of heavy, waxy leaves, willing them to fall on the woman's forehead and end that disgusting embrace.

The leaves fluttered downward . . . downward . . . separating, missing their mark. But as Tricia watched breathlessly, one landed on the Duke's ear.

He jerked back, looked around, grabbed at his ear, and stared at the leaf in his fingers.

Lady Flitcroft wobbled off balance and gave him a killing glance.

The Duke said, "The most curious thing!" He looked at the other leaves sprinkled on the stairs.

Tricia knew that next he would look up, so she pulled back into the darkness, her pulses pounding.

Was that sound diminishing, or did it grow louder? When she realized that footsteps were firmly running up the marble stairs, she fled in panic. She scrambled at her door lever and slipped inside. As she shut the door, her voluminous nightshirt stuck in it. Not daring to open the door at this juncture, she held her breath in the dark, her back pinned to the wooden door.

The footfall halted outside. What would he do? If he confronted her as she was, he could easily discover she was a female. As a boy, she had no excuse to refuse him admittance in his own house.

She felt a slow tug on her nightshirt. Her eyes widened in alarm as it kept pulling. There went her hem until, to her chagrin, the shirt had ridden up about her thighs and she was wrapped tightly against the door.

Terrified as she was, she must remember to be Patrick Raven. "Aw, Your Grace," she cajoled.

"Yes, Patrick?" drawled the Duke.

"I'm mighty sorry!" was all she could think of to say.

"Open up!"

"I can't, Your Grace. I'm stuck against the lever."

It moved against the small of her back. She felt

her nightshirt loosen. With a lunge, she made to run and leap into bed, but she had no freedom. The Duke inched into the room, holding fast to her garment.

"Please, Your Grace, let go!" cried Tricia, an edge of desperation to her voice. "I won't do it again!"

She found herself free, and bounded into bed, knowing her boyish scampering was silhouetted against the windows. She flopped about in the sheets and pulled them up to her eyes as if in shame at what she had done.

Rowan towered over her narrow bed. "Patrick, there is no need to think I'll take a pitchfork to you as Ramsbottom may have done, but I demand an explanation."

She whispered, "Your Grace, you said you were escaping her!"

In the dim light, she saw his fingers tighten into fists. "Your intervention must mean you think I lack the wherewithal to keep myself—or her— under control."

Silence fell as Tricia fought between honesty and prevarication. She eked out, "It didn't look like Your Grace was controlling . . . anything." There! Now she would be forcibly struck and turned out for good.

The Duke grabbed her ankle through the blanket and held it hard. "How dare you refute my self-control?" he spat beneath his breath. Abruptly he let go his grip and straightened to a semblance of dignity. "*Touché*." His tone was diminished and he shook his head slowly. "Forgive me."

Tricia reached out and started to say she forgave him, and ready to beg for forgiveness herself, but the door swished wide open.

Something glistened. In the semi-darkness, Lady Flitcroft glided toward them, her bracelet catching light from the windows. She inquired with what sounded like bottled-up fury, "Why must you race up here *now,* Lucas?"

Tersely he said, "I am having a word with my newest employee."

"What? Are you out of your mind? If you run away from me again to speak to servants, why—*I* shall have words with them!"

Tricia lay like a ramrod.

"I'll see you in the morning, Patrick."

"Yes, Your Grace."

Lady Flitcroft warned, "Do not trouble the Duke any more, or you shall have more than a lecture from me in the morning, and that's a promise!"

Glaring at her in the darkness, Tricia scarcely breathed until they left the room. She swiped at the air with her pillow, trying to chase away the suffocating smell of that woman's perfume.

Tricia knew she was in trouble deep. Her feminine feelings had almost betrayed her. She had gone much too far with her impetuosity. How had she dared to interfere with the Duke of Rowan's personal life?

The trouble was, her personal life had become the Duke of Rowan.

CHAPTER 5

Portrait of a Gentleman

The next morning, Tricia gave a tug to her teal coat, smoothed her knee breeches, and hurried down the grand, curving staircase to the floor below. She wanted to be ready when the Duke needed her.

She arrived outside his suite just as his valet, Eldred, came striding toward her in a haughty manner. He ignored her as he knocked three times on the tall, gilt-edged door. Eldred wore his graying blond hair in forward curls that seemed to grow out of the high points of his collar. The Duke's deep voice bade him enter, so he went in and pointedly snapped the door shut in Tricia's face.

"Oh my!" she expelled. It seemed that the valet and footmen feared that her presence in the house would impinge on their own territorial duties in some way. She wondered jealously if Eldred had massaged the Duke's sore neck last night. She did not want it to be Eldred. What, then, did she want? —to be asked to perform that service again herself? She sighed. It was a perplexing situation, this chaos in her mind.

Eldred stuck his head out. "The Duke requires

you on the instant," he said, and snapped his fingers at her.

Ignoring him, she entered a majestic chamber with sky blue-curtained windows topped and tasseled in burgundy and silver. The Duke faced away from her, busily writing at an inlaid desk. He wore a poetic-looking nightshirt and his long legs were bare. She strove to keep her eyes from looking at them, but she was not successful. This position of page seemed to be one in which she must run in and out of his private rooms no matter what she would find his state of dress or undress to be. She had not foreseen this complication when she agreed to serve him.

Rowan's plumed pen waved as he wrote. He dipped it in ink repeatedly, adding lines, while she waited. He read his letter, wrote his signature, and ended with a flourish. He looked over his shoulder at her. "Good morning, Patrick." For a moment, his dark eyes met hers and held. Was she in for punishment after she had separated him from Lady Flitcroft last night?

She bade him a good morning and bowed her head. She wasn't a bit sorry.

"Seal this, will you?" He stood and indicated the letter on the desk. "Convey it to Highcourt House in Cavendish Square. The London map is in the library, printed on a window shade. Ask Aldwin to order you the town chariot to convey you there."

She could not avert her eyes from him in his nightshirt without appearing evasive so she summoned courage and smiled into his eyes. "Yes, Your Grace." He was so appealing, all the more so in this half-light and in his relaxed attitude.

"I will see you again when you bring me a reply." He moved to receive an aromatic cup of coffee from Eldred. The man had poured it from a carafe on the dumbwaiter which had arrived with a click and a whir. The Duke sipped with a lusty sigh and strolled from window to arched window overlooking Hyde Park. He pushed opened a pane to the chirpy bird voices.

Did he always wake so cheerfully? Or was That Woman responsible for his vigor this morning? Tricia looked hastily around the room, but there were no feminine trappings in sight. Good. She prayed that he had gotten rid of her immediately after she had come smelling up Tricia's room and threatening her. She did not dare to ask him, though.

On his desk, she found his prepared seals in an ivory box. She licked the salty back of a red crested wafer and affixed it over the edge of the letter. On the other side was the name *Lady Caroline Claremont.*

Not daring to look at what Eldred was doing toward dressing or undressing their master, she sidled toward the door. Since the Duke said no more, she glanced back to see if he had dismissed her from his mind as well as his presence. Perhaps he had, for with a quick pull over his head, he threw his nightshirt to Eldred, who said, "Your bath is ready, Your Grace."

Tricia ran toward the door, her gaze skewering the carpet. This would never do! How could she manage to absent herself while he took off his clothes?

As she dashed toward the stairs, she heard his

voice behind her. "Patrick!"

She whirled.

"Are you getting along all right?" He leaned out of the doorway, his broad shoulders bare.

"Yes, Your Grace, I am fine now." One look into his eyes and she blurted out, "But I started off wrong, Your Grace. When Stefan made fun of my brother's trousers, it made me so mad! I kicked him."

"You *kicked* him?"

"In the shin, with feeling. They are my brother, David's."

The Duke's brows lifted. "Right. Where are your bruises? Your black eye?"

Tricia grinned. "He wrestled me to the floor, but Mrs. Pollard broke it up. Later, he tricked me into eating butter that he said was ice cream."

"Butter?" The Duke screwed up his forehead. "What is my household coming to? I leave London for three days—"

"Do not concern yourself with the butter," said Tricia. "I think that may have ended our feud. I expect he feels like the victor now."

The Duke shook his head in half-smiling wonder. "I expected you would make your presence known, but the sort of behavior I require is hardly to kick my footmen, Patrick."

"Oh, I agree! That was the last time. I am sorry."

"It sounds like you had provocation." He grinned ruefully. "But curb your instincts next time."

She could have said that to him, too, but she put a hard clamp on her tongue. At least he said nothing about how she had interfered with those leaves.

* * *

In Highcourt House, Tricia waited for a reply to the letter she had delivered from the Duke. Minutes ticked by, but the Claremont butler did not return.

Tricia moved sidewise, studying the portraits along the first-floor gallery. She worked her way from the ruffs to the powdered wigs, then on to the more recent pictures. One young gentleman had such a familiar face that she stopped and drew in breath. He looked just like her father! Her amazement grew as she took in the happy, intelligent eyes, the upturned smile, and the neat brown hair. "His walking stick!" she exclaimed. There, indeed, was the setter's head carved on the staff which had helped Leigh Ravenscar up and down the hilly streets of Robin Hood's Bay since Tricia could remember.

Her heart thumped loudly as she wondered why his picture hung here. He had been a leading citizen of Robin Hood's Bay, but she had never heard him speak of any connection with London.

"Pardon me, but who are you?" said a woman's voice close behind her.

Tricia whirled. "Oh! You startled me."

"*I* startled *you?* Young man, you startled me, a stranger standing right outside my rooms."

Tricia was face-to-face with a fashionable lady with inquiring hazel eyes. Her high-piled brown curls were streaked in subtle gray at the temples while her smooth, pretty face looked to be about five-and-forty.

"I beg your forgiveness, Madam," said Tricia with

a little bow.

"Granted. Now tell me who you are." Her voice sounded kind.

"I am Patrick Raven, Madam."

The woman frowned slightly. "I don't know that name, do I?"

"I am the Duke of Rowan's page."

"You don't say. Rowan sent the invitation with you?"

"Yes, to Lady Caroline Claremont. Would that be you, Madam?"

"Yes, but I am called Lady Caro in conversation. You can bring this reply to him." She handed over a folded letter. "Do our pictures interest you?"

"Yes," breathed Tricia, "especially that one." She indicated her father's likeness. "He appears a very amiable man."

"Oh, he was."

"Was?" prompted Tricia, trying to mask her eagerness to hear more.

Lady Caro folded her arms over her aqua ruffled bodice and said, "He left us at such an early age, only twenty years old."

"Why did he leave?"

Lady Caro shook her head sadly. "He made a mésalliance with a shipping merchant's daughter. She was lovely, and I don't blame him because she made him so happy, but we never had the sound of his laughter here again. His departure was not his doing, mind you, but our father's. He was angered that the marriage was not equal in rank and wealth. I, by the way, am the gentleman's elder sister."

Tricia stood flabbergasted. If that portrait really *was* her father, it made this aristocratic woman her aunt!

Lady Caro pointed to an earlier painting of a man in a white bagwig and stern countenance. "That was our father, who showed Leigh and his bride the door. It made my heart sick, but I could do nothing about it."

Tricia's pulses pounded. Her father's Christian name *was* Leigh. "Did Leigh, your brother, live in this house?"

"Yes, of course."

Tricia tried to sound detached. "What name did he go by?"

"We suspect he stopped using his courtesy title, Lord Claremont, when he was ousted from here. He, being the oldest son, was the heir apparent to our father, the Marquis of Wyndhurst."

Tricia gave a gasp of amazement.

Lady Caro sank onto a soft bench and lifted her hands in futility. "Leigh died last year without my even seeing him again. His death was a shock to me, and especially to my younger brother, Clive."

"Why a shock, Your Ladyship?" Tricia's heart was pounding fast.

"Because Clive assumed that Leigh died long ago. That was because he disappeared so completely that he could never track him down."

Tricia's thoughts whirled. Why had her father never told her any of this? "Did the title, which belonged to Leigh, continue?"

"Oh yes. When Father died a year ago, Clive took up as the Marquis of Wyndhurst." Lady Caro's eyes popped wide. "It was an erroneous step; a great presumption. Leigh is the one who really became the Marquis of Wyndhurst when

Father died. But he was never here to claim it. Clive declared him dead after he received no reply to his request in several newspapers to come forward. Clive felt free, then, and took up as Lord Wyndhurst." Lady Caro gave Tricia a darkling look. "He gulped when the news reached us that Leigh died only eight months ago. What if he had come back and found that Clive had usurped his position?"

Tricia met her eyes with speculative wonder.

"Clive is Lord Wyndhurst right and tight now," said Lady Caro, lifting her chin. "He has a wife and a daughter, Lady Jewel. They lapped up their new titles like cats at clotted cream. They've certainly kept the engravers in business." Twisting her handkerchief, she sighed. "How I miss the good old times with Leigh. He was a wonderful brother."

Tricia's eyes misted over. "I feel bad that he had to die!" She lifted her hand to cover her trembling lips.

Lady Caro looked strangely touched. "Why *thank* you, dear boy. You are a sensitive soul." Her eyes riveted on Tricia, and she stared. "Come here and let me see your hands!"

Tricia wondered why she asked such a strange thing. She went forward apprehensively.

Lady Caro straightened out Tricia's fingers, and then did the same to the other hand. "I don't believe it."

Tricia thought wildly that Lady Caro had discovered she was a girl. Would she tell the Duke?

"Put your hand palm-to-palm with mine, Patrick. Don't look so scared. Just do as I say."

Tricia wondered what on earth would come of this physical examination.

The woman pressed their fingers together for an instant before she crowed, "Look at that. Our fingers match! They're even the same length and slimness." With eyes alight, she said, "No one I've ever met, in my vast circle of acquaintance, has second and third fingers the same length as you and I do. There is only one other person who had hands like ours, and that was Leigh. How *odd* it is that you were attracted by his portrait!"

She continued to eye Tricia, turning her chin from side to side. "Is it my imagination, or do you look like his wife?" Lady Caro continued. "Turn this way, more into the light. I only saw her once, but yes, you do have those huge, eloquent eyes and that seagull-in-flight mouth. Mercy sakes, you bring it all back! Who are your parents?" she cried.

Tricia schooled herself sternly into Patrick, ready to deny everything until she knew what was safe to do or say. "Mr. and Mrs. Raven."

"Answer me this: where did the Duke find you?"

"On the Great North Road." She did not understand what the ramifications of this interview might be, so she bowed respectfully away and said, "The Duke awaits your reply. By your leave, I must hurry back to him. Thank you, Your Ladyship."

"Next time, we'll talk more about that painting," said Lady Caro over the balustrade as Tricia hurried down. They locked eyes. The Lady meant it.

On her way out, Tricia sensed the elegance of the house in a blur. Was it true that this was the home her father left when he married her mother? Had he really been Lord Wyndhurst?

He had married a lovely shipping merchant's daughter, so that part was true. But as far as Tricia knew, he had been Mr. Leigh Ravenscar of Robin Hood's Bay all her life. If he should have become the Marquis of Wyndhurst on his stern father's death, why had he not acknowledged his title?

Outside, the sun broke through the cobalt clouds as a curricle dashed into windy Cavendish Square. To Tricia's delight, the driver under the black hat was her Duke. "Do you have a reply?" he called, pulling his white horse to a halt.

"Yes, Your Grace." She ran and put the missive into his hand.

"Thank you. Hop up here. I can't read this with the square looking on." He glanced uneasily at the many stories of windows that eyed them from all directions.

When she landed in the leather seat next to him, he motioned away the parked chariot in which she had arrived. The driver touched his hat. Tricia felt privileged to be riding off with her Duke. He drove out of Cavendish Square and said, "You may read it to me now."

The letter stuck out of his waistcoat. He nodded, so she drew it out and broke the seal. "My Lord Duke," she read, "I accept with thanks Your Grace's invitation to Lady Jewel and myself to attend the opera in your company. We will expect you to call for us this evening at eight. It will be a great pleasure to us both. Yours faithfully, Lady Caro."

The Duke groaned. "Why did I do it?"

"Did you not want them to accept?"

"I have no objection to Lady Caro, but the prospect of squiring that eligible *jewel* on my arm throws me into a freak."

Tricia laughed in a puzzled way. "Why, Your Grace?"

"This sort of thing is *not* my métier."

"Then why did you invite her, and not just Lady Caro?"

"Because I *have to get an heir!*" he shouted desperately, arm lifted. He ducked his head into his shoulders as he saw refined ladies pass by in an open barouche. Two of them stared after him with lively interest.

"I knew those people," he said, flushing under his skin.

Tricia giggled. "You can be sure that you still do."

"Rowan!" came a masculine halloo amidst a clatter of hoofs. A tanned-faced young man with fair hair and a blue coat rode a sleek horse in mane-slapping speed after them.

"Ah, here is my friend, Lord Bixby." Rowan lifted his whip in salute.

"Whither so fast?" the young man called, his eyes narrowed in friendly censure. "Weren't we supposed to meet at Hyde Park Corner a quarter hour ago?"

"Believe me, Bix, I set out to meet you, but after my detour here, I'm afraid I forgot your very existence."

Bixby eyed Rowan, half smiling. "Could only mean one thing: a woman." He caught Tricia studying him curiously. "Rowan, you have a new acquisition there."

"Yes, he's my page. Name's Patrick. This is Lord

Bixby."

"A neat article is Patrick. A shame he's not a girl."

Tricia crossed her arms and affected an insulted jut of her chin.

Rowan said dryly, "It is a good thing he's not a girl, or you'd try to hire him away from me like that nice parlor maid I once had."

"She is still with me. But Rowan," Bixby pressed, riding near the curricle, "which member of the fair sex has so irritated or enthralled you that you forgot your rendezvous with your great friend, Bixby?"

"The adjective is your own," said Rowan, and grinned at him. He neglected to say a single word about the woman.

CHAPTER 6

High Stakes

Passing from Piccadilly Street to St. James's with Rowan and Lord Bixby, Tricia had a quick view of a street devoted entirely to man and his various needs and pleasures. She saw windows of haberdashers and high-priced tailors, as well as snuff shops and a delicious-smelling coffee house. She glimpsed elegant houses which, though unmarked, were gentlemen's clubs, as the Duke told her.

The exclusive White's Club at the top of the street was his destination, and it was, indeed, white. Awnings shaded a curved bow window near the door, and above it, a black railing traversed a balcony. Eight pillars soared past medallions toward the London sky.

Rowan and Bixby handed their hats to the old porter. Rowan indicated that Tricia remain in the plush waiting room. She felt young and out of her depth among the liveried footmen who joked and gossiped there. She crossed her arms and tried to look world-weary and bored. But she was thinking of how privileged she was now. What other female could race around town with a bachelor Duke and enter an exclusive gentleman's club like this?

Ladies and non-members were strictly not allowed.

Ten minutes later, the gray-haired porter strolled in. "Who serves the Duke of Rowan?" he rasped.

"I do," said Tricia, instantly on her feet.

"His Grace requires you. Here is a message just delivered for him, so bring that along. Keep your presence in the rooms brief."

With the scented note in hand, Tricia entered a spacious card room. Rows of portraits lined the walls and a blazing chandelier lit the white mantel. Searching the occupied tables, she passed by a group of men in a rousing political debate and several others slapping down cards.

The good-looking Lord Bixby stood, a glass in his hand, watching a card game over Rowan's shoulder. Tricia could see the Duke's frown. It looked like not only a concentration frown but also a harassed one. What was happening?

Across the table from him, with his back toward Tricia, sat a man in a broad-brimmed hat with queer black tassels hanging from it. She had never seen the like. He wore a frieze coat and leather mitts with the tips of his thin fingers uncovered. Even from a distance, she could see that he had dirty fingernails.

Lord Bixby signaled her to halt her approach until Rowan had played his hand.

When Bixby beckoned her, she whispered, "Why does the Duke's opponent wear such an odd get-up?"

Bixby's lips twisted in disgust. He whispered behind his glass, "He hides his eyes with the tassels so he doesn't give himself away. He claims to shade them from light with the brim. Very shady, isn't it? The mitts apparently protect his cuffs. He parks himself here for days when he comes to London."

The Duke looked stiff around the mouth. His eyes softened a bit at sight of her, and he raised an eyebrow in the summons he had taught her.

With a swelling heart, she went to him.

His breath tickled her ear as he whispered, "Listen carefully. I want you to look into the pockets of that rust-colored coat which hangs on my opponent's chair. Don't be obvious, but see if you can discover cards or a card case. If so, nod your head as you leave the room. If you find nothing like that, just walk out."

Tricia took a deep breath. It was a scary mission. "Yes, Your Grace. Oh, here is a letter that just came for you."

After one whiff of the perfume, he held the billet at arm's length and impatiently cracked the seal. He ran his eyes over the curlicue hand. He leaned toward Tricia and said low, "Tell the person in what is sure to be an orange and black vehicle that I am engaged this evening." His voice held annoyance as he crushed the letter. He threw it with precision onto the fire, where it blazed up and soon fell to ashes.

"Yes, Your Grace." Tricia eyed him approvingly. She would soon see what woman had sent him an invitation at his private club. She rejoiced that, on his orders, she could march outside and turn her down.

Her pulses pounded. First she had to peer into that strange man's pocket. How could she contrive it?

The man sat unmoving, his face in shadow.

Rowan called the next bet.

She had no time to think long, for it was obvious the Duke had dismissed his page. Noting the position of the rust coat which dragged on the floor, she strode in front of two men moving to the table to see what action was taking place in the Duke's game. She purposely bumped into a man's paunch, tripped over his shoe, and stumbled. She grabbed the coat on the chair as she went down.

She heard its owner swear. His boot kicked her sharply in the rib.

Wrath infused her. Breathing hard, she groped at the velvet as if trying to pull herself up. Her hand closed around a quizzing glass in a pocket, and as she rose, she felt coins.

Her arm was suddenly gripped in vise-like fingers. "What a clumsy creature!"

The way he said *creature* terrorized her. She looked up at the face beneath the black tassels. It was Lord Kilver! Tricia had escaped his clutches in Robin Hood's Bay, but here and now he held a painful grip on her. And he was playing against her Duke! Rowan had suspicions about his integrity, and Tricia knew they were founded. With a surge of devotion, she vowed she would champion her Duke against Lord Kilver to her last breath.

"Let my page go, if you please," the Duke ordered crisply.

Kilver angrily complied, making her fall off balance. She was still on her bottom creating a brouhaha, so she went on bungling, pulling at the coat to help herself up. Her busy fingers closed over something hard in the sleeve. Despite his close-set black eyes boring down into her, she ascertained that the rectangular object could, indeed, accommodate a pack of cards.

Her voice sounded boyish as, with averted head, she rose to her feet and begged, "Forgive me, gentlemen." Flushed, she bowed and streaked for the door.

Because Lord Kilver watched her, she dared not look back at the Duke with her verdict. She nodded without turning her head, but a waiter appeared in front of her and smiled at her, confusing matters.

She said to him, "Please, Sir, do something for me. Nod at the Duke of Rowan. It's a signal he expects. Does he look this way?"

"He keeps glancing up, yes."

"Then please give him an obvious nod."

The waiter did so.

"Did he see that?"

"He nodded back."

"Thank you ever so much." Tricia hurried down the staircase and saw herself in the large, ornately-framed mirror on the landing. Her pupils were dark, and her face terror-stricken, so she paused there, pulling herself into order. She smoothed down her blonde hair, wiped the perspiration from her upper lip, and pulled her shoulders back.

Outside, a town chariot with an orange door and wheels waited, blocking traffic in front of White's. Two feminine occupants of the vehicle were laughing and talking when Tricia approached the carriage. An eager black glove stretched out.

"His Grace desires me to convey the message that he is engaged this evening," recited Tricia to a lace veil which swathed a black bonnet.

"How dare you!" cried a petulant voice which could only be Lady Flitcroft's. She leaned out. "Here, take *that* for your vile tongue!" and she slapped Tricia across the face.

As Tricia fell back in shock and pain, the woman knocked her parasol end on the ceiling. The orange wheels of her carriage rattled away.

Raging inside, Tricia backed against the spiked iron railing and nursed her cheek. Tears swam in her eyes. Breathing deeply in and out, she told herself that it didn't matter; she would endure anything for him.

She felt relieved that Rowan had sent Lady Flitcroft a set-down. That must mean that she had not succeeded in her plan to trap him.

The door to White's opened, so Tricia straightened to a semblance of dignity.

Out stepped Lord Kilver. He wore the rust-colored coat and he was setting a tan beaver on his sparse hair, oiled so heavily it looked black. He apparently kept his tasseled hat inside the club.

"Clever," he intoned in his nasal drawl, "ve-ry clev-er." Thin eyebrows framed his insolent eyes and his straight slit of a mouth curled at one side as he sneered. "So you thought to hide by parading as a boy? Hah!"

"Leave me alone," she warned, rigidly alert.

"That's what I've done too much of, Creature. But I won't cause a scene outside the most famous window in town. I merely take the air, you see?" He swaggered away, took out his snuffbox, and noisily inhaled a pinch from between his knuckles. He whirled back before Tricia could bolt, his close-set eyes piercing her. "I know where to find you now."

"You do not!" *Oh dear God, please save me!* Tricia prayed frantically.

Lord Kilver's nose twitched from side to side in exultation. "You have no chance. I won money from the Duke. Shall I ask for you instead of . . . let's see . . . a twentieth of the money?" He thought his insult amusing, but his humor halted in mid-cackle when Lord Bixby came out of the door.

The fresh-faced Bixby placed his hat at a dapper angle against the sun and stood whistling on the top step. A servant came out and began raising the awnings on the bow window.

Lord Kilver made to reenter the club without acknowledging Lord Bixby.

"Say, Kilver," Bixby arrested him genially, "let me feel that crushed velvet. Is it the new style to wear this during the day?" With enthusiastic questioning, he touched the torso of Kilver's coat.

Kilver eyed him suspiciously and backed away. He halted when they saw, strolling through the doorway, an impressive dark-haired man in a black coat and a blinding white cravat.

Bixby smiled and beckoned him over. "Brummell, what do you think of Kilver's coat? It's good velvet, but is the garment well cut?"

Mr. Brummell, the arbiter of men's fashion, drawled, "Do turn around and let us have a look, Lord Kilver."

Kilver seemed torn between unease and a desire to accept such a supreme boost as Beau Brummell's attention on the steps of White's Club would mean to his social éclat. He turned from side to side.

While Brummell scrutinized the coat through his quizzing glass, Bixby descended the five steps to observe the garment from the back. Out of the side of his mouth, he asked Tricia, "Where are the cards?"

With a frisson of anticipation, she whispered, "Underside of the left sleeve."

"Beau, what do you think of his tailor?" insisted Bixby, vaulting back up and sliding a hand in friendly style down Kilver's left arm.

Tricia could hardly stand the suspense.

Brummell gave a long-suffering toss of his long curls and moved closer with his quizzer.

Kilver eyed him nervously and tried to edge away.

In loud curiosity, Bixby crowed, "What is this lump?"

Kilver jerked away from him, eyes fiery. "I have no lump!"

Bixby clucked his tongue. "Why do you carry a weapon into the club, then? Against the rules, Kilver!" His voice was hard.

Kilver became a dynamo. "I carry no weapon!" he lashed out.

"You had better prove it."

"I told you I have none!" reiterated Kilver between clenched jaws.

Mr. Brummell said, "Let me see what it is in your sleeve that so ruins the hang of it, then."

"Deuce take it, I told you it's not a pistol! Can't you take my word of honor?"

Brummell said airily, "If you decline to show us, how are we to believe you *have* a word of honor?" He turned away.

That did it. "It's—it's just a snuffbox, gentlemen!" Kilver drew out a box and flashed it at them, revealing his two missing teeth in a desperate smile.

He was trying to slip the box back into his cuff when the Duke of Rowan pushed up a pane in the bow window and leaned out. "Hand that interesting box here, Bix. I've never seen a snuff box that size, and I inherited quite a collection."

Lord Bixby wrenched it from Kilver by lightning force and gave it to Rowan over the spiked railing.

Tricia cheered within.

Kilver gobbled, "The *outrage!* –taking a man's possessions without a by-your-leave!" He clattered into the club looking frenzied.

Beau Brummell looked from Tricia to Lord Bixby, dropped his quizzer on its chain, and shuddered. "Oh, that man!" he said. "Dreadful, dreadful."

* * *

It was on the sunset drive home that Rowan proudly thumped Tricia on the back. "You, my page, did the unheard-of at White's!" His smile bathed her in his delight.

"What did I do?"

"You ferreted out a cheater."

"Kilver *cheated* you? Oh!" She clenched her fists. "I'm not a bit surprised!"

"You're not?" he queried as he tooled his horse adroitly through the press of traffic. "What do *you* know about him, anyway?"

In confusion, she replied, "He . . . he *looks* evil. He

acted guilty, didn't he?"

"Yes. I wasn't sure how I could prove my suspicion. By carrying out my request so well, you saved me a great deal of money, Patrick."

Tricia rejoiced at that, but she felt deeply troubled. "Your Grace, why did you even play with such a man?"

"That was an error indeed. I was upset by what I planned for this evening, and I grabbed the first diversion that came along." He shook his head. "I vow I'll never play another game that involves money."

"That is an excellent resolution!" she burst out, feeling that progress of a great magnitude had been made. "What happened after Lord Bixby handed you Kilver's card case?" She had had to stay out in the waiting room.

"The club called the game void when I showed them the box with cards left in it. That blackguard had arranged the other ones in a pattern and switched them with the club's pack before our game began. Bixby showed everyone how Kilver's cards in the box made a complete set of the rest."

"I am so glad you caught him!" breathed Tricia, her hand on her heart.

"You caught him, Patrick."

"You suspected him, Your Grace. I fear I disgraced you by acting such a complete nincompoop in there."

Chuckling, the Duke said, "No, it worked." He touched a hand to Tricia's knee. "It had to be God who led you to bound across my path. I find myself humbly thankful."

"You could hardly be as grateful as I am, Your

Grace." The vitality of his hand upon her knee had weakened her in the strangest way. If only she could lay her head on his shoulder and ask him to take care of her. If only she could tell him how frightened she was of Lord Kilver. If she did tell him, he would have to hear the reason. She lifted a quick look at his face. Her heart swelled. She could not spoil what they had by telling him that she was a woman.

CHAPTER 7

A Nerve-Wracking Opera

As Tricia eased her slim legs into silken hose and her feet into flat evening pumps, she shivered. The pierce in Kilver's eyes when he glared at her in front of White's showed that he meant what he said. He would track her down and force her back to his house in Robin Hood's Bay. She was safe from him in this ducal residence, but outside these walls there was no such assurance.

Should she beg protection from Rowan? The trouble was, he would never keep her employed as his page if he knew she had a legal guardian of Lord Kilver's status. Rowan would never really understand her predicament unless she admitted she was a female. She must continue to pray, stay close to the Duke, and avoid Kilver like the plague.

A knock sounded. She buttoned her white breeches and grabbed her teal coat. Her chamber door was flung open by Stefan, the first footman. "His Grace wants you in his dressing room. Move!"

Tricia said, "Thank you," and moved past him, buttoning her waistcoat.

He stuck his boot in her way, but she hopped over it and hurried down the stairs. He scowled at her over the banister. So he was still bent on scrapping, was he?

When Eldred, the valet, admitted her to the inner sanctum, the Duke was setting his opera hat onto his brow. He looked resplendent in a coat of dark forest green. His waistcoat bore stripes of the same hue in silk on black velvet, dark and rich against his white cravat. Tricia sighed in her feminine heart.

"What's the matter, Patrick?" he asked, eyeing her in the mirror.

She had slipped her guard. "My breeches," she blurted out, "are too tight. But never mind, I'll stand straight tonight, Your Grace."

He laughed. He seemed preoccupied nonetheless, and tapped his walking stick against the balustrade as they rushed down the staircase, his evening cape flaring behind him.

As they careered into Cavendish Square inside Rowan's polished coach, Tricia straightened her wrist lace with a boyish jerk and slid a gaze over him in the light of the carriage lanterns. What an unconscious aura of greatness he carried in his well-shaped head . . . that intelligent brow, the kind, dark eyes, and the noble profile. She flicked her admiring gaze away before he caught her again. Lady Jewel Claremont was a privileged woman, Tricia thought with a pang, to have the Duke of Rowan calling for her.

When they had congregated beside the Rowan chariot following the fray at White's, Lord Bixby had asked the Duke to join him for dinner in his apartments tonight. Rowan had declined. In a droll manner, he told Bixby he was sentenced to convey Lady Jewel Claremont to the opera. He added that he was sure to spend an excruciating afternoon trying to think how to conduct himself.

Hooting in laughter, Bixby tried to brush his fears aside. "You do not need to do a thing, Rowan. Just sit there. Women melt into puddles at every blink of your long eyelashes."

"Cut line!" retorted the Duke, rolling his eyes.

Bixby grinned and sighed. "Alas, 'tis true."

Tricia had inwardly agreed with him. But now she saw that her Duke had plunged into throes of anxiety anyway. She wondered how she could be of any help to him.

She, herself, was uneasy because the ladies they were calling for were her relations, if all that Lady Caro had revealed to her proved true.

They arrived at Highcourt House as the first stars twinkled above London. My, but they were hard to see here. In Robin Hood's Bay, they were bright and clear, and there were so many of them.

Rowan was received with great obeisance by the butler. Tricia had not expected the thud in her heart which hit her when she saw Lady Jewel Claremont. Alas, she was an attractive women. With white skin, high cheekbones, and marked black brows, she carried her tall figure regally in a high-waisted gown of liquid burgundy silk. Her lips were a sculpted pair of thin red petals. Her black hair was piled to perfection and topped with a ruby tiara. The only fault Tricia could find was with her nostrils, which were long and thin. They gave her a haughty look when her chin was lifted, and that was often.

Tricia watched the Duke. He dropped his gaze, took Jewel's gloved hand and kissed it, and flashed the woman a little smile before he rose to his full height. He looked much too attractive! Tricia felt as if she had been slugged in the stomach when she saw Lady Jewel basking in his notice.

She said in a high, aristocratic voice, "Your invitation is my great pleasure, Your Grace."

Lady Caro descended the stairs, lovely in an ivory gown and lacy headdress on her piled-up curls. "You are early, Rowan, but we are ready to hear that opera. Ah, I see you brought your new page. I like him. Good evening, Patrick." She smiled at Tricia, who affected sheepishness and bowed to her.

Rowan took no notice. He was politely replying to the eligible lady on his arm.

As the carriage was full of Rowan and the ladies' gowns, Tricia had to ride on the perch outside. She was forced to resist Stefan's exaggerated swings every time they rounded a corner, for he tried to make her fly off. She proved stubborn, and jumped down in disgust when they halted before the Royal Opera House in Covent Garden. She felt like shouting, "Grow up!" but was trying her best to curb her violent instincts as the Duke had directed her.

In the box in the second tier of the theatre, bathed in the flattering light of an enormous chandelier, Lady Jewel Claremont preened. She used her extraordinary eyes to advantage whenever Rowan favored her with a glance. Although watching the two of them pained her, Tricia praised the Duke silently for his conduct, knowing how he had doubted his abilities. Any woman would give face and figure to be in Lady Jewel's seat now. There wasn't a man in the place who possessed the heart-stopping good looks and modest charm of Tricia's Duke.

He was so unattainable to Tricia that her heart hurt.

Seated in the chaperone's chair, Lady Caro watched the opera from between the silhouettes of Jewel's high braided coiffure and Rowan's well-shaped head. Tricia stood behind Lady Caro at a good vantage point.

Lady Caro turned and conveyed by a smile and a point to her fingers that she wanted to continue their discussion begun beneath the portrait of her father.

Tricia, suspecting that Lady Caro might see her worry in the light from the stage, wondered what to do. For now, the close quarters of the box allowed them no private discourse.

Though the singing in Gluck's *Iphigenie en Tauride* proved admirable to Tricia, it did not penetrate the awareness of a portion of the audience. Opera glasses and quizzers were aimed in all directions from the gilt boxes and from the seats in the pit. It amazed her how long and often some persons stared at Rowan and Lady Jewel.

Tricia watched her lean toward Rowan and whisper behind her fan. She had a manner more sophisticated than her twenty years. For one thing, she maintained erect posture which accentuated her good but wide-shouldered figure. She spoke in a cultured drawl with care to the words she used. Watching the subtle way in which Lady Jewel showed the Duke she was worth looking at, Tricia felt a dreadful hopelessness. She, herself, was bent on being the best page and confidante to Rowan that she could possibly be; hoping, even, to become invaluable to him. But Lady Jewel could become far more important to him than any page. Then what would happen to Tricia?

She backed into the shadowy corner, feeling strange in this world of lofty looks and costly gems and soaring voices. She felt lonely, for here her Duke was not hers by any means.

At the first curtain, the Duke turned, smiled at her, and said, "Will you fetch cordials for us, Patrick?"

She had been told to expect this duty and said, "Yes, Your Grace." Leaving the opera box at the rear, she wove through the people who milled about knocking on private box doors. As she reached the stairs, she felt a tug on her sleeve.

With her heart in her throat, she expected to be harassed by Stefan, who had been left to kick his heels in the vestibule. But confronting her was Lady Flitcroft, a-glitter with jet beads and diamonds and mustard silk.

Tricia flinched and stepped back.

"I won't slap you if you'll do my bidding," said the widow without preamble.

With stiffened spine, Tricia said, "I only serve my master."

"Oh, I'll serve him, too," Lady Flitcroft replied in a throaty voice. "Where did he find such a beautiful boy as you?" She grabbed Tricia's cheeks and squeezed them together painfully.

"Thtop it!" Tricia flung the woman's hands off.

"I could give you a better position in my house. I'll double your pay. Come work for me," the woman coaxed.

"*No*, thank you."

"Then tell me something, Impudence! Who is that haughty-faced female with him tonight?"

"It is not my place, Your Ladyship, to relay information." Tricia darted away and hurried upstairs to order the cordials at the crowded counter. She felt proud that she served the Duke, and glad that she had refused to knuckle under to the demands of Lady Flitcroft.

Balancing three goblets on a tray, Tricia descended the stairs. When she reached the bottom step, a man's dusty beribboned pump appeared beneath an alcove curtain, and the brocade swished aside. Face-to-face, she encountered Lord Kilver.

She gasped, almost tipping her tray.

"Fine pair of legs, Creature." He smirked and looked her over. He moved in close until she smelled his tobacco breath.

"The better to run with," she retorted angrily. "I wish you the same, for it would behoove you to do some serious running."

He cackled. "After you?"

"Out of the country! For cheating at White's!" she finished loudly.

His eyes blazed, and his eyes swiveled from side to side to see who had heard her reveal such a heinous social crime.

She sidled against the wall, praying she could escape him.

He changed his tack. "Tricia," he said, trying to pull her by the elbows into the alcove without spilling the goblets, "come away with me. We'll go to the Continent on *The White Dove* now the war's over and Napoleon is banished to St. Helena." His nostrils twitched in that horrid excitement she had seen when his eyes were glazed upon her. "I've been taking the ship out, and she certainly flies!"

She wanted to rail at him about *The White Dove*, which belonged to her late father; but now her personal safety remained uppermost. "Go away!" she shouted in a voice meant to carry. Even so, he kept a grip on her arms.

Blessedly, she heard a voice call, "What's wrong, Patrick?" It was Rowan, rounding the corner.

"Your Grace!" she beseeched him, her eyes eloquent with terror. She was suddenly free of Kilver's pinioning hold.

"Kilver?" queried the Duke in what looked like flaring rage. "What business do you have with my page?"

Kilver half shut his eyes and looked knowing.

Rowan moved closer and growled, "I warn you not to develop any unsavory interest in him!"

Kilver chortled.

Rowan held him with a steely stare until Kilver's eyelids dropped.

"Patrick, the ladies await their cordial," said the Duke.

Tricia thankfully glided away.

The orchestra began a number, the curtain went up, and she willed her hands not to tremble as she served the Claremont ladies their goblets.

The door opened. Expecting the Duke, Tricia stood aside, ready to serve him. But it was not Rowan. In squeezed Lady Flitcroft and her cloud of perfume. She looked down at the Claremont women, her red mouth hanging open in affected surprise. "Have I got the wrong box? I was sure I had worn a distinct path to this one by now."

Jewel lifted her profile and eyed the woman icily. "The wrong box, yes." She turned pointedly away.

Tricia saw a twinkle in Lady Caro's eye. "If you want the Duke of Rowan, you have the right place, but he stepped out. Care to leave your name?"

Lady Flitcroft smiled and gushed, "Yes, tell him that Nadine dropped by. Say I regret I turned him down for tonight, but I'm relieved he found someone to accompany him. Who am I addressing, by the way?"

"I am Lady Caroline Claremont and that is my niece, Lady Jewel."

Jewel shot her aunt a rigid look of disbelief.

"I am the Lady Flitcroft." After a glance at the back of Jewel's head, she said, "Chilly in here, isn't it? Lacking in the usual heat I've found in this box." She winked at Lady Caro and left.

Lady Caro grinned impishly at Tricia.

"Aunt!" exploded Jewel, "what on *earth* possessed you to speak to that tart? I heard she is trying to stick her hooks into Rowan!"

"Has she succeeded?" asked Lady Caro with interest.

"She is utterly the *last* person you should acknowledge! Oh, you're back, Rowan! Just listen to this virtuoso. I've been so hoping you wouldn't miss him." Lady Jewel's countenance changed, like a mask falling, from venomous eyes to a brilliant smile for him.

Like Jewel, Tricia feared that Nadine Vavasour, Lady Flitcroft had already sunk her talons too deeply into Rowan to do him aught but ill. At least by taking these Claremont ladies to the opera, he made a public statement for respectability. But had the onlookers seen Lady Flitcroft in his box, confronting them? How could anyone have missed her showy golden gown and sparkling hair plumes?

Tricia's heart sank, not only for the wagging tongues but mainly over the possibility that her Duke was publicly announcing his intentions. Had he not declared aloud that the reason he invited Lady Jewel tonight was because he needed an heir?

That thought made the night pure misery for Tricia. She did not like Lady Jewel. She could not be the kind of woman his mother would want for her son, could she?

The rest of the performance remained a blur. She not only had to endure Jewel's flirtation with Rowan, but also live in the knowledge that her lecherous guardian lurked in the theatre. He would not give up, would Kilver.

Lady Caro turned to Tricia and their eyes met. "Patrick."

"Yes, Your Ladyship?"

"Will you take a stroll with me? I need some circulation in my legs. I am not used to sitting still this long."

As they left, Jewel was already taking advantage of her aunt's departure. She leaned her puffed sleeve against the Duke's arm as she whispered to him.

Tricia closed the door without a sound but for the rending in her heart.

"Now, Patrick," said Lady Caro as they moved through a long, vacant corridor, "tell me quickly: who are your parents?"

"I cannot tell you, Your Ladyship. I am very sorry." She had thought long and hard that, if she revealed who she was, she would be forever in Society's black book. Well-born girls did not get themselves up in livery to serve single men.

"Please." Lady Caro's hazel eyes begged for the truth. "I wish you would answer me. There are reasons why I *must* know."

Tricia felt bereft of words.

"I see I shall have to ask you point-blank: was Leigh Claremont your father?"

Tricia blinked and asked, "That lord-person in your portrait gallery?" She felt hot beneath her collar. "Your Ladyship, what are you saying? I am only a page."

"No need to look so undone, Patrick, but there's the matter of our hands matching. Don't you think this is worth delving into?"

"It could be a coincidence, Your Ladyship." Tricia clenched her hands behind her back and strolled beside the frustrated woman, passing a couple enjoying each other's company rather than the performance.

Lady Caro whispered, "Are you afraid, Patrick? Afraid, perhaps, that you are an illegitimate child of my brother, Leigh's?"

Tricia's whole being sparked in anger. "The very idea!"

Interest jumped into Lady Caro's eyes.

Tricia knew that she had to rid this lady of that ignoble idea. "Lady Caro, I am very apprehensive to confess this, but I do believe that the man in the portrait, whom you called Lord Wyndhurst, was indeed my father. My *legitimate* father."

"A-ha!" Lady Caro's face shone. Excitedly, she pressed a door lever. In a room hung with costumes, she said, "Close the door. We'll talk in here."

Tricia whisked ballet dresses from a dainty chair and offered it to Lady Caro.

"I've sat long enough, thank you. Tell me why on earth you're serving the Duke of Rowan if you're my brother's son," she demanded, amazement written all over her face. "It's preposterous."

"I certainly never knew I was the child of a Lord Wyndhurst. I only knew my father as Leigh Ravenscar."

"Leigh Claremont disappeared after his wedding, and apparently took up an alias, using his wife's surname of Ravenscar. Where did you live?"

"In Robin Hood's Bay, south of Whitby."

"That must be where she was from. Tell me all about how you came to meet up with the Duke of Rowan. Begin after your parents died, if you please."

Tricia related how her aunt's husband, Lord Kilver, escorted her straight to his house after her parents' funeral and the reading of the Will. "Lord Kilver was never a friend to my parents, though he was married to my mother's sister. After the Will was read, he said it meant I must stay with him and Lady Kilver from that day on. When I tried to flee to my home, Kilver's footman stood before the door and prevented my leaving. Lord Kilver insisted that an orphan could not live alone."

"Well, that's true," said Lady Caro.

"I did not believe that Lady Kilver wanted me in her house," said Tricia, "and she downright unnerved me. Lord Kilver made sure I stayed. He said that, according to the law, he was in charge of my affairs, and would handle my inheritance for me."

"What did your inheritance include?"

"A ship, my father's merchant shipping business, and our new home called Soaring Gables, plus whatever money he left."

"Isn't all of that customary for a guardian to manage until one comes of age?"

"Not to the extent of locking a youth in a bedchamber!" retorted Tricia. She must be sure not to reveal that she was a female.

"True! So how did you escape him?"

"I waited until night, and with a sack slung across my middle, I opened the laundry chute in my room. I sat on the opening, thrust in my legs, and as I began to slip downward, I pulled the door shut. I whizzed down a dark tunnel."

Lady Caro looked taken aback. "Oh my! Tell me more."

"It made a turn, intersecting with the chute from Lady Kilver's bedchamber, and again from Lord Kilver's, but I expected something of the sort and kept my limbs close. I landed in a pile of laundry. What luck that the laundress was slovenly in her duties that week."

"Well, yes." Lady Caro's eyebrows stayed aloft for several seconds.

Tricia did not say it, but she still suspected that the chute had been built for the passage of smuggled goods more than for the convenience of washing, for there was a door opposite to where she landed which led into the neighbor's cellar.

"I could never count on townspeople to help me leave Lord Kilver's house, for everyone lives in awe of him. He's the only *noble*man in town." Her voice dripped sarcasm. "I stood on a table where I was eye-level with the cobbles of the street and watched. When I saw Lord Kilver stalk into the pub. I hefted myself up out of the window and bolted away from my town."

"My, but you're an amazing lad. However did you survive alone?"

"By keeping behind the stone walls, and later, the trees and hedges, and away from villages and roads. I walked for two days. I stopped at the remotest-looking farms, where I bought bits of food. I inquired for work at two kitchen doors and three stables. Everywhere, I was refused."

Lady Caro's hand covered her eyes at that. "If Leigh only knew!"

"After my fifth rejection, I tried more positively, out of necessity, you realize, and landed a job with a Farmer Ramsbottom."

"Good gracious! You worked for a farmer?"

Tricia grinned ruefully. "Mrs. Ramsbottom looked me over piteously, but her husband demanded hard work for every morsel."

Lady Caro threw up her hands. "My own nephew brought to such horrid, menial circumstances! It's a crime! I shudder to think of the indignities you must have suffered." Stricken, she gazed at Tricia with a mixture of disbelief and compassion. "My word, you are the rightful Marquis of Wyndhurst now!"

Worried to an intense degree by this new and startling idea, Tricia waved her off and said, "Oh, no, I'm not. I couldn't be. You are really my aunt, though?"

With a joyful voice, Lady Caro trilled, "I am sure of it! Oh, God be praised! I am so tickled I can hardly think." She grabbed Tricia's arm, suddenly looking appalled. "But now you're working for the Duke of Rowan! You will halt such toil at once, and come live with us."

Tricia felt dismay. "Oh no! I must continue to serve him for awhile yet. Please do not say anything to the Duke about all this. With respect, Lady Caro, I implore you!"

The lady looked doubtful. "How can I allow you, the son of Lord Wyndhurst, to lackey for anyone, even if he is a Duke? You are our long-lost heir!"

In desperation, Tricia cried, "Please don't think that way! I must! He needs me, and I promised to serve him after he rescued me. I must break this news to him myself when the time is right."

Lady Caro seemed overjoyed by her discovery that Patrick was now the rightful Marquis of Wyndhurst, and not Clive, her brother the usurper. While Tricia knew this was not true due to her sex, Lady Caro was all a-twitter over the truth as she saw it. It was very difficult for Tricia to procure her consent for silence.

Finally she agreed, but with great reluctance, saying, "You must do as you feel is right, then, my boy, but do not prolong your revelation a minute longer than necessary. After you have told him, fly to me. Highcourt House is your rightful home from now on, dear Patrick."

Tricia sighed in relief. She had a reprieve. Pain had forked through her heart at the prospect of leaving the Duke. After all, he needed her as a fellow soldier in his battles against scheming women. The way things looked tonight, she knew he needed her skill and weaponry without delay.

CHAPTER 8

An Eye-Opening Night

After the opera, the Duke's mansion seemed unusually quiet. Eldred did not glide down the stairs at the Duke's signal bell. "Where is he?" Rowan asked Stefan.

The footman did not know, but said he and Eldred did not have the evening off as most of the other servants did.

"I may as well look in at the Clarendon," murmured the Duke, "but first I'll change this cape and hat. Come, Patrick. You can take Eldred's place."

Tricia's heart skipped. *Just get his cape and hat,* she thought. She could handle those.

As they circled their way upstairs, the Duke asked, "Was Lord Kilver making you uneasy when I came upon you tonight?"

What an understatement. "That he was, Your Grace. Terribly!"

"He is enraged that you discovered his card case. I will have to keep a good watch over you."

"I would greatly appreciate that," she said with all her heart.

When they reached his chamber, he went in, saying, "Only one candle? Eldred expects me to change in darkness? Has he turned thrifty, or have his wits gone begging?"

"I'll light the lamps," said Tricia, and touched the candle to the wick under the nearest globe.

Under the domed bed, the curtains were closed, a fact which seemed to prick Rowan's curiosity. He flicked back the embroidered velvet.

Because he reacted with a startled sound, Tricia held up the lighted lamp and gaped. A woman lay curved on the Duke's blue counterpane. With russet hair spread loose like a mermaid, Lady Flitcroft had arranged herself in an alluring way.

"Well, well!" said the Duke, tugging at his snug collar.

Lady Flitcroft, wearing a thin, revealing chemise with her black lace scarf covering her face, feigned slumber.

The whites of Rowan's eyes flashed as he snapped the curtains shut. "Patrick," he whispered, "you should not see such things! But stay." This he added pianissimo with a touch on Tricia's arm as he passed by her.

She watched breathlessly to see what he would do.

He went into his bathing chamber and quickly reappeared. His eyes glinted in the candlelight as he parted the velvet bed curtains, swung the spout of a porcelain pitcher above the widow, and splashed an arc of water onto her face and neck.

She sprang to life. "Eee-yi! Lucas! Stop it!" she shrieked. Looking up at his stern face, she pushed back a wet tress and yanked off the soaked lace. Her face was flushed and angry. Swiftly, she changed her tune and affected a throaty voice.

"What game is this, Lucas, you original man?"

With a disgusted roll of his eyes for Patrick, Rowan snapped, "One that I hope will cool your ardor—for good!"

Her expression turned to indignation.

It made Rowan laugh, though he tried to sober himself.

At sight of Tricia's twitching lips as well, Lady Flitcroft furiously heaved herself up. "You dare to horse-laugh! What a cold soul you are!" She dragged the wet counterpane with her, heavy as it was, and disappeared into His Grace's bathing chamber. The door connected with a bang.

The Duke strolled over and spoke through it. "Shall I send in your clothing?" He pointed to the floor. "Patrick, I spy some alien garments under the bed. By the way, Madam," he called, "what have you done with my valet?"

Through the door, she explosively retorted, "I sent him off to fix us a supper, but since he does not cook, he opted to ask your neighbor's cook to conjure up something."

"Oh, thank you," said Rowan, "that will look very good. Do you mean to say Eldred gave you the entrée to my rooms?"

"I'll never tell. Fussy as he is, he at least appreciates a beautiful woman." She opened the door and in a trembling voice asked, "Why on earth don't you?"

"I very much enjoy looking at beautiful women, yourself included," returned the Duke with undue generosity, "but I beg your understanding, for I fight the enemy of temptation that accompanies you."

As her mouth opened, his voice hardened. "I will not succumb to an invasion of my bedchamber . . . or my life!"

Tricia sent her Duke a wide, congratulatory smile. She dove to retrieve the woman's mustard gown, hose, shoes, black gloves, bracelets, and beaded reticule.

Lady Flitcroft's eyes narrowed on her through the crack in the door as she snatched her clothes. "You! Go at once to your room!" She pushed Tricia's chest, causing her pain. "Send that one straight up to bed, Lucas."

"Hey, hey, be careful." Rowan steadied Tricia and set her out of the woman's reach. "Can Patrick call you a hackney first, or does your coachman wait in the next block?"

"He's waiting," drawled Lady Flitcroft. "What are *you* waiting for?" she snapped at Tricia. "I said go!"

Tricia felt her glare until she backed out of her sight.

"Patrick," said the Duke, following her into the corridor, "could you find me some tooth powder and a brush? Mine are inaccessible at the moment, and I must get going. I'll wait for you here." He ran a hand through his hair in a distracted manner.

It had not been easy to do what he had done and say what he had said to the woman, Tricia surmised. Tension had crackled despite his stabs at lightheartedness. She prayed to God that her Duke could continue in strength against his temptresses.

Upstairs she groped on her bureau top for her candlestick, and carried it to the landing, where she lit it from the wall sconce. Back in her room, she opened her top drawer and took out her own extra tooth brush and powder box that Mrs. Pollard had provided, for she did not know where the Duke's extras were kept. Just as she blew out the flame, she caught a whiff of something burning, more pungent than her charred wick.

It was pipe tobacco smoking.

From behind her bed, a man's silhouette moved like lightning, the door snapped shut, and she stood in darkness.

She screamed, but her mouth was clamped by a vise-like hand.

* * *

Rowan knew he must say extremely firm words of farewell to Lady Flitcroft, but he was not about to do it in his bedchamber. It must be downstairs in the entrance hall with his supportive page at his side. He looked up the stairwell, waiting for Patrick.

A latch clicked, and Lady Flitcroft emerged from his room looking mussed-up and defiant.

"Will you come down to the hall with me?" Rowan asked her. "I owe you an apology."

"Yes, you do, but first of all, have you no servants at your beck and call this time of night? I cannot fasten myself up the back; it is most provoking."

He knew that far more provoked her than dress fastenings. With great reluctance, he said slowly, "Let me, ah, help. Most of my servants have the evening off." He shot a look over his shoulder. Still no Patrick. Rowan found the tabs and managed to connect three of them with their hooks.

His touch must have stirred the widow, for she gazed at him over her shoulder. Her voice throbbed with emotion. "*How* can you throw all this away, Lucas?"

He knew what a clunch he seemed, having accepted her invitation to Yorkshire without suspecting her intentions. But how could he undo all that?

He could not, so he sang lightly as he fastened:
"Mrs. Gill is very ill;
Nothing can improve her
But to see the Tuileries
And waddle through the Louv-wah."

Lady Flitcroft giggled at his rhyming of Louvre. With a sigh, she said, "I wish you will tell me exactly what naïve reason you have for curtailing what good times you and I could have together." She positioned herself in another attempt to entice him.

He warned, "Lady Flitcroft, cease fire!"

She looked as if she had been slapped. "You louse! Why is it Lady Flitcroft all of a sudden? I have been Nadine to you for years."

"You and I have no leave to continue this first-name informality, or to perpetuate further encounters than that which we had in conversation and games of piquet and all the rest."

"The rest?" she screeched. "What rest? Those few shared poems in my garden? Our fevered, interrupted kiss here the other night?"

"You must forgive me if I hurt your feelings, but I decline your proposed liaison. As for fevered—" He waved his hand expressively, for he could not agree. Hers had been the surprise onslaught.

Why had he not thrown her out the minute she entered his house? Ruefully he thought, because he was too much of a gentleman. One did not eject ladies from one's house in the normal course of things.

Lady Flitcroft was raging at him. "Lucas! You're so inexperienced!" That was meant to sting.

"Becoming more experienced all the time," he said under his breath.

Why didn't Patrick return? His footsteps would be audible on the marble steps, but Rowan could hear nothing but Nadine Vavasour complaining, "We were on the brink of happiness. My grief was gone! But now I find you so icy and supposedly *noble* and tossing it all to the wind! Could it be Lady Jewel Claremont who has done this to you? Is it that snooty chit who caused your turnabout?"

"My convictions have nothing whatever to do with Lady Jewel, or with anything but my own conscience." He bowed his head. "I am repenting my lapse into libertinage."

"Repenting!   Libertinage?" she squeaked in disbelief.

"Yes, thank God," he returned firmly. "One does not go on with actions which bring one to guilt. Do you understand? You know what your intentions are toward me; you've made that startlingly clear. I cannot, in good conscience, see you more. I'm sorry I ever—"

"Ever what?" she attacked. "You didn't *do* anything! You make me so mad! I wonder if you like women at all. Except," her eyes glistened in remembrance, "I saw your eyes follow me, in the mirror once."

Rowan needed to loosen his cravat, but kept his hands clasped resolutely behind his back. He was not able to look longer on the woman. She embarrassed him.

She ran and flung an embrace around him which trapped his arms. "Lucas," she coaxed, "why not marry me?" Blinking her short lashes, she looked intensely up into his eyes.

Her perfume and closeness smothered him. He detached her clinging arms and cleared his throat. "It is with me in marriage as in, ah, dueling," he prevaricated. "I'll be anything rather than a principal. I have long disapproved of either practice as a means of *obtaining satisfaction*." There, that should do it.

As her eyes flashed, he quoted, "*No man is wise at all hours*. I hope you can forgive my lapse in judgment."

"*Forgive* you? For spending time with me? What do you take me for?" She was on the warpath now. "Lucas Beaufort, may your search for love end in complete disaster!" She slapped his face.

It stung. Endeavoring to remain the gentleman he felt he was no longer, Rowan indicated the stairs and stonily gestured her down ahead of him.

She was rooted to the spot, blinking in rage. "You will pay for leaving me! I'll ruin whoever is dear to you!" She moved down one step.

"No, you won't," he said calmly. He sent a prayer to God that she would not be able to do that.

Footsteps sounded from the landing above, and Stefan dashed into sight, to the Duke's profound relief. "Your Grace, something's going on in the attic! Somebody screamed, and Lionel shouted,

'Fetch the Duke!'"

Lady Flitcroft grabbed Rowan's arm with great strength. "Don't go!"

"Lady Flitcroft, let go! If someone screamed in my house, I'll know the reason."

She hung on vehemently. "Send that incompetent footman to investigate," she cried. "It's one of the servants having a nightmare. What else could it be? Rowan, we must finish our talk *now.*"

"We *have* finished it. Sit there and take a damper!" Against his every finer feeling, he flung her backwards onto the upholstered settee behind her on the landing, where she bounced and stared up at him. Her face showed more fascination with him than ever.

Was there no ridding himself of that woman? Rowan vaulted up the steps three at a time. He arrived on the servants' floor just as the back stairs door closed in the distance. He would have streaked for it immediately had not Stefan cried, "Look at Lionel!"

The dark-haired footman lay on his face on the floor. The Duke bent to feel his wrist. "Is he the one who screamed?"

"No, he doesn't scream. He heard it, too. He told me to check the maids through Mrs. Pollard, and he would check on Patrick. The maids' rooms were all quiet, Mrs. Pollard said."

Rowan's heart beat hard. "It looks as if Lionel was knocked down with a deal of force." He pushed the door into Patrick's chamber, calling his name. He felt hurriedly over the bed and found it empty. He noticed the scent of tobacco pungent in the room. It smelled like the Turk's Delight Lady Flitcroft had given him.

"Does Patrick smoke? No? Then my page has been taken from under our noses! Stefan, you see to Lionel, bring him round. I'm going after whoever made off with Patrick."

"Alone, Your Grace?"

"There's no time to wait for anyone! Go get rid of that woman who invaded my house," he ordered.

Rowan could hear Lady Flitcroft calling him as he ran to the far door and plunged down the narrow wedged steps of the servant's staircase, round and round, nearly hitting his head on the steps above. Tobacco pervaded the closeness of the air. Someone had actually sneaked into his house and kidnapped Patrick! The boy was handsome as an angel, intelligent, and sensitive. He was a caring listener and a willing doer. Someone must covet the lad for his own entourage. Or worse.

Rowan began to seethe. Through the kitchen and the garden he ran, over flagstones and past the ornate iron gate that should not have been hanging open. A crunch of hoofs on gravel started up past the trees, and an unlit carriage wheeled off down the private alley and curved out of sight.

It would take forever to get one of his horses from the mews. There was a parked carriage just ahead; Lady Flitcroft's, to be sure. She had nerve parking so close to his house. Rowan hoped that bad intent could turn to good result. "Look sharp!" he shouted, running toward it.

The slumped coachman turned and opened one eye.

"Give me one of those horses, quick! Groom, come loosen this animal. It's an emergency! Yes, I am the Duke. Thank you for your speed."

With the animal between the knees of his silk breeches, Rowan set off at a gallop in the direction the carriage had gone. He saw but one coach without lights, so he tracked it through the streets, keeping it in sight even though he could not catch it for the press of traffic. It veered onto New Road and out to the countryside.

He expected to overtake it, but when they reached the end of the paving stones, the wheels sent dust rolling into Rowan's face in such a choking cloud that he was forced to veer into the ditch to clear his eyes before urging the coach horse onward.

Ten minutes later, loping desperately past houses and farms, he saw the vehicle halted ahead, its lanterns being lit. Rowan knew that he could catapult himself into a futile situation without a weapon to bank on. How could he hold up a coach with nothing but his voice? He must seize his chance in a more calculated way.

The black coach rattled on, its side lanterns throwing out two tunnels of light. At the edge of the walnut-scented lane cantered Rowan, fighting to control the awkward horse in its carriage harness.

Suddenly, the vehicle was nowhere to be seen. When the dust cleared, he saw that he had passed a high stone wall surrounded by ancient trees. He heard the heavy clink of an iron latch ahead, so he reined in at the gate.

The coach in question jounced down a cobbled

lane inside. Though the Duke shook the gate in fury, it was solidly locked.

He tied the horse to a gnarled walnut tree and felt for branches stout enough to support his weight. Standing in the V of two limbs, he peered over the wall and saw the coach in a porte-cochère attached to a brick house.

There was Patrick's blond head emerging into the light of a lantern, his face white and terrified. A lanky man, opera hat pulled low, gripped him by the shoulders. When the man spoke, Patrick struggled and cried, "No! Get away!" in a high pitch.

At that, the man jerked him around. Patrick ducked his head.

Rowan was galvanized by shock. He moved like quicksilver across a thick branch and onto the crumbling brick wall. Whoever this lecher for young boys was, he would feel the pain of Rowan's outrage.

"You're back under my control, Creature," the man was saying in a familiar nasal voice.

In a flash, the furious Duke recognized Lord Kilver.

Patrick dodged violently, elbows and legs everywhere.

"No use resisting or shouting," Kilver sneered, grappling to subdue his quarry, "for this vacant house belongs to a friend of mine. She's keeping someone busy at the moment. Can you guess who that is?"

Seeing red, Rowan shot up from his crouch on the wall and leaped eight feet down.

Patrick screamed as Kilver pinioned him with

arms behind his back and marched him toward the house.

To snatch a chunk of brick at the wall's edge and hurl it at Kilver was the work of an instant. Rowan's aim carried with it the precision born of righteous rage. The brick thumped with stunning impact behind Kilver's ear.

He jerked aside, his eyeballs sank into his head, and he fell back and landed motionless on the ground.

Patrick was yelling, "I'll fight you to my dying breath! You *won't* have your way with me now or *ever!*"

That is for sure, vowed Rowan, running toward his page.

Patrick turned with a look of wonderment and cried, "Huh? Your Grace?" Joy flooded the white face and widened, glistening eyes.

As he reached Patrick, the boy's eyelids fell in what looked like great relief. With a glad murmur of "My Duke!" he fell into Rowan's outstretched arms. Rowan held his trembling page, thankful to God that he had been in time.

He saw Kilver move. He stirred and sat up slowly. He snarled at the Duke, "You can't have her! She's mine! By law!"

The Duke blinked. "What are you talking about, you blackguard?"

Kilver, seeing his bewilderment, crowed, "The girl!" He grabbed Patrick's foot. "You still think she's a boy?" His thin mouth made an ugly hole. "Ha ha ha! Never tell me you've been fooled all this time, Duke? That's famous! Wait till I tell Nadine!" He slapped his thigh as he emitted cackles.

The Duke angrily wrested Patrick's foot away from Kilver's grip and kicked his chest, sending him rolling.

Rowan swallowed. It took him several seconds to consider the idea that Patrick, his page, could be a young woman.

He looked down at the fair face beneath the sheen of pale hair and saw the long lashes downcast with guilt.

CHAPTER 9

The Disastrous Truth

"You vile rat!" Rowan loomed over Kilver, making him cower. He reached down and grabbed the man's ear, only to find it bloody from the brick he had hurled. Rowan pinched it and yelled, "Is there nothing to which you will not stoop? Touch this child again, you dastardly scum, and I'll—"

Lord Kilver was staring at him in fear when he went slack and fell back, apparently in a faint.

Rowan raged at the inert form, "For these offenses tonight, as for your cheating at cards, you are blackballed from the clubs and ostracized from Society! –but how I long to do more! Much more!"

As he turned to his wide-eyed page, he growled, "God help me to remember that vengeance is the Lord's, not mine."

The Duke looked powerful and frighteningly wonderful to Tricia. Melting love for him overrode all else, even the horrible ordeal of Kilver's abduction and attack on her. The Duke had saved her! She thanked God in choking gratitude for sending him.

As Rowan, breathing hard, stared down at her, his jaw looked tight.

Tricia's heart jumped. Oh, but the truth Kilver

had blurted out! The Duke now knew she was a woman!

The Duke motioned her to follow him. At the garden wall, he insisted on giving her a leg-up and told her to climb down the tree on the other side. She could not see his face for the darkness.

As he loosened the reins of a horse waiting there, his eyes looked hard in the faint moonlight. "What," he inquired tersely, "was your reason for deceiving me?"

This was worse than she had feared. With a shaking hand, she pointed back over the wall. "*He* was my reason, Your Grace."

The ride home, with two of them close together on Lady Flitcroft's leader, was horrid. The glacial silence maintained by the Duke made Tricia want to cry, but tears would not come. What was he thinking? Why didn't he say more? She felt sick with apprehension. She wanted to explain despite his stilted reserve, so she asked, "Will you hear my reasons, please, Your Grace?"

Woodenly, he said, "Tell me."

His arms felt warm about her as he held the reins in front of her, but she felt dry in her throat because she knew she had lost her Duke's confidence. "All right, Your Grace, I will. After my parents died, Lord Kilver took me to his house and kept me locked up." Her voice faltered. "He did strange things . . ."

"Like what?" snapped the Duke.

Tricia hated to relive such sordid episodes. "For example, when I was alone in the laundry, he grabbed my waist from behind and flung me upward toward the ceiling. He twirled me around so that I fell against him. It was revolting!"

"That fiend! What did you do?"

"I hit him in the teeth and gave him a bloody lip."

"Good. And?"

"We heard Lady Kilver's footfall. He got away with that because I didn't dare to tell her about it. She is a strange woman. But he was cockier than ever after that."

"Tell me more," Rowan said severely near her ear.

Tricia spoke with her face half-turned so he could hear her over the horse's *clip-clops*. "One evening, while his wife worked at her tambour frame, he told me to play the spinet. He came to turn my pages, not knowing when to do so, but waiting for me to tell him. He leaned against me, and when his wife wasn't looking, he . . . he pinched me." Tricia felt her face flame. "Your Grace, it's mortifying to tell you of these sordid episodes."

"I expect it is, but I need to know. *He* is the scoundrel. Do not take guilt upon yourself. Didn't Lady Kilver do anything at all to help you?"

"When I dashed away from him to sit on her footstool, she took one look at me and told me to go to bed. She must have sensed something. In my room, I dragged two heavy chairs and rammed them against the door. I did not undress, but lay in bed, jumping at every creak. It was an hour later when I heard a key turn in my lock. The door opened, but it didn't go far, for the chairs were lodged tightly. Lord Kilver said through the crack, 'Think you're clever, don't you?' He gave up then, for Lady Kilver called him." Tricia shuddered against Rowan's chest. "I knew I could waste no time in leaving that nest of iniquity."

Rowan whistled. "How did you manage it?"

She told him she knew her moment had come when she heard a knock on the downstairs door, and overheard that *The White Dove,* her late father's ship, had landed.

"I suspect Lord Kilver is using that ship to smuggle contraband into Robin Hood's Bay. He sneaked out of the house, whispering with someone, so I grabbed my chance and worked by the light of a full moon gleaming through my window. I pulled on my brother, David's, clothes. The only problem was my hair."

"Why?"

"It fell nearly to my waist. Those scissors chilled me at first. I was afraid of what I was going to attempt. I held up a tress and prayed to God for help to escape from Kilver, no matter how petrified I was." Tricia sighed deeply, and shuddered. She felt so thankful that she was on this side of that terrifying night, and this present one.

"After I cut my hair, I was ready." She told the Duke about whizzing down the laundry chute, climbing through the window, and how she sneaked through the narrow, twisting streets and up onto the moor.

Despite his considerate listening attitude, Tricia feared that the Duke had retreated from her. He was strange and distant because she was not Patrick. She had known that the truth would make all the difference in the world.

Now the gulf between them felt vast and awful. She could not bear it. With her heart full to bursting, she said as they rounded the corner into Park Lane, "Things will never be the same again, will they?"

"You mean where you are concerned?" He dismounted. "Certainly not. How *can* they be?"

Despair flooded through her.

When he lifted her off the horse, she rejoiced in the strength of his hands, but felt injured by how coldly and quickly he released her.

"What is the worst part of this matter, dear Duke?" she begged. "What is making you so terribly furious with me?"

"Women!" he expelled. "You are all deceivers!"

Tricia watched him march up his marble steps. She burst out crying. He was right.

* * *

Minutes later, the Duke roused Mrs. Pollard by pounding on her bedchamber door.

Tricia hovered in the shadows of the third-floor corridor, for he had curtly bade her to follow him, ignoring her tears. He did not even smile at his housekeeper as he usually did. "Excuse me, Mrs. Pollard, I need your help. This whole farrago should be explained to you, but for the moment, please find feminine sleeping garments for—what is your name?" He rounded on Tricia. "It's certainly not Patrick."

Why did he have to sound so pitiless? Breathlessly, she eked out, "Patricia—that is, I prefer Tricia."

"See that *Patricia* has what she needs for the night. Thank you, Pollard. Keep her until I decide what's to be done with her. Good night."

"Yes, Your Grace. Good night." Mrs. Pollard turned to stare at the trembling young person, her kind face all amazement.

Tricia sniffed wetly and waited for the Duke to bid her good night. He did not. His handsome head disappeared around the corner. She heard him ask someone how Lionel had recovered.

"He's still got his faculties. Did you find Patrick?" asked Stefan, sounding as if he cared.

"My former page is found," stated the Duke. "I am obliged that you alerted me when you did."

Former page. His words made Tricia feel sick.

Mrs. Pollard took her arm gently. "Come, dear."

A sob rose within Tricia as she stumbled into the housekeeper's chamber. She let herself be nudged into a cushioned rocking chair. The bedside candle's flame blurred through her tears. She covered her eyes, and rocked, and wept.

Mrs. Pollard's white braids brushed Tricia's hands as she grasped them, exclaiming, "A girl, are you? My dearest dear, you are nothing but a slip of a girl!"

Tricia nodded. Her heart felt too full of misery to hold back the tears that kept flowing. Ample arms pulled her near as the anguish flowed gradually out of Tricia, ending with soft shudders.

Mingling with the fresh cotton of Mrs. Pollard's nightdress were the soft tones of her voice crooning, "You've been our Duke's page! My goodness gracious, you are a brave girl, you surely are. What's he going to do with you now?"

CHAPTER 10

The Duke's Dilemma

The Duke of Rowan, alone at his dining room table, looked more intimidating than Tricia had ever imagined a rich, irritated Duke could look. "Come here, if you please," said His Grace.

She hung back apprehensively in the doorway. She heard harshness underlying his voice when he spoke to her now. There was no question of her pulling out his chair at table or lingering for confidential talks. Gone were those dream days.

Mrs. Pollard said Tricia had been summoned after he sent Eldred, his former valet, out of the house "with his final pay and his nose out of joint for conspiring with that Flitcroft hussy!"

Rupert, the footman, shyly told Tricia that the household was in an uproar unprecedented in the life of this Duke. Rowan was slow to wrath, but his ire had been sparked into a towering conflagration since last night. Everyone in the house felt singed. They slunk silently, peeked around corners, and cringed at his appearance as if they were all guilty of something. And it was only lunch time.

Mrs. Pollard dressed Tricia in a pale blue gown acquired from one of the chamber maids. She ushered her downstairs, whispering, "Take courage!" and left her standing in his awe-inspiring presence.

With downcast eyes, Tricia winced at the tone the Duke had used toward her. She knew she deserved whatever he chose to mete out as punishment. What reason did she dare to give him? She moved closer as he commanded her, knowing she could not tell him the truth. She could not say, *I wanted to stay near you because you drew me by your warmth, your gracious nature, your wonderful appeal . . . and I thought you needed me to help you fend off deceitful women.*

Now he classed her as one, too.

He appeared to wrestle inwardly. He got up, slung the door shut, and lashed out. "Barring a host of other vital questions, answer me this one: how could you gawk at me in my bedchamber while I undressed without letting on that you were a female?"

Sure enough, that was a shocking crime, and she knew it. Gripping a carved chair back, she fought for a steadying breath while her heart palpitated. She felt far too feminine in the airy gown belted below her bosom. She had visualized throwing herself on his mercy, hugging his knees, and softening his heart by her tears. She could do none of those things because he looked relentless.

His dark eyes kindled as he said, "I have all sorts of suspicions about you."

"What suspicions? I am not like Lady Flitcroft! I never *meant* to see you like that. When I was called into your room to take your letter, I had a hard time knowing *where* to look!" Her cheeks felt hot. That vision of him from the back, silhouetted as he threw off his nightshirt, remained glorious in her mind's eye. What was he so angry about?

"At the George Inn," she hurried to explain, "you asked so nicely for me to massage your soreness away that how could I be disobedient and leave you to that aggressive maid?"

He crossed his arms and put a hand to his brow, shielding his face from her.

Tricia stared. Surely he wasn't laughing!

He passed a hand over his mouth, turned back to her, and demanded, "Then tell me why you became my page under such a monumental falsehood."

"Your Grace, if you will kindly recall, I did not ask to be your page. All I begged was a lift far away from Ramsbottom. You urged me to travel farther, which was wonderfully helpful, so I did, with gratitude. When you persuaded me that you needed a page and nearly *told* me I should be yours, I knew I could not refuse. I was, and still am, indebted to you for saving me. What else could I have done here in London, where I knew not a soul?"

From under lowered brows, he watched her during this speech. "Halt this trumpeting of your virtuous behavior. I see what happened, but you still lied to me."

"Yes, my untruths began with telling you I was sixteen when I am eighteen. You assumed from my dress that I was a male, as I intended as protection in my work, and I gave you the false name of Patrick Raven. I had to be a boy in order to run away from Lord Kilver's house and find work. Please show me an ounce of mercy, Your

Grace."

"Yes, but you could have taken me into your confidence, and not skulked into my private and personal doings!" Rowan expelled.

"I never expected to be called to your bedchamber as part of my duties, Your Grace. I have known nothing of pages and their work, yet I could not refuse to do your bidding once I had the job, could I? I was alarmed when you pulled off your nightshirt so that's why I ran out of your room."

"You could have told me you were a woman then!" he shouted. He whirled to tug the velvet bell pull.

"Told you *then?*" echoed Tricia. "Oh, no. I thought that would have really embarrassed you."

The Duke flipped vigorously through his mail on the sideboard. When his face appeared in profile, she was sure he had been fighting some emotion again. His voice was stern as he demanded, "Why on earth didn't you reveal yourself later?"

Tricia blinked and swallowed. Here was the crux. "You would have thrown me out."

* * *

The Duke took a few steps closer to her and squinted at her menacingly. "You only delayed the inevitable."

Her face fell; that beautiful, luminous face with the vulnerable lips, eloquent eyes, and delicate arching eyebrows. Rowan knew now why he had felt such unorthodox sensations at times when his page had sat near, or laughed, or looked so fetchingly beautiful. A sudden draft swayed her flounced blue hem and there, to halt the charged moment, came Mrs. Pollard, having thrown open the door in answer to his bell.

Rowan turned, his eyes still glued upon his transformed page. She looked so contrite, and he regretted to see the wetness in her eyes and spilling over.

Of his housekeeper, he asked in exasperation, "What am I to do with her?"

Tricia spoke up softly. "I expect you must bustle me out without a reference, just as you did Eldred."

"I gave him a reference."

Tricia took a deep breath and would likely have said something more had not Mrs. Pollard gripped her arm. "Listen to His Grace, now, my dear. I am sure he will take care of you in the best way." She nodded at Rowan.

There was a long pause as he tried to decide what he should do. Finally, throwing down his unread mail with a slap, he said, "You may stay on as my parlor maid. I have not got one at the moment, and I have a musical soirée scheduled for tomorrow afternoon. You may help the footmen."

"Oh, I couldn't do that, Your Grace!"

"Why not? Have you an objection to working as yourself?" he heard himself fire at her.

Tricia said wanly, "I cannot bear to stay here as baggage underfoot."

Rowan snapped, "You would not stay here in that capacity." He said to Mrs. Pollard, "Take her under your wing and have Aldwin help you instruct her in her duties as a parlor maid."

Mrs. Pollard said cajolingly, "But think how those

footmen will pester her now. Why, she is a very lovely girl, Your Grace."

Rowan felt reluctant to admit that out loud, but he let his eyes travel from her slender figure up to her angelic face with its soulful eyes. "She is not precisely a girl. A girl would not know how to exercise such cunning on me."

Tricia's jaw dropped and her eyes sparked at him.

He ignored that and continued, "Give the footmen a lecture before-hand. Dress her appropriately for drawing-room duties. You told me once that you can fetch and carry," he challenged Tricia, "so you may serve sherry and cakes to my guests. You will fit more easily through the rows of chairs than the footmen do."

"Your Grace, doesn't the sight of me irk you intolerably? After the way I deceived you and put you to such horrendous trouble? Why should I stay?"

His eye contact tangled with hers. The feeling she evoked in him was unsettling. She made him want to take her in his arms and tell her everything would be all right. He felt like assuring her that he would care for her until his dying breath. But with his pride and Mrs. Pollard in the way, he could only stalk toward the door, saying, "I cannot let you out of my sight. Kilver is out there, remember?"

When his footsteps echoed around the curve of the stairs above, Mrs. Pollard expelled, "I do declare, this was the strangest interview I have ever witnessed. But you are to stay, dear Tricia; that's all that matters. I will lend you my embroidered apron for tomorrow. Oh, don't look so undone. Aldwin will show you how he wants to serve the guests. Are you easier now, my dear?"

"Easier?" echoed Tricia. "Things are far more difficult for me than ever!"

* * *

The Duke, as he usually did on Wednesday afternoons, rode to White's to congregate with his circle of friends. He found Lord Bixby in the front room, and regaled him with a terse account of "Patrick's" abduction by Lord Kilver. He left out the part about his page's true sex.

Bixby listened agog. At the part about Kilver attacking Patrick, he jerked back and cried, "What a greasy eel! Let me at that crackpot! I hope you gave him what for!"

"I did." The Duke twisted his lips. "I suppose I'm lucky the brick didn't do him in. But it galls me that he is still prowling loose."

"Yes, and you can't just haul a peer like Lord Kilver in to the law. Unfair, but that's the way it is."

The club was filling fast. Rowan and Bixby sat, not with their usual crowd in the bow window, but at a coffee table apart because Rowan had hoped to find solace in Bixby's confidence. It hadn't worked. Rowan was still on edge. He wished he had Patrick to pluck him up.

At this unbidden thought, he frowned deeply. His little Patrick was gone . . . gone forever. In his place was an enchanting girl whom he had verbally abused, over and over. The sensitive thing was surely hurt by his inability to say what he felt. Instead, he had been so cruel to her.

"What's the matter?" demanded Bixby, watching

him. "There must be something awful that you haven't told me."

He might as well spill it. He had to confide in someone. With a deep groan, he said, "Wait until you hear." He leaned across the table, locking eyes with his friend. "Patrick is not what you think," he whispered. "I discovered that Kilver has been after the scamp for months because the scamp is a young woman."

"What? A young *woman?*" screeched Bixby, his blue eyes popping wide.

Rowan grabbed his jaw to hush him up.

Bixby flushed, and then fell into a rush of whispering, "Your page, who you took around everywhere—even here into White's—is a *female?* And you didn't know it? Ho, Rowan!" He grinned in awestruck amazement. "No need to look so mortified, my friend. Of all the luck in London, you always have more than your share. I *say!*"

"Squelch it, Bix!" Rowan clapped a newspaper at his friend's mouth, drawing even more curious looks from men conversing and reading nearby.

Lord Alvanley and Beau Brummell rose as one from their seats in the bow window and approached. Brummell, smiling urbanely, twirled his quizzing glass. "You absent yourself from us today, Duke, Bixby. I miss you two."

"It's this blackball business," growled Rowan. "Thank you for your support, and for yours, Alvanley. I have so many black balls in this sack, when one would do, that we have effectively expelled Kilver from this club."

"Can you believe," drawled Brummell, "that a club member should have sunk into such moral turpitude? Unthinkable!" He shuddered. "But what," he said in a new voice, "was Lord Bixby in transports over when you shushed him up? Was it something about a female?"

Lord Alvanley asked, "Who is she?"

Rowan cast Bixby a look of warning not to say.

Bixby teased, buying time for Rowan, "Young ladies are of prime importance in any conversation, are they not, Beau?"

"Absolutely. Who is the woman of the hour?"

Rowan looked around at his rapt audience of three. He returned Brummell's charming smile. "Lady Jewel Claremont." As Bixby's brows shot up, Rowan asked, "What do you think of her, Beau?"

Brummell crossed his arms and looked at the chandelier, considering. "Lady Jewel Claremont has . . . an air."

"That's sure death," said Bixby, who looked grateful for deliverance from their true topic.

Mr. Brummell chuckled at Bixby's comment and turned to the Duke. "That is, an air of elegance, Your Grace. Is she not perfectly elegant, gentlemen?"

"Surely," murmured Lord Alvanley, looking bored.

"Is she yours, Rowan?" queried Brummell slyly.

Rowan shrugged. "I haven't the slightest idea."

The Beau remarked, "I do think she has too cool an elegance for you, my friend, or do I err?" He lifted a dark eyebrow and, with Alvanley in his wake, strolled away to dinner.

Bixby looked at Rowan with penitence. "Sorry I caused you all that probing. But the more I think over what you've said, the more I can't *stand* that

Patrick was kidnapped by that slime, Kilver. That she was subjected to a carriage ride and pawing by him just boils my blood! What a shocking thing for a girl to endure!"

"Yes, the whole thing makes me want to strangle him!" Rowan flexed his fists. "Over and over!"

Bixby said, "I admire how she so cleverly served you as a boy, though. Her actions and attitude were well conducted and convincing, weren't they? I see now how brilliant she was."

Rowan had sunk in his chair, pressing his throbbing forehead with his palms. He eyed Bixby and said, "Don't forget that the little baggage deceived me."

"Convincingly, too! Good for her. Duped me completely." Bixby grinned. "Remember I said it was a shame Patrick wasn't a girl? Remember?"

Rowan got up, replaced his chair with a shove, and strolled darkly out of the room. On his way up the portrait-lined stairs, the mirror showed him the furor of his thoughts. He cleared his brow with an effort. How had Patrick—Tricia—gotten so quickly under his skin? The way her blue-gray eyes had beseeched him when she begged for an ounce of mercy! How her tender lips had trembled when he chastised her . . .

"Stop it!" he snarled at himself. He saw Bixby hurrying to catch up with him. "She tricked me!" he threw over his shoulder. "For days!"

"She must have had serious reasons." As gentlemen flowing down the staircase perked up at that remark, Rowan shot his friend a black look.

Bixby held his tongue until they reached the billiard room. "Don't take it so to heart. What of real harm did she do to make you this wroth?"

Rowan grabbed Bixby by the lapels. "She listened to me talk about my problems with women! She looked me over when I was undressing!"

Bixby's jaw dropped. "You don't say!" He laughed.

"Howl away if you must! She took unfair advantage!" Rowan stalked over to the billiard cues.

"Where did you give her such opportunity?" Bixby gobbled, grabbing Rowan's arm to peruse his face with interest.

Rowan snatched a cue stick. "In my bedchamber, which I have long considered a sanctum in which to doff a nightshirt away from the eyes of women."

Bixby grinned hugely. "Did she show any reaction? Or, do you recall?"

Rowan said through clenched teeth, "Stop grinning, will you, and listen to this: I asked my page, Patrick, to give me a back massage in the inn room we shared in Huntingdon. Yes, Bix, she slept on a trundle in my room. But first she put me to sleep with a most effective back rub, and woke me in the morning with coffee in bed."

Lord Bixby looked rapturous. "You *are* the luckiest man alive!"

"There's more," said Rowan, scowling darkly at his friend's enjoyment.

"What else?" asked Bixby, avid for more sensations.

"My page stood at my side when whom should I discover in my bed last night but Nadine Vavasour!"

"You . . . keep . . . Lady Flitcroft?" whispered Bixby disbelievingly, his eyes wide with shock. "I've been absolutely denying the rumor."

At that, the Duke hit the billiard table with his fist, making the balls jump. "It *is* a rumor! I am *not* keeping her! Never have! I've been trying my utmost to get rid of her!" He turned his back on the other men who had walked in, and lowered his voice. "The worst part was that Patrick—the girl—witnessed the whole sordid scene."

"Ah," said Bixby, shaking his fair head, "that is too bad."

The Duke let out a stressful breath. "She probably thinks the woman has been there before!"

His friend stared at him. "If she knew your morals, she would not think that. Does she know much about you?"

Rowan, remembering his discussions with Patrick, felt better on that score. "She does. I ranted to her about how I strove to escape that woman, and a lot more drivel about how I have to dodge grasping women all the time. I shudder to think of all that I spilled to my *page*."

Bixby, standing awestruck beside the billiard table with a ball in his hand, expelled, "Zounds! You told her all of that?"

"I did," he said, and changed the subject abruptly. "By the way, I heard Lord Kilver boast to her that he and Lady Flitcroft had a joint plan. Get this: she was meant to seduce me while he kidnapped my page! What if it had turned out the way they planned?" Wrathfully, Rowan lifted his brows at Bixby. "What if I hadn't gotten to Tricia in time?"

His friend's eyes rounded in alarm.

"Unthinkable!"

Rowan thrust a cue stick at him.

"What will you do with Tricia now?" asked Bixby. "You'll have to keep her doubly secure, won't you, since Kilver's after her?"

Rowan hit a one-cushion carom and said brusquely, "I have given her parlor duties."

"Really? Well, well! She must look quite something dressed as a girl. Can I ask her to come and work for me? I appreciate beautiful scenery."

"Don't even think of it!" snarled the Duke. He had to get something else off his chest. "Do you know what she told me about Kilver?" He waited until two old club members ambled out of earshot. "She suspects he receives contraband in Robin Hood's Bay."

"Oh? That's interesting. Hmmm . . . like velvet, perhaps?" Bixby went silent for awhile, looking speculative. After he missed a ball, he straightened up and said, "I have an idea. Let's ask the Beau if he would like to look over Kilver's supply of stuff and velvet. Kilver told us he has more where his vulgar coat came from. If Brummell will cooperate, that should be a carrot in front of Kilver's nose, especially after being booted out of this club. We want him exposed for at least some of his crimes, don't we? He should jump at any notice from Brummell."

"Yes," said Rowan, making a carom by cracking a crotch shot, "and if he's into illegal dealings, you will have him locked up neat as cheese. Is that it?"

"Contraband goods could be difficult to prove, but it would be worth it to get the upper hand with that cheating abductor of an innocent girl!"

Rowan gave his heated friend an approving glance. "It sounds as if you've made up your mind. Go ask Brummell if he wants to help ferret out the snake. But say nothing of our feminine reason, will you? The less people who know about her the better."

"Of course. But tell me something else. Why did you expose Lady Jewel to Brummell and Alvanley like that?"

"To elicit their opinions of her suitability. Did I err?" Rowan threw Bixby a slanted look.

"You were certainly frank. Confident as well. I should think they'll be after her themselves now that they know that you have singled her out. But no, Brummell didn't favor what he termed her cool air."

"Are you coming to my musical tomorrow?"

"I usually yawn at concerts, but if Tricia is to be glimpsed, I'll be there."

Rowan slammed his cue at a ball, and missed.

* * *

The next afternoon, Lord Bixby sauntered up to Rowan in his sunset-filled music room and said conspiratorially, "Brummell and I have arranged to meet Kilver tomorrow morning. We are buying velvet." Bixby raised his chin, expecting kudos.

"That was fast. Excellent work. Where did you find Kilver?"

"At the Clarendon, wolfing down Jaquiers's genuine French *diner*. When I mentioned that Brummell wanted stuff for new waistcoats, Kilver perked up. He promised the Beau thirty pounds' worth and me twenty, but I stipulated we get to see all he has, and we'll only purchase if the stuff's superior. He insists it couldn't be finer. Hinted that it came from the Continent."

"Does he take you for dim-wits?" asked Rowan, spying Tricia in the doorway holding a large silver tray. My, but she looked fragile and ethereal. Was he right to make her carry trays for him?

"Shall we set out from my place, then, at the break of dawn?" asked Bixby.

"I think you better go without me," Rowan replied. "Kilver will take instant umbrage at sight of my face. In light of his recent abduction of my page, he'll turn tail on the whole project. He knows I could hand him over to the Lords if I wished to raise the dust."

"Would you consider that?"

"I feel it would not be in my, ah—Tricia's—best interest. We must keep her out of the scandal sheets, and give her a chance to shape her life somehow . . . first."

"Ah, yes," murmured Bixby gravely. Rowan saw him watching her graceful figure with admiring eyes.

* * *

Ladies and gentlemen chatting and laughing breezed into the Duke's ground floor ballroom in couples and small parties. Tricia entered the salon with a heavy, ornate silver tray arrayed with three kinds of colorful sweets. She saw Lord Bixby talking with Rowan.

The Duke paused in his attention to Bixby when

he saw her.

She swallowed against a lump in her throat and hurried to work.

Lord Bixby soon left the Duke. "Have you something good to eat?" he asked her with a wondering smile that reached his eyes.

As she offered her tray of petit-fours, she saw his gaze move from her pink puff-sleeved gown and dainty apron up to the cap of delicate lace that hid most of her short hair. He whispered, "I say, this beats all! You were a complete hand as Rowan's page, and I admire you excessively for all that you have done. Now you make the prettiest parlor maid I ever saw. Think about this: I would pay you better than Rowan does." He wiggled his eyebrows up and down and cast a challenging grin across the room at Rowan. He received a scowl from his friend in return.

Tricia said quietly, "No, I won't come, Your Lordship, but thank you very much. Would you like one of these cakes?" As he smilingly took two, the Ladies Caroline and Jewel Claremont were announced.

The Duke moved to receive them. There was a swish of white plumes behind his dark head, and Tricia saw Lady Jewel lift her face to be kissed. Rowan touched the air near her cheek with his lips, and then air-kissed Lady Caro. An old gentleman moved to offer Lady Caro his arm, and the two couples strolled in state to the front of the gilt chairs which were set in a fan shape before the musicians.

Jewel looked like a fairy-tale snow queen with her swansdown wrap close about her chin.

Diamonds glinted in her black braided coronet and dangled from her ears. The hem of her white gown, lavishly embroidered with silver and gold thread, completed her queenly appearance. She maintained an almost perpetual smile upon the Duke.

Tricia's heart felt clenched into a knot. Was she wicked? She did not want Lady Jewel to have the Duke. She could not stand the thought of his dear nature thrown away on that superior beauty who dropped her high-toned comments about people as from a great height. There was something about her that was too brittle and falsely assured. Tricia knew the Duke needed a real woman: someone good and warm and loving. She needed to be someone who would listen to his concerns with an open heart; someone who would help him through life. She couldn't imagine Lady Jewel helping him in any way. She seemed absolutely self-serving.

Aldwin announced Lord Alvanley and Mr. Brummell. Tricia stayed away from those two famous gentlemen, remembering that they could well have taken note of her at White's when she, as Patrick, made such a commotion and found the card case.

The seats filled with ladies and gentlemen to whom she carried refreshments. Footmen were apparently too large to make that a discreet operation between the rows of chairs, so Aldwin had directed her to do most of it while the footmen filled the trays and handed them to her outside the door. Tricia was grateful to have the butler on her side amongst the scandalized staff. Aldwin had shown no adversity toward her; only support and solicitude.

Lionel and Stefan, Rupert and Theodore were all agog over the feisty Patrick having turned into a parlor maid. Mrs. Pollard had given them all a warning lecture, and so far they had dared say nothing derogatory out loud. But they looked at her aghast and with wonder. They didn't quite know how to behave toward her now. Tricia wondered if Stefan felt guilty for having insulted and wrestled a female to the ground. She hoped he did, and that he remembered how capable she was of fighting him back.

The orchestra members had taken their places after bowing to the Duke and his guests. A harpsichord player, a violinist, and a cellist took positions, and Mozart's *Concerto in D Major* soared through the room.

Tricia, nearer the door than anyone, heard a feminine voice that rose shrilly in the hall behind her. Alarmed, she beckoned Stefan to follow her. He looked hesitant to obey her, but when she heard the voice again, she conveyed to him such desperate urgency that he grudgingly detached himself from the wall. Outside, she whispered, "I hear a woman arguing. We must not let anyone disturb the Duke's concert."

They rounded the corner into the marble entrance hall. There was Lady Flitcroft, dressed to the hilt in glittering purple, remonstrating with the newly-hired porter. Aldwin was nowhere in sight. "Without an invitation card, I am not allowed to admit you. It is regrettable, Your Ladyship, but there are no more seats."

"I shall sit on His Grace's lap if I have to!"

declared Lady Flitcroft, hitting him with her long pearls.

Tricia told Stefan, "Stop her!"

"Get the other footmen," he said.

"Right! Use force with her if necessary," Tricia added boldly, eyeing Lady Flitcroft's progress past the babbling new porter.

Tricia raced to the three footmen standing like liveried ornaments. Under cover of the music she ordered them, "Come and help! A person who means mischief wants to make a scandalous entrance. Stefan needs to use force to remove her. That new porter is not succeeding. It's up to you men."

They went, streaking out importantly.

Tricia caught the eye of the Duke as he turned halfway in his chair. He must have seen her excited face, for he raised an eyebrow in the summons he had taught her as a page.

Her heart skipped. *Oh, my dear Duke,* she whispered under her breath, *why did we have to lose what we had before?* She wondered if she had to explain to him what was happening. She did not want to trouble him. With trepidation, she went to his side. She bent and put her ear near his face.

"Is anything wrong?" he whispered.

The nearness of him and his breath upon her cheek made her heart rise up in his defense. "Something untoward is occurring in the hall," she replied quietly, "but do not go yourself, Your Grace." She touched the fine wool of his coat, for he looked about to rise.

"What is it?" he asked, their eyes magnetized together.

Tricia broke their breathtaking eye contact and put her lips next to his ear. "Lady Flitcroft," she whispered.

He closed his eyes and groaned.

"Not to worry; I sent your quartet of footmen to take care of it," she assured him.

That was all she could say, for Lady Jewel turned a quizzical glance at them and leaned closer to Rowan, presumably to hear what was going on.

"Thank you," he sighed in Tricia's direction.

She curtseyed and made a graceful beeline for the hall.

Aldwin stalked toward her in the corridor, his upper lip sporting beads of perspiration. "They took the woman off, but heavens! —when this leaks out, I'm fired, we're all sacked! This sort of thing is just not done! Not *ever* to a Lady. I should not have left the hall."

"She is not a Lady!" returned Tricia before she could stop herself. "Don't let her connive any of these menservants into doing what she wants in the future, Mr. Aldwin. Please warn them all so they don't end up like Eldred."

The butler turned stiffly and stared her down. "A parlor maid telling me what to do? Tricia, you are relegated to the bottom of the Lower Fives as of this instant." Then he winked at her.

"That's where I am anyway," she said, shooting him a little grin.

Lionel entered the front door, followed by Stefan and the others, all looking flushed and triumphant as they filed back into the ballroom.

Behind them, the shaken porter slid the bolt into place.

"What did the footmen do?" Tricia hurried to ask him.

"I have never seen the like! Duke must be a hard one to issue a command like that. Took her by each arm, would've escorted her out, but she stamped on Stefan's foot—poor chap, second time in a week he's been assaulted in this hall, he says—but the Lady refused to exit."

"So how did they manage it?"

"Stefan picked her up and Lionel told her she was a lovely lady, much too nice to suffer embarrassment, so they must return her to her carriage. She slapped and swore, so they all had to grab a limb, so to speak. This staff bribed her coachman to drive her away against her will. Mr. Aldwin forked over quite a sum. But that's what His Grace wanted done, apparently," he finished, lifting his hands helplessly.

CHAPTER 11

Departure from His Grace

"Lady Caro Claremont, please," said Tricia to the lofty butler at Highcourt House the next morning.

"Whom may I say has called?" The corpulent man put a quizzing glass to his eye. When he saw what type of simply-dressed young person it was, his hairy nostrils flared.

Tricia knew that of course she looked unworthy to call. She wore a kitchen maid's plain gray spencer over the pink muslin frock. The coal-scuttle hat was one of Mrs. Pollard's, a charcoal color that framed Tricia's small face in ludicrous overstatement. "Please tell Lady Caro that it is the person whose hands she wanted to examine." Tricia saw the man's bristly brows shoot up at that.

"Hands?" he rasped. "This is no gypsy's house, so scram!"

Tricia said sweetly, "Don't you remember me? I have been here before." Pretending a confidence she did not feel, she slipped past his stomach and into the hall. "Where shall I wait? Believe me, Lady Caro asked me to call."

The man looked as though he would love to toss her out, but grudgingly he indicated a salon draped in gold bombazine. "Do not sit on the settee," he warned. "It was just reupholstered." He waddled off, making floorboards creak.

Tricia lowered herself onto the bolstered silk settee. When the butler reappeared, she sat serenely eyeing him.

"Follow me," he said in a much milder manner.

At the back of the house, overlooking the garden, Lady Caro wielded a watering can in a room warm with sunlight and hung with chartreuse ferns and shelves of herbs in clay pots. The basil smelled lovely. Lady Caro pulled off her work gloves and set them next to three pots of purple violets. "Mercy!" she cried, staring at Tricia. "A familiar face, but . . ." She motioned at the butler. "Leave us, Hopkins. Thank you."

Tricia began to bow to Lady Caro, but hastily swooped it into a curtsey. "Lady Caro, forgive me."

"Dear Patrick! What is the meaning of this?" She laughed. "You dressed up like a girl? You sure make a good one! My word!"

Tricia told her in a rush that she was the former Patrick, and that she had lied all along because she was really a young woman named Tricia. "You were the only person I could think of to come to in my dilemma, Lady Caro. If you will hear me out and *then* turn me out, I will at least have tried."

After her great astonishment had subsided, Lady Caro said, "Perch here on this stool and tell me everything, dear girl. I will try to keep my questions until the end. You look so troubled; you're scaring me."

"The Duke found out that I am not the boy he thought his page naturally should be."

"Gracious! I can sympathize with his incredulity. How did he react to the knowledge that you are a girl?"

"He was bewildered, naturally, and then very cold toward me. I am *history* in his regard. Oh, Lady Caro, I duped him shamelessly. The only service I can render him now is to remove myself from his sight."

"Why? Did he say you're not welcome in his house anymore?"

"No, but he was roaring angry when my perfidy was unveiled. He has since treated me with more charity than I deserve, telling me to stay and be his parlor maid. I did so for one day, but no longer."

"Why, what happened?"

"Yesterday, I ordered Lady Flitcroft trounced bodily out of his entry hall while the orchestra played for all of you invited guests. By the way, I made sure that you did not see my face."

"Lady Flitcroft tried to intrude on the party? That flagrant widow? You say *you* ordered her out?" Lady Caro's eyes grew huge.

"No, but I told the footmen to do it so she wouldn't bring undeserved gossip on His Grace's head." Tricia added miserably, "But the gossip will swirl after all, for now she will tell all of London."

Lady Caro laughed and laughed. "If you had been thrown out of a Duke's house, would *you* tell all of London?"

Their smiles at each other grew.

"Lady Caro, you have such a way of comforting me. Oh, I pray there's some way you can help me. My life is in tatters."

"If you're in as bad a scrape as you say, why, of

course I'm your man. But it's only fair to let me know your identity first. I'm dying to know who my Patrick's replacement is."

Tricia hesitated.

"You must not deceive me any longer, my dear. I *will* have the truth this time."

"Yes, Your Ladyship. My name is Tricia Ravenscar. Leigh and Lucretia were my parents."

With a gleeful screech, Lady Caro snatched Tricia off her stool and swung her about. "You are my niece! Oh, I have a new niece, not a nephew! Heavenly days are here again! I haven't really lost a relative after all!" She kissed Tricia soundly on the cheek.

A wave of joy engulfed Tricia as she freely returned the hugs of her flesh-and-blood aunt.

After Tricia recounted how her parents had died when their coble, carrying them out to Leigh's ship, was caught in a gale, Lady Caro said solemnly, "Since they are gone, Tricia, you aren't going anywhere but here. I am *so* thankful to have you!"

Tricia felt tears prick her eyes. It was a new experience to find herself as the reason for gladness. "You are thankful to have me here? Why?"

"Dear Tricia, you don't know what it means to have my dear brother Leigh's own daughter before me. Mine has been rather a lonely life, and now I have you to care for." Her smile sparkled. "I want you reinstated, not only to your family, but also to your rightful place in society. We will now call you by your rightful title: Lady Tricia Claremont."

Tricia started. "I'm not a Lady!"

"Oh, but you are. I will thoroughly check this out

with the Lords for form's sake, but I am certain. Perhaps we won't announce you just yet, but soon everyone will know that you, my niece, have arrived from Yorkshire to stay for the Little Season."

Tricia stared at her in heart-thumping apprehension. "But my stupid employment has ruined me! There is no need to even consider taking me out amongst your friends, Lady Caro."

"Shadowing the Duke as his page was unorthodox, to be sure, but who will know you did that if the Duke or I do not tell anyone it was you?"

"Many people know. Lady Jewel for one, and Lord Kilver for another."

"Lord Kilver! My stars, we have *him* to deal with! I can see I'll be busy. Well, first thing to do is to give you a room and get you into a better gown."

Tricia felt nervous about staying, especially as she recalled the lofty attitude of Lady Jewel. "Shouldn't you ask the Marquis, Lady Jewel's father, first?"

"Absolutely, I shall tell my brother and his wife, and they will be pleasantly astonished, you'll see. They're in Paris, but when they return, they will welcome you as I do. As for Jewel, so what? Even if she should object, she's the leader of the smartest set of ladies in town, so she has nothing to fear from you, does she? I will make her keep her tongue. Oh, but this is sweet, having you turn up when we didn't know there *was* a you. Come, follow me, dear Tricia. You know," she said behind her hand as they mounted the main staircase to the picture gallery, "it's much better that you're exactly who you are, not Patrick, because it would have caused a tremendous upset to Jewel's father if he had to give up his new title of Marquis to you."

"That's true," breathed Tricia.

In glorious spirits, Lady Caro called the housekeeper, who summoned two housemaids to open a guest room and air it. Tricia stood looking around at pink striped bed curtains on a domed bed, with pale blue bows and matching chairs in dainty French fashion. This sunny guest chamber was to be hers.

"Remove those painting things," Lady Caro directed. "Jewel sometimes does watercolors in here, as the light is good. Jane, will you take Tricia's measurements? We must find her something to wear, and then, of course, see Madame Yvonne for a wardrobe. Excuse me, Tricia, while I write a letter to the Duke."

Tricia panicked. "What will you say to him?"

"That I have you safely ensconced here, and that we shall all keep mum about where you came from, where you have recently lived, and what you have recently been."

"If only such silence can be achieved, but servants talk, don't they? Who can keep the Duke's footmen quiet?"

"Servants! –hang the lot of them! The Duke and I will put the fear into them. Oh heavens, we must do something about your poor hair."

Tricia ran a hand self-consciously over her boyish crop which curled up slightly at the ends from having been under the bonnet. "I had to cut it off." She brightened. "But I brought my long tresses with me."

"You did?"

"Yes, I wrapped them in a cotton casing I made. I tied it under my bosom when I had to look like a boy. Here it is."

Lady Caro watched as Tricia groped in Mrs. Pollard's bandbox. Tricia ripped out basting stitches and unfolded the cotton to reveal the silky, pale blonde mane.

"Your own hair? Why, this is capital! We can have it made into a chignon or a bunch of lovely curls. What an ingenious young lady you are. Take good care of that." Lady Caro patted it and went humming down the corridor.

The maids brought garments into the room and laid them on Tricia's bed.

"Whose gowns are these?" she asked.

"Cast-offs of Lady Jewel's," said the fair maid named Jane. "I wonder if we can make some fit you in a pinch, Lady Tricia. You are slimmer than she is."

It was a jolt to hear herself called *Lady Tricia*. "What if I just wear this round dress I have on until we have something made up?" She didn't even feel comfortable with that idea, for it meant someone would bear the expense for her new gowns. She had no money unless Lord Kilver allotted her some.

"Orders is orders, Lady Tricia," said the friendliest maid, Sarah. She and Jane curtseyed to Tricia and left.

Tricia could see herself in the looking glass. How her eyes bespoke her worry! She picked up a silver-handled brush, made a part in the middle of her hair, brushed it behind her ears, and took out half of her long hair from the bundle. Holding it at the side of her face, she sighed. She wished now that she had not had to cut it off.

"What are *you* doing here?" came a cold feminine query. In the doorway, carrying her easel back into the room stood Lady Jewel. She wore a puce dressing gown and her dark hair flowed loose. She set down the easel and lifted her eyebrows, waiting for an answer.

Tricia lowered her handful of hair, feeling foolish.

"Who are you and what are you doing here?" Jewel repeated while advancing to stare at her blonde tresses.

"I . . . this is my hair."

"How queer." Lady Jewel raked her critically with narrowed eyes. "I've seen you before." She pointed triumphantly. "*You* are Rowan's parlor maid! Why are you here in my studio clad in only a chemise, holding loose hair up to your face?"

Tricia's heart thumped. "Lady Jewel," she said, "I *was* His Grace's parlor maid as a disguise. That is now over. Please don't mention it to anyone. I beg your discretion."

"My discretion? Why?" Jewel's eyes snapped with an angry thought. "You were *disguised* as a parlor maid? So what does that make you really? Oho! I get it!" In a perforating voice, she cried, "So that's how one Duke cloaks his peccadilloes, is it? Parlor maids! Well, you can get out of my house right now! I cannot imagine why you are standing in this room."

Through the doorway came Lady Caro. "Jewel! Whatever is the fuss?"

Lady Jewel's long nostrils quivered and she

tightened her lips. "Who is this?" She made a jerky motion at Tricia.

"Why, this is such a treat." Lady Caro smiled. "I have the great privilege of introducing you two as first cousins. Jewel, as you are older—twenty years versus Tricia's how many years?"

"Nearly nineteen," she supplied miserably.

"Jewel, let me present to you your first cousin, Lady Tricia Claremont."

Jewel stared as if turned into a gargoyle. Only her eyes revolved to glare in disbelief at Tricia.

"I am happy to meet you, Lady Jewel." Tricia offered her hand.

"How can *this* be my cousin?" snapped Jewel with a derisive gesture.

"Jewel, I have the pleasure to inform you that she is your Uncle Leigh's daughter."

"But—!" sputtered Jewel, "Leigh married an unacceptable person and left, and has since died, and his wife along with him."

"Jewel, we didn't know it, but Leigh Claremont, Lord Wyndhurst, had a son and a daughter. The son succumbed in the war against Bonaparte, but the daughter is here now. I have begged Lady Tricia to stay. Isn't this a miraculous day for us all?"

It appeared to be a devastating day for Lady Jewel for some reason. It felt like it to Tricia, too, as she faced her antagonistic cousin.

"Then pray tell why she has been working in Rowan's household," Jewel stabbed out, piercing Tricia with a censorious look.

Quietly, Tricia said, "The Duke rescued me from a dangerous situation. He doesn't know who I really am."

"And must never know, I presume?"

Lady Caro said, "Jewel, we must not tell anyone that Tricia was Rowan's recent employee. That much is certain."

Jewel masked her face with a new expression and said, "Of course not. How long will you be staying with us?" she asked frigidly.

"Always," announced Lady Caro joyfully, eyeing Jewel's face as she pulled Tricia into a heartfelt hug.

CHAPTER 12

A Clash of Wills

Tricia spent the night in the domed bed, assailed with fits of misgiving. She kicked her legs and punched her pillows into different positions for two wakeful hours.

She had deserted the Duke after all he had done for her. What did he think of her now? She wanted to weep, but she hugged a pillow to her eyelids and could not shed a tear. Memories deluged her. They all featured him.

At ten o'clock the next morning, feeling heavy-eyed and exhausted, she stood before the mirror in one of Lady Jewel's old frocks. It was a murky gold hue that Tricia did not like. It had too many knobby bows on the bodice and looping brown decorations at the hem.

"Sarah, try that rose and cream stripe on Lady Tricia," Lady Caro directed the maid as she, herself, perused a fashion periodical. "That and the periwinkle can be altered next. I don't like this one on her. What is it?" she asked of Jane, who hovered in the doorway.

"Your Ladyship, you have a caller."

"Who is it?"

In a reverent voice, Jane said, "It's His Grace the

Duke of Rowan, My Lady!"

Lady Caro alerted, and then smiled at Tricia. "I shall receive him in the drawing room."

Lady Jewel paused in tossing aside gowns she wanted to keep after all. She said archly, "But whom does he wish to see, Aunt?"

The maid boldly said, "He asked to see Miss Tricia."

Jewel's eyes needled into her, and then revolved to Tricia.

Lady Caro said perkily, "Well, Tricia? Here's your chance to set all to rights."

"How can I receive him this way? My hair!" It was the only excuse she could think of.

"Very true," said Jewel, eyeing her.

Last evening at dinner she had inquired why Tricia's hair was so short, and had been informed by Lady Caro that Tricia had been the Duke's page out of dire necessity; that she had cut her hair in order to leave Yorkshire anonymously. That was all she would reveal no matter how many shocked and probing queries Jewel persisted with.

Lady Caro suggested, "Make a pair of curls out of some of that hair. Sarah, put the curling iron on the fire, and by the time we get Lady Tricia into that periwinkle frock and you have tied the sash snugly under the bodice, we will have her looking prime-up-to-the-rig."

"Where will we put the curls?" inquired Tricia.

"Pin them at your temples, under your hair. I think you will look charming."

Jewel said, "Well, *I* shall not be accused of rudeness. For the Duke of Rowan to be kept waiting such an inordinate amount of time for the sake of her toilette is unthinkable. I am going down."

"An excellent plan," said Lady Caro, winking at Tricia. "I'll be in on your heels, Jewel. Speaking of heels, Tricia, I have a pair of pink shoes which might fit you. They're exquisite, with scallops, but alas, too tight for me. I'll send them in."

With Lady Caro out of the room, Jewel streaked to the mirror and said to Sarah, "Touch up my tendrils with the curling iron, quick! Yes, you heard me. Mine first."

Sarah bit her lip and complied as Tricia separated slim strands of her own hair from her bundle.

When the maids had stepped out to fetch things, Jewel said to Tricia, "I believe I can help you save face."

"What do you mean?"

"When I go down, I'll receive whatever message the Duke has, and give it to you after he's gone. You know that Aunt Caro means well," she said confidentially, "but those curls you fix are going to look silly. They'll never stay on. Until you have a decent wig made, I'll aid you by being the go-between so you don't have to sit under the scrutiny of our morning callers. They notice *everything*." She laid her cool fingers on Tricia's hand and gave her a condescending smile as she passed.

Tricia felt coerced by Jewel, and did not like it. She also quaked at the prospect of seeing Rowan face-to-face after she had fled from his home without a by-your-leave. To Jewel, she lifted her chin and said, "If you want to take a message for me, please do. His coming here could regard something embarrassing like a settlement of my wages."

"Wages?" Jewel stared in disbelief. "Unthinkable! But I suspect you'll want them, hmm? I can at least save you the mortification of receiving money."

Tricia watched Jewel hurry out. "Wait, Lady Jewel. If there is anything else he wants, please call me down." She felt regret already. It would be so heavenly to look at him again.

"I will. I'll smooth this over. I saw your expression when he was announced. Everything will be all right. Trust me."

"Thank you," Tricia forced herself to say. She saw Jewel stop at the landing mirror, where she adjusted her bosom up in her scanty bodice.

With her heart in her throat, Tricia leaned over the rail and whispered, "Jewel, I am acting cowardly. I should face up and see him."

Jewel waved that away with an airy smile. "Nonsense. There's no need to be such a martyr."

Tricia suddenly wanted to apologize to him, to explain her actions, voice her gratitude to him for saving her from Lord Kilver.

With a tug of her heart, Tricia returned to the bedchamber and put her feet in the pink slippers Sarah held for her. Her longing to see the Duke grew more poignant. As the pink ribbons were tightened around her ankles, her resolve grew. Why should she not see him when he had called especially to see her? Just because Lady Jewel did not want her to? She must show her she could not divert her from what was right.

Tricia felt that the periwinkle gown looked nice, but she worried aloud over her hair. Sarah tied thread tightly around the tops of the two curled tresses, then pinned them under her hair in front of each ear. This set long, gleaming curls falling next to her cheekbones. "La, but you're gorgeous, Lady Tricia!"

"Thank you, Sarah." Tricia did look feminine again, thanks to Lady Caro and her vision.

Putting on a very wide-brimmed black hat, Tricia said, "I would like to go out on the steps for some air." Slipping gingerly down the staircase, she saw the open drawing room door through the banister. There was the Duke's shiny boot and fawn-colored pantaloons. She heard a murmur of his deep voice and Jewel's artificial laugh.

Tricia's heart thumped. How could she walk in there and meet his eyes? She could do nothing when she faced him but beg his forgiveness. That was what she needed to do. She hid beside the open door. Should she enter and blurt it all out?

No, not with Lady Jewel sitting there. What if the Duke lectured her again? What if he eyed her coldly? Tricia could not endure it. She was rocked by a see-saw of emotions.

Rowan's voice sounded louder. Was he walking toward the door? "Saturday evening then, Lady Jewel," he said. "Good day, Lady Caro."

Tricia panicked. Where could she run? The stairs were in full view. She almost made a dash past the drawing room, but at sight of his dark head, she pulled herself back up against the wainscoting.

"Yes indeed, eight o'clock, Rowan." Jewel must have seen Tricia's hat brim, for there was a startled silence on her part, then she added, "But did I show you my latest painting? It's over here."

"Show it to me Saturday," he said congenially. "I will have that to look forward to, Lady Jewel."

Tricia scurried across the hall as if her skirts were on fire. She kept going, straight out the front door. Oh dear, the Duke was sure to come this way, but it was too late to change course now. In the breezy Square, she did not know which way to flee. This was utter lunacy, for a lady would not walk anywhere in London without an escort.

She could invent no motive for an amble outdoors until her glance fell on the brightest spot in Cavendish Square: purple foxgloves. She made for them as if starved for flowers, hoping the milk cart passing behind her would hide her from the Duke.

With no shears or finesse, she yanked at a thick stem with rows of purple finger-stalls rising three feet high. Roots and all came up. She labored to detach the dirty roots from the bottom of the stem with no success. Others, she managed to pick without roots. The wind whipped her bonnet off kilter, so she had to adjust her swooping hat brim until its deep dip covered one eye. Now the Duke would not be able to see her face.

"Tricia!"

With a leap of her heart, she determined not to answer to her name. She would pretend to be somebody else, and he might think he was mistaken.

Here came his footsteps down the flagged walk, firm and purposeful.

She turned to him, the foxgloves clutched to her pounding breast.

His direct gaze left her devoid of any refuge.

"Good morning, Your Grace," she said nervously. She curtseyed very low. The flowers swiveled out of her grasp and splayed over the grass. She grabbed at the nearest one, and bumped hats with him. His black beaver tipped off upside down.

She scooped to retrieve it, and brushed the grass off. "I'm sorry," she said, handing it back to him.

"My fault."

She was to recall his look later in her waking dreams: first a searching glance over her face, then a blink of dark lashes, and the most peculiar softening in his eyes. He gave her a white grin which devastated her by its shy sweetness. "Thank you, Miss Tricia."

So they had not told him she was a Lady. All the better.

He picked up her stolen purple posies one by one. "You were not at home to me," he accused as he presented her with the willowy bouquet.

"No, Your Grace, I could not be. Will you forgive me?"

"May I ask why not before I forgive?"

"My hair is not long enough, Jewel said, and I haven't any well-fitting clothes."

"You were my page, for crying out loud! I saw you in quite a dirty, woebegone shape when we met." His voice changed as he said softly, "You look exquisite now, and so right as a girl."

"Thank you," returned Tricia, feeling her cheeks heating up. "Lady Jewel says she knows best about what females do and don't do. They don't walk outside in London alone. But Your Grace, I need to talk to you."

"I am here. I am listening." He drew her into the

shade of a tree.

"If only I can screw up my courage."

Rowan reached into his pocket. "While you're doing that, I must take care of a certain matter. Lady Jewel reminded me I owe you wages."

Tricia was aghast. "She reminded you?"

"I owe you for excellent service to me, and I want to pay you without delay." He handed her a purse that clinked.

"Thank you, but I absolutely do not want to take—"

He cut her off. "You are about to tell me why you left my house, Tricia. I did not dismiss you," he said, eyeing her sternly.

She bit her lip. "I did something terrible. If I stayed on working for you, I would ruin your life even more than I already have."

"Ruin my life? Whatever did you do?"

"I sent Lady Flitcroft out of your house during the concert. She planned to come in and sit on your lap because I said there were no more chairs. I told your footmen to carry her out whether she liked it or not. They assumed the order came from you, so they did it. Physically!"

The Duke's brows skyrocketed. He stared at her until he cracked out into a disbelieving laugh. "Carried out? Physically, by my footmen? Ho, she must have loved that."

"Yes, but aren't you appalled that I gave an order in your house to treat her in such an ignominious way? I fear that I have ruined your reputation beyond belief."

The Duke put a hand to his forehead and sang out, "I am *wretched!*"

"Your Grace! Why do you laugh?"

Touching his hat brim in salute, he said, "My own tactics with Lady Flitcroft were anything but effective. You were a witness to her most devious ploys. Following each of my rebuffs, she has pestered me all the more. But you trussed her off, which I would not have dared to do in quite that style, and I get the credit." He bowed. "I am deeply in your debt." He was chuckling with wonder and merriment.

Tricia dropped her lashes. "I do not think so at all." Tears squeezed out of her eyes.

"What are you saying?" He reached for her. "Are you weeping?"

At the touch of his hand on her face, Tricia's heart filled with bittersweet longing. She sank her cheek into his palm and gloried in the moment. Thank God he was no longer angry with her! "Please forgive me for all my sins against you," she said.

Rowan gathered her close behind the trunk of the tree and said he forgave her.

"Oh, thank you," she breathed, clutching his fingers. "What would we do without Jesus so that we can forgive each other?"

"Very true. Forgive me, too. I have treated you so badly," he mourned.

As she put her arms up to assure him, a shout came sharply across the park. "Tricia!"

Its vehemence made Rowan's hand drop from her back. Peering around the tree, they saw Lady Jewel on the steps of Highcourt House, spying in their direction with opera glasses.

"I must go!" said the Duke and Tricia in chorus.

She swiped at her tears, smiled, and would have fled, but the Duke placed a discreet grip on her elbow which kept her walking casually at his side.

"Please don't run off until you've answered my questions, Tricia. In what capacity are you living here with the Claremont women?"

"I was invited to stay by Lady Caro."

"You chose to leave my house and my care? You won't be back to fetch and carry for me?" He looked sad despite his attempt at lightness.

Tricia felt bewildered. "No, Your Grace."

"Of course not. A guest is far better than a servant any day."

"But no, it is not!" Tricia refuted, meeting his eyes. Her heart ached.

They were now within speaking distance of Jewel, whose inspection looked like jealousy. "You have found little Tricia, I see. How gentlemanly of you to escort her back, Rowan. She does not know anything about London behavior yet."

Tricia knew that what Jewel thought was nothing charitable toward her. Adding to her admonishment, Jewel meticulously reminded Tricia that she needed a companion for strolls in the Square. She then smiled and bade the Duke a flirtatious adieu.

He drove off in his coach, and instantly, Tricia found herself gripped sternly by the arm as Jewel marched her into the house. Inside, she felt the wrath that propelled her cousin, although to all the servants along the way, the two of them must have appeared as amiable girls walking arm-in-arm. When they reached Tricia's new bedchamber, Jewel nearly pushed her in. "What do you call that kind of behavior? Answer me this minute!"

"What behavior?"

"You deliberately waylaid the Duke out there! Were you his doxy? Are you still?"

"Heavens no!" cried Tricia.

Jewel smacked a fist into her palm. "Wait until everyone in the *haut ton* hears about it!"

"I'm not anyone's doxy! And I am not in the *haut ton,* either."

"Not yet, but my aunt has some trumpery notions in her head; grand plans for you to enter Society," Jewel hissed, her eyes narrowed.

Tricia was appalled by her cousin's fury. "Lady Jewel," she said, "I cannot let you judge me so falsely. What you surmise about my character is simply not true."

Indignantly, Jewel cried, "Don't talk to me like that, you little strumpet! Duke-chaser!" She grabbed the cotton bundle lying on the bed and shook out its contents. "*That's* what you get!" and she hurled Tricia's blonde hair into the fire.

"No!" Tricia screamed. In helpless disbelief, she watched the remainder of her long hair licked by rising flames, curling and sending forth a nose-crinkling odor. "No!" she cried again. "How could you do such a thing to me?"

With barely-controlled fury, Jewel spat, "Easily! You deserve it. I saw you and him hugging. I know illicit goings-on when I see them."

Tricia cried in desperation, "I was asking forgiveness from him! He did the same of me. You should not be jealous of that!" Falling to her knees hopelessly before the fire, she shed tears and watched the last of her hair charred to nothing.

"What is going on here?" cried Lady Caro, marching into the room. "What's that acrid smell?"

Jewel jerked her chin up and pushed out of the room past her aunt.

"What on earth happened?" cried Lady Caro, stooping to lift Tricia by her shaking shoulders.

"My hair," wailed Tricia. "She burnt my hair!"

CHAPTER 13

The Illicit Purchase

The Duke turned the pages of his social diary. For Saturday next, he wrote in his engagement with the Ladies Caroline and Jewel Claremont. Yesterday, Lady Jewel had walked into the drawing room at Highcourt House in high spirits. He had risen and kissed her hand, flushed under her frequent smiles, and for awhile almost forgot his reason for calling.

Lady Jewel had first attracted his notice last spring when they had both been guests at a dinner party. He thought her expressive, dark-eyed beauty rather fascinating to watch. She gave him just enough smiles to indicate that she liked him, but she did not follow or flatter him as many women did. She had played it very cool.

Rowan knew her aunt, Lady Caro, better. He had partnered her in several card and parlor games. After the first such evening, they had sought each other's company because they enjoyed conversing and laughing together. The Duke found her a safe haven from all the blushing and nervous attempts of young ladies who strove to hook his interest.

Lady Caro was a woman of Christian principles; that was clear. Rowan figured that her niece, Lady

Jewel, was likely of the same persuasion and therefore a lady who was safe to cultivate. After all, he had to find a wife, and must get to know some suitable ladies.

Yesterday, Lady Jewel had handed him a china cup of hot chocolate which the butler brought in. She said, "Your Grace, I regret that your maid, Tricia, cannot see you. However—and forgive this indelicacy," she lowered her lashes while shaking her head, "she will certainly accept her wages."

"Ah! Yes, of course. In fact, I brought them." He touched his breast pocket. Irritation swept over him. Why would Tricia not see him herself?

Lady Caro, breezing into the room with her fichu lappets fluttering, welcomed Rowan warmly. She sat next to him on the red and yellow striped sofa and talked gaily about up-coming events. Rowan fancied he detected the dear woman pairing Jewel and himself at every rout and soirée she mentioned. He considered that it might be all the better to have Lady Caro's help.

Lady Jewel, if he let himself think that far, would make a suitable Duchess if she proved to be as good and genuine as she was artistic to look at. As she flashed him a smile from beneath her mother's portrait, he mused that she would have been a far more worthy subject for the brush of George Morland than the unremarkable older woman in the frame.

Lady Caro said, "Rowan, I wish to invite you to a coming-out ball honoring our friend, Miss Hobart. Everyone is asked to bring guests, especially the male variety." She winked at him. "The Hobarts know too few unattached men to make it a successful début. Would you and Lord Bixby deign to come with us?"

"Yes, I'll come. I will ask Bixby. He may enjoy obliging you."

His reply appeared to please Lady Jewel.

As he rose to leave their golden drawing room, it jolted him to see the pretty figure in a large black hat fleeing out the front door. By the time he extricated himself from the Claremont ladies, the sprite was in the center of Cavendish Square, yanking at blossoms as though it were her task to denude the place. So Tricia could have seen him if she chose. Her note beneath his chamber door that morning had said:

> *My Lord Duke:*
> *I resign my post, although it is very difficult to do so. I have been invited to Highcourt House. With all my gratitude,*
> *Your (Dis)obedient servant,*
> *Tricia*

> *PS: Please forgive me, Your Grace, for everything I did to deceive and anger you. I am very, very sorry. I did not mean to hurt you in any way. Please believe me.*

By the time he had read through her beautifully-formed words, he felt choked. He went to question Mrs. Pollard, but found her reticent. He suspected that she had let the girl slip out, and possibly even aided her. Aldwin and the footmen, however, were astonished to hear she was gone.

In Cavendish Square, when Tricia dropped the

foxgloves at his approach, he was shaken by how lovely and forlorn she looked under her curvy hat. The long, blonde curls at her cheeks and the soft gown which showed her figure made a different creature of her. Her tender mouth looked so innocent amidst the world's guile, he thought. But it was those magnificent eyes that lifted to his, and her eloquent, sweeping brows which tugged at his heart. In place of the protective camaraderie he had felt for Patrick, he experienced an odd longing mingled with awe for the delicate girl. She had fought so hard to keep her virtue and her life strings together. He remembered her fierce struggles against Lord Kilver.

"It's over with!" he exclaimed, slamming his fist onto a pile of documents. He must not keep wishing to bring her back. He must stop dwelling on all of those moments.

He lit his pipe, which he smoked when he was upset, and crossed his booted legs on his desk. He tried to picture Tricia ordering the oxen-willed Lady Flitcroft carried away by his footmen. A laugh escaped him.

He thought of how wonderful it had been to forgive Tricia in person. His own heart felt free of his burden of anger against her. He had been asking her forgiveness for his harshness toward her when Lady Jewel had so high-handedly interrupted them. He needed to talk to Tricia again soon.

He gazed out the French windows at the blue hydrangeas bobbing in the breeze, and wondered in what capacity she had fled to Lady Caro. Perhaps she was accepted as something of a companion. Caro had said that she took a great liking to Rowan's former page. So long as Tricia was safe, he must try to relax on her account.

But he couldn't relax. He swung down his boots and withdrew a sheet of crested paper from a marble box. Dipping his pen, he wrote:

> *Dear Lady Caro,*
>   *Keep a close vigil over Tricia. She is the object of Lord Kilver's lewd designs. This is serious.*
>
> *Rowan*

As he licked a salty seal and pressed it to his letter, he sobered. Tricia's eyes had glistened with sincerity when she argued that being a guest of the Claremonts was not better than being his servant. What had she meant by that?

A knock drummed on his library door.

"Enter," he called.

Aldwin stepped through the arch and said, "Lord Bixby, Your Grace."

The Viscount Bixby, Rowan's friend since their Oxford Balliol days, marched in and halted. "Smoking your pipe? What's wrong, Rowan?"

"Good to see you. I could use a friend. What's all that?" He pointed his pipe stem at a bandbox and a huge, brown-wrapped bundle that Theodore dropped heavily onto a table. "Moving in?"

"Capital idea," said Bixby, shedding his blue coat with the footman's help. In a sober tone, Bixby added, "I heard you have a vacancy."

"Two vacancies amongst my staff, yes," said Rowan, looking away. He did not want to talk about Tricia in front of just anyone. He groped for his letter. "Theodore, deliver this at once, if you please."

When they were alone, Bixby looked wise and said, "It's been a successful morning."

"How so?"

"We met him, Brummell and I."

"Kilver?"

"Yes, indeed." Bixby tugged at a string on the large parcel. "I have something rather interesting to show you."

Rowan leaned on his forearms, all attention.

Unwrapping tissue, Bixby crowed, "See what I bought?" He held up a bolt of pale gray velvet stamped in large purple fleurs de lis. "Look at that."

Rowan went to lift the silk plush. He smiled. "Do you dare to wear this? Granted, the war's over and we English swarm to Paris these days, but I don't exactly see our shops flaunting Napoleon's lilies in their windows, do you?"

"I'm not worried about that. What concerns me is that Kilver is lining his pockets over this kind of thing. I'm dead sure that duty was never paid on any of it." He continued to unroll the cloth until about a dozen yards were draped over Rowan's Sheraton chairs and library table.

"All right, already!" crowed the Duke, chuckling, "I can see that it's elegant stuff. What do you need so blooming much for?"

"Never mind, I want you to see this." At the end of the fabric was a board dove-tailed together, about two inches thick. Bixby pointed to where the end of the fabric was tacked to it. There was a break in the wood, and he pushed on it.

Something white showed beneath. He handed it to Rowan. "Take a peek at the surprise."

Rowan pushed his finger in. "What is it? It feels like material of some sort. Lace, maybe?"

"I have a feeling it is. Let's crack it open."

They did so with a heavy, crystal-handled letter opener. Bixby extracted a narrower bolt. On it were wound three patterns of intricate lace.

Rowan marveled, "You certainly got your money's worth!"

"Didn't I? I'm convinced Kilver knew nothing about this extra bonus that he handed over to me."

"Did you ask him where he got the velvet?"

"I tried to tease him about contraband; that we all get our hands on it, y' know, but he stiffened up and said in that nasal voice of his, 'Duty is paid on all this, never fear. I inherited too much velvet for my own use, so buy what you want, gentlemen.' That's what he said."

"Inherited!" Rowan scoffed.

"What shall we do with this lace?"

"We?"

"I say it belongs to both of us, Rowan. I would like to leave it here with you in case my female relations should come across it at my house and try to snap it up. We may need all this for evidence, you know. Eventually I'll go pay duty on it and keep it for some young and beautiful thing. My lucky bride, I mean."

Grinning at Bixby, the Duke said, "I'll stash it here, then. That way, you can't touch it until I approve your prospective bride." He removed the bust of a Greek maiden from her pedestal and stuffed the bolt of lace down inside the column. "I have a feeling that Lord Kilver is a smuggler, but not a very experienced one. He overlooked the possibility of anything hidden inside. By the way, what made you buy that whole bolt of velvet, Bix?"

"I have to admit it was vanity, actually. While I had Kilver unroll most of it so I could check for flaws, I decided I would have a waistcoat made for myself, and then to match it, some new curtains for my library window. I thought it would look good for the portrait I'll have painted in front of it."

Rowan looked at Bixby's reddening face and laughed out loud. "That's all right, Bix. A little overkill, I'd say. A lucky thing you bowed to the dictates of vanity, though, because you acquired valuable evidence against Kilver. What did Brummell buy?"

"Didn't condescend to buy a thing! It was the Beau's way of assuring Kilver that he is to be cut for his treachery toward you at White's."

"My, my, classic Brummell. Was Kilver sore?"

"Mad as fire! That's when he packed up and forgot his hat. I brought it straight to you."

"Why to me?"

From the bandbox, Lord Bixby lifted a black beaver in the style Rowan favored. "Tell me," he said, eyeing the inside, "how Kilver came by one of *your* monogrammed beavers?"

The Duke stared. "Toss that here!" He recognized his hat at once. "I recall only one house where I left a hat, and that was at the late Lord Flitcroft's estate in Yorkshire."

"Indeed? How so?"

"In the dark, I took the only hat from the hall table early that morning. It was dark when I made my departure," said Rowan defensively. "I could not face a second breakfast across the table from that grasping widow." He shot Bixby a long-suffering look. "Down the road a ways, I had occasion to note that the hat on my nose was not mine. It was ringed with Macassar oil, as this now is!" With a grimace, Rowan tossed the hat onto the neatly-laid wood in the fireplace.

"So you left with Kilver's hat? What was he doing at Lady Flitcroft's? Did you see him?"

"No, I did not. He could only have come during the wee hours."

Bixby whistled.

"On the night Kilver kidnapped my page," said Rowan, dropping into his hooded leather chair, "Lady Flitcroft was here, endeavoring with all her might to keep me occupied. In fact, she insisted Patrick go to his room. That was because Kilver was there, waiting to snatch him—her!"

"Kilver and that woman are in cahoots!"

Rowan frowned. "What I want to know is, why?"

"Something deep, I fear." Bixby assumed a thinking stance. "What lady would throw her reputation to the wind, as Lady Flitcroft has done in pursuing you, unless she had something wonderful to gain by it?"

"Do you mean me?" queried Rowan, hiding a smile behind his fist.

"No. I mean something more than you. Money!" Bixby chuckled. "Well, that's you, too, isn't it? I suppose you *could* be a great enough lure without your money."

"Cut the garble!" snapped Rowan laughingly. "So now we know: those two have a scheme afoot."

"We must sniff it out."

"Yes. It's vital since Tricia is involved." The Duke told him all about her flight to Highcourt House.

"Well, dash it, that's what Aldwin reported when I asked after her health."

Rowan looked at Bixby thoughtfully. "Why would a Viscount ask after a parlor maid's health?"

Bixby dimpled guiltily. "Why did she go to Highcourt House?"

"I haven't the vaguest notion. She's a guest, however; not in service, so it's a great come-uppance for her."

"I'll say. She deserves it."

"By the way, we're invited to Sir Henry Hobart's daughter's come-out ball on Saturday," Rowan remembered to tell him. "Can Lady Caro count on you?"

Bixby had been listening avidly to the tale of Tricia, and had to adjust his thoughts. "You're asking me to go with you?"

"Mmm, yes, with Lady Jewel and her aunt."

"Oh, oh, I see! While you take the beauty on your arm, I am to escort the maiden aunt, right?"

Rowan grinned and clapped him on the shoulder. "Always the bright one! Yes!"

CHAPTER 14

The Coming-Out Ball

Tricia entwined her lace-gloved fingers together and tried to subdue her nerves. The Bixby coach in which she rode swerved into queue before Sir Henry Hobart's house in Seymour Street. The mansion windows glowed with light. Faintly, the tinkle of music reached her ears through the press of carriages, calls of grooms, and chatter of guests arriving on foot with their torch-bearing footmen.

Lord Bixby was handsomely rigged in an upstanding collar, a cravat tied into a bow, a yellow figured waistcoat, and a dark green coat. He said cheerily to Tricia, "I hope you'll have a rollicking good evening."

"Yes indeed," chimed in his grandmother, Lady Bixby.

Tricia quipped, "Taking me to look at the high realms of life should prove diverting for both of you."

The Bixbys laughed and prevaricated. "Everyone will be looking at *you*," predicted Lady Bixby, checking her white curls in the mirror inside her fan.

Tricia admitted, "I almost wish this evening over already."

Bixby protested, "No, why?"

"I fear that I might appear gauche, and make noticeable gaffes."

Lady Bixby patted her hand and assured her that she would be admired, and not to worry about a thing. "You naturally have good manners, and that is all that really counts."

Tricia smiled gratefully at her. She looked out the window when their carriage moved again to see if they were in position to alight. She saw, two vehicles ahead of theirs, the Duke of Rowan's town chariot, polished to a gleam. He emerged from it, dressed in black with a snow white collar against a black coat, with a beautifully-tied cravat. When Tricia saw his face, she wished she could have ridden with him. It proved to be Lady Jewel and Aunt Caro whom he handed down from his carriage. They looked festive in their aqua and peach gowns and matching head embellishments.

Earlier, when Jewel had learned that Lady Caro truly planned to make Tricia one of the party, she objected that they would never all fit in Rowan's carriage. To which Lady Caro had replied that two carriages was the solution. Another chaperone was needed, but nothing could be easier, for Lady Bixby planned to attend.

Lady Bixby, intrigued by her grandson's enthusiasm for an unknown Miss Claremont, had asked that the young woman ride with them. How surprised she was when Lady Caro introduced the girl as her niece, *Lady* Tricia Claremont, Lord Wyndhurst's daughter from Yorkshire.

After Lord Bixby jumped down out of his coach, Tricia put one hand on his arm and lifted the skirt of her silk gown. It shone pale ivory in the lantern light. Looking down, she saw the pale blonde sheen of her long curls touching her bodice and glimpsed, in the dark coach door window, the silk roses that held the curls at her temples.

The maid, Sarah, had achieved a sweet arrangement with a well-matched switch of blonde hair looped and curled at the crown of her head. The effect was young and charming, and prettier than Tricia had ever thought her hair could look. She supposed that, if she invested the burning of her own hair with meaning, she could be thankful that a part of her former life was gone. Her purchased chignon felt as foreign to her as this entrance into Society, but her side curls were her own.

"My Lord," she whispered as Lord Bixby lifted her pale aqua shawl back onto her shoulder.

"Yes, Lady Tricia?" he asked, fingering the long fringe on her shawl and examining her face with pleased attention.

"Will you take pity on my inexperience, and help me over the rough spots tonight?"

"Lady Tricia, it will be the greatest honor." He smiled charmingly. "But I doubt if you'll need any help. You do know how to dance, don't you?"

"Several country dances, yes." Her mother, brother, and even her father had taught her in the privacy of their own drawing room. Her parents had enjoyed dancing, and it was where they had met and fallen in love: on the dance floor at an Assembly. Tricia added, "But I've certainly never waltzed."

"I only took lessons in that new dance this past

summer myself. You can observe until you've had some instruction, and until the patronesses of Almack's approve you to waltz."

"Lady Caro warned me about them."

"Don't worry; you'll meet some of them tonight. You need only say how-do-you-do and yes."

"Yes? To what?"

"To me, when I ask you to dance. You can say no to anyone else you please." He grinned, and his grandmother tittered.

Lord Bixby proudly escorted Tricia toward the receiving lines which snaked up the split staircase. Lavish ladies, including Jewel and Lady Caro up ahead, were bedecked with winking jewelry and adorned with headdresses of silk and satin, flowers and plumes. Curls fell over their ears and in cascades from their crown knots.

The men of various builds looked sophisticated in dark coats and pale breeches or trousers, and there were so many of them at close range that Tricia, now a female and unable to mask herself behind a page's uniform, felt self-conscious under their interested looks.

Lord Bixby glanced at her often as well. Quietly, he asked, "Has Rowan seen you tonight?"

"No."

"I want to see his face when he does."

"I don't!"

Bixby looked curiously at her. "Will you tell me what propelled you out of his house?"

"Shhh, someone might hear."

"Sorry."

Lady Caro waited for Tricia while the butler announced their arrival to Sir Henry and Lady

Hobart and their daughter, Isidore. The young lady making her début had a pale complexion and red-gold curls. She smiled at Tricia while sneaking a hitch at her white lace bodice.

Tricia gave her a sympathizing smile. She, too, felt odd in a new gown of the latest fashion with an expanse of exposed neckline and ankles in patterned silk hose. Isidore eyed Tricia in a friendly way as they exchanged civilities.

Lady Caro said, "My niece, Lady Tricia Claremont, has come to live with me. I've brought her as the guest which you allowed on your invitation."

"I am so glad," said Isidore. "Will you sit at my table at supper, Lady Tricia? Lord Bixby, may I ask you to escort her?"

Bixby said, "I will be utterly delighted, Miss Hobart. Thank you."

They were announced again at the entrance to the ballroom. Tricia happened to spot the Duke of Rowan as the butler shouted in his reverberating cadence, "Lady Tricia Claremont!"

The Duke looked her way, and did a double-take. First, he looked quizzical, then stunned.

Tricia grasped Lord Bixby's arm, and they followed his grandmother into the crowd. What was the Duke thinking now? She dreaded that her title distanced her even further from him because they were now socially closer in rank. It felt awkward. She did not know to behave around him if they should meet face-to-face. It would not be comfortable, as when she was Patrick at the Duke's side, serving him.

When the music began, Sir Henry Hobart, with

perspiring forehead, partnered his daughter and took the floor. Isidore's eyes were pinned on his while she kept a tremulous smile in place. Tricia thanked Heaven she was not in Isidore's shoes as the débutante.

They were followed to the floor by couples who seemed to have been designated beforehand, Lady Jewel and the Duke among them. Tricia sighed in admiration as she watched the Duke dance. What shoulders, what a head of thick, wavy hair, and what breeding he exuded as he danced with skillful grace. Every female eyeing him must have had the same thought: If only I could dance with *him!*

Jewel kept a smile pasted on her lips and her chin at a haughty tilt. The couple drew much attention, which she obviously realized, so she preened.

"Will you partner me in the first country dance, Lady Tricia?" It was Lord Bixby smiling at her, his blue eyes twinkling.

"I would love to, if I know it."

Bixby took that as acquiescence, and led her hastily to the floor as soon as the waltz music died away. "If you can do one country dance, then you know the basic steps. If you haven't done this dance, I will help, and after one sequence, you will know it." A couple arrived next to them, and another, and many more until they formed one of two long lines of men facing ladies down the length of the ballroom.

"Oh no, we're at the head of the line," moaned Tricia.

"We are. I like being number ones all the way down, don't you? Ones usually get the best part."

"I agree, but what is the dance?"

"It's called 'Once I Loved a Maiden Faire.'" He lifted his eyebrows. "Do you know it?"

"I learned it many months ago."

"Then we'll do fine."

When the music began, the caller's voice came loud and clear right next to them as he shouted the dance moves. Lord Bixby took her hands and they glided down the line between the men on one side and the women on the other. That put them next to another couple, with whom they exchanged partners for a turn. As soon as Lord Bixby finished hand-in-hand with Isidore, Tricia had to cross over to honor partners with who but her Duke!

She locked eyes with him for a split-second before they revolved together. Her heart rejoiced at the feel of his hand holding hers.

"The *Lady* Tricia?" he said low.

She felt presumptive, seeing the baffled look on his face, as if she was found guilty trying to push into exalted circles where she had no right to be. She said nothing.

The next couple came swishing down the line. Tricia circled with the gentleman. It was Beau Brummell. He observed her from the corner of his eye. Could he possibly remember her as Rowan's page at White's? Tricia grew uneasy. But who would expect a page to turn up as a Society miss? She must squash her qualms and go on with confidence. That was Mrs. Pollard's advice.

Bixby skipped to meet Brummell's partner, Lady Jewel. As they parted, Jewel threw Rowan a smile. While so doing, she stepped on her twirling train and toppled off balance. It was a ludicrous sight. Jewel's gloved hands flailed and her smile fled.

Everyone moved, and she landed chest downward on the outstretched arms of the Duke and Mr. Brummell.

"Oh!" she uttered, straightening up, looking around wild-eyed. She lowered her eyelids and composed her flushed face. "Your Grace! And Mr. Brummell, too. What female could ask for a more gallant pair to rescue her?" Though her face was red, she smiled at each man in turn, and allowed them to straighten her to her feet.

The music had ceased, for they were making other couples pile up, and the dance could not go on. Jewel announced quite loudly, "I have turned my ankle." She affected an elegant wince. She did not seem to care that the other dancers were at a confused standstill on her account.

Bixby was all chivalry in shouldering blame which was not his. "I am sorry if I—? May I escort you to a chair, Lady Jewel?"

"I believe that I should beg help from the largest man around, for I don't expect I can walk." She glanced pointedly at the Duke, and when he didn't move, she beckoned him with a gloved finger.

He said obligingly in front of his audience, "By your leave, Lady Jewel, may I help you?"

"Ah, yes," she breathed. To Brummell, she said an eloquent thanks as the Duke picked her up. "Tricia, you follow along," she said, pointing at her.

The crowd stared as Lady Jewel was carried from the midst of the dance floor by the Duke. Tricia excused herself to Lord Bixby with great regret, for this caused him to drop out of the dance as well.

It was such a *faux pas* to leave a country dance because it messed everyone up. It just was not done. She had no choice, though, so she followed Lady Jewel, feeling like a zero. How cleverly Jewel had turned her clumsiness into a grand display of herself, with the attention of the most desirable men in the room upon herself.

The Duke bore his heavy burden into a chamber which had been set aside as a ladies' visiting room. To a maid, he said, "Be so good as to fetch Lady Caro Claremont." To another one he said, lowering Jewel onto a fainting couch, "Help this lady in whatever she needs. Do you want a doctor, Lady Jewel?"

"Thank you ever so, Your Grace, but no. I will recover here." She leaned herself back and gave him a seductive look. "Care to stay?"

Rowan passed a hand through his hair. "I must go. This room is for you ladies only." He backed into Tricia. "Pardon me, my dear . . . My Lady," he added quietly, meeting her eyes. He steadied her by the shoulders with a warm squeeze, and strode out the door.

Jewel's eyes narrowed on Tricia. "I require needle and thread the color of my fringe. Go find some, hurry!"

A maid hovering behind Tricia said, "Right away, Ma'am."

Tricia inquired, "What can I do to help you, Lady Jewel?"

"That Lord Bixby is a clumsy oaf!"

"What did he do? I thought you tripped on your train. I have found that trains are impossible for me to dance in."

"What? Are you standing up for Lord Bixby? I suppose I can see why you are. You're grateful to him for partnering you."

"Please, Jewel."

"Listen to me, Tricia. While dancing with the likes of Bixby exalts you, since you are an unknown fresh up from the country, I must advise you about something. Should you accept a dance from any man higher in rank than a Viscount, your behavior will be cause for censure from everyone present. That goes for Mr. Brummell, since he is the Prince's friend and the supreme judge of who is who, and who is not."

Tricia blinked her long lashes slowly during Jewel's vehement speech. "I would not try to raise myself to exalted heights. In truth, I never dreamed I would dance in London at all."

"It's all Aunt Caro's fault! —but yours, too, for coming. You are flopping about like a fish out of the sea. You know that you don't belong, but since you are here, keep your place. Now sew this on, will you?"

Tricia moved to take the needle, skein, and scissors from the maid.

"Oh no, Miss," she protested, "you must not do it! I must sew the tassel on for Milady."

Jewel gave the maid a freezing stare. "She shall sew it on. She has been a lower servant than you until recently."

"That was uncalled-for," said Tricia, glaring at Jewel.

The maid looked shocked. Tricia feared the whole story would now be out, and knew it was exactly what Jewel wanted.

"What on earth happened?" asked Lady Caro, hurrying into the room as Tricia strolled angrily out. "I've heard a dozen reports on my way from the card room. Did Rowan really carry Jewel out in a romantic passion?"

"Hardly, Aunt. Jewel tripped on her own train during our dance, pitched onto Rowan and Brummell both at once, and directed the Duke to carry her here. She said she couldn't walk."

"Stars above! What next? You go to Lady Bixby's side, Tricia, while I see to Jewel."

They locked eyes. "Gladly."

"Why, here you are, dear," said the white-haired Lady Bixby, beaming at Tricia, and holding out her gloved hand for hers.

"On that cue, I put in my appearance," said a male voice. "Please introduce us, Lady Bixby."

It was Beau Brummell, fixing his dark eyes on Tricia in a friendly way.

The introduction was made.

"May I take her to dance, Lady Bixby?"

Despite Jewel's warning, Tricia felt her own brand of alarm. Dared she dance with this arbiter of taste, this intimate friend of the Prince Regent's?

She managed a smile as she said, "I am honored, Mr. Brummell. But my cousin has warned me that I am unworthy to dance with you."

Curiosity lit his handsome face. "On what grounds could you be unworthy, as you so charmingly put it?"

Flushing, she said, "Mr. Brummell, will you be so good as to allow me a quick word with Lady Bixby? It is a message I meant to relay to her."

"Certainly. I did interrupt your course, I realize that." He stepped aside and watched her go.

Lady Bixby looked totally awash. "What are you

doing, Lady Tricia? Putting off the man you most want to keep on your side?”

Tricia squeezed her hand. “Please help me. How do I refuse him without hurting his feelings?”

“Refuse? What folderol is this?”

“I’ve been warned I must not dance with Mr. Brummell or with anyone higher in rank than your grandson. How do I extricate myself from Beau Brummell? He is ranked among the Prince Regent’s inner circle.”

“Tricia! Who on this earth gave you such a stricture? Surely not Caro!”

“No, my cousin, Lady Jewel.”

“Jewel! That snake! I’ll have a thing or two to say to her! You are the daughter of a rightful Marquis. You go this instant and dance with all and sundry who ask you. But not twice in a row, or three times total with the same man, do you understand? Now be charming to Mr. Brummell, of all people!”

“I am sorry to have kept you waiting,” Tricia said with a genuine smile for Mr. Brummell.

Behind his shoulder, Lord Bixby asked, “You kept the Beau waiting? I never knew of a woman who dared before, eh, Brummell?”

He smiled at Lord Bixby. “Few are worth the wait.” Gallantly, he offered Tricia his arm.

She could see Bixby’s wonder as she was led out to dance. Did it really mean so much that Beau Brummell had chosen her?

“Oh *no*,” she groaned as the music began in three-quarter time. “Mr. Brummell, is this a waltz?”

“It most certainly is.”

“Then I cannot,” she said, meeting his eyes in regret.

"Have you not been approved?"

"No! I haven't even met the patronesses."

"Not been to Almack's?"

"Heavens no! I only just arrived."

"Come with me." He led her toward a striking dark-haired lady whom he introduced as the Countess Lieven. Tricia had read of this patroness in the newspapers. The Countess had an airy confidence and a fine, long neck.

Brummell made Tricia's title and connection with the missing Lord Claremont known to her. Tricia wondered how he knew that much, but doubtless gossip ran rife in these circles.

"Yes, I have just heard all that," said the Countess. "Charmed, Lady Tricia. What is it you'd like from me, Beau?"

"I would like to waltz with her. Will Your Ladyship permit?"

"Hmmm. How old are you, Tricia?"

"Nineteen next month."

"Have you been presented?"

Brummell saw Tricia's blank look. He inserted, "At Court."

"No, Your Ladyship."

"She just arrived."

"Hmmm, it isn't every day I get to bend the rules. Let's give those dowagers something to hiss about. Go ahead, Beau." The Countess winked at Brummell and moved away with her own waltz partner.

Tricia felt flustered. "Thank you for what you did, Mr. Brummell, but I dare not embarrass you."

"Embarrass me? How?"

"I can't waltz."

"You mean you tried and failed? Or you've never given it a go?"

"I've never had instruction."

"I am thrilled. Come with me," he said, his lips curving.

Curious looks followed them as Mr. Brummell led her past the dancers until he gained the gallery overlooking the staircase.

"In this salon, we can still hear the music." He gestured her into a room where he moved aside a small tea table.

Tricia nearly pinched herself. She realized she was being taken up by very important people, and wondered how on earth to go on with this one.

Brummell poked his head back out, hailed an elderly couple coming up the stairs, and introduced them as Lord and Lady Dondervan. "Will you supervise our waltz lesson?" he asked them with a little bow. "You would do us a great service."

"Certainly, Mr. Brummell." Pleased, they were introduced to Tricia, and settled next to one another on a sofa to watch.

"Now, My Lady, we join hands," Mr. Brummell said, taking hers in his. "Your other one you must put here on my arm even as mine encircles you . . . so."

Tricia had seen cartoons depicting the close proximity of waltzers, and here she was, embraced in person by the pleasant-smelling Mr. Brummell. She was grateful for respectable chaperones, but her blush still rose.

"The steps are like this: *one*-two-three, *one*-two-three . . . " While Tricia lightly stumbled around his highly-polished evening pumps, he gradually got her to move in time with him by disengaging himself, doing it alone, and having her rejoin him. She was determined to learn quickly.

"That's prime." They practiced for many minutes until she was gliding around at his leading, and smiling with joy. When the next waltz number began, he danced her toward the door. "Keep it up, Lady Tricia, and we shall now move into the ballroom. That first number did not count because we were practicing."

As they danced across the gallery, Tricia saw the Duke of Rowan standing there, gripping the railing, as though he had been watching them for some time. At sight of him, she tripped on Brummell's foot. "So sorry!"

"Never apologize. It's nothing." His dark eyes smiled into hers. "It's the fault of these distractions—hello, Duke—so ignore these people and focus on flowing with my lead. Yes, Lady Tricia, you are moving superbly now."

She kept time with him. Although she was still learning, she felt rushes of delight in his graceful swoops. Her silk gown swirled and her curls swung. She had the feeling, when she finally curtseyed to Mr. Brummell's bow at the finis, that something extraordinary had happened to her. He applauded her with his pristine white gloves.

"That was wonderful!" she said, smiling at him in true delight as she curtseyed.

How glorious it felt to be free of Jewel's stricture not to dance with high-born gentlemen. At the back of her mind, Tricia wondered uneasily what Jewel would do about this defiance of her orders, especially if she had seen her with Beau Brummell. For the rest of the glorious evening, Tricia was inundated with gentlemen clamoring to partner her.

* * *

When the Duke saw his former page at private waltzing lessons with Mr. Brummell, he nearly stormed in after them. How could the Beau do something so ruinous to the girl? It was only when he approached and heard a cough within the salon that he discovered Lord and Lady Dondervan sitting there, chaperoning them in all propriety. So the Beau thought of everything in order to get away with the unheard-of.

When Tricia waltzed with him onto the gallery, it was easy to see that she was Brummell's new protégée. That said a great deal. He was dancing her out in the public eye, Rowan's own little Patrick whom he rescued from Farmer Ramsbottom. The Duke exhaled and watched them with admiration and a modicum of pain. What would become of her now? A fear niggled at him. She might be spoiled by all this attention. It annoyed him that Brummell had perked up out of his boredom to take up Rowan's own discovery.

When the Duke had heard, at the beginning of the ball, that the angelic nonpareil in the ivory gown was styled Lady Tricia Claremont, he had stared in spite of his manners. Could it be true? What was Lady Caro trying to pull off by calling her that? The Duke went straight to her for intelligence.

With excitement, Lady Caro had divulged that his page and parlor maid was indeed a genuine Lady. She was her own niece, in fact. She proudly regaled him with the details of their discovered connection.

It took Rowan some time to digest the significance of it all. As he saw Brummell conclude his dance with Tricia, there went Lord Alvanley, like a streak, to take the Beau's place.

Rowan, because of his height, was visible to anyone who might seek him, and that was how Brummell found him. Lord Bixby converged with them, exclaiming, "Brummell! Tell us—although we already know what *we* think of Lady Tricia— what do *you* say?"

Mr. Brummell crossed his arms, eyed the chandelier, and appeared to search within himself. "She is more alluring and tender than a newborn—"

"Lamb?" guessed Bixby.

"Dream!" decided Brummell.

"Ahh," sighed Bixby, "that's poetic." His eyes followed Tricia's graceful progress down the set with Lord Alvanley. "But she had better remain a dream to all of you gentlemen, because I—well, I'm her escort."

Rowan eyed Bix icily, and Brummell laughed.

Bixby reddened.

Brummell said, "She's out there dancing her way into all of our hearts, gentlemen. Snuff, Duke?"

"No, thanks!" he snapped.

Mr. Brummell leaned toward him. "How goes it with the Lady Jewel? What do you think of *her* by now?"

Rowan had forgotten all about her. "Never mind what I think. What do you think of the Jewel?"

"She's striving to have one on her finger by the end of the season," Brummell predicted.

"You've nothing else to say?"

Brummell drawled, "Whom she marries depends upon who is strong, and who is susceptible."

Rowan forced a grin. "You sound like a man who doesn't want a wife."

"And you sound like you're leaning into the camp of those who do."

Rowan mused how, when Lady Jewel had tripped, and when he had lifted her in his arms and carried her out, he involuntarily made a comparison. She was much heavier than Tricia and felt different: much larger of frame. He almost staggered carrying her. But she had a brilliant smile, did Jewel, and those half-closed eyes, when he laid her down, promised . . . what? It had made him leave the room, for he was gun-shy.

Rowan noticed Lady Caro beckoning him with her fan. He excused himself from his friends. "May I be of service, Lady Caro?"

"I hope so, Duke." Worriedly, she whispered, "As much as I've tried to scotch it, word is flying amongst the dowagers that Tricia worked for you in breeches. What are we to do?"

The Duke sighed in exasperation. "Brummell has countenanced her. Did they not notice? That should out-weigh any gossip."

"That *is* something. It's far more of a triumph than I ever hoped for. Even Jewel can't be that sure of Brummell's approbation. But what shall I say to those clucking hens?"

"Tell them nothing."

"Your Grace, I can think of something that might help Tricia, if only you would . . ."

"What, dear Lady?"

She patted his hand. "Dance with her."

Rowan smiled ruefully. "I would love to, but will she have me?"

Lady Caro's jaw dropped. "Look around you, dear Rowan. As I speak, I see scads of girls who are dying slow deaths because you have not noticed them. Look, there's another smile gushed at you, the forty-year-old green frock. Can you doubt your acceptance with any lady, young or old?"

Rowan pursed his lips in embarrassment. "I do doubt. But I need to have a serious talk with her, not just dance with her."

"Why don't you forget serious talks for now? Go and make her happy. All the other men are endeavoring to do that. Here, let me take your glass."

The Duke gave it up gratefully, and circumvented the room, looking for that certain fair head. He was jostled and greeted by numerous friends along the way, but he smiled shyly and made excuses and kept moving. It felt like they all knew what he was up to, but that was ridiculous.

"Absolutely, it's too true!" sang out a familiar voice as Rowan rounded a pillar. His heart sank. It was Lady Flitcroft.

Another woman queried shrilly, "A page? For the Duke of Rowan? She was?"

Deliberately, the Duke leaned his shoulder against the pillar, crossed his arms, and waited. His eyes sent darts into the back of Lady Flitcroft's russet curls. Another woman glanced aside and did a double-take, her eyes popping at him. "Your Grace!"

Plumes and turbans spun. The women's faces registered guilt. Lady Flitcroft knew she was caught when Rowan directed a furious squint at her.

"Why, it's our devastating Duke," she exclaimed nervously. "I believe he's come to ask me to dance." She undulated toward him, long black fringe swinging from her dark purple gown.

"You are in mourning," he informed her coldly. The look he gave her friends in turn made them all stand straighter. "Ladies," he said distinctly, "take caution about what you say. Someone might believe you." Being a powerful Duke had its advantages. They all looked suitably cowed.

"Tell me, Lady Flitcroft, who originated that gossip back there?"

"Everyone knows about your lackey-turned-lady. But it was Augusta Sylvester who brought it up."

"Who told Miss Sylvester?"

"One of her friends, no doubt. I suspect it was that Lady Jewel Claremont."

They could see Lady Jewel embracing an elderly gentleman and smiling as they parted. She looked so kind that Rowan shook his head. "I don't think Lady Jewel would spread such a tale."

"Do you not? But you think *I* would?" Furiously she attacked him on another score. "Why did you treat me so horrendously? Was I not good enough to be invited to your musical evening?"

"Such questions. Listen, I have reason to believe that you knew my page was to be abducted by Lord

Kilver that night you were in my house."

She looked trapped. "I knew Lord Kilver had an eye on Tricia, so I thought he should *have* the little sneak. After all, she ran away from him, and he's her guardian."

Savagely, he whipped out, "So you knew all along that she was a female?"

"No! He told me that night at the opera."

"So you furthered his kidnapping scheme? What a vile-hearted thing to do!" He glared at her terribly.   "Listen here, I won't have you broadcasting anything more about Lady Tricia, do you hear? I still don't understand why you aided Kilver. Tell me why!"

She pouted, "I wanted to be with *you*.   He proposed a delightful mission for me that night."

"You two are despicable! Vile! Evil!" He left her, his hands in tight fists.

There in the distance against the blue-draped windows went Tricia, dancing with an Army officer in a red coat. As they went skipping down the set, her two long curls bouncing, she smiled at Lord Bixby standing against the wall sipping tea. His face brightened and stayed that way as he watched her. Many other men had admiring eyes trained on her, too.

Rowan backed into an alcove and put his hand to his hot forehead.

Another quickly replaced it, a woman's cool hand. He pulled it down in surprise and blinked. "Lady Jewel!"

"Does that feel better, Your Grace?" She glanced around to see if anyone observed them. Since they were behind a row of potted palms, she reasserted her bold touch.

The Duke, abashed, took her hand down again and let it go. "I am obliged to you, Lady Jewel but how is your ankle?"

"Infinitely better. I can walk again, thanks to your timely aid." She fanned herself and asked, "Was that blowsy widow pestering you?"

"Lady Flitcroft?" The Duke cleared his throat, not exactly knowing what to say to a well-bred Lady about such a one.

"Have you told her to jump off a cliff?" Jewel cast him a straight look. She meant it.

The Duke, taken off guard, gave a small laugh and said, "Let's not talk about her. Would you like one of those cordials?" He moved around the palm to lift two goblets off a footman's tray. This put the two of them into a more public spot. He knew how tongues flapped about every move he made. Following their former display when he had carried her out, cozying together now behind palm fronds would add to the scandal-broth. He searched the room for Lady Caro. She saw him, so he beckoned her subtly with his head.

Jewel said, "Lady Flitcroft crashed this ball. Augusta said she barged in through the servants' entrance."

"Oh?"

"She came to see you, Rowan. Are you now forewarned?"

"I caught her gossiping about your cousin, Lady Tricia," he growled.

Jewel sipped, her lashes paused at half-mast.

He added, "I beseech your help in counteracting any rumors you hear which could hurt her."

"Why, of course. But what does it mean to you, Rowan?"

"I, ah . . . I feel responsible for her. I brought her to London in the first place."

"Why did you?" Jewel was watching him closely but he maintained a cool dignity.

"Lady Caro, would you care for this cordial?" he asked as she gained his side. "I haven't touched it."

"You never touch them, do you, Rowan? I'll gladly take yours, for at this moment I feel extremely put out. Jewel dear, I must talk with Rowan. Will you kindly join Lady Bixby around the corner there?"

"Oh, Aunt!" huffed Jewel from the side of her mouth as she moved away, frowning.

The music was mounting to a finale, and Rowan had his eye on where the red Army coat and the pale gown circled around each other in the gypsy move. "Lady Caro," he said, "I was interrupted in my purpose to request a certain dance, so if you'll pardon me, I'll try again as soon as this number concludes. But first, what was it you wanted to say to me?"

"Only that, unless we *do* something, Tricia will be spurned by this whole set by morning! You should hear how quickly the story travels, and how it's changing! That coarse Mrs. Kerberts hissed that Tricia has been your doxy!"

"Pray to God no one believes that." He nearly pushed his way through the crowd in his urgency to get to Tricia. When he reached her, she was surrounded by a bevy of women. Lady Jewel was there with Augusta Sylvester and Isidore Hobart.

He heard Augusta say to Tricia, "We switched

tables so Isidore can be more prominent as the débutante. Now, because she can have only two friends and escorts at her table, she has to ask you to sit lower. You do understand, do you not?"

With a blink of her long lashes, Tricia replied softly, "Of course." She smiled at Isidore.

When Lady Jewel and Augusta turned away, Rowan heard giggling, and the two of them nearly collided with him. Jewel looked up at him with a start of surprise. He saw how ashamed Isidore Hobart looked, so he approached her. "You're not the one who contrived this new arrangement, are you?" he put to her gently.

"Oh no, Your Grace, but I agreed with Lady Jewel and Augusta before I realized that Lady Tricia would be left out." She glanced at Tricia who had moved out of earshot. "I feel so bad, Your Grace. I should not have hurt her like that. I like her, so I invited her to join my table at the outset, but now it appears that I've gone back on my word!"

"Then make it up to her."

"How?   The table order has already been changed, Your Grace."

"Ward off any gossip about her," he said, "and call on her tomorrow."

"Yes, I shall," said Isidore, smiling up at him with relief. "I can see that you and Mr. Brummell and Lord Bixby all like her very much, so she must be as lovely as she looks. Thank you, Your Grace, for your advice."

Rowan admired Tricia's slim neck and fetching curls as he followed her down the middle of the room. Before another gentleman on a collision course could claim her, he caught her hand from behind, turned her to face him, and smiled. "Hello there, Lady Tricia."

"Oh, Your Grace, please don't call me Lady in that way," she begged, her large eyes beseeching him. "I feel so presumptuous."

"You do? Well, I think it sounds nice."

"Where are we going, Your Grace?"

He hadn't realized it, but he had a proprietary hold on her hand and was leading her out of the ballroom. "Hmm, that's right; I was to dance with you first."

Tricia turned a suspicious look on him. "Excuse me?"

"I so need to talk with you that I forgot we haven't danced," he corrected himself.

She retained a skeptical look, but when the music began in three-quarter time, she smiled and said, "I am still learning the waltz."

"You've had quite a teacher, too."

"Yes. It was good of Mr. Brummell to ask Countess Lieven if I could waltz, and very long-suffering of him to teach me."

Rowan rolled his eyes. "Indeed, on both points." They both grinned.

They swayed and revolved together. Something about the way his hand fitted over the middle of her shoulder blades pleased Rowan immeasurably. Before long, he could not breathe properly. She smelled divine. She was such a tender, vulnerable young thing. He let his gaze roam over the corn floss curls shining on either side of her smooth forehead and followed them over the arch of her delicate brows, down her pretty cheekbones ...

"Your Grace?"

"Call me Rowan."

"I couldn't," she said. "Your Grace, I want to know if you approve of what has happened to me."

"What is that?"

"My being discovered as the daughter of a missing Peer, and having to be one now."

"Put it this way: I knew you weren't of the Ramsbottom realm."

She laughed. "Thank you for that."

"I think it's providential that you found your family, Lady Tricia. However, whenever I think of my taking you into service, I am mortified."

"Oh no, don't feel that way, for I will be forever grateful! Remember that I would still be dodging about the York Road if you had not taken me up."

"Thanks to God for that, then. Are you happy at Highcourt House?"

Tricia looked away. "Yes," she returned in a small voice. But her fingers tightened touchingly around his.

CHAPTER 15

The Letter

The sweet scent of flowers filled Highcourt House. Baskets and tissues of colorful bouquets were piled upon the marble-topped table in the entrance hall. Hopkins puffed and wheezed as he artfully arranged the overflow of floral offerings up the edge of the stairs.

Lady Caro called, "Here's another one for you, Tricia, from someone I've never heard of. Forget-me-nots! You garnered admirers unceasingly at the ball, my dear."

Tricia, seated at the writing table at the back end of the hall, looked up and smiled.

She saw Jewel scowl and pass over two new bouquet cards until she found one with her name on it. She remarked in her high pitch, "Callow young men always try with the newest female on the scene. Look Aunt, Lord Alvanley has sent me this bouquet of narcissus."

"Narcissi! Now, why would he send you those?" Lady Caro grinned roguishly at Tricia. "What is that new arrival, Hopkins?" Lady Caro strode to the closing door to examine two bouquets of roses the butler bore. "My, my!" she reported. "The Duke of Rowan sends red roses to you, Jewel, and these white ones to Tricia.”

Jewel, in alt, cried, “Red roses mean love!”

“On the Continent they do, but not here,” Lady Caro corrected her bluntly. “White ones mean purity and spiritual love. Here, Tricia.”

“Purity? He got that wrong!” snapped Jewel.

“Shame on you!” expectorated her aunt. “You, who are usually a pattern of rectitude, talking so disgracefully to her! Apologize to her at once.”

“Pardon me,” said Jewel, fluttering her fingers in Tricia’s direction. It sounded like lip service, to be gotten through quickly.

Lady Caro said, “If we’re analyzing meanings to all of these, then Mr. Brummell’s jasmine to Tricia is a tribute to her waltz lesson with him last night. Jasmine means grace and elegance.”

Jewel appeared frustratingly tongue-tied, for she had just apologized.

Tricia was gratified by the roses from the Duke. Her eyes rested fondly on them as she opened another in a stack of invitation cards. She had pleaded with her aunt to give her tasks to do, for she did not want to live at Highcourt House without contributing in some way. She could keep track of their social calendars and write some of their letters to begin with, Lady Caro conceded.

Setting aside an invitation for a rout party, Tricia came upon a letter with *Tricia* scrawled across it. That spiky hand! She flipped the letter over as if it were hot, and took one look at the brown seal. “Oh, Aunt, come here!” Her heart beat like galloping hooves. “I can’t open that.”

“Whyever not?”

Tricia flung the letter away from her. It slipped

off the escritoire and sailed across the floor.

With an alarmed look, Lady Caro asked, "Can you see bad news through paper?"

"Yes!"

Jewel, interested, swooped up the letter. "*I'm* not afraid to read it."

"Of course you're not. Give it to me, Jewel," said Lady Caro firmly.

Jewel unwillingly thrust the missive across her swans-down muff. They were about to leave for church.

Lady Caro cracked the seal. Her eyes grew wide and then narrowed as they flicked along the written lines.

Tricia was wondering what she read when Hopkins opened the door, spoke with someone, and turned to announce, "Lady Hobart and Miss Hobart have arrived, Your Ladyships."

Lady Caro continued to peruse the paper with consternation until she belatedly heard what the butler had said. Deflated, she ran a stunned glance over Tricia and pushed the letter into her reticule. "Good morning, Lady Hobart. You're coming to church with us? How nice. Isidore, come in. How beautifully you conducted yourself at your ball last night. Have posies arrived for you this morning?"

Blushing, she said, "Yes, My Lady."

"Ever so many," inserted the skinny Lady Hobart, smiling widely under her long nose.

"That's delightful," said Lady Caro distractedly. "Are we ready?"

In the barouche-landau, Jewel patted the seat beside her for Isidore, so she sat there; but the débutante included Tricia in her conversation all the way to church even though she had to talk across. As they bowled along, Tricia felt warmed by her friendliness.

Last night, the change in the supper seating had hurt a little, but Tricia had enjoyed many laughs with Lord Bixby, his grandmother, and Lady Caro. The only real thorn had been watching the Duke of Rowan fêted in force by Jewel, Augusta, and by Isidore herself.

"Tonight," said Isidore to Tricia, "there are to be fireworks in Hyde Park. Are you coming?"

"Of course," said Jewel.

"Famous." Isidore smiled at Tricia. "Let's go together. May we, Lady Caro?"

"Perhaps."

Tricia knew that her aunt was upset and could hardly think of other things than what the mysterious letter had contained.

In church, Tricia had a hard time hearing the sermon at first, for her heart was full of anxiety. But gradually, as she listened, she let her problems slide from her shoulders. She heard the account of Jesus fasting in the wilderness and then being tempted by the Devil. She loved the way Jesus defeated him in every instance by speaking the Word of God. It encouraged her, and reminded her what to do in her own battles.

At the close of the service, the song they sang continued in her heart. *"Come, Thou long-expected Jesus, born to set thy people free."*

She walked out to the strains of the organ, thanking God for strengthening her faith. Though evil pursued her, Jesus promised never to leave her nor forsake her. He was the "joy of every longing heart." He had made her spirit free, and that was the most important aspect of her life.

At the back of the church, Mrs. Pollard and Aldwin, Lionel, Stefan, and Theodore waited respectfully for the Nobility to pass. Up in the balcony, leaving his private pew, was the Duke himself.

Lady Caro gave a nudge to Tricia's back. "Go out with the others. I'm staying to speak with Rowan when he comes down the stairs."

"What did the letter say?"

Lady Caro put her finger to her lips and said, "Later, Tricia."

She obeyed and emerged between the columns, blinking at the sunshine.

Isidore accompanied her mother to speak with an old lady. Jewel had joined a group of young people. Tricia moved to join them, but a young lady, who had been present at the ball, looked at Jewel and lifted her parasol to block Tricia's entrance to their circle. It was very deliberate.

Tricia felt a bit sick, and turned away. The feeling abated when Isidore came gaily over and put an arm about her. "Have you ever been walking in Hyde Park at night?" she put to her with lively eyes.

"No, I've never stepped foot in Hyde Park. I have only passed by it in the street." She had seen it through her window when she was page to the Duke.

"Oh, you must come! When there are fireworks, you get all sorts of people out, and it's so diverting. The last time I went was when Colonel Blucher came to London. The crowds! It was such a squeeze. There are so many good-looking bucks to encounter whom one never sees otherwise."

"Really? Does your mother let you talk to them?"

"No, but I can wink at them during the explosions, for Mama is always distracted by the spectacle above."

Tricia saw Stefan, Lionel, and Theodore emerge from the doorway in the church portico. Mr. Aldwin was already escorting Mrs. Pollard into a carriage.

Tricia called, "Good morning!"

They eyed her and looked taken aback. Mrs. Pollard immediately curtseyed low and said, "Good morning, Your Ladyship." Aldwin bowed his head with deference, and the footmen followed suit.

Tricia's smile faded as she realized what had happened. She had become a Lady. "A blessed Sunday to you all," she said unsteadily.

"Thank you, Your Ladyship, and to you."

She followed the Rowan servants with wistful eyes. Stefan glanced back from his perch, and she couldn't help it: she lifted her hand in a small salute.

He acknowledged her with a slight nod, but that was all.

Isidore was staring at her, awestruck. "Tricia! It's true then, isn't it?"

"Yes. I was one of them."

"Do you wish you still were? Merciful Margaret! I've never heard of such a thing. Was there something good about service, then?"

"Yes, there was but please don't repeat any of this, Isidore. I see I am not to speak to my old friends, for that is what I felt them to be after a few days."

"Lady Tricia, I think you should know something," Isidore said suddenly, drawing her aside. "Jewel is not only telling people that you were Rowan's page, but worse." She looked at Tricia with grave significance.

"What do you mean, worse?"

"It's too awful. I don't think I should tell you, but someone should, and I like you too well to leave you in ignorance."

Tricia felt alarm as she looked at Isidore's earnest face. "Go on."

"She says Lady Flitcroft has proof that you are some Lord's bird of paradise, or some such word, and to crown the whole, she insists that you were also the Duke's!"

Tricia's anger flared. "As dreadful as that sounds, I am not entirely surprised! My cousin has shown me in many ways that I am not to be a part of her world. Is that why she slanders me?" They could see Jewel in her group of young ladies, leaning their heads together, chattering and laughing.

"She is obviously envious of you." Isidore quietly added, "Those lurid stories aren't true, are they?"

"Of course not! I've never even kissed a man, much less—"

"Shhh! Here comes Mother. I'll tell everyone that what Jewel has been broadcasting are outright lies!"

"Thank you. They are!" Tricia hugged her with gratitude. While doing so, she saw the Duke emerge from the church. He looked divine in a charcoal tail coat and ivory pantaloons. As he fitted his top hat to his head, he saw her releasing Isidore.

He walked directly to see them, smiled, and said, "Good morning, Lady Tricia, Miss Hobart."

"Thank you for coming to my ball, Your Grace, and thank you for the orchids," returned Isidore in a rush.

"You deserved them. You certainly were a success."

Tricia had no opportunity to thank the Duke for her white roses, for Isidore's conversation with the Duke hurried on, fueled by her nervous admiration.

When the five ladies were wheeling along home, they decided to ride together to the fireworks. "But we must have a male escort," said Lady Caro. "We cannot go to such an event at night without one. With my brother off in Paris, I cannot think who we could ask."

"Papa will come, won't he?" queried Isidore.

"He cannot," said Lady Hobart, "for he went hunting. He only stayed for your ball, and was off first thing this morning."

Jewel said loftily, "Why not ask the Duke?"

"What makes you think we can call on the Duke of Rowan any time we wish?" returned Lady Caro incredulously. "He has been extremely obliging to us already, considering the large circle of friends he has, and the myriad activities and clubs he must give his attention to. No, we cannot ask him."

"So what did Tricia's fearsome letter say?" Jewel taunted when they returned to Highcourt House.

Lady Caro said, "It is a private matter." As she removed her bonnet, she added, "I know that isn't going to please you, Jewel, but you have to accept it. Tricia, I need you to come with me."

In Lady Caro's bedchamber of yellow flowered walls, Tricia slumped in the window seat and stared at the garden through shivering maple leaves. With her arms crossed tightly, she said, "I hate the sight of that writing, and I don't want to hear what he says."

"I understand, Tricia love, but I must read it to you. You can explain to me what it's all about. It says, 'Tricia. I am your guardian and you know it. If you don't come back home with me obediently, I will take strict measures. You tell those Claremonts that I have the legal document to prove it. Unless they give you up today, I will make things very unpleasant for them, and especially for you. I have my ways. I am coming to fetch you, so you better be ready. Uncle Lord Kilver.'"

"Oh!" Tricia slammed her feet on the floor and made furious fists. "That fiend! He is *not* my uncle!"

"Why, that part nearly made me faint! Why does he claim to be?"

"His wife is my aunt," Tricia admitted, "but *he* is nothing to me."

"Rowan warned me to keep you safe from him, Tricia, so I showed him this letter at church."

Tricia sat bolt upright. "What did he say?"

"He is furious. I don't know what he'll do, but the letter galvanized him. After all, he rescued you from that man in the most horrendous moment imaginable, and I know he cares what happens to you."

"But Kilver demands by law to force me back!" wailed Tricia. "If he succeeds, that will be the worst nightmare of my life!"

CHAPTER 16

Fireworks

"Look, Tricia, it's the Congreve Rocket!" exclaimed Isidore. The swishing noise and the powerful pink streak surging up into the night sky captured the attention of hundreds of onlookers in Hyde Park.

Someone touched Tricia's arm. Since she wanted to watch the bursts of blue, red, and gold until they died away, she dragged her eyes away reluctantly. There, shadowed beneath a tree branch, stood a woman in a veiled bonnet. Her features were impossible to see.

"Miss," she whispered urgently, "will you please watch my little girls for a moment while I try to find my boy? I am so worried! He just slipped away, and anybody could snatch him."

"How awful!" replied Tricia. The crowds were thick around the water of the Serpentine. To lose a child in this motley crowd was unthinkable.

"There they are, on that bench." The woman pointed. "My girls." Two bonnets were upturned, for the sky arced over with fantastic sparkles, exploding and crackling and accompanied by a chorus of awed voices.

Tricia assured her, "I will watch them."

"Oh, thank you." The woman darted away.

"Come with me, Isidore," said Tricia, pulling her sleeve, "I must sit with those children while their mother finds her missing boy."

Isidore's pupils grew wide in the semi-darkness. "Tricia, who *was* that woman who asked you to do such a thing? Where's her nurse?"

"I don't know, but I can't leave her daughters alone."

The Duke of Rowan observed their distressed dialogue and disengaged himself from Lady Jewel and Lady Caro. He came to ask, "Is anything wrong?"

Tricia hurriedly explained.

Rowan had been implored by a note from Lady Caro to escort them tonight after all. She did not dare to come without a man's protection, nor did she wish to stay home for fear Lord Kilver would come to demand Tricia as he had threatened.

Lady Jewel, upon hearing that the Duke agreed to escort them, had looked elated. She had opened her new bottle of perfume. Tricia could smell it now, for it had rubbed off on Rowan. Jewel had been hanging on his arm for the past half-hour, chatting non-stop. She called to any acquaintances she saw, obviously wanting all and sundry to notice her there with him. Tricia had steamed. Feeling anger and frustration, she had moved away and tried to talk with Isidore between the fireworks.

The Duke had taken Tricia aside briefly tonight as he was handing the ladies into their barouche. With concern drawing his brows together, he had said, "I wrote to Kilver, Tricia. I told him not to try anything, for you are well guarded."

She discovered, to her great surprise, that he had sent Stefan and Lionel to stand guard in Highcourt House. Theodore and Rupert would relieve them for the nights, the Duke said. Tricia was very touched.

It felt good to have him here in the park, striding beside her now toward the little girls seated on the bench. When the older one looked up and saw them, she said, "Run, Dorcas, run!" She slipped quickly from her seat, pulling her sister with her. With little cloaks flying, they raced past the legs of a group of men and away into the dimness of the throng.

"We must catch them!" cried Tricia, "or they'll be lost!"

Rowan sprinted, coattails flying.

Tricia dashed after him.

Isidore was soon panting behind her. "Imagine! A reason to run from Mama, and in such a place, too. She'll probably screech at me. Look, he's caught the little naughties."

The Duke had each miscreant by the arm. "Do you know where your mother is? No? Then why are you tearing loose like this?"

They looked up at him, tongue-tied.

Lady Caro had gained their side and said breathlessly, "Let me talk to them." In a honeyed voice, she asked the oldest one, "Where is your brother, little girl?" When she had gained answers to her quiet questions, she said a few words to the Duke and pushed the girls toward him.

"We don't have any brother," she mimicked as she returned to Tricia and Isidore, Jewel, and Lady Hobart. "Our mama is the beautiful Lady

Flitcroft."

Jewel's eyes flashed. "That woman! She teaches her brats to call her *the beautiful!*"

"Isn't she the lowest?" hissed Lady Hobart to the other ladies huddled together near a lamp post. "To use her own children so! I don't know what is going forward here, but it is despicable."

Jewel remarked acrimoniously, "She's nowhere near beautiful!"

The Duke approached and asked Tricia, "Was that Lady Flitcroft under the veil?"

"I believe it was," she surmised. "But what is the purpose of her trick?"

Rowan hunkered down and quizzed the girls, "Where were you going just now?"

"Over there," pointed the little one, "to uncle Kilver's coach."

"*What?*" In fear, Tricia's eyes locked with Rowan's.

He growled behind his glove, "Another kidnapping attempt, I see! He and Lady Flitcroft are scheming together." His jaw muscles clenched.

A male silhouette in a top hat disengaged from the shadows and made straight for them. Tricia reached out and grasped Rowan's arm as she recognized the quick, nervous stalk of Lord Kilver.

A brilliant rocket exploded. By its light she saw Kilver's straight slit of a mouth in angry determination as he kept walking jerkily straight at them.

She cringed. Memories flooded back.

Jewel moved next to Tricia, having seen her hand on Rowan's arm. As Kilver came into the lamp light, Jewel declared loudly, "Whoever he is, he doesn't look nice."

Isidore quavered, "Oh, God help us! What's he going to do?"

The Duke thrust the children at the ladies, and planted himself in Kilver's path.

Tightly gripping the arms of the little ones, Tricia watched Kilver halt before Rowan. The bangs of the fireworks became so deafening that she could not hear what they said, but she saw the Duke speak, Kilver whip out answers, and both of them go rigid.

When the sounds diminished, Kilver shouted, "Dorcas! Daphne! Get over here!" He motioned angrily at the little girls.

Tricia looked quizzically at the Duke. Should she give up the children?

Rowan nodded ruefully.

Kilver came and snatched their hands.

"Where did Mama go?" cried the smallest one.

The elder piped up, "Did we run fast enough when we saw her, Uncle Kilver? She chased us like you wanted. Do we get our cherry ices now?"

"Hush up!" The glare Kilver turned on Tricia at close range made her heart thud. "Get my letter?" he spat.

She forced a blank look.

"I will make it legally clear." His look knifed through her. He flicked his glittering, narrow eyes to Jewel and raised his brows in avowal.

Jewel looked down her nose at him and challenged, "Are you, by chance, in league with that new widow who flits from man to man? If so, your taste is execrable."

"Why, you—!" Kilver reacted with quick fists

upward near Jewel's taunting face.

The Duke snatched Jewel out of Kilver's reach.

Lady Caro planted herself before Lord Kilver and cried, "Leave us at once!" She continued to tell him that he could not take Tricia by fair means or foul, to which he snarled back that he would come fetch her with the arm of the law.

But Tricia's attention had riveted to Lady Jewel. With a secret smile, she had swiveled purposefully toward Rowan when he pulled her out of Kilver's way. She hurried and twined her arms around the Duke, even though he had just released her. She tripped backward with a little cry and a wobble, causing him to grab her so she wouldn't fall. Like lightning, she hugged his dark head with grasping white hands and kissed him full on the mouth.

Tricia gasped and stared. The kiss went on because Jewel was straining to hold his head fast to her.

Kilver pointed at them. With a cackle, he jeered, "Look at the old libertine!"

At that, the whites of Rowan's eyes widened. Looking panicked, he disengaged from Jewel's lips. He appeared to Tricia as though he could not believe what happened. She could not fathom it, either.

Kilver slunk away with his charges, making that gulping sound which, for him, constituted glee. "I'll be seeing you," he called nastily to Tricia.

She paid him no heed. Her heart convulsed with hot pain as she watched the Duke suffer through his bewilderment and chagrin at Jewel's action. How did she dare to be so conniving? She made it appear to all watching that he pulled her to him for that kiss.

Ignoring Rowan's discomfiture, Jewel proceeded to lay her head on his waistcoat, smiling like a woman who had just been kissed in public because she is so adored. "My *dear* Rowan!" she exclaimed, squeezing his ribcage. "I suppose we should have waited until we got home." She glanced sidewise at her audience and smiled slyly.

Rowan's mouth opened and shut. He tried to dissemble with a stunned half-laugh as Jewel clung to him.

The ladies all gaped at the two of them. Tricia was sure no one but she had seen how cleverly Jewel had engineered her *coup de théâtre.*

Lady Caro gripped Tricia's wrist, casting her eyes about to see if anyone else witnessed the scandal of her niece and the Duke of Rowan making love in public. Scores had seen it, for the fireworks were over, a nearby lantern had illuminated them, and the crowd was on the move. In fact, there was Mrs. Drummond Burrell, a feared patroness of Almack's, coming to a standstill before Rowan and Jewel.

"A-ha! So that's how it is, Duke." She looked him and Jewel up and down through her quizzer.

Jewel smiled brilliantly and said, "Mrs. Burrell, we're so happy to see you."

The Duke obviously wanted to refute what the woman had seen—what they had all seen—but Mrs. Burrell roved a knowing look over their whole group and moved off with her party, seemingly bursting to divulge the news.

"Wait until I get that Jewel home!" vowed Lady Caro, shaking with emotion.

Isidore inquired, "Mama? Are they engaged?"

Lady Hobart's eyes popped wide. "They had better be!" she exclaimed.

CHAPTER 17

The Honor of a Gentleman

"That's it!" said Lord Bixby with the cheerful tone of a death knell. "You have to marry her."

"I know, I *know!*" Rowan kicked a stone off the pavement with undue force.

"You don't sound too elated. Then why did you kiss her on the mouth in front of everybody if you didn't plan to marry her? It's just not done, you know."

"I didn't! I pulled her away from an altercation with Kilver, and the next thing I knew, she wobbled off-balance. I steadied her, and she kissed me so fast you wouldn't believe it! I couldn't believe it. She took me totally by surprise. I feel like the biggest fool in nature."

Bixby stared at him incredulously. "Is *that* how it was?"

"She obviously plans to marry me." Rowan leaned miserably over the saddle of his patient horse. The leather was warm from the sun but it failed to impart comfort to his aching head. He whirled and snatched a leaf from a tree and tore it to shreds. He wished he and Bixby could have ridden far out into the country, not only around St. James's Park. "Why did I, like a fool, return to

London?   Equally puzzling: why did I go to Yorkshire? Is there no place where I can be safe from the treachery of women?" he ranted, throwing a tragic look at Bixby.

His friend pursed his lips and listened in helpless puzzlement.

Rowan added in a shaking voice, "I would never have dreamed that Lady Jewel Claremont, paragon of social correctness, would do such a thing. She made it honestly look like *I* grabbed and kissed her." He still couldn't believe it.

"I'm not too surprised, because she blamed me for her trip-up at the Hobart ball," Bixby reflected, worrying his riding crop through his gloves. "But I never thought you, my friend, would be out-maneuvered by a woman. You did well when you ordered Lady Flitcroft carried out when she tried to crash your soirée. But then what happens? Lady Jewel puts her seal on you in Hyde Park. It passes everything!" He clanged his crop against the iron railing, and the horses, as well as Rowan, flinched. "But I thought, when you told Brummell in White's about Lady Jewel, that you were seriously considering her."

"I was at first, as a possibility. However, I don't know her. Does she serve anyone but herself?" Rowan queried uneasily. "I can't marry a cold-hearted, conniving, or superficial woman. What does she believe and value?"

Bixby said, "I don't know her, either. Just because the Jewel goes to church with her aunt doesn't mean much. As I've noticed, she is very strong willed, and leads those other women in her flock to do whatever she wants. I'd say again, you need to get to know her."

"I was trying, but now it's too late to pull back." The Duke squinted at a troop of sedan chairs carried up Park Lane by chairmen in an array of livery colors. "Heaven preserve us! It's the Countess," he groaned.

"Lieven and her Ladies, out before five?" asked Bixby. "Taking chairs to the park? What next?"

Countess Lieven's lively eyes were visible through the window of her white and gold sedan chair as she ordered her chairmen to halt. She was set down before Rowan and Bixby. She pushed her door open. Sitting amongst her squashed skirts, she smiled at the Duke and crooked a finger in a blue glove for him to approach.

"What can I say to her?" Rowan asked Bixby below his breath. With an attitude of inevitability, Rowan strolled to greet her.

Bixby tipped his hat from a distance and held the horses.

"Did I hear correctly, Duke?" asked the Countess, her face alive as she searched his.

"On what score, Countess?" he asked, knowing he must force himself to appear calm, and not screwed as tightly as he felt.

"Your engagement, Rowan! Is it true?"

"Ah," he let forth an ironic sigh while his heart twisted, "one's secrets are always out before one even . . . creates them."

Countess Lieven laughed and flourished her fan sticks at him. "You are being evasive."

"Where did you hear about an engagement, anyway?"

"Hear? Why, Mrs. Burrell *saw* how it was last

night! You are quite the lover-boy!" She shook her head in wonder. "I must confirm this to my friends." She winked laughingly at the row of sedan chairs with their fashionable occupants in the shade of the trees, all watching the Duke. One of them had her quizzing glass raised at him.

Rowan coughed with embarrassment behind his glove. "Be kind enough to wait until I am gone. Ladies can fawn over a man too much."

"Especially a man of your caliber," twinkled the Countess. "A good day, Duke. You've got yourself a . . . jewel." Her laugh tinkled as he turned away.

Clenching his jaw, he mounted his horse, although Bixby retained a grip on the bridle. "So you didn't refute it?" he whispered, his face agog.

"How could I?" Rowan snatched his reins. "People saw what they saw. I can never prove that it wasn't that way. Kilver didn't help matters, either, yelling, 'Look at the old libertine!'" Rowan's horse grew restive. "Are you coming?"

"Where are we going?"

"To the gallows: Highcourt House."

All the way there, Rowan felt dazed. In his heart, he asked, Why did this have to happen? To retain all honor as a gentleman, I must marry her. Help me, Lord!

When they dismounted in Cavendish Square, it seemed to him that all the windows held curious eyes watching him "come up to scratch" at Lady Jewel's door.

Lord Bixby asked, "Now that we're here, what do you want me to do? Hold the noose for you?"

Rowan strove for patience. "While I speak with the aunt, you may keep the young ladies amused."

"That's a change," said Bixby. He did not offer any more attempts at levity.

When Rowan's boot touched the paving-stones, he had a sudden vision of Tricia and the moment he had encountered her here in Cavendish Square. He saw a few foxgloves swaying in the breeze, the few she had not pulled up. He wondered what expression would fill her eyes when she heard that he was to marry Lady Jewel. The thought made his insides twist.

He knew Bixby feared that he had fallen into a trap. He had. But for a day or two, he had envisioned Lady Jewel as his Duchess, anyway—hadn't he? The trap, he told himself, would prove pleasurable in the end—wouldn't it? Silver linings and all that?

* * *

"Rowan! What a relief it is to see you."

"And I you, Lady Caro," sighed the Duke, closing the door behind him. "I have a question to ask you."

"Fire away, dear Rowan."

He seated her in a chair in her private sitting room. He paced from the table of flower pots to the marble fireplace and back. "In the Marquis of Wyndhurst's absence, do I postpone asking for Jewel's hand in marriage?" If he could do that, maybe he could fall off his horse and break his neck and die in the meantime, he imagined hopefully. "Or do I ask you?" He ventured a look at her.

"Ah!" Lady Caro fixed him intently. "So you've

come to do the honorable thing."

Rowan tore rose petals off a flower in the vase, not knowing what he did.

"You know that Jewel would be ruined without your proposal of marriage, don't you?" Lady Caro asked him gently.

"Yes, of course, everyone knows that," he said impatiently. "I am afraid I left Countess Lieven believing your niece and I are engaged already."

"You did?" said Lady Caro, alerted by the disclosure.

The Duke tried to loosen his collar with indiscernible movements of his shoulders. "Leagues of ladies are blabbing it all over London now because I couldn't deny it."

"But how do you feel? Do you want to marry her? Where is your heart in all this, Rowan?"

His heart was in misery, he acknowledged inwardly. He had planned to wait for the woman God had created just for him, and he didn't think it was Jewel.

The door burst open and Hopkins, the butler, barged in, his eyes wild. "Your Ladyship! Somebody sneaked in through the servants' entrance. He wouldn't give his name, but poked his head into the music room, the dining room, bedchambers, and even the broom cupboard! He's still on the loose!" He waved his fat hands ineffectually. "The Duke's footmen and I tried to stop him, but the intruder made his way into the drawing room where Lady Tricia is. She looks terrified!"

At Tricia's name, the Duke locked eyes with Lady Caro. They both leaped to their feet and said,

"Lord Kilver!"

Rowan ran. In the drawing room, he saw Lord Bixby trying to yank Lord Kilver away from Tricia. She cowered in an armchair, her eyes huge with angry fear as Kilver clamped her by the arms.

"Take him off me!" she screamed, and Stefan and Lionel promptly added their strength to Bixby's in pulling at various parts of the jerking, swearing Kilver. The tug-of-war obviously hurt Tricia's arms, for Kilver kept a determined grip on her.

The Duke roared, "Let her go, Kilver!"

When he snarled and would not, Rowan punched him in the stomach without compunction.

He crumpled to the floor with a loud thud.

Tricia fell back into her chair, her eyes full of thanks for Rowan.

Lady Caro shouted, "How dare you sneak into my house to hurt Lady Tricia?"

Kilver ignored everyone but Tricia. "Come now, without any fuss!" he hissed at her. "As I just told you, I have your father's Last Will and Testament to prove that I am your guardian."

Lady Caro, brandishing her fan sticks, shrieked, "Remove your hands from my niece this instant! Don't ever touch her again!"

He whirled to face Lady Caro, fire in his close-set eyes, his hair disarranged in oily strands over his forehead. "Hush, woman!" he spat up at her as he struggled to his feet. "She's my ward, and she's disobeying me!"

Jewel queried, "What if he's telling the truth, Aunt? He stated that he's Tricia's guardian, and that he can prove it. If that's the way things are, doesn't she have to accept it?"

"Oh, Jewel, have a heart!" yelled Lady Caro.

Jewel touched her bosom and tried to look innocent under everyone's glares.

Tricia's spirits had plummeted painfully at Jewel's statement. Kilver, too, looked so sure of himself that it scared her.

Rowan said, "Kilver, Lady Tricia's closest male relative is not you, but the Marquis of Wyndhurst, her uncle. Therefore, he is her legal guardian."

"Nay, nay!" Kilver shook his head in denial.

Lady Caro cut in starchily, "I wrote to the Marquis all about this, and he is on his way from Paris as we speak."

"A wasted effort!" barked Kilver. "The Will declares that I am her guardian. Ask my solicitor. He's sitting in my carriage *as we speak*," he mocked.

"Then call him!" commanded the Duke. "And you show some respect, Kilver, or you'll be catapulted out the door without another word."

As Kilver clattered out of the room, Rowan followed. He said through his teeth, "Tell me what drives you in your incessant efforts to seize Lady Tricia."

Kilver curled his mouth in a sneer. "Why wouldn't I want to take her from strangers to whom she doesn't belong? You, Duke! –using her for a page to do your bidding! How can I stand by and see her mistreated so?"

The Duke saw red. "She was already forced to masquerade as a boy because of your perfidy! She preferred to pluck chickens for a farmer rather than stay in your house. That sets me wondering: What kind of a life did she live under your roof that she took such extreme measures to leave you, cutting her hair and running away?"

Kilver pointed at the Duke and snapped, "Her father's house had to be closed up. She couldn't live there alone. Lady Kilver and I gave her a good home. My wife misses her, and I vowed to bring the obstinate girl back, and I will!"

"There's a lot you're not telling me. Answer the most looming of my questions: Why did you kidnap her from my house and throw her on the ground at Lady Flitcroft's cottage?"

"That girl has wiles!" Kilver shot back. "Has she never tried them on you? It's more than a man can take!"

"I don't believe you!" Rowan yelled back from the middle of the entrance hall, although all the servants were hovering in the corners, agog. "You have shown that you want nothing so much as to ruin her! It would be better that a millstone be hanged around your neck, and you dropped into the depths of the sea!"

Kilver, nostrils flaring, grabbed at something in his pocket.

Rowan held his every move in keen observance, as did Lionel and Stefan, so Kilver halted in whatever he intended to do. He continued to look murderous, and viciously pushed the large butler out of his way.

Rowan grabbed Kilver's garish velvet sleeve as soon as he crossed the threshold out to the Square. "What about the fact that you went aboard a ship called *The White Dove* last night at the Thames port docks? Lady Flitcroft and daughters boarded with you. Don't deny it; my servants followed you. Was it your plan to sail away, taking Tricia with you after you snatched her during the fireworks?"

"Huh! You can't prove that."

"In time I will. That's all I have to say to you."

Rowan slipped into the small entrance salon, slammed the door, and dropped his forehead against the wall. "Dear God Almighty," he prayed in a harried voice, "help us in this hour of need!"

His voice shook as he whispered, "Oh, Tricia, darling Tricia! If I were free of Jewel, I would ask to marry you! I would keep you safe forever from that devil." As his nightmarish life now dictated, he was forced to wed Lady Jewel.

Though his head pulsed with pain, his heart surged with the determination never to let Kilver take Tricia back under his thumb, no matter what he had to do to prevent it.

* * *

Kilver's solicitor appeared in the doorway to the drawing room. Tricia judged him on sight as a coarse, red-faced incompetent. Coupled with his thatch of blond hair, his head looked like a pile of straw on a boiled beet.

"Mr. Roger Snipley, Your Ladyship," Hopkins announced with distaste.

The ill-dressed man went around bowing to Lady Caro and them all, looking overawed by the finery of the women as well as of the inlaid Italian table into which he stumbled. Emitting apologies, he backed and seated himself next to Lord Bixby, who instantly moved aside.

Kilver stalked into the room, looking tense. As soon as he saw the company looking dubiously at his solicitor, he jutted his chin out with a hostile attitude.

Tricia fiercely ignored him. She couldn't stand the sight of his insufferable face.

Rowan walked in with his footmen, looking deadly. Tricia yearned to run and throw herself onto his chest and beg for protection. *Please, dear God, let the Duke help me somehow,* she prayed silently, fervently.

Lady Caro narrowed her eyes at Lord Kilver, then at his nervous solicitor. "Mr. Snipley? Explain to us this Will that Kilver keeps referring to. Who is my niece's guardian?" she demanded.

"Your Ladyship, that is Pultney Slugmore, Lord Kilver, here present."

Tricia burst out, "My father would never have assigned me to *his* guardianship!"

"Why is that, Miss?" Mr. Snipley asked.

"Because he and Lord Kilver never had more than a nodding acquaintance. My mother and Lady Kilver were sisters, but we rarely saw her husband. We were certainly not friends."

Kilver made a furious noise through his nose.

Tricia pressed Mr. Snipley, "Were you the solicitor with whom my father drew up that will?"

Mr. Snipley nodded.

Tricia watched his evasive eyelids. She really wondered. As a child, she thought she had seen a very small, white-haired lawyer shown to her father's study on occasion. It was possible, of course, that he had changed solicitors for the drawing up of his Last Will and Testament. The old man could have died.

Lord Bixby spoke up. "Do you feel that your

client, Lord Kilver, assumes he is her guardian because he believed he was her closest male relative, not knowing about the Marquis of Wyndhurst?"

Mr. Snipley said, "There is that, of course, by law. If no other guardian is appointed in writing, then the closest male relation has custody. However, I tell you that the actual will states that Lord Kilver is guardian of Tricia Ravenscar as well as her possessions until she comes of age."

"Possessions!" cried Tricia. "He certainly grasped at those. But what I object to most is that he imprisoned me in his house. I lived in fear and danger there. Don't you see? You must help me, Mr. Snipley!" Her voice quavered and she felt near to tears.

Rowan moved to her side.

She felt she was losing the battle. With her eyes, she beseeched him and whispered, "I cannot go with him!"

He put one arm about her shoulders, whispering, "Tricia! It is not over yet. Pray!"

"Well?" stabbed Lady Caro as Mr. Snipley sat open-mouthed. "Are you going to help her?"

Kilver guffawed from the corner where he stood chewing nuts out of Lady Caro's crystal bowl.

Mr. Snipley shifted uneasily. "How can *I* help her?"

Lady Caro stared at him. "You can show us that Will, you idiot!"

"But I do not have it, Your Ladyship."

"Where is it?"

"Lord Kilver has it."

Rowan said, "I thought he said you had it. What

kind of rigmarole is this? We must see it now, Kilver!"

"Fine, fine. I thought as much. Do I have it? I thought you carried it, Snipley. Well, well, here it is." He extracted a folded paper from his pocket and strode across the carpet and insolently tossed it onto Lady Caro's lap. He hovered until she glared him away.

She snapped the paper and frowned at it.

Tricia felt wretched. The suspense, with Kilver standing in the midst of them all, smirking with such insolence, made her ill with foreboding.

Lady Caro closed her eyes after several minutes of reading, and let the page fall.

Tricia rose shakily, went and took up the paper, and saw the statement that declared Lord Kilver was her guardian. A pain forked through her. She stared at the signature. "I don't think that is my father's hand!" she cried out. It looked very like it, but it did not have the free flow of the pen, and the curlicue at the beginning of the L was too thick, as though it had been gone over.

"Of course it's his!" Kilver scoffed. "No use quibbling. This is lawful, and you have to admit it."

Rowan took the paper from her trembling hand and read it.

With her heart in her throat, she whispered, "I think the signature is forged." She pointed it out to the Duke.

He said to Kilver, "In the case of wills, there should be more than one copy. Where is another one so Tricia can examine it?"

Lord Kilver crossed his arms and looked cocky. "In Yorkshire."

Rowan put straight to Mr. Snipley, "Where in Yorkshire?"

Lord Kilver put up his hand. "It makes no difference, it's the very same as this. The signatures are authentic, never fear. As your legal guardian, Trish, I command you to pack your things. You're coming home."

Tricia slumped.

Rowan's arms closed around her.

To ease her faintness, she breathed in deeply of the breezy scent of his riding coat. "I can't bear this!" she confided.

He whispered, "Tell him you will be ready by tomorrow at two o'clock."

Tricia lifted her face to stare at him in disbelief. She saw a strange light in his speculative eyes.

"Say it!" he urged without moving his mouth, for all eyes were on them now, especially Jewel's jealous ones. He released her.

Fearfully, but trusting Rowan, she cleared her throat. "I—I cannot be ready until tomorrow after two o'clock."

Kilver's eyes narrowed. "Be ready by noon. I'll be here to take you back to Lady Kilver at that hour and no later."

"I won't be staying in your house," said Tricia calmly. "I will stay at Soaring Gables if I go to Yorkshire."

Lord Bixby remarked, "That's only right and reasonable."

Kilver shook his head firmly. "Nay, she can't do it."

"Her own house after all, Kilver," said Bixby firmly. "And be sure you show her, and witnesses, that other copy of the Will."

"There is no other. She'll be convinced e'er long," he avowed. "What tongues these modern misses have, eh Snipley? Issuing commands in a hoity-toity manner. That's dangerous."

Tricia's heart pounded. She knew, from the assessing look Kilver raked over her, that he would *try again* the moment he got her away and alone.

Lady Caro stood up. "I advise you, Kilver, to be ready to show two copies of proof to the Marquis of Wyndhurst when he returns. Otherwise, by law, he is Tricia's guardian, not you."

"Nay, I have proven otherwise," said Lord Kilver, "before a man of the law and all of you witnesses. That's all I need to do."

It was hopeless. As soon as Lord Kilver and Mr. Snipley left, Tricia turned her extreme puzzlement on the Duke. "Why did I have to say I'll go with him, Your Grace?"

"Because now I can spirit you north before he gets here at noon."

"You can?" Infused with a sudden leap of hope, Tricia found it wonderful to think he would spirit her anywhere to get away from Kilver.

Jewel, who had been silent for ever so long, had slipped to the Duke's other side. "It looks like Lord Bixby, there," she pointed, "wants to take up the gauntlet if you would but let him, Rowan. No need to trouble yourself."

"I would be honored," admitted Bixby, flushing and looking fondly at Tricia.

Rowan, ignoring Jewel, said levelly, "Thank you, Bix, but I must delve into this business myself. It is my responsibility to settle this score with Kilver.

Do you accept my services, Lady Tricia?"

"Oh, yes, Your Grace!" With gratitude shining from her soul, she blinked away tears.

Behind Rowan, Jewel's long nostrils sniffed in displeasure. This was not going her way.

Lady Caro announced, "I'm coming with you, Duke."

Jewel looked taken aback and then turned her annoyed frown into a winning smile for Rowan. "You can count on me to support you," she said, pressing his hand, "that is, if you really mean what you say."

"Why wouldn't I mean what I say?" he snapped.

"I wish *I* could go," moaned Bixby, "but I've just remembered, my uncle arrives tonight from Cornwall, and I promised to take him to buy some horses at Tattersall's. Drat!"

"That's all right, Bix, stick to your plans," said the Duke. "We'll leave in darkest secrecy. Everyone be ready at five o'clock in the morning."

Jewel made a squeak of dismay.

"By all means," said Lady Caro, "the earlier the better. Up at three-thirty, ladies. I'll go tell my servants to glue their lips shut on pain of death, and have Hopkins order my traveling coach."

"I'll supply the coaches," said Rowan. "Since I have arrangements to make, I must leave you now. Haste is necessary if we're to out-fox Kilver."

"Thank you, Your Grace," said Tricia with breathy excitement.

He bowed his head to her and made for the door.

Though Jewel, weaving past the tea table, looked about to accompany him, he pretended not to notice and bolted toward the door calling, "My hat, if you please!" When Stefan handed it to him, the Duke said, "Watch Lady Tricia like a hawk."

"Yes, Your Grace."

Lionel solemnly offered the same response.

Rowan set his beaver firmly on his head and strode out into the wind, noting, in his peripheral vision, Lady Jewel hurrying down the stairs.

He had come to dutifully ask the woman to marry him. That detail remained an onerous item left undone. The truth was that he didn't want to.

He glanced up at the house and saw Tricia at the drawing room window. He smiled with his whole heart and touched his hat to her encouragingly. She smiled back, and then moved out of his sight.

Rowan gloried in her need of him. How quickly she had trusted him to help her through her dire straights. His chivalry had risen to the fore.

The house door opened behind him. "Rowan!" It was Lady Jewel's high-pitched call.

He turned, wanting to forget all about their unfinished predicament. But he must be a man of honor and give it his full attention now.

She came striding elegantly, a red shawl clasped about her white muslin dress. "My dear Duke!" she said, smiling, "I just wanted to say thank you for everything you are doing for our Tricia—again." She rolled her eyes.

"I have accomplished nothing yet."

"You make the most unnecessary sacrifices. I realize how much you want to please us, and how you care for others. Don't shake your head. You do, Rowan." She squeezed his arm. "Even at the fireworks," she went on, her eyes dancing evasively, "you were absolutely wonderful, saving *me* from that horrid Kilver. You know how much I appreciated it. I will remember it all our lives."

Since he said nothing, she dropped her eyelids and said, "You will always know that you did the right thing." She paused for him to speak. Nothing moved but her red shawl fringes on the breeze.

He felt words stick in his throat, but he forced himself to ask, "Why did you kiss me in the park, Lady Jewel? Not only from gratitude, surely. A simple thank you would have sufficed."

"Oh, I have great affection for you, Rowan." She smiled widely up at him, but she looked uneasy.

Rowan took a deep breath, knowing he was stumbling in the dark. "Are you a sincerely-believing Christian, Lady Jewel?"

She looked startled. Her face changed. "What? Oh, of course, Rowan. What do you mean, and why do you ask such an odd question?"

"Because that is the most important thing to me."

Her mouth dropped open, and she looked bewildered.

He took a few steps and untied his white horse. "We shall talk again tomorrow. As you know, we have a pressing situation on our hands, and I must put the wheels in motion. Until morning, then, if you really mean to come." He touched his brim.

"Yes," she said with a parting curtsey, "until morning, Rowan dear. God bless you in all your efforts. You are *so good!*"

Rowan huffed below his breath as he cantered off, "I am not good." He hated the sound of those words in connection with himself. Christ was the only good one, and if any good was to come about in Rowan's life, he knew it would be by his help and guidance. He asked again for wisdom from Heaven in his perplexities. Could he keep Tricia from Kilver? He must! Could he marry Jewel and be happy? Was she the one God intended for him? He did not know. He did not like the prospect. *Please show me, O ignorant wretch that I am, Thy good and gracious will, O Lord,* he prayed, *in Jesus' name, Thy will be done.*

Rowan rode his horse home, more keyed-up than he had ever felt before. If, through discussions on their journey to Yorkshire, he discovered that Jewel was not a believer in the God he worshipped, what then? What could he do? He wanted his own children, should he be blessed with any, to be brought up as he had been by his parents, in the nurture and admonition of the Lord. He did not presume to judge, but he did not feel the right spirit from Lady Jewel.

The hard fact remained, of which she was well aware, that a gentleman could never cry off from an engagement.

CHAPTER 18

A Published Item

"Just read this, Tricia!" said Lady Jewel at half past four the next morning. She was dressed for traveling in a deep rust spencer over a tan carriage gown and a hunter green bonnet with matching plumes. Her eyes sparkled as she dashed into Tricia's chamber.

Tricia, who had just donned a new white velvet pelisse to go over her pink gown, was hurriedly doing up the pearly buttons. They must hurry on their journey to Yorkshire. Jewel laid a newspaper before her, pointing to a big heart which she had drawn around an item of print in last night's Society column. Since the sun had not yet risen and the room was dim, Tricia took up the paper, went to her window seat, pushed aside the chintz curtain for more light, and read: *A kiss in Hyde Park was the illuminating announcement of one Lady J.C.'s engagement to every woman's darling, the one and only D. of R. A reputable source says that, while R was too shy to tell the world his secret, he seemed to confirm it this evening. Let hopeful maidens weep.*

"What?" gasped Tricia under her breath. She turned a carefully controlled face to Jewel's gleeful one.

"There you have it!" Jewel cried. "It's my engagement announcement!" She hugged herself and twirled, and grasped the bedpost and lifted her chin while eyeing Tricia sidewise.

Tricia stared at her in pained bewilderment. Hadn't anyone else seen how Jewel herself initiated that kiss? Rowan had had nothing to do with it! Tricia's head reeled. "Did the Duke *ask* you to marry him?"

"Yes! This is Rowan's surprise to me, do you not see? It's his unique way of proposing. Is it not the most romantic, poetical thing you have ever heard?"

"Not if he didn't actually ask you."

Jewel grabbed the paper angrily from Tricia. "This is *it!*" she spat, and flipped the column with her nails as if explaining to a dimwit. "By his actions, I have known he meant to ask me. This should be no surprise to anyone who knows me. The opera, the musical evening where I was the guest he honored –you saw it all, you were his servant. Oh, but if you only knew how he kisses, Tricia! But that is something you will never know!" she trilled vaingloriously. "He is *mine!* The handsomest, richest, most sought-after Duke in London—mine! Doesn't it sound well? Jewel, the Duchess of Rowan." She smiled smugly at herself in the mirror.

Tricia suffered acutely through this speech. If she showed any negative emotion, Jewel would triumphantly brand her as jealous. "Then I wish you well, Jewel," she said, fighting to keep her utter despair from showing.

"Oh, thank you, Tricia!" Jewel patted her

shoulder as she whisked by. "But drat this trip north! How can we have engagement celebrations if we are not in town? If I point out that fact to Rowan right away, I am sure he will postpone the Yorkshire thing. I must write to Augusta this minute." She glided to Tricia's writing desk and applied pen to paper. "You must support me in convincing him!"

Choking with emotion, Tricia walked blindly to Lady Caro's chamber. Her aunt's dresser poked her nose out and let her in. Lady Caro, her auburn hair half hanging down her back, was seated at her dressing table quickly dabbing a tint of rouge to her cheeks. "Dear Aunt!" said Tricia, "let me finish your hair. I need to talk to you."

"Yes, go bring my bandboxes down, Jane," she told the maid. "Whatever is the matter now, Tricia?"

"You'll think me despicable when I confess my feelings."

"No, I won't. Out with it."

"Jewel is going to *marry* the Duke of Rowan," Tricia faltered.

"Ah! I had an indication of that yesterday."

"From whom?"

"From him."

Tricia raised stricken eyes to her aunt. She groped for the hairbrush.

"I know, dear, it's hard for me to understand why Jewel is to come out smelling like a rose after what she did."

"You saw it, too? How Jewel so cunningly pulled him into it?"

"I saw!" said Lady Caro with feeling. "Oh Tricia, I

see it affects you more deeply than outrage against propriety. My darling girl! I wish I could ease the pain I see in you."

"Jewel must never know," Tricia whispered, rapidly pinning up her aunt's heavy hair into a curving chignon and thrusting in pins.

"How did you hear of it, Tricia?"

She told her about Jewel and the gossip column.

"Isn't that strange! I wonder if he ever got around to asking her, with all that chaos about the Will yesterday."

"Jewel sounded to me like he didn't actually propose in person."

"But it's in the paper?" crowed Lady Caro.

"Yes."

When Tricia dashed back to her room, Jewel had a finished missive on one edge of the desk, and was writing another. As Tricia took her pink bonnet out of the armoire, she saw the upper corner where Jewel had written her return: *Jewel, Duchess of Rowan, Highcourt House.*

What utter presumption! thought Tricia. Styling herself the Duchess of Rowan already! That was a very foolish thing to do.

"Are you still planning on this long journey?" queried the bride-to-be, glancing around to see Tricia closing her traveling case.

"Of course. It is of the utmost importance that I investigate the Will. Can you try to understand that?"

"But what if your father really thought it best for you to live with Lord Kilver? I wouldn't get away with crossing *my* father's wishes."

Tricia turned to give her cousin a hurt look. "I

wonder if you have any idea what I went through, living in constant peril of Lord Kilver."

"No, I have no idea. Tell me what the peril was."

"His designs were lewd, Jewel. He never succeeded, but I won't go back under his jurisdiction no matter what it costs me."

"Well, why don't you find an available bachelor and marry? That would get you out of this whole situation, wouldn't it?"

"Thanks heaps."

"Well? Isn't it a good solution?"

"No one has asked me to marry him."

"You can make it happen," said Jewel.

"What would you suggest? Kiss a man in public?"

Jewel's eyes flashed, and the tongue-lashing Tricia received proved to her that such was the whole truth about Jewel's victorious engagement. It enraged her to no end that she was found out.

Tricia felt sicker than ever as they waited for the Duke's carriage. The air smelled of rain and there was a bite in the wind. The trees swished half-empty branches to and fro, sending a swirl of dead leaves at her face.

When his crested black coach hove into the Square followed by a baggage coach, the sight of the familiar white horses in the pre-dawn darkness made her long for the day she met him, when he had halted on Gunnerby Hill in her behalf. She took one look at her Duke and felt an ache in her throat. He looked grave and determined as he jumped down, dressed in a black coat with shoulder capes and a dark red stock and snowy collar.

As Jewel went to meet him, fluttering the

newspaper in her gloved hand, Tricia ran back up the steps into the house, pretending she had forgotten something. She could not forever postpone greeting Rowan, but she could not contain her tears, either. She sped past the Rowan footmen who were carrying out luggage, and prayed for composure as she pretended to search in her reticule, her bonnet brim hiding her face. She caught a whiff of the white roses Rowan had sent her, so she paused and took one out. She put her nose into it and made her way outside. The Duke was waiting for her, having already tucked in the other two Claremont ladies.

"Congratulations on your engagement, Your Grace," she said softly as he came to meet her. Before he could hand her down the steps, she reached up and tucked the white rose into his buttonhole, avoiding his eyes. "Thank you for the white roses," she said.

"What did you say?" he asked, bending down, his eyes searching her face. How sweet he looked, thought Tricia. He was still the same wonderful man, even after Jewel had kissed him.

"Thank you for the roses after the ball. I love them. And also, about your engagement to Jewel, Your Grace," she hurried to add. "Congratulations are in order?"

His face was impassive. His jaw clenched as he looked away and asked, "How did you hear?

"Jewel showed me the newspaper in which the society gossip appeared."

He huffed. "Yes, she showed me, also. I was surprised to see that."

"You were?"

"Yes." He offered his hand and ushered her carefully into the carriage.

Jewel's eyes were narrowed on her, glaring through the open coach door. She quickly bathed Rowan in a beatific smile. She chattered about how enjoyable it would be to stop at an inn before long and take refreshments together.

"We must rush," he said. He saw Tricia settled by herself on the backward seat. There would have been room for him in the coach, as Jewel repeatedly pointed out, but he declined, touched his hat to them all, and vaulted up to ride with his coachman.

Lady Caro's hazel eyes fluttered over Tricia sadly.

Jewel, however, sat like a queen bee that had everything going her way.

CHAPTER 19

Robin Hood's Bay

Tricia was well aware that Jewel had not relished the journey north. She declared often how she hated the jouncing caused by potholed roads, rising before dawn, and the inability to stop at most of the inns they passed. These irksome discomforts merely added to her pique that all had not gone her way. She groused about not staying in London, where she had responsibilities galore to take care of now that she had her engagement ball and wedding to plan. She sulked and complained after Rowan refused to take luncheon with them instead of seeing to the new teams of horses himself.

According to Lady Caro, he had stonily refused Jewel's plea that they give up this trip. He had told her she could stay safely in London while the rest of them went to search for the Will. But Jewel would have none of that. Apparently, she was not going to let her recalcitrant, betrothed Duke out of sight. All of this Lady Caro whispered to Tricia when they were momentarily alone in the breakfast room of an inn.

It put Lady Jewel out of all patience to be bumped down the steep hill at Stoupe Beck at the end of their second breakneck day of travel. Her starched sleeve crushed when she was thrown together with her aunt, and that seemed to be the final insult she could bear. She lashed out at Tricia. "You should have submitted as is proper, and come on this trip with your guardian!" She tried to pinch her sleeve up to fluff it out. "It's totally unfitting that a Duke of the Realm should have to put himself out personally because of your objection to a legal Will!"

"Jewel!" cried Lady Caro furiously.

Tricia, ignoring them both, gazed out the window and said, "The mountains of alum stone have grown since I left."

Jewel looked disdainfully at the quarry above the beach. Workers in dark leather vests and broad-brimmed hats shoveled into wheelbarrows the shale they had loosened by pick-ax from the cliff sides. They paused to stare at the black coach and horses as they sped by.

"Isn't this weird and dangerous, driving through sand? What if we get stuck?" Jewel cried, panicked. As they splashed through an inlet, she gasped, "The water is too high!"

Tricia could see that the tide was rising. She said, "As long as Rowan keeps his horses at a fast trot, I don't think we'll stick." She looked back, her cheek pressed to the glass. The coach left distinct tracks in the crescent of damp beach. Rowan had made his four footmen get off the back and run after the vehicle. Tricia smiled at the sight of them grinning and racing each other, sand flying from their booted heels as each one strained to win. At least those four seemed to be enjoying the journey.

Lady Caro said, "I see seaweed clinging to those

rocks. Never tell me those end up under water!" She pointed at dark boulders that loomed sharp and forbidding, as tall as the coach roof as they sped by.

"Oh yes, we have fifteen to twenty-foot tides here. Those standers are completely covered with water."

"So this road, as you call this beach, is totally obliterated then?" Jewel queried incredulously.

"Yes."

"How does one get in or out of town, if that's the town ahead?"

Tricia smiled impishly. "Hardly anyone finds it convenient to come to Robin Hood's Bay. The townspeople have all they need to live right here. We see very few strangers, and hardly ever any strange women."

"I can see why." Jewel tightened her grip on the strap and looked askance at the waves galloping toward them. "I wish I had never come!"

"No one forced you," Lady Caro reminded her.

Beyond Ness Point, Tricia could see that the cobles were out fishing. They had gone with the morning tide as they had done since she could remember. Their brightly-colored hulls were dotted just short of the horizon: blue, red, yellow, and green.

At sight of the russet brick and white-washed houses clustered ahead, she felt a pang of joy. She loved her homely town of crooked lanes sliding steeply from the high cliff down to the sparkling blue bay. If only her parents and brother were here to welcome her.

In an interested voice, Lady Caro said, "I've never

seen a place quite like this. Those cliffs above make me dizzy."

"How will this carriage ever make it up the streets?" asked Jewel. "It looks like a maze to me. Those narrow streets go every which way."

"You're right. The coach will be useless in Robin Hood's Bay. I always walked everywhere, but I think there's an old sedan chair to be had at one of the hotels, if you'd like that, Lady Jewel." Smiling, she added, "Look at the people stare. I imagine the last vehicle to demand such observance in this town was in seventy-four when the Raven Hall Inn was built for King George to recover in."

"Really? Our poor Majesty came here?"

"Yes, Aunt, he came to stay. Old folks still talk about it as the great event of their lives."

The coach halted. Lionel, breathless, reached the door first and, smiling in victory, opened it for the ladies with a flourish.

Tricia smiled and congratulated him. "Please tell His Grace that we will alight here on Wayfoot so the coach can be pulled up more easily to the Dock. The tide is rolling in." As Stefan's hat wanted to leave his red head in the stiff breeze, she turned and told him, "That won't stay on in Bay Town; not unless you tie it with ribbons under your chin."

"Yes, My Lady," he said, trying not to laugh, and secured the hat under his arm. The other footmen did likewise. Rowan, noting this in amusement, doffed his top hat as well.

The Duke descended from the driver's box, thanking his coachman, Shepperton, for seeing them safely to their destination.

Tricia gave him a smile of appreciation. "Your

Grace, that was wonderful driving you did across the beach."

"Thank you. I think Shepperton was nervous." His eyes glistened as he looked about him. The wind ruffled his hair.

Watching him, Tricia thought, *how I love him!* Her heart swelled.

She brusquely returned to her problem. "Do you think Kilver is here yet, Your Grace?" With the Duke on her side, her resolve had grown strong to best Kilver. But now, somewhat fatigued by the journey and Jewel's ill humor, she felt relieved to shelter in the Duke's presence, and to take courage from his commanding presence. She did not want to think about Kilver's coming after them, but they had to face the inevitable, and plan.

"I don't think there is any way he could have beaten us, Tricia; especially as he was to fetch you at noon yesterday. We have at least seven hours' head start on him. With only four hours of sleep last night, we're leagues ahead, I believe. Try not to worry."

"Thank you, Your Grace." She felt happy walking up the terraced street with her arm through his, the focus of curious stares and barking dogs. She wondered how Jewel liked the sight of her with the Duke, for she and Lady Caro followed behind with two of the footmen trailing, and the other two bringing up the rear. Only two people could comfortably walk abreast in most of the streets, and Tricia was Rowan's guide.

They were assailed by the familiar smell of fish spread out to dry on the stone steps and hung on the walls of houses. The welcoming smiles of the old men and women, who were not out working, put a sparkle into the eyes of Bay Town's daughter.

Watching her, the Duke said, "You look glad to be home. I think that's a good sign. Now where does Lady Kilver live?"

"I will show you. Shepperton will have to bring the coach around tomorrow by the circuitous route if you think you'll need it on the moors while you are here. As you can see already, the streets are narrow, and have ridges and steps. The horses could never pull your coach up them. Be careful," she said as the Duke slipped on the cobbles. Involuntarily, she grabbed his hand. "It's the salt and sand."

He squeezed her fingers warmly before he released her. "How does sea water get this high?"

Tricia tried to think, for her senses were humming from his meaningful squeeze. "Storms are one way. And when the fisher wives carry catch to load onto the donkeys at the top of the town, sea water trickles out of their baskets."

"What else do donkeys carry out of here, I wonder?" he mused quietly.

Tricia leaned close. "Tea, spirits, tobacco . . ."

"A-ha! I thought as much."

A woman at an upstairs window dropped her knitting into her flower box and cried, "Miss Ravenscar! Tricia, as I live! Is it really you?"

She smiled and lifted her hand. "Yes, and I'm happy to see you again." She knew that Bay people were wondering what on earth she was doing back after her disappearance. They would wonder even more about a handsome gentleman of the highest quality at her side, arrived in a coach with a ducal coat-of-arms on its doors.

But the Duke was Lady Jewel's, she reminded herself bitterly. She had no right to glory in the appearance they made together. She would have to set the town straight.

"There is Lord Kilver's house," whispered Tricia as they walked into The Square. They faced a neat row of staggered houses, whitewashed with small paned windows. "The largest one is his, of course." Her heart clutched with dread at sight of that evil prison.

Lionel stepped up to knock.

Lizzy, the Kilver parlor maid, jumped back at sight of the liveried giant. She looked boggled to see Tricia dressed in the first crack of fashion and accompanied by an attractive gentleman and two stylish ladies whose fancy bonnet brims fought against the wind.

Rowan smiled. "May we see Lady Kilver, please?" He handed the girl his card.

Tricia knew the maid couldn't read, so she said, "The Duke of Rowan, Lizzy."

The maid gasped, dropped a gangly curtsey, and ran in, letting the door bang.

Tricia winked at Rowan. "Forgive her terror."

"We're a bit out of place here," he murmured.

"Duke, Duke," Tricia reminded him, and they laughed together.

Jewel looked jealous of their banter. She walked a few steps as if assessing her surroundings, letting the wind lift her gown high at the hem, showing a great deal of ankle. She asked Rowan to aid her to fasten her parasol shut, and hung on his arm, watching while he did it. She pouted her lips and threw a little thank-you kiss up at him.

Tricia chanced to meet Lady Caro's eye. Was she groaning, too?

The door reopened. Lizzy stood straight, pinned her eyes on Tricia, and recited, "Lady Kilver will see Your Grace now . . . Your Grace," she said to the Duke.

"Thank you very much." He smiled and gestured Tricia ahead of him.

Lady Caro touched her shoulder and murmured, "Take heart, Tricia dear. We're all with you."

She nodded.

Lady Kilver, pushing pins into her gray crown knot, rose from her chair and stared at the crowd entering.

Tricia recognized the smell of hartshorn and lavender which Lady Kilver often whisked beneath her nose when she wasn't feeling well. "Hello, Aunt." Tricia greeted her with a light hug.

Lady Kilver clung a moment, which surprised her. "Well, Tricia, this is something."

Tricia introduced the rest of her party. Lady Kilver bowed her head to them all and looked around distractedly, trying to find places for the extra ladies to sit in her cluttered parlor. Most of the green striped sofas held her pillows of lace-making as well as knitting projects, for, as Tricia knew, Lady Kilver tired of one form of work after several hours and took up another.

"I apologize, Lady Kilver, for descending on you without notice," he said, smiling kindly, "but our trip was quite unpremeditated. Is Lord Kilver at home?"

"No, Your Grace. He is in London, I believe."

"Have you heard anything from him?" Tricia asked. "Has he sent orders for my house to be opened?"

Lady Kilver squinted in disbelief. "Soaring Gables opened? No, nothing like that."

"Can you open it for her, Lady Kilver?" asked the Duke with a charming smile. He looked so irresistible that Tricia wondered if her aunt would be able to refuse him anything.

"Well, I—" She bent down, pushed her sewing basket under the footstool, and said as she rose with a redder face, "I suppose I . . . could. But where have you been, and what are you doing now, Tricia?" Tricia assumed she meant what on earth was she doing hobnobbing with the Nobility?

"I made my way to London through His Grace's kindness, and have since discovered my father's family. Lady Caroline Claremont, here, is my father's sister. Yes, I was astonished, too! Lady Jewel, there, is my cousin. Can you believe all this, Lady Kilver?"

The broad-faced woman with the deep-set squinted eyes could say nothing for many moments. She seemed not to be staring at the relatives, but thinking far-away thoughts. "Well, I told him that one day you would find the Claremonts . . ."

Tricia stared at her in utter bewilderment. "You *knew?*"

"Your mother married into that Claremont family."

Tricia exploded softly, "Why did no one tell me about it?"

The clock wound up, chimed the quarter hour,

and continued ticking. Lady Kilver looked at Lady Caro cautiously before saying, "It was a fact that Leigh and Lucretia decided to keep hidden. Else their family in London, which apparently is your Ladyships, would find out where they were."

Tricia, frowning, asked, "Why didn't they want them to know?"

"Because, although we Ravenscars had wealth enough, the Claremonts did not approve of Leigh's marrying my sister. For that reason, he would not allow there to be any taint known about his happy marriage. He never let himself be known as a Peer here in Robin Hood's Bay. He wanted to drop out of sight, so he called himself Mr. Ravenscar. Local folk thought he was a third cousin of Lucretia's and mine with the same surname. We used to live in Whitby, so Lucretia and I were both foreigners when we married and came to live in Bay Town. Everyone thought I got the bigger catch," Lady Kilver added with a strange little laugh the likes of which Tricia had never heard. "But Lucretia married an Earl, I a Baron, and I was the one given precedence."

Lady Jewel said, "We were sure Lord Wyndhurst was dead long ago."

Lady Kilver replied, "Well, he wouldn't have minded your thinking that."

Lady Caro was quick to explain, "After our father passed away, my brother searched extensively for Leigh. What belonged to him then—that is, the Marquisate—was finally petitioned by my younger brother, Clive."

Jewel was piqued. "My father *is* the Marquis! Tricia's father is dead!"

"Yes, Jewel, that is so now. Don't go into the vapors, dear. But rightfully, Tricia would have taken precedence over us when Leigh was alive and my father dead, for Leigh was the rightful Marquis."

Lady Jewel looked away, obviously seething at the very idea.

Lady Kilver asked, "So are you putting Lucretia's daughter in the way of being a Lady now?"

"That is who she is: Lady Tricia," said Lady Caro decidedly.

"Then what do you want from me?" asked Lady Kilver. Glancing at the maid huddling in the alcove, she said, "Bring tea."

The Duke said, "There has been a misunderstanding, we believe, about the guardianship of Lady Tricia as it now stands. Lady Kilver, do you know the whereabouts of her late father's Will?"

Tricia wondered what her aunt would say. Tricia had never been allowed to read it.

"There's the Will, yes, the one my husband has." To Tricia's amazement, her aunt lowered her crumpling face into her hands and wept with a strange, chilling sound. It rose like a mourning wail. The others looked at each other wide-eyed and askance.

Tricia moved to sit on the arm of her aunt's chair and put her hand on the trembling shoulder. "Aunt, I miss them, too," she whispered, assuming the reason for Lady Kilver's emotion. Her own tears were welling up. When she had lived in this house, they had never talked about missing her parents. She had never known for sure how much

Lady Kilver had cared for her sister, Lucretia. In retrospect, Lady Kilver had very few friends that ever came a-calling or sent her invitations as Tricia's mother had.

"Pardon me," quivered Lady Kilver, groping in her ample bodice for her handkerchief and applying it to her eyes. "I assume, Your Grace, it is because you know what that Will says that you are here."

"That is correct, Your Ladyship."

"With no offense intended," asserted Lady Caro, "I must say that Clive, the Marquis of Wyndhurst, is otherwise Lady Tricia's legal guardian and caretaker of all that belongs to her."

"Yes, you would think that," said Lady Kilver, and blew her nose.

The clock's pendulum ticked back and forth, loud in the silence. Lady Kilver said, "But the Will makes it all different."

Suddenly they heard a clatter of hoofs on cobbles from the back of the house.

Lady Kilver gasped. "He's here!"

The tension moved like lightning through the others. "Quick, Lady Kilver," cried Tricia, "tell me, is there another copy of the Will? I must see it!"

Lady Kilver raised her hand to hush them as she went to the curtains and peeked out. Her mouth worked, and she looked to be struggling within.

When they heard Lord Kilver's voice delivering orders at the back door, she said very low, "Go find Mr. Septimus Flint of Whitby." She gave Tricia an inquiring look, ascertaining that she had heard clearly.

Tricia repeated the oddly familiar name and sat

back, thinking. When she was a little girl, she had heard it. Septimus Flint. Was he that old solicitor? With a leap of hope, she looked significantly at Rowan.

He cocked an eye at her and wrote the name with his small pencil on the back of one of his calling cards and shoved it into his waistcoat. He gave her a small wink.

Lady Kilver hurried to the door while calling, "Lizzy! The tea, hurry! Oh, Pultney, good afternoon. You're back. We . . . have visitors." She avoided his eyes and gestured at the parlor full of people.

Lord Kilver stood on the threshold scratching his head as he passed his piercing black eyes over each guest in turn. He looked thunderstruck that they had outwitted him. "So! You're all here," he said curtly. He directed a suspicious stare at his wife.

The serving cart came rolling in, but poor Lizzy caught it on a lump in the carpet created by his rough tread. The resulting clink of china and spoons gave him cause to turn his irritation on her. "Need lessons in cart-pushing, girl?"

The rest of the visit was short, just long enough to sip the tea and make a show of sampling the few stale biscuits on the plate. Lord Kilver would not sit, but remained in a stiff stance against the light of the window in silhouette, making everyone uneasy. Contemptuously, he said to Tricia, "You raced ahead of me to find the Will, eh?"

She did not reply or even look at him.

"It's no different than the one I showed you in London."

Tricia maintained an air of self-possession and

smiled slightly at Lady Kilver.

He said to his wife, "She must eyeball it for herself, I warrant. *If* she can find it." He guffawed, and spat into the cold fireplace.

Lady Kilver took up her blue knitting and said nothing.

* * *

The Duke, wanting very much to throttle Lord Kilver, closed the visit for Tricia's sake. He knew she was upset beneath her brave exterior. He tried not to imagine what kind of a life she had endured under this oppressive roof. He said, "You may as well show us the copy of the Will here and now, Kilver."

"Nay. Don't have it. You'll just have to live without it." He cackled. "Trust me."

Everyone darted disgusted looks at him.

On their way to the door, Lady Kilver gave a slight tug to Rowan's sleeve, unseen by her husband. Rowan hung back, pulling out his gold watch on its chain, checking the time and stuffing it back, stalling while waiting for Lady Kilver to return from another room.

Lord Kilver was rapt with attention for Tricia, who was already out the door. He was telling her she would stay in his house from this night on, and where was her trunk?

Lady Kilver saw him gesticulating at Tricia out in the street, so she grabbed her chance. Above her broad cheeks, her squinted eyes looked nervous, but her mouth was set in determination. She pressed something hard into Rowan's hand.

He gave her a word of mystified thanks, tipped his hat respectfully, and went out to intercede for Tricia before she let loose whatever horrified words jumped into her mind. He said to Kilver, "We plan to give this town some custom by staying at their inns."

"Which inns?" Kilver inquired.

"We have not decided yet."

"Stay away from any down at The Dock. When storms come up, the water whips high along those walls. Lady Jewel, there," he gestured, "would have a hard time sleeping with the sea vibrating the walls and spray hitting her windows. Tricia would feel like she was on a ship about to go down."

That was cruel, for her parents had drowned in the sea. "Thanks for your concern," growled the Duke, and turned abruptly away.

A half-hour later, Tricia had guided Rowan through five small inns called Ye Dolphin, Old Mariner's, The King's Arms, The Fisherman's Arms, and the Robin Hood's Bay Hotel. Rowan decided to ensconce his womenfolk in The Fisherman's Arms at Tricia's suggestion. She chose it because she said she wanted to see the cellars.

She held touchingly onto Rowan's arm as they left the inn and headed down toward the water. She explained, "When my brother, David, worked in the Customs House over there," she pointed, "he told us how the Revenue Men surprised a gang of smugglers just as they were in the act of delivering a run of spirits into the cellars of The Fisherman's Arms." Her eyes were alight as she looked up and awaited his reaction.

"Was your brother one of the Revenue Men?"

asked Rowan. He stilled her by his other hand so they could admire the broad red sunset glittering on the bay and beyond.

"No, he was a clerk. If he had been a Revenue Man, what occurred would never have happened."

"What was that?" asked Rowan. He enjoyed watching her animated face and dancing curls as she talked.

"There was a fight," she said, "and for once the Revenue Men were victorious. During the fuss, one of the kegs sprang a leak, so—can you believe it?—the Revenue Men celebrated their triumph. In the morning, they were all found snoring-drunk!"

"Oh?" Rowan was amused. "And?"

"The smugglers and the booty had vanished."

Rowan grinned. "But of course." He wished her good reminiscing at her inn.

"Where will you be?" she asked.

He told her he and his servants would be nearby in the Robin Hood's Bay Hotel, if they had enough rooms. "I want to be right there on The Dock where I can see what activity might go forward at the water's edge, especially since Kilver does not want me there. What do you suppose is his reason?"

"It's time to tell you," she said.

Rowan offered his arm, and she slipped her gloved hand through it again. The sunset gave her skin a golden glow. His heart picked up speed as they turned and walked in step down the curving cobblestone street. It felt like a stolen wonder to walk arm-in-arm with her beautiful, trusting presence. He was glad they had left Jewel having a better tea than Lady Kilver's at The Fisherman's

Arms.

The bay, in sparkling splendor, dropped away before the stone steps at Rowan's feet. Seagulls set up a raucous mewing as they dipped and dived over a net flopping with catch that two men were tugging out of a boat. It all fascinated Rowan.

Tricia's voice came quietly, "In this innocent-looking town, there are smugglers running rife beneath the very noses of His Majesty's Revenue Men. To profess to be a smuggler would never occur to anyone of respectability, but many otherwise honorable people are guilty. My father, Your Grace, was honest as those wind-washed cliffs. He was jeered at, and even threatened by some of these people because he paid the King's taxes."

"I am glad to hear that he stuck to his principles."

"I discovered," she said, looking around to ascertain that no one could overhear them, "that Lord Kilver was smuggling with *The White Dove!* It made me so angry because that ship was my father's!"

Rowan was suitably struck. "That is despicable!"

"Yes, so that evening, I shoved a nightshirt and other necessities into a sack. I was already desperate to escape from his house. A trio of fisher lads ran by in the street, talking in excited whispers, each pulling a donkey whose hoofs were muffled by woolen socks. Those animals would soon carry contraband across the moorland."

"Was that when you cut your hair and slid down the laundry chute?"

"Yes. After I squeezed out the window from the basement, I edged along the walls of the houses, ducked below window casings, and darted from one shadow to another. When I reached the street called The Bolts, I bolted up the hill as fast as I could." She told him how, in the darkness, she rested on her pack, her heart palpitating. She buried her nose in the fragrant grass. It was the sweet essence of God's nature, and she thanked Him for letting her escape that grievous house. More hopeful than she had been for months, she ventured a look back above the fronds of bracken.

The water of the bay had shimmered faintly. Almost indistinguishable in the gray expanse was a ship's dark hull halfway to the horizon. There were two cobles forming tell-tale wakes as they left the shore from separate locations.

Rowan asked, "Where were the Revenue Men?"

"That's what I was wondering. I prayed hard that they would notice. I could not go back to warn them that *The White Dove* had sneaked in without lights, surely carrying contraband."

"So what happened?"

"Just then, I heard hoofs drumming along the ground, and a horseman cantered into the copse of trees. I hid myself, and as he rode by with a lantern, I recognized him as one of the Customs Officers my father had known. I yelled, 'Mr. Richard!' He asked who I was and shot the slide across the front of his lantern to shine it on me. I said I was the son of a fisher, and said that it was a night they should investigate down at The Dock. I said, 'There's activity in the Bay. See that dark ship and those cobles? They're out for a reason.' He looked over the dim sea, and thanked me, and threw me a coin."

Rowan said, "You certainly did your duty."

"I was satisfied with that, and felt most daring for informing on Lord Kilver. I was very glad for the glittering coin that he left me because I needed it for the journey ahead. See how God provides?"

"I do indeed."

Tricia turned her faraway eyes to his. "You've heard the rest. I don't know if they caught him at it or not. If they did, he was probably immune from any consequence because he is a Peer."

"That could very well be the case if he exercises control over people in this town. I don't know when I've seen a man with a more tyrannical nature." Rowan breathed in deeply of the sea air blowing at them in cool gusts. "You were extremely brave, Tricia. I thank you for telling me all this. I will watch that character with new eyes. Let's keep quiet about what we suspect."

"You mean to say you want to expose his smuggling?" Tricia gazed up at him, looking apprehensive.

"Of course I do."

"Is it not dangerous to meddle with such a viper and hypocrite as he is?"

"Yes, but if he's landing contraband with a ship which is yours when you come of age, what's to make him stop such activity then?"

"Oh, but Your Grace, you've done so much for me already," she objected. "How can you think of delving into such a terrible nest of iniquity? I worry that you will come to harm."

Waves crashed nearly over the tops of the huge boulders that they had driven past earlier on the beach. "Thank you for caring so much for the right, Tricia. I'm sure you bring a lot of joy into this world." He quickly touched her chin and added, "Try not to worry. Just keep my efforts in your prayers, will you?"

* * *

Tricia took the Duke's arm again to walk back up the street. She felt too full of emotion to trust her voice for a full minute. Her thoughts raced, and her heart was calling him her *dear Duke*. It was so sweet to be with him; to know that he, in return, cared about her affairs so much that he made this long journey on her behalf. "I keep you perpetually in my prayers," she said before she could edit her words. She chastised herself silently, recalling that he was now engaged to Lady Jewel.

Slowly retracing their steps uphill, Rowan stopped and rummaged around inside his coat's inside pocket. He glanced around and whispered, "Lady Kilver slipped this to me before we left. Do you know what it unlocks?"

"Why, it's the key to my house!"

"That was good of her, considering she may be in trouble with him for giving it to us. Where is your house?"

"There, my Duke, you can see three of the chimneys." She pointed up the six-hundred-foot cliff on the north end of the town. "Can we go first thing in the morning? If we went now, we would soon have to light candles, and Lord Kilver might see that we're there and come running."

"True. Well thought out. Tomorrow morning, then, early. What about Lady Caro? Is she invited?"

"Yes, she should come to safeguard my reputation, I expect." Tricia gave him a droll look.

"We three will go after an early breakfast."

"Won't Jewel mind?" asked Tricia.

"If it's a walk to the cliff top, I believe she will prudently sleep rather than rise for such an excursion. I think the journey was wearing quite thin with her."

The journey had worn thin with Rowan, too, as far as Lady Jewel's comfort was concerned. He had heard her hints of complaint that he hadn't provided them with better inns at which to stop. There had been no time for planning such an impromptu trip, he said. The other ladies found fault with nothing. Tricia had been buoyed by their quick pace, and thanked him more than once for all he was doing for her.

When they had been unable to acquire a private dining parlor last night, and were obliged to settle for a table in the so-called Gentry Supper Room, Jewel had smiled up at him while she declared it insupportable. In fact, Jewel accompanied most of her remarks with questioning smiles at him.

He made it a point to talk to her. "Jewel," he began when they were alone in the carriage while it was being hastily and sloppily washed. The others were partaking of a quick bun and coffee. "I'm sorry, but this is the only place and time I have found for us to speak to each other."

"Yes, Rowan?" she breathed, an alertness apparent in every line of her body.

"About the engagement gossip in the paper which you showed me—"

"Yes?"

Flustered as a schoolboy, he asked, "Did it shock you?"

"Dear Rowan," she said, trapping his wrists with cold fingers, "are you asking me if I *want* to marry you, as you have been hoping since you put that item in the paper? I'm gloriously glad to tell you that the answer is *yes!*" She leaned toward him and twined her perfumed arms about his neck. Because he was prepared this time, she was not able to kiss his lips, for he presented the side of his head. "Yes, yes, and yes!" she expelled all over his ear.

No, no, and no! he thought. Get off of me!

Gazing at him, she cried, "You are so shy, Rowan! I am very much thrilled to marry you."

"I . . . see." He honestly did not know what to do. There was no backing out now; that was as obvious as the desire in her voice. He felt like an animal in a snare. Anything he did tied him tighter.

He knew that Society would highly approve this match. Jewel seemed to be the young set's social leader, and she knew how to make things happen her way in tonnish circles. Many of his friends had married far worse-looking, worse-behaving women than Lady Jewel. Many of the regulars at White's, for example, did not look upon a wife as having much to do with love. Just so the estates joined were advantageous, that they could beget children as their heirs, and most of all, that there was plenty of money, old or new, in the wife's dowry; those were the things that mattered. The freedom remained with them to fall in and out of love anywhere else they chose, some of them said.

But, raged Rowan inwardly, *they do not fear or love God if that is how they think and live their lives.* The whole idea of marriage under their rules scalded him. He wished he could have a marriage of love such as his parents had had. He cared nothing whatever about any money Jewel might bring, but he owed it to the realm to get himself an heir. This thought caught him short, back to the lengthening silence between him and her.

Her hot breath came near his ear and she kissed his cheek in rapturous, one-sided pecks. Rowan saw, in the light radiating at the inn door, a willowy figure: Tricia.

He politely set Jewel back, told her she was crazy to think so much of him, and closed his eyes. He didn't know if he moaned aloud, but it issued from his heart, and. oddly for him, he felt like weeping.

"We must wait, Rowan dear," whispered Jewel, readjusting her dress. Apparently she perceived herself disheveled. "You are having a difficult time waiting, too, aren't you?" she said, and put her hand on his knee.

"Let's go in," he growled, pressing the door lever. Was she purposely misunderstanding him, speaking at cross-purposes so he couldn't voice his true feelings? Did she realize that he was far less than thrilled with the engagement she had foisted upon him?

Rowan forgot that the ostler was scrubbing the coach, and stepped on his fingers, for he was toiling away on the muddy step. "Sorry, man, sorry!" He gave him a coin.

He figured Tricia had seen their heads together through the wet windows, for she turned deliberately back into the lighted inn. Lady Caro appeared after her, and the look she gave Rowan indicated that she, too, could see that all was settled; and that he and Jewel were betrothed.

Rowan hated himself for the rest of the night. He could not converse decently through their evening in the Gentry Supper Room, and he could not smile.

Jewel smiled for both of them. She kept sliding her hand into his on the sofa. She had told the landlord it was their official engagement announcement, and ordered champagne. Rowan, who hated the stuff, touched none of it.

From eleven o'clock on, sleep eluded him. He kicked off the sheet, punched his pillow into thirty different positions, and finally woke Lionel, asleep on a cot in the room, and asked if he would kindly go fetch some hot milk. Yes, milk.

After two slowly-drained glasses had relaxed him into hopeless thinking, Rowan at last turned to prayer. He fell asleep in the middle of the Lord's Prayer, which always concluded his other petitions. *Thy will be done, in earth as it is in Heaven.*

Now in Robin Hood's Bay, walking with Tricia's light grasp on his arm, he actually smiled. Her lively face, bright from their exertions, brought a beam of happiness to his heart. Her positive nature continued to amaze him, and it was impossible not to eye her natural beauty with appreciation and yes, longing.

His jaw tightened when he saw his betrothed waving at him from a window in The Fisherman's Arms.

CHAPTER 20

The Crashing Tide

In the wee hours of the night, Rowan woke to the sound of loud waves crashing. He sat up, alarm seizing him. What was going on? It sounded like he was sailing madly aboard a tossing ship. He threw his covers aside, went to the window that faced the sea, and nearly jumped back at the sight below. Waves were rushing at the wall, *Whoosh!* . . . *Whoosh!* . . . *Whoosh!* Continually they crashed, loudly, rhythmically, and insistently. To look down and see slamming water at the base of the outer wall below his window was the eeriest feeling. Just water! The sand beach and the flagstone walks had all disappeared. It felt like he was looking down from the prow of a ship on a threatening ocean. It was startling that the tide had completely deluged the beach that he had driven his coach upon during the daytime. With awe, he felt and heard the mighty force of the sea.

Fascinated, he kept watching the foaming white waves below by the light of the stars and the waning moon. When he finally laid his tired body down on the bed, he listened for a long time. *Whoosh!* . . . *Whoosh!* . . . *Whoosh!* He hoped that the boisterous sea roiling so close beneath him was not some sort of a sinister omen.

* * *

A scream woke Tricia. As she jerked awake from a sound sleep, she realized that it was the herring gull, and she was in Robin Hood's Bay. Beyond the flowered curtains of the carved bed stretched a dark beam in the ceiling, salvaged from a wrecked ship. This was her town, and the sun slanted pinkish gold through the diamond window panes, cheering her.

The Claremont servants had arrived last evening, their baggage coach much slower than Rowan's. Sarah, the chambermaid, was now at Tricia's beck and call, snoring in the dressing room.

"Sarah," said Tricia, shaking her cot.

"Ooh! I should be the one waking you, My Lady. Pardon me, I'm so sorry!"

"Never mind, just help me dress. I'm going out."

"Yes, My Lady. This early, going out?"

"I am going to my home." Tricia smiled. "Wake Jane so she can help Lady Caro. But let Lady Jewel sleep as long as she sleeps."

They met on the ground floor in the little parlor Rowan had reserved for their meals. It had black beams and half-timbering against white plaster walls. Lady Caro looked puffy round the eyes as she entered. It looked suspiciously as if she had wept last night. Tricia wondered why, but dared not ask her about it.

Rowan walked in. His dark bottle green coat and buff trousers looked well for Robin Hood's Bay. She admired the small paisley print of his waistcoat, the high boots, and the informal black stock. But there was something wrong with his eyes. They wouldn't quite meet hers.

On their way up Chapel Street, Lady Caro told Tricia to take Rowan's arm and lead the way through the narrow streets and turnings. Lionel took up the rear, giving his arm to Lady Caro. Tricia laughingly noticed that his black curly hair caught on an empty sign iron and made it clear that there was no room for four to walk abreast.

A woman in a white apron over a dark wool dress stepped out of her cottage door and nearly bumped into Tricia. Goggling, the red-faced woman put her hands to her kerchief and cried, "It's Beany!"

"Mrs. Willoughby, how nice to see you."

"You escaped from that Kilver house, did you? I was a-prayin' for you, Love. Has the good Lord kept you careful?" Her eyes swept over Tricia's well-dressed companions.

"That He has, Mrs. Willoughby. Thank you for your prayers. I need them still."

The woman nodded, and then looked concerned.

Tricia introduced the Duke and Lady Caro. She almost wished she hadn't had to, for the Bay woman looked genuinely speechless, and bowed so low and paused there so long that Tricia feared what would happen when word spread that she, herself, was now styled Lady Tricia. She preferred "Beany" in this town, although it had rankled as a fourteen-year-old when she was straight and skinny.

Their climb to the carriage took them past fishermen carrying nets down the streets. One old man fretted to a youth that he was late, and his crab pots still had to be loaded. As they watched, a green coble launched from the beach and floated out on the heavy surf, its three passengers pulling at the oars.

"I tried to talk with some fishermen this morning who were lifting their cobles into the water," said Rowan privately to Tricia. "They are mighty leery of strangers here, aren't they?"

"Oh yes. For all they know, you're connected with His Majesty's Customs House."

"I see." Rowan rubbed his chin thoughtfully.

"If you want to learn about this smuggling business, ask around discreetly amongst the fishermen for those who will help you unload some cargo around the dark of the moon," Tricia teased.

"Ah. But were I to claim such plans, wouldn't I have to direct them where to deliver?"

"No, you needn't tell your schemes in the beginning. Smugglers are accustomed to short shrift."

"What is all this . . . talk of . . . smugglers?" puffed Lady Caro, following them up the steps which formed the top of Chapel Street.

"Local flavor," replied Rowan. "Here is the coach to relieve you, Lady Caro."

The ducal coach wheeled them along the breathtaking cliff top from which they could see the glorious expanse of ocean stretching in deep blue to the horizon. The ride was short, and soon they halted before Tricia's three-storied pale stone house. The windows were long arches, and above the central doorway, a fanlight caught a glint of sun. On the red pantiled roof, a kittiwake set up a cry.

"No one has been here for some time," she said, "or that snowy-headed bird would be long gone." When she pointed, it leaped and flew to the edge of the cliff.

"This is an impressive place." The Duke breathed in deeply and said, "I feel on top of the world here. We have the same view as the gulls." He handed Tricia the key Lady Kilver had given him in secrecy.

As they approached her mansion by the flagstone walk, Tricia noted the long shoots on the rose bushes, the waving dry grass, and the hazy windows. "This place needs care," she said, longing to put it back to rights.

The key wouldn't fit.

"It looks like a new lock," observed Rowan.

"It is." Tricia stared at the shiny brass with rising anger. "Does he think he can keep me out of my own house?"

"Is there another way in?" asked Lady Caro.

They tried the garden door at the back, but it, too, sported a new bolt.

"That's all there is." Tricia turned her face to the Bay breeze and vowed, "I *will* get in."

"How about the windows?" Rowan tried to rattle some loose but found them tight. He continued all around the large house on the ground floor.

"If we could reach the first floor windows, we might come across one that's open."

"I'll stand on the coach roof," Rowan offered.

Shepperton drove the coach beneath the row of south windows, but he shook his head when the

Duke made to step on it. "I'm afraid it'll bust right through, Your Grace. See how it gives already?"

Tricia said, "Let me. I'm not very heavy."

"Oh no, Tricia," said her aunt.

"I must try."

Rowan smiled. "Come, I'll lift you up."

She sighed in pleasure as he grasped her by the waist and set her on the driving box. "Be careful," he warned, and stepped onto the driving box beside his coachman. "Shepperton, keep the cattle still. Lionel, stand below her in case she falls. Tricia, can you move the pane up at all?"

Working from the coach roof, she strained to lift the sash of her father's office window. "No. Next one, please." She looked over her shoulder. Rowan had his arms outstretched to her and his brown eyes gleamed in an invitation to hang onto his hands while they moved forward.

One look at him made her toss prudence to the wind. She let him grasp her hands to steady her while the horses moved a mere yard forward. He made her feel like something precious.

As she reached up and tried to lift the next long window, she wondered what Lady Caro, with her bright eyes, thought about what she saw, or if she realized what love Tricia felt for him. If Jewel knew, her fury would know no bounds.

Shepperton said suddenly, "Your Grace, there's someone comin'."

Glancing at the wiry figure stalking up the hill, a flat cap low on his forehead and a walking stick plying the ground with each rapid step, she said, aghast, "It's Lord Kilver!"

"No need to look caught in the act, Tricia," said

Rowan, "but come here so you don't fall down."

She wiggled the window of her own bedchamber to no avail. She put her eye to the small gap between the curtains and could see herself in the gilt mirror with her shining pencil curls and the white gathered lace around her throat. She put her forehead on the window and shaded around her eyes. All over her room lay strange bundles wrapped and tied.

The Duke urged her to hurry, but she angled her eye a different way and tried to see what those bulky heaps were. They were tumbled all over her Italian settee, her bed, and the carpet.

"There's something peculiar stored in there," she whispered portentously as she abandoned her peering and descended to Rowan's waiting arms.

"What did you see?"

She told him. "The shapes were like bales of wool, but too smooth. Maybe silk," she whispered.

"So he does have a reason to keep you out!" The Duke cleared his throat and turned. "Is that you, Kilver?"

He squinted and studied them up on the coach box. "Trying to find the Will?" he sneered. "Think you'd see it lying on your father's desk, Trish?"

Rowan said, "Lady Tricia wants to see her home."

Kilver felt his pockets. "Hanged if I don't think that key is back in my study."

"Why are there new locks on the doors?" she inquired.

"So none of the old servants can get in and loot while the house is empty," Kilver replied. "What were you doing? Trying to catch a look at your dolls?" he mocked.

"What if I was? I miss my things."

"You are too sentimental. I'll have to get the key, then. Come back tomorrow afternoon. I'll show you round the place."

"How about today?" Rowan asked.

"Nay, can't do it. I'm on my way to Whitby. Won't be back till tomorrow."

"Without a horse?" queried Tricia.

"Thanks for your kind observance, girl. As it happens, I'm buying a new one. Puttin' her through her paces this afternoon. Care to look her over tomorrow morning, Duke?"

Tricia imagined the suggestion was more than Rowan could stomach. He ignored him.

Lady Caro was more for cutting the man, as she later told Tricia in suppressed indignation, and therefore the unwelcome encounter on the breezy cliff-top concluded.

Rowan said to the ladies as the coach wheeled down the slope, "A few of us at White's know he's been selling goods from the Continent to men of means in London. Bixby bought yards of velvet from him only to find expensive lace concealed inside the center of the bolt."

"Indeed?" Lady Caro was intrigued. "What kind of lace?"

"Elegant and costly lace. I wouldn't know what it's called," said Rowan with an apologetic smile. "Kilver claimed he inherited the fabric, which we do not believe, but we are sure he knew nothing about the lace he inadvertently sold to Bixby, or he would have sold it separately. We think Kilver is new at landing contraband and does not know all of the smugglers' tricks. Tell me, Tricia, is it possible for him to have the necessary funds to buy a merchant ship full of goods?"

Considering this, Tricia replied, "It was some time after my parents died that Kilver said he had to send *The White Dove* out for refitting. The ship didn't return until last month, the night I ran away from here, so it was gone quite awhile. I know that the end of the war with France allows Lord Kilver much more freedom to do what he wants with it. My father had to curtail his shipping in Europe during the war years, of course. As for money, I could not tell you about Kilver's finances, but he could be using *my father's* money, which is supposed to be mine in due time." Tricia sighed helplessly.

Lady Caro exclaimed, "That is despicable!"

Tricia added, "Kilver has an estate called Fylingstone here in Yorkshire, but I don't know whether it's profitable or not."

Lady Caro remained flabbergasted. "That eel! He cannot steal Tricia's money, Rowan!"

He said, "If he's doing it, he must be stopped immediately. He is going to Whitby now, or so he says. That is where his wife told us to see someone. I feel we should beat him there and find that person named . . ." he took out the card and read, "Mr. Septimus Flint."

"I think," said Tricia, excited by old memories, "that he could have been my father's solicitor."

"I hope that's true," said the Duke. "Shall we trot up to Whitby now?"

Lady Caro said enthusiastically, "Yes, it's essential to arrive there before Kilver does. Jewel will sleep late; and anyway, she has our maids to care for her.

Let's be off!"

Tricia caught their spirit of adventure. "You are both so good to do all this on my behalf."

When they wheeled onto the Whitby road over the moor, they passed a stone church which caught Lady Caro's curiosity.

"That's Saint Stephen's," said Tricia. "We can go there next Sunday, if you plan to stay that long." Tricia wondered what time frame the Duke had in mind.

He said, "Certainly, I'll be here. How about you, Lady Caro?" he asked, adjusting the window shade to keep the sun out of her eyes.

Lady Caro sniffed her pretty nose and said firmly, "I'm not moving from this town until Tricia is safe from that reptile, Kilver."

Tricia was touched. "But what if he proves beyond a doubt that I must remain under his roof?"

"Then we will hide you!" said Lady Caro. "Heavens, I will not allow that libertine near you again, much less let you live in his house, Tricia."

"Amen," said the Duke.

Tricia thanked them both with shining eyes.

As Shepperton drove them across the heather moors, whose purple color had grown subtle with the late summer days, Tricia remained uneasy. Would any of these proposed investigations do any good?

It was on the road a mile short of Whitby that she saw a rider trot by whom she recognized. "Your Grace, will you stop the coach and hail that man? I think he can help us so we don't have to scour all of Whitby for Septimus Flint."

With a blast of the coach horn and a sprint by

Lionel, the deed was done.

"Good day, Mr. Richard," Tricia greeted the Customs Officer. The last time she had seen him was the night she cut her hair and bolted out of town. He had thrown her a crown for her information about *The White Dove*. She wished she could thank him for his generosity, which had provided her with food for three days before she found work with Ramsbottom, but she must remain discreet.

"Miss Ravenscar!" His thin face lit up. "What a relief. We thought you had gone missing. Some even said drowned. I don't know when I've been so glad to see anyone."

"Thank you, Mr. Richard. I'm happy to see you, too." Rushing on to avoid explanation, she introduced the Duke, who indicated that the man should remain in the saddle. They shook hands.

Tricia said, "Mr. Richard, do you know where we can find Mr. Septimus Flint?"

"Flint?" The man looked taken aback. "In his cave, I should imagine."

"In his cave?"

Mr. Richard gave a helpless lift of his shoulders. "They say the old man's gone crazy. For the summer months, he has lived above the beach at Ravenscar. I visited him on a night when we searched for barrels of wine that we knew had come ashore. I wondered if they had been hefted into his cave by smugglers, but there he sat with his lantern at his feet, reading the Holy Word, his place as clean as a bosun's whistle. We found nothing suspicious in his abode."

With great interest, the Duke asked, "Can you

direct us to this man, Mr. Richard?"

"I can draw you a map, but it's a difficult spot. It's impossible to reach except at low tide. Are you sure you want to see him? He may have gone completely loony."

CHAPTER 21

The Hermit

"So Mr. Flint is not in Whitby after all," murmured Lady Caro, her eyes wide under her auburn curls and bonnet brim. She grasped the carriage strap as they began to move.

"My aunt Kilver's information was well meant, but not quite up-to-date," murmured Tricia. "She doesn't go out, and sees very few people."

Ominously, Lady Caro said, "She is probably trying to lead you astray. No offense, Tricia, but do think! Would such a weak-mannered woman dare to go against that kind of a husband?"

Tricia lifted her eyebrows. "It seems that she is. I think it's brave of her."

Rowan sat across from the ladies and pointed to the X on Mr. Richard's map. "Mr. Richard said it's above the beach to the south, beyond Ravenscar. I assume you know where that is, Tricia?"

"Yes, Your Grace," she replied as the coach jounced around in the heather and headed back toward Robin Hood's Bay. "It's south of the alum works."

"But you, yourself, won't want to climb to a cave on a cliff-side," he said, watching her from the corners of his dark eyes.

"Oh, but I *will*," she returned with feeling. Then she saw his teasing twinkle.

He gestured over her flimsy cambric gown and matching lavender half-boots. "But you are too clean and ladylike. How can you climb in that exquisite rig?"

She shot him a withering glance.

He laughed. "Never tell me you're going to wear boy's clothes."

"What else?" She grinned at Lady Caro.

"*No*, Tricia," said her aunt. "You are a Lady now."

Tricia grasped her gloved hands. "Dear Aunt, please understand that I *must* search out this solicitor. I saw him visit my father when I was a girl. What if he knows something? Is he not my only hope? Kilver is hindering us as much as he can, and I think it's because something is wrong with that Will. Mr. Flint might at least remember my father even if he didn't write up his Will. Perhaps he can advise me what to do."

"But, Tricia! You heard that he is mad."

"I don't care. I must see him."

"Then go with Rowan; he will protect you. But take extreme care not to let anyone *see* you in boy's garb. We have your reputation to safeguard. Word can fly from here to London; believe me, it can." She caught Tricia's eye and held it.

Tricia thought of Jewel and said, "Yes, Aunt."

Her heart skipped at the thought of going with the Duke on such a mission, just the two of them.

As soon as she burst into her chamber at The Fisherman's Arms, she sat Sarah down to make a list. She told her to go buy black trousers, wool socks, high-heeled boots like the fishermen wore, a shirt, and a knitted Bay Town gansey small enough to fit.

"Fit who, My Lady?"

"Me, of course."

Sarah goggled at her.

"Do not tell Lady Jewel, whatever you do. Here, trace my foot so you'll get the boot size right."

The maid bent to do her bidding, plying a pencil around Tricia's slim foot as she stood on a piece of paper. "Leave room for the socks," she said as Sarah left with directions to the shop in her hand. "They can be used boots; I do not mind."

Jewel knocked and walked in.

"Good morning," said Tricia. "Did you sleep well? Have you breakfasted?"

"No on both points. Have you?"

"Why, yes, but I'm hungry again. It's past noon."

"What on earth is there to *do* in this ghastly place?"

Lady Caro bustled in and cried, "Shop, of all things! Who would like to go shopping around town with me?" She threw Tricia a private wink and regaled Jewel with what she had glimpsed in quaint little windows as she walked about this morning. "I do so want to go back and look at that jet jewelry. They have such a great variety, and unusual patterns that I really liked. One necklace I saw would highly become you, Jewel."

"Where's Rowan?" Jewel asked, peering out the window.

Lady Caro said airily, "Out and about, I imagine. There's much for a man to explore around here, I would think. Crab pots and such. You don't want to take up all his time, Jewel. Men, even engaged ones, need to feel a bit of freedom, don't you think?"

"Please!" huffed Jewel. "Leave off!"

Tricia and Lady Caro exchanged cautious looks. Lady Caro said, "I'm sorry; I wasn't suggesting you had taken up his time, for, of course you have barely been with the man, but—"

"I know what you mean. Not to expect him to run circles around me. To *amuse* myself as much as possible. Why did I even come here?"

"Because you wanted to help Tricia, of course. We all commend you for your kind heart," murmured Lady Caro, sending Tricia another ironic look.

Jewel lifted her chin, her long nostrils in evidence.

"Shall we have something to eat?" Tricia proposed.

Tempting aromas drew them to the parlor, where they were served a nuncheon of crab and eggs, scones with blackberry jam, and an unusual tea. Lady Caro liked it very much. Tricia suspected it had come in duty-free from some far-flung land.

When Tricia saw Sarah enter the front door and make for the stairs, she excused herself, having seen her arms full of packages.

"Where are you going?" Jewel asked.

"I want to visit someone."

"Who is it? Someone we all should meet in order to engage in some social life around here?" asked Jewel ironically.

"What a thought," commended Lady Caro, casting Tricia a sly look.

"Well?" Jewel insisted ludicrously. "Is it someone young and of good family?"

Tricia said, "He is an old man, Jewel. Are you interested in coming to his home on the cliff top? I have to walk there."

Her eyes grew wide with disgust. "An old man? Forget it."

Lady Caro laughed and said, "Oho, but consider *me*. I might be interested in old men." She and Tricia laughed.

Jewel rolled her eyes.

Lady Caro said, "Come, Jewel, I itch to shop. Everything is in such quaint proximity here, and we will see such different things to buy. I saw such pretty flowers in the window boxes, too, and there's a house that's shaped like a wedge and as narrow as this little parlor. Come see! You will never see the likes of this humblety-tumblety town again. I expect the Duke will be around in the evening, and then we can all dine together."

"I won't see Rowan until evening?" screeched Jewel.

Thanks to Lady Caro's continued dialogue and her private wave, Tricia escaped. She almost felt sorry for Jewel, who was so dependent upon the Duke to buoy her spirits now that she was away from her London friends and fancy trappings.

Tricia had to admit, as she set a black cap onto her short hair, that her own spirits were on the high wire because she was dressing to meet the Duke. She thrillingly anticipated the search for a cave-dweller who might know something vital to her future, and she rejoiced in her chance to do so with the Duke.

Lady Caro had generously not mentioned chaperonage. She knew that on such a mission, conventions were but in the way. She knew that what was going forward was serious business.

Tricia rubbed a little dust onto her face and kept to the narrow shadow along the wall as she sauntered, boy style, down to The Dock. She sat to await Rowan outside the door of the Bay Hotel.

Up from the beach came three men carrying a weathered red coble. Tricia moved back into a corner to let them set the boat near the hotel steps, where more of the boats were lined up when not in use. She hadn't realized that one of the men was the Duke because the first thing she had noticed was the worn sealskin cap on his head. As he straightened up, she stared in fascination. He was attired in a white collarless shirt and dark breeches and boots, much as she was, minus the knitted wool gansey, but she noted with approval that he had an old blue one tied around his waist. She smiled. He looked the part of a Robin's Hood Bay fisherman. But what was he doing?

"Thank ye," said a fair-haired, stocky young fisher, looking respectfully at Rowan.

The other, a tough, weathered old salt, stowed the wet oars neatly over the wooden seats, two pairs of them.

"Thank *you*," returned the Duke, touching his cap to the elder. "Again, I appreciate your promise of assistance."

The old man turned at that, looked sharply at Rowan from under his white brows. "If tha sez that again, Ah'll fettle thee!" Spying Tricia grinning at him, the craggy-faced fisherman advanced, saying,

"Tha git! –or Ah'll gie tha a claht over t'eead!"

She scampered up the cobbled steps between the hotel and the corner shop, looking suitably terrified. She held her grin back with her hand and listened out of sight.

"Wat's yer name?" the harsh voice demanded.

"Rowan. And yours?"

"Y'earnshaw."

"Have you lived here all your life, Mr. Earnshaw?"

"Not yit."

Rowan must have choked back his laugh, for his voice was full of it when he said, "I hope your health improves."

Earnshaw made an impatient sound. "Ah might just mucky another cleean shirt afore t'day's over."

When the Duke appeared, Tricia leaped up and strode ahead of him up Albion Street as they had planned. Before she curved out of his sight up the Flagstaff Steps, she looked back.

Rowan grinned at her, and motioned for her to continue. She supposed it amused him to see her in breeches again. It couldn't be helped. She led him up through a wood on the hillside and emerged on the flat grassy expanse where they could walk side by side unobserved.

"This is right up your alley, isn't it?" he asked mirthfully as he gestured over her fisher costume.

She smiled and said, "I hope no one recognizes me."

"Must I call you Patrick Raven again?"

"Oh, no. Word might get to Ramsbottom. What were you doing hand-in-glove with old Earnshaw? Did you just bow and strike up a conversation? People around here don't fuzzy up to foreigners.

That's a strict rule."

"I loudly observed, as he staggered out of his coble, that the view was tremendous. He replied, 'Aye, but it weean't pay t' rent.'"

Tricia laughed at Rowan's rendition of the Yorkshire yammer. "That is very good!"

"He didn't look well, either, and had an unpleasant odor about him. So, along with his son, we rinsed his boat out by dousing some buckets in the surf. I found out quite a bit for five minutes' acquaintance. He detests Kilver, and hoped I was a Revenue Man."

"Really? What is his particular reason for detesting Kilver?"

"Apparently he rowed goods for him and didn't get paid enough. If he hadn't kept a barrel of rum, he wouldn't have had much to show for a long night's dangerous work."

"Mercy! Kilver *is* smuggling then!"

"We knew it, didn't we? Earnshaw is bitter."

"So is he willing to help you?"

"Yes, he said he is. I asked him if he could use some extra money, and now we're friends of sorts." Rowan chuckled. "He had his son procure me these clothes."

"Perfect," she said, smiling. They walked along the grassy meadow until a long, slippery path led them down to a bridge. "Let me help you," he said, descending first.

"No, Duke." She giggled and looked around. "Someone might see us."

"Who is here to see? I see only squawking gulls." He took her hand and hurried down the slope and crossed the bridge over what Tricia told him was

Mill Beck. The water gurgled and splashed below them.

"Now, again." Rowan hauled her up the treacherous bank on the other side. "Our horses should be waiting for us before Stoupe Beck. That was not it, obviously," he remarked as they climbed over clumps of tough heather, mud, and stones.

Two of Rowan's black carriage horses were waiting at the little beck, their bridles tied firmly to a ring stake in the ground. They alerted and whickered.

"Who brought them here?" asked Tricia, looking around, seeing only the workers at the distant alum quarry.

"I hired them walked up from the stable at my hotel."

"Did they think you strange to have them left here?"

"They said there were rings they could tie them to, and locks. They gave me the key."

Tricia said, "Ah, they've used these rings many times before. Waiting donkeys, you know."

"Yes, I see. These are very handy for us. Do you ride?"

"Oh yes. My father bought me a pony when I was about four." She accepted Rowan's leg-up, and threw herself astride. "You need not help me too much, Your Grace. The workers might see. I'm a boy, remember?" She pulled her cap low and urged the horse up the path. But it was secretly wonderful to receive the Duke's kind attentions. When she looked back at him for a response, he was watching her, and had not even mounted his horse yet. His gaze made her feel aware of her femininity, and her shape in the trousers, especially.

After circumventing the alum quarry with its working men and sounds of shoveled stone, they cantered by stone-walled meadows and a farm. Tricia kept her face averted, mindful of Lady Caro's concern for her reputation. Finally they vaulted up the bridle road which wound them up the hill to Ravenscar.

Rowan came thundering up to her on the splendid, windy crest. "I'd like to sit there and look at the map," he said, pointing.

"On Robin Hood's Butts?"

"What did you call those?"

"Robin and his outlaws used them for their archery practice," she told him, slipping down from her horse. "It's probably why they protected Whitby so well from the Danes."

"What revered ground we tread," Rowan said, pacing from one earth mound to another and smiling. He sat down and leaned against one. "Now, I think we must be too high up. Somehow, we have to find this track." He pointed to a line Mr. Richard had sketched leading from the bridle path past the next alum quarry, and Ravenscar, and then down to the sea.

"Come, that's farther on," said Tricia, scanning the panorama of Robin Hood's Bay. It was low tide and the Bay had the appearance of a half-submerged, sliced onion showing a hundred concentric curves eroded by waves. The cluster of houses with their russet red roofs fell pell-mell from the cliff top steeply down to the beach. White gulls with yellow bills flew and dipped and mewed sharply over the chimneys.

Rowan and Tricia cantered on, past the imposing Raven Hall Inn near the cliff, and again Tricia looked the other way to hide her identity.

"Let's try here," said Rowan suddenly as he paced the cliff ten minutes later beside a clump of trees. "This must be it." He secured their horses to separate scrubby branches, leaving length enough for them to graze.

Following the quick stride of the Duke, she noted the blue gansey he had acquired. It had the Robin Hood's Bay pattern stitched vertically from the base of his shoulder blades up to his broad shoulders. Failing to watch her steps, she sloshed into the mud of the trickling stream and caught her own gansey on a snag of branches, which pulled threads.

On their steepest descent, rocks rolled, and so did she. She cried out a warning to the Duke, as, out of control, she slid on her heels with dirt and loose rocks. With arms waving, she crashed into Rowan's boots. He tried to prevent his falling backward onto her, but as he dove to make a protective arch over her, his fist hit her in the temple.

She saw stars.

* * *

Mortified, Rowan grasped her soft face and saw her pupils dark and wide. "Tricia, I am so sorry!" He was mortified. "Did I hurt you badly?"

Her long eyelashes lowered, she blinked a few times, and looked up at him with those dramatic eyes. "Ow," she quipped. "My pride stings."

In relief, he laughed and lifted her gently to sitting. "Move all of your limbs and your head to make sure all is well."

She did so. "All as normal, Your Grace."

"But I struck you somewhere," he insisted.

"In the head." She put her palm to her temple. "After that burst of skyrockets, I think I'll forever see more clearly."

"Oh, no! Well, now I should carry you."

Tricia wiggled her eyebrows at him.

Rowan was delighted by it. "My Lady, you asked for it!" He grabbed her up in a struggling bundle until her face was inches from his.

"No, you can't carry me!" she gasped.

"I can. Just until I make sure my blow to your head has not knocked you silly." He hummed in jollity as he held her to him and started down the grassy clearing.

Tricia was, to his joy, hugging him tightly. She sighed near his ear. Much affected by the warm and lovely burden he carried, Rowan felt the moment to be an elevated dream which must, alas, soon end. He stopped and looked into her eyes for the briefest moment. Then he kissed her.

* * *

Startled by his warm mouth telling her sweet and glorious things, Tricia felt a flood of love for him. Rapturously, she gave herself up to kissing him back. She told him of her wonder, her reverence, and her trust in him, and ended with the sad fact that she could not have him.

His dark lashes parted and his agate brown eyes

met hers. "Tricia." He groaned as from the depths of his heart. He pulled her head to his until their foreheads touched. "I am sorry! Temptation, you know."

Surprisingly, that made both of them chuckle.

He hefted her against his shoulder so she could no longer see his face but had to view the terrain they were leaving behind.

He had kissed her! Oh, singing angels! –and she had kissed him! Tricia's head felt giddy with their illicit actions.

Rowan ran with her down to the bottom of the slope so she was forced to hang tightly to him. She took her chance to grasp the back of his thick, silky hair and slide her hand down his strong neck for a good grip. This was the vital man she loved.

As soon as they reached the sandy beach, he held her close to his beating heart, paused, and said, "Listen."

A thin strumming sound issued from somewhere, borne to their ears by the lack of a breeze. They looked at each other questioningly, and Rowan set her down.

An enthusiastic, thin old voice sang the words, "O God, our help in ages past, our hope for years to come . . ." It was a familiar hymn. That boded well, thought Tricia.

Propelled by curiosity, they hurried over rocks along the beach. The lyrics came louder, and the singer sounded higher than they were. As they passed a huge black rock in the tide pools, a sudden clap made them jump. On the other side of the stander, hundreds of large wings flapped as a flock of black birds rose, crying and screeching.

"Jackdaws," said Tricia with a hand on her heart.

"Were they his audience?" Rowan pointed up the cliff side.

A shadowed hole gaped high above them in the sunlight. A thin brown leg dangled out, swinging to the incessant twanging of a stringed instrument. The voice burst out again while the strumming went on furiously in the same chord, "Our shelter from the stormy blast, and our eternal home!"

"Your man of the law?" asked Rowan while they watched the bare foot kicking dust loose in time with the music.

Tricia stared in disbelief. "Whoever that leg belongs to, he could be a hermit, all right." It looked as though they could climb the cliff face, for the man had carved himself a footpath that traversed back and forth straight up to the cave at steep angles.

"I know this whole thing looks dubious," whispered Rowan, stepping over ragged seaweed, "but Mr. Septimus Flint, whom I assume this to be, is one bit of hope in an otherwise bleary prospect. Come. Let's try not to startle him."

"He startles me."

The singing became expressive. "Under the shadow of Thy throne Thy saints have dwelt secure! Sufficient is Thine arm alone, and our defense is sure!"

"He's right," said Tricia, smiling with a sense of peace. "I often get so caught up in my problems that I forget."

"I, too," said Rowan. "Tricia," he said, causing her to face him by his earnest tone, "the Bible says that if any two of us, his children, agree to pray for something, it shall be done unto them. Let's put these perplexities that each of us faces into God's hands, shall we? Let's follow where He leads. I don't want to start thinking I can accomplish things alone. I can't. It may not be right if I do things my way."

"Thank you, Your Grace. That is exactly how we should pray."

They crossed wet sand littered with lug worms and periwinkles. As she stepped over a dog whelk shell, a hairy leg thrust out. She jumped back and gave a little scream.

"Shh," said the Duke, "you disturbed the hermit crab."

They looked at each other, and up at the cave, and giggled.

The voice above had ceased, as had the strumming. The man's small foot was no longer in sight.

They approached the base of the 600-foot cliff. The cave was two-thirds of the way up. The height made Tricia stagger. She felt Rowan's hands on her back as he steadied her. Gulls mewed insistently over their heads, challenging their right to scale the cliff.

"Let's go, Duke," she said breathlessly.

"You first, so I can catch you if you tumble."

Tricia, aware that he would have quite a view all the way up, tiptoed bravely up the narrow path. She reached down for Rowan's hand when she rounded a perilous switchback. He supported her by holding her ankles until she felt safer. When at last they could see the ceiling of the large cavern, she squatted and clung to a wide ledge that stuck out of the cliff side. The sea spread wide in an aqua panorama, littered near at hand with black boulders, jagged standers, and splashing surf. Her spine tingled, and she ceased to look down.

Rowan leaned his head toward hers and whispered, "Remember to look friendly." He gave her an encouraging nudge. They had decided that she would look less intimidating to a stranger unannounced, so she should appear first.

Biting her lip, she raised herself on bended legs to look into the cave. At eye level, she saw a cut crystal goblet winking in the sunshine. Perched at an angle in it was a toothbrush. There was nothing else at all but the hard dirt floor of the cave diminishing into blackness.

"I don't see him," she whispered to Rowan.

"Hmm." Rowan placed his hands on the edge of the precipice and pulled himself up until he sat on the wide entrance. He lifted Tricia up until she stood on the solid floor. Again she felt giddy as she looked down. Far below were a dozen dark cormorants flying swiftly across the tips of the waves in a straight line. They dove into the surf.

"I wonder where our host went." Rowan stood and pulled his gansey off over his head. "That was a warm climb."

"What if he saw us, and is loading his musket? He could shoot us down in all freedom from that dark hole. He's probably taking careful aim now. Is it at you or me?"

A sound, abounding with echoes, issued from the depths of the cave. It sounded something like, "Visitors, ho!"

As their eyes became accustomed, they saw the

small, frail figure scurrying toward them. When he drew into the light, he stopped. "Aye-yi!" he trilled, staring up at Rowan's magnificent height.

Tricia gave a gasp. A yard of white hair streamed back from the little man's curved, lined forehead. A splayed-out beard framed his wizened face. The rest of his lean brown body was utterly bare.

"Good day to you," said the Duke, bowing his head.

Tricia tried to look friendly, but stupefaction warred on her countenance as the bare-limbed hermit did an astonished little jig.

Rowan, choking on silent laughter, stepped forward and thrust his fisherman's gansey at the man's middle. The little fellow jerked back, grasped the garment in surprise, and stared hard at Rowan with round, liquid eyes, trying to comprehend what he meant.

"A small gift," said the Duke.

The old man nodded his head sagely. "In lieu of payment, I see. Well, thank you, Sir."

Rowan said, "Allow me," and turned the man's front away from Tricia and lowered the blue wool over the beautiful white head.

Tricia knew her cheeks were aflame.

"Septimus Flint?" Rowan addressed the head that popped out.

"That's me!" He thrust his arms into the overly-long sleeves. "Septimus Flint, Solicitor!"

When he turned to Tricia with a pert bow, it was all she could do to keep from laughing at the sight of the spindly legs emerging from the knitted hem. He tenderly pulled his hair and beard out of the neckline.

"I am happy to see you again, Mr. Flint. I am sure it was you who my father consulted when I was young."

Rowan nodded encouragement to her.

"Oh no, not so long! Not so long." Folding up the gansey sleeves, he turned to the Duke. "What did you say your name was, Sir?" My, but sound swirled oddly in the cavern.

"I'm Rowan. And this is—"

"Do not tell me!" cried the little man, his blue eyes excitedly jumping as he pointed at Tricia. "It's David!" He slapped his bare knee. "They thought he died in the war!" He laughed at such stupidity and then wheezed to a stop. "I never saw him die, did you?" he put seriously to Rowan.

Tricia's astonishment increased. "So you know Leigh Ravenscar's children, Mr. Flint?"

The little man strode straight toward her, examining her face. "How could I not? I even danced with your mother the other night. Nobody else knows she is a Countess, my boy, but I do, I do!" He leaped again in that odd little manner, feet moving so fast they almost blurred.

"You *do?*" pressed Tricia.

"Come admire my view," said Septimus Flint, motioning them to the front of the cave. "Pardon the mess," he said, grabbing up the goblet, "and sit down."

They lowered themselves on either side of him, legs dangling over the dramatic edge. Tricia could see why his skin was so brown if he sat here every sunny day in nothing but his beard. It was surprisingly warm in the sheltered cave.

Rowan said conversationally, "Do you get many

visitors, Mr. Flint?"

"None as leave their calling cards." His eyes crinkled up. "Had some sitters trying to take over this property, offering me tobacco for it, but—hee hee!—I don't smoke!" He enjoyed his mirth, tapering off in high wheezes.

"Sitters? You mean Customs Officers? Revenue Men?"

Mr. Flint nodded rapidly. "They said they needed a look-out. I said I can look out as well as any of them."

"Is that what you like to do?"

"Oh, yes, I have a good spy glass."

Tricia asked, "Has Mr. Richard been to see you?"

"The same. He's an honest man. Few of those. Your papa is one of the noble, fighting ones. And you are, too, aren't you now, young fellow? You spoke out against that drunk at The Fisherman's Arms. That takes courage in this wicked and gainsaying generation. It is never easy to stick to the truth when you believe you're the only one." He cocked his head and asked, "How old are you?"

Tricia said carefully, "Do you not think I am old enough to work in the Customs Office?"

"Oh, but you do work there. I beg your pardon."

Tricia said, "You have been very valuable to my father, Mr. Flint. Have you not drawn up the most important documents of his life?"

"That I have. Can I serve you some smoked herring?"

"No, thank you," she said, for her pulses raced with excitement, and she wanted to get on with her questioning.

Septimus Flint objected, "But you must. I

smoked it myself on that ledge." He pointed down to an outcrop above the water mark.

Tricia saw the tide frothing in. There was much less beach now; only a hundred feet of the brown, sparkly sand.

Rowan winked at Tricia and said, "We would love some herring, if it's no trouble."

"No trouble a-tall." Septimus Flint jumped up and hurried away.

Tricia whispered, "What do you think, Rowan?"

He looked gratified. "I think you've gotten a lot out of him. Well done! Let's go in and see what we can do to help him."

He was exhibiting great energy in lighting a candle stump with a tinder-box. He set it on a discarded coble seat set up as a low table, and lit two more candles from the first.

Shadows jumped into the irregular recesses of the cavern. The light showed crockery jars stashed neatly into hollowed-out shelves and holes everywhere. There were not only containers but also the lute he had been playing, and a short broom, a teapot and kettle, pyramids of potatoes, carrots, onions, leeks, and a store of garlic, dried fish, and crab legs. Gold-edged porcelain dishes gleamed in an open chest. Farther back, in a room angling away, myriad rolled papers stuck out of holes in the cavern wall.

"Mr. Flint," said Tricia, pointing, "pardon my curiosity, but what are those?"

"My work. Those represent hours of composition based on knowledge of the intricate laws of the land. Do you take tomatoes with your herring?"

"Of course," said Rowan, meeting Tricia's eyes mirthfully.

"That is your legal work, then," affirmed Tricia with suppressed eagerness. "Do you . . . do you have any documents that you drew up for my father?" She waited breathlessly.

"Who's your father?" he asked, screwing up his forehead.

"Leigh Ravenscar," she said, but Rowan, surprisingly, put up his hand.

"The Earl of Wyndhurst," he said.

"How do *you* know he's the Earl of Wyndhurst?" the solicitor challenged.

Rowan blinked and said, "Because I'm the Duke of Rowan."

Tricia laughed out loud. Rowan had used his title in a superior manner for once.

The solicitor's eyes bored into hers. "Do you believe that? The Duke of Rowan? Here, in my home? Why, this beats all!" He looked gleeful. "Your father will have a reception for the Duke. I can dance with the secret Countess again, hee-hee! Shhh . . . I won't divulge their secret."

"Has my father made up his Will yet?" Tricia asked.

"Oh, yes."

"He *has?*" Too quick.

Sure enough, the hermit was backing away, going to get the herring he had since forgotten. "Made it up, but his children can't look at it until he's dead. Hope that's never."

Tricia and Rowan exchanged a defeated look. Tricia bit her lip and silently called herself a dolt. "Mr. Flint," she said, taking a deep breath, "My father *is* dead."

The man whirled and two smoked herrings slid off the plate. He picked them up, clucked his tongue, and stalked to the opening of the cliff. There he made a high, piercing cry like the sea gulls, and threw up the reject herrings. The snowy birds swooped and caught them in mid-air.

Septimus Flint marched back, anger in every line of his spare frame. "How dare you try to gammon me with that story? His Lordship tried to convince me once that that was so, but did I believe him? Never!"

Rowan said, "I'll gladly try some of that herring, Mr. Flint." When the man gallantly laid a plate of them before him, admonishing him to wait for the plates, Rowan said casually, "By His Lordship, you mean . . . ?"

"Lord Kilver, of course. Here; now I've set this table properly. Sit up, lad. I never believe people have died until I have seen them in their . . . coffins!" To their dismay, Septimus Flint burst into sobs, his head bent into his trembling hands.

Frowning in great puzzlement, Tricia moved to the hermit's side. With her hand on his thin, heaving shoulder, she asked gently, "Mr. Flint, have you lost someone dear to you?"

His head came up in a flash, his eyes flooded and shining. "Jenny! That's who I lost!" His white head dropped again, shaking from side to side.

"Oh, Mr. Flint," said Tricia, "was Jenny a woman you loved?"

"That's it . . . my love she was," he cried through his twined fingers. "My little wifey!"

Rowan looked sympathetic. "Can you explain to

me why you don't believe someone has passed away unless you have seen them, Mr. Flint?"

The hermit's eyes shone wildly into space. "Because they told me she was dead once before, but she wasn't."

"No?"

"She didn't drown; she was stranded by the tide and couldn't come back till next day. They were wrong. But I suffered hours of agony just the same." His voice was strained and he seemed furious. "She shivered all night!"

"But she came back to you?" asked Tricia.

"High tide!" shrieked the hermit, leaping up like a grasshopper to race to the cave's opening.

Rowan and Tricia followed hastily to look down.

"He's right," said Rowan.

The water was rolling in closer with every wave thrown upon the shore. Hardly a yard of sand remained at the cliff's base.

"You have to go! No delay, no delay!" Septimus Flint flung his arms about, doing that jig again. "Don't forget your caps." He thrust them at the Duke and Tricia.

"But—!" said Tricia, looking longingly at the man's legal documents.

Rowan asked, "Can we get back in time if we run for it?"

"That's it, run because your lives depend on it— run!" He nearly pushed Tricia over the side after Rowan. "The hidden standers ers are dangerous when the water hides them. Don't fall down as you go. It's easier to crouch in some places. Be ye careful!"

"Thank you!" Tricia gasped out with a quick smile for him.

"You look like your mother," he marveled. "Come a-calling again. At low tide, early."

"We will!" she shouted back, watching the swirling foam surge over their path below. The whole world seemed to be moving and glittering with the pounding surf.

When they made it to the bottom of the precarious, narrow trail, Rowan snatched her hand. Into the water they splashed together, through the sucking backwash. She sometimes tripped on the uneven gullies, but they managed to keep each other upright. When Rowan pulled her up out of two feet of cold water to the grass-tufted bank, she said breathlessly, "What a strange and sweet little man he was! I say, that was worthwhile."

"I'm glad you agree. Shall we dance?" He sprang up and tried to imitate Septimus Flint's jig.

Tricia hugely enjoyed seeing the usually dignified Duke cutting such a caper, his boots sloshing water. She laughed without sparing him. Feeling exhilarated, she swung her arms up to the cloud-filled sky and twirled precariously on the grassy outcrop, filling her lungs with the fresh and salty smell of the sea.

Rowan caught her cap as it fell. He snatched her to him, and replaced its tweed brim above her graceful eyebrows. He slid his hand down from her elbow until he caressed her fingers. "Tricia, my sprite, we'd better go or the tide will swallow us up."

The glow in his face when he looked at her, his relaxed voice, and the free swing of his hand holding hers—all served to propel her joyfully up the steep slope.

CHAPTER 22

The Raid

The Duke grinned as he parted ways with sodden, disheveled Lady Tricia at the wooden door to The Fisherman's Arms. If she could sneak past her aunt and Lady Jewel and get herself cleaned up of water, sand, and horse hair, and then properly spiffed into a young lady before dinner, she was indeed something. She was indeed something anyway, he mused, running a finger thoughtfully over his lips. Those big eyes sparkling with life, and that exquisite, vulnerable mouth. He had given way to his loving desire when he kissed her. And, mercy!—how she kissed him back!

A clatter of feet sounded on the cobbles behind him. Before he could turn, someone grabbed his arms with power and wrenched them backward. Another strong hand clamped his jaws painfully.

Rowan riveted into action, fighting for control. He had nearly thrown the two assailants off when he saw a third man raise something above his head and come down with it. He tried to dodge, but two pairs of muscled arms held him fast. A crack on his head followed. Darkness flooded him.

* * *

Tricia had just gained the landing in The Fishermen's Arms when she heard, "Where on earth have you been?" Jewel emerged from her room in a high-waisted sprigged gown, goggling at her in disbelief.

"To see the old gentleman," she replied, self-consciously hiding one soaked boot behind the other.

"Dressed like *that?*" Jewel wrinkled her nose and grimaced horribly as she studied the hideous garment covering Tricia's upper half and the snug black breeches, sodden and stinking of wool.

"Jewel, he lives by the sea, and when the tide comes in, one has to be prepared to run through the water. I stayed too long, and that's what happened."

Lady Jewel remained absolutely horrified. "Did you dress this way when you lived here?" she demanded.

"No, never."

"I should hope not! I must reprove you here and now. Do not ever again put on male garments! If you are to be one of our family, you absolutely will not shame us so. Act like a lady from now on, *if* you know how!"

The door below burst open, and before Tricia could say a word more in her defense, burly men filled the tiny hall, moving, one up the stairs and the other into the lower rooms.

Tricia saw the sun-browned faces and sailor's caps. "No!" she screamed. "Alert! Alert! It's the *Press Gang!*"

"Come 'ere!" The sailor grabbed for her as she

ran up the stairs.

As Jewel squealed, Tricia ducked against a door, kicked the sailor's outstretched hands, and shouted, "Get away! You can't take me! I'm not a boy!"

As the man got hold of her wet boot, it came off. While Jewel shrieked with hysterics, Tricia fell against the upstairs door. It opened, and she looked up into the face of Lady Caro.

The man dove for Tricia.

Jewel, of all people, kicked him in the ribs, shouting, "Servants! Landlord! Throw this ruffian out! Let her go, I say!"

Lady Caro stepped over Tricia to slap her beaded reticule as hard as she could across the man's face with a resounding *whack!*

"Now see here, woman!" he growled, showing the whites of his eyes while rubbing his reddened face.

"That's *Lady*. I am a Marquis's daughter from London, and what you think you are doing accosting my niece, who is also a Peer's daughter, is beyond me! You shall answer for it in a court of law! What is your name?"

The man shrank back. His protruding eyes revolved from the grand Lady before him to the fair-haired waif she indicated as an Earl's daughter. He eked out, "Daughter? That's a daughter?"

Jewel cried, "Can't you tell the difference between a man and a woman, you revolting snipe?"

Tricia unfolded herself and stood up. "By what ungodly authority do you swoop into an innocent town to brutally kidnap men?" she screeched at him. "Why do you idiots think you can press them into the Navy against their will?" In furor, she shouted into his face, "It's against the law!"

The cowed man eyed her uneasily and muttered, "I have me orders," and thundered down the stairs.

Tricia raced after him. They would soon take someone else.

In the taproom, Mrs. Gunnthorpe, the landlady, stood wild-eyed behind a table, the object of three sailors' inquisition. She said to the men, "You get on your way now. There is no one here, as everyone goes out during the afternoons. To answer your question, my husband is seven-and-fifty, with rheumatics. You won't find him suitable for your Navy." She snatched up a rag and scrubbed vigorously at the table. Two of the sailors clattered out the door, but one was still down in the cellar, Mrs. Gunnthorpe told Tricia. "I don't hear the drum yet, so I better warn the Bay folk meself." She ran for a pot and spoon, opened her front window, and banged them together with a deafening clamor, and kept on banging hard and fast.

When the sailor emerged from below, he dashed for Mrs. Gunnthorpe and wrested the pot and spoon away, threw them across the room with an oath, and, with dire warnings lest she take them up again, left the inn with a shuddering slam of the door.

Tricia, with a hand on her heart, looked admiringly at her hostess. With her nose pressed to the window, Mrs. Gunnthorpe suddenly cried, "Who is *that* townie?" and pointed up New Road. "He's gonna get himself hooked for certain, the fool!"

It was ludicrous, for coming down the narrow street was a well-dressed young gentleman in high spirits, flicking his coach whip against his glove. Tricia could not believe her eyes. "It's Lord Bixby! I know him; he's from London!" Was he unaware of the state of siege in the town? She streaked out the door and heard a couple of sailors emerging from the post office as they spotted Lord Bixby.

He halted at sight of her running figure. "What the blazes? Dashed if it isn't Lady Tricia! What *are* you wearing?" he crowed, staring at her with an incredulous grin.

She grabbed him by the arm and said urgently, "Run with me, don't delay! Don't look around you and don't ask questions. Just duck in here, quick!"

Mrs. Gunnthorpe slammed the door behind them and slid the bolts. "Get him into the tunnel! I don't know if I can keep them strong men out; they might break me windows."

"What's going on?" queried Bixby in puzzlement. "I heard an awful banging commotion a minute ago."

Tricia asked, "Will they dare to touch him, being a Peer and all? Surely not!"

"They *shouldn't* dare," spat Mrs. Gunnthorpe, "but there's no tellin'. I will not be responsible for a Lord's scurvy treatment, so if you don't mind, Your Lordship, we'll hide you right and tight."

"Hide me from *what?*" insisted Bixby, still at sea.

"*The Press Gang!*" cried Tricia and Mrs. Gunnthorpe in unison.

They dashed down narrow brick steps into the damp, moldy-smelling region below the inn. "Where do you hide your men in cases like this?" Tricia asked Mrs. Gunnthorpe.

"In here." She yanked the bedclothes off a built-in bed, lifted the mattress, then the wood supports, and said, "Slide that board aside, Yer Lordship."

Bixby did so, asking, "Where on earth are you sending me?"

"Into the tunnel," said Mrs. Gunnthorpe.

"There's a tunnel down here? Where does it lead?" he asked as he lowered himself in his fine traveling suit into the hole under the bed.

"Under the town. Go through that door before you, and stay down there until we ring bells for you. Otherwise, you may find yourself on the high seas with a cat-o-nine-tails for a tutor. We don't want that, Lordship. God keep you."

Tricia, her heart racing, allowed herself but one glimpse of him reaching for an iron door lever in the wall below the cellar before she slid the panel back and helped her hostess square the bed supports back into place. They decided to grab piles of laundry to haul back up from the cellar to give them a reason for being down there. She threw some onto the bed as well.

A member of the Press Gang was coming through the window, with broken panes at his feet. He looked Tricia over, but she side-stepped adroitly. He rumbled down the cellar steps.

Mrs. Gunnthorpe hugged the laundry and looked harassed. Together, they went to the public room window, where they watched the sailors storming other doors.

Tricia prayed that Lord Bixby was safe, and that the bed and its secret would not be detected.

* * *

Rowan was jerked along as he half reclined against a ridge of hard wood. The sound of water splashing at intervals made it clear that rowing was the motion that lolled his head back with each pull.

While his eyes remained closed, his other senses flew awake. He leaned against a body that reeked of sweat. Feet intersected with his, and shifted slightly. The air was quite still, and smelled of salt water. He heard a fish jump. A pair of gulls went over quite low, squabbling over something.

Judging by the brilliant orange light through his eyelids, the sun was near setting. That meant he had been unconscious for quite some time. He had never had his lights put out before, and the feeling that he had lost time unnerved him. These men had been able to do with him as they pleased, even tie his wrists behind his back.

"There's another one," said the man next to him in an excited, predatory tone. He stiffened his muscles and prepared for action.

"Let's nail 'im," said the other, and stilled one oar to turn the boat.

Rowan remained limp, letting himself fall backward as his keeper lowered his set of oars into the water. The boat lurched forward and Rowan's head hit the side. It sounded worse than it felt, for he caught himself.

"What about this chap?" Rowan felt his boot kicked.

"He's banged 'is head. Should keep him out for awhile longer. We'll tie our two prizes together. Row fast now!"

Rowan felt water splashes land on his face. He cracked open his downward eye. The bay water shimmered with golden light from the dropping sun. Ominous on the horizon was a three-masted Navy ship.

So that was their destination.

How dared the Navy barge into peaceful English towns and knock out men and filch them for service? Rowan clenched his teeth. As a Peer of the Realm, he would tongue-lash that vessel's captain, then the Admiral, and report this in the House of Lords. That should wake them all up. That was, if he wasn't knocked into grueling servitude first. He would be freed only if he were believed. Dressed in the Bay Town fisherman's gansey, he had nothing on his person to prove who he was.

The boat made straight for a red coble with two men in it. They had their backs turned, hefting their fishing net.

Rowan squinted, trying to see. Wasn't that old Earnshaw and his son? Sure enough, it was the men he had met that morning. The Press Gang would hurt young Earnie and filch him for the Navy, and the boy wouldn't have the thread of a chance to get free. He and his father could never defend themselves against these brawny sailors.

As soon as a forceful pull at their oars made it plausible, Rowan lolled the other way. He sneaked a peek at where his boots rested. The dinghy was well weathered, the wood old. He would take quite a risk.

The two argued in hisses about how to position their boat to attack the coble and who should grab the lad.

While they were thus preoccupied, Rowan gave a

mighty kick of his heel to the inside of the dinghy. He heard a satisfying crack and a splinter.

It was enough. As water pulsed in, cries of stupefaction split the air. Before the men could drop their oars to grab him, Rowan heaved his head and shoulders to the side and dove into the sea.

The water was shockingly cold. It was frustrating to be constricted with his hands tied behind his back. He saw his air bubbles rise against the green water filtered with light. Bowing his head, he kicked himself away using the bottom of the stern as a springboard. Undulating his upper body, he kept well under the surface and headed in the direction of the Earnshaw coble.

From above, the tumult of the rocking boat he had just left, and the wild beating of the oars spread through the water, muffled and echoing. After kicking powerfully and holding his breath with a calm vengeance, he aimed toward the surface and hoped he was far enough from the sailors to prevent their hitting him on the head with their oars. His face broke free and his lungs expelled the little breath he had left. He filled his lungs with sweet air.

Old Earnshaw rowed steadily toward the sailors. They were yelling, begging for his help.

Rowan bellowed, "Earnshaw!"

The old man and his son turned astonished eyes on him after a boggled search over the water.

"'Tis Mr. Rowan!" Young Earnie said, pointing at him, utterly gob smacked.

Between the yells and flailing from the other boat, Rowan swam toward the Earnshaws, shouting each time his head came up, "Don't help them . . . they're Press Gang . . . they want Earnie!"

That produced results. Earnshaw swung his bows around and barked at Earnie to "hold t' ship still." He leaned over and motioned at Rowan to hurry, and he stuck out an oar.

Rowan shook his wet head as he approached, out of breath. "Can't grab it . . . my hands are tied."

"By gum! Three sheets to t' wind, t' tosspot Navy! Fetch tha knife, Earnie."

Rowan was grabbed at, inadvertently pushed lower, and reached for again by the old man. Rowan rose up again for a nose full of air and an unplanned gulp of briny water. He saw the coble tip perilously, old Earnshaw lean out to reach him, and his son lean mightily the other way to counterbalance the craft.

The Duke felt himself secured by the scruff of his collar and the top of his trousers. He was pulled up by degrees. He banged and scraped as the men heaved his weight over the edge, and he fell, coughing, onto a catch of fat salmon splayed over the bottom.

Old Earnshaw took at once to his oars, muttering furiously against the Navy, while he ordered his son to "Cut 'im looase."

Rowan turned himself to allow his wrist ropes to be severed. Between coughs, he raised his head to view their pursuers. "I thank you, Earnshaws, thank you indeed! Look at that boat sink."

They all took in the extraordinary sight. The top rim of the dinghy lowered to the surface of the water, the men in it still standing, waving their arms and an oar, and cursing ferociously. The boat went down, disappearing smoothly. Water glided after it to fill its shape. Splashes followed as the men took to their limbs.

"Which way they goin' t' swim?" jeered old Earnshaw, and burst into gulps of laughter.

"They're not comin' with us," said Earnie with a fierce yank of his oars. He and his father rowed fast toward shore in unison, experienced boatmen that they were.

From under white eyebrows, the old man eyed the shivering Rowan with solemn gratitude.

Ahead, the tumble of Bay Town was silhouetted by evening sun. Sides of the roofs were turned to wine, the occasional white wall dyed pink. People ran on The Dock and nearby Wayfoot, their voices raised to warn their neighbors in the fishing cobles streaming for shore.

Two other boats rowed away, one running up a square sail. It was ineffective in the calm, but he was obviously trying to cut out toward the north.

Rowan asked, "Are those two Press Gang boats?"

"That's them, all right," returned Earnie, yanking his dark cap lower and thrusting his oars into Rowan's tingling hands. He stood in the bow, cupped his hands over his mouth, and yelled, "Press Gang, ho! Headed for West Scar!"

The old man told his son that he wouldn't take the risk of heading them off. "So get going t' other way."

Earnie reluctantly agreed.

Explosions of gunfire came from shore.

Rowan could make out two strings of people running north along the bank as well as on the cliff, the women's white aprons over black dresses speeding past the old men and little boys. Puffs of smoke appeared, followed by the sound of each shot aimed at the Press Gang boats.

Then he heard a strange clatter which, after a minute or two, grew in volume: the sound of tin pans beaten by spoons in various parts of the town. Voices shouted angrily, and women derided and condemned the Navy men in no uncertain terms.

"We ain't goin' t' dock," declared Earnshaw.

"No, not with the Gang on the rampage. Where to, then?"

"T' south," growled the old man. The boat carved a crescent wake toward Ravenscar.

Rowan fingered his sore head and asked, "How long do you expect they'll be on the prowl?"

"Until they have their quota of able men, or till they're chased out o' town. Where we dockin', Father?"

As Earnshaw seemed to be scratching his head about that very problem, the Duke said, "You went out again today, Earnshaw. I thought you were ill."

"T'aint."

"I'm sure God made you such a tough old walrus for a reason, and I'll thank Him in my prayers for that tonight."

"Tha's gawmless as a suckin' duck! Tear tha top clothes off 'n put this on." Old Earnshaw thrust his dark blue gansey at his drenched passenger.

A light came into the Duke's eyes as he, with shivers running down his bare back, complied. "I declare," he said in a new voice. "I know a chap who might just take us in."

CHAPTER 23

Passions Under the Surface

When the sun had sunk over the moor and the clanging of pots and spoons had ceased for the moment, Rowan had still not turned up. Tricia was very worried.

With Lady Caro and Jewel, she walked into the Bay Hotel, where Jewel demanded to see the innkeeper. "Where is the Duke of Rowan?" she challenged without preamble.

"I have not seen His Grace since breakfast, Madam," responded Mr. Simby. His countenance took on a look of alarm.

Tricia, seeing this, queried, "Didn't he return about an hour ago?" That was when they had parted after their excursion to Mr. Flint's.

"No, Beany. I mean Tricia."

"Will you ask all of your servants if they have seen him, please?"

The landlord nervously excused himself to do so, suggesting the ladies wait upstairs in the public room.

Jewel's spoken fear rose to a frenzied pitch as she climbed the narrow staircase and said, "Do you suppose they *took* him?"

Lady Caro, tripping on her hem, recovered and

said, "You heard Mrs. Gunnthorpe's precaution for Lord Bixby. Apparently gentlemen and nobles *can* be snatched, especially if it isn't obvious who they are."

Tricia, perusing the shimmering bay from the window, woodenly stated, "That Navy has no mercy. One time a whaling ship was driven back to Whitby by weather. As soon as the crew disembarked, the Press Gang descended to nab them."

Jewel asked, "Were they taken?"

"Those men managed to ditch the Gang through the town and flee to the hills, but it isn't always like that. My brother's friend was taken in a raid when he walked his dog on the beach." Her tears welled up as she feared for the Duke.

Jewel's next outburst made her want to cover her ears. "That is the outside of enough! How can it go on? The *Duke of Rowan* is missing! Just wait until my father hears!" She strode to the wooden bar, calling sharply for servants.

When Mr. Simby came up the stairs to the taproom, Jewel demanded of him pen, ink, and paper. Upon acquiring these, she swooped to a table and began composing her indignant summons to her father.

"Well?" said Lady Caro, her voice a portent of menace. She eyed Mr. Simby's twiddling fingers.

Nervously, he said, "The Duke has not been seen since breakfast. But so much has happened that we can't keep track of everyone. I hope someone hid him." His voice lowered to a whisper. "We put half-a-dozen guests and the Duke's footmen into hiding; some through our cellar, two in the priest's hole, and one up the chimney. There they must remain until the Gang is gone."

He wanted to be off, Tricia could see that. It must be a terrible burden to know that a Duke of Great Britain, staying at his inn, remained unaccounted for at a time like this.

"Perhaps," she proposed to Lady Caro and Jewel, "I should go into the tunnel myself and find out who is there. It leads from so many houses and inns that when smugglers bring in goods, a barrel or a bale of silk passes from The Dock at the end of King's Beck, and makes it all the way to the top of the town without ever seeing daylight."

The ladies' eyes grew wide with incredulity. "Is that where they hide everyone?" asked Jewel. "In a tunnel? Hurry and go down there, Tricia. Find the Duke immediately. Tell him I've been waiting all day!"

"I will try, but there are many hiding places in this town. Some houses have false floors. I know men who have lain below them for hours with only mice for company while the Press Gang trod over the top of them. Mrs. Willoughby hid her husband in a compartment under her daughter's bed years ago, with her girl pretending to be asleep in it with smallpox. That's how Lord Bixby went into the tunnel, through a similar bed."

"You mean Rowan could be lying somewhere with *mice* running over him?" squeaked Jewel.

* * *

At The Fisherman's Arms, Tricia had to pound on the old wooden door with its whorled thick glass window many times. When no one came, she rattled the letter box handle and pounded the round ring handle. "It's Tricia!" she yelled, trying to make her voice carry through the stout nailed door with its ancient fleur de lis ironwork. As she waited, she noticed the date above the door: 1680.

Finally, Mrs. Gunnthorpe realized it was Tricia pounding for entrance, and let her in. Alas, she had not seen the Duke of Rowan. At that devastating news, Tricia declared that she was going down into the tunnel. Jewel, arriving with Lady Caro at her heels, urged her on.

Tricia teasingly asked Jewel to join her, but her cousin desisted, saying, "I wouldn't know what to do or where to go. You are certainly acquainted with this town, I can see that."

Lady Caro said, "This plan of yours is commendable, Tricia, but first find Lord Bixby down there and have him help you search. Do not try any heroics on your own." She gave Tricia a stern look, and then a hug.

Tricia enlisted Mrs. Gunnthorpe's help in procuring an old black gown suitable for traversing the stream inside the tunnel, for this was no time to don male garments.

When Tricia lowered herself through the bed, Mrs. Gunnthorpe ordered her maid, Meg, to follow with two lanterns, one for each of them.

As soon as she pulled the iron lever, the salty sea air wafted in. The girls stepped over the threshold and into a passageway hollowed out of the earth. They bent down and moved hesitantly toward the intersection with the tunnel. Tricia vowed to ignore anything small and living, whereas Meg gasped and started. "Don't peer into corners, Meg, and don't step into the water, you see?" They had come upon King's Beck flowing under the town to the sea. They tiptoed, crouching, along the wall, trying to avoid getting their boots and clogs wet. Past the trickling sound of water, they heard echoed voices and footsteps. "Shh! Listen!" Tricia whispered.

Something creaked shut and the voices ceased, but footsteps grew louder. Around the bend, a man came into sight. The light of Tricia's lantern illuminated the furrowed face, thin mouth, and piercing black eyes of Lord Kilver!

Her heart leaped into her throat, and she grabbed Meg's arm to protect her.

"O-ho! Who have we here?" Kilver called, his nasal voice echoing. "Girls out for an evening's airing?" He cackled and advanced upon them. "Well, well, if it isn't Tricia! Is this your fashionable promenade these days?" He hiccupped with mirth.

"Lord Kilver! What are you doing here?"

"Odd that you should ask," he drawled. "Hiding from the Press Gang, of course."

"Why should you have to hide? You're not young or able-bodied."

She had said the wrong thing. He glared strangely at her. She feared that glittering look, and her mouth went dry. Her heart raced and she wanted to back away as Meg was doing.

"I am looking for someone," she said firmly. "Step aside so I can continue."

"Not before I've assured you of my devotion, Creature," he said, darting out his hand and grasping her by the neck. She knew he aimed to smear his lips on hers, so she did what she had to: she jabbed the sharp corner of her lantern where it would do the most damage.

Kilver's eyes popped wide. He clutched at himself, doubled over, and was eerily silent in his grimaces of pain.

Tricia grabbed her chance and gave him a hard shove. It landed him in the beck with a marvelous splash. Glad it had worked, but terrified at what would happen to her now, she dashed on, pulling Meg.

"He's sure to come after you now, Your Ladyship!" wailed Meg. "Oh God, help us!"

Sure enough, Kilver was grimacing but trying to rise from the water, his eyes full of murder.

* * *

"A light!" said Rowan. He pointed at a glimmer high on the cliffs of Ravenscar.

"We canna get in there," returned young Earnie. He paused in his rowing while he and his father argued about the shoreline.

Rowan continued to keep the cavern in view. A dark shape passed before the light. He cupped his hands to his mouth and bellowed across the water, *"Mis-ter Flint!"*

The Earnshaws were mightily startled. There was a sickening crack, and the coble jerked sideways.

"We've hit!" cried Earnie, his voice high in desperation. He and his father maneuvered the tiller and oars with great energy, but to no avail, for the unseen rock had wrecked the coble.

"Ah'll be swimmin' fer it now," old Earnshaw

announced as if it were up to the others to do as they pleased. Rowan watched him lower his bulk over the side into the water, take his two oars and his rolled-up sails, and push them floating before him as he kicked.

Rowan and Earnie stared after him. They glanced at each other as the pulsing water swirled in around their feet.

"You're next," said Rowan.

"'Tis enough to mek tha brains rattle," Earnie muttered in fair imitation of his sire. He rolled over the side into the surf. He, also, found it expedient to save his oars, and guided them before him. It was probably a good precaution against other hidden rocks. "It'll make you heavier, but leave your boots on, Mr. Rowan," he called back. "And yell again in your forty-acre voice."

Rowan let loose another bellow. *"Mis-ter Flint! Men overboard!"*

* * *

As Lord Kilver gave chase after Tricia through the murky tunnel, her glance back showed that he was grasping at Meg. The maid struggled and cried out.

Tricia screamed, "Someone! Ladies need your help! Over here! Hurry!"

As she ran on, searching for the men who were supposed to be hidden, she heard a rapid footfall from around the bend ahead.

"Who needs help?" came a familiar voice.

"Lord Bixby! Oh, thank God!" She fell headlong into his arms. She pointed back and cried, "He's got Meg!"

"Lady Tricia! Who's got Meg, and who's Meg?"

When she told him, rage leaped into his eyes. "That swine! He's plaguing you *again?*" He thrust Tricia behind him and ran, his feet splashing and echoing. "Look here, Kilver, accosting women will cause you to repent! You have me to deal with, here and now." He punched the scowling Kilver hard on the jaw and wrenched the maid away.

Tricia held her breath when Bixby took his coach whip out of his waistcoat and snapped it in the air with a crack. He moved fast, which surprised her, but Kilver was mean and wily, grabbing at the end of the whip.

Bixby flicked it away and slashed him around the chest. At each crack, Tricia winced but rejoiced that she had not had to endure Kilver down here without a man to save her.

Meg came creeping out of the shadows to Tricia's side, trembling.

Tricia asked her privately, "Does Lord Kilver smuggle goods through this beck?"

Meg's small eyes went wary. "Oh, My Lady, I couldn't never say."

"You'd be thrown into prison, is that right? Just tell *me*."

"No, My Lady, I canna tell you." She looked petrified.

How frustrating! No one of the lower orders ever dared oppose a Peer no matter what he did.

Lord Bixby had driven Kilver so close to the beck that with the next whip lash, he toppled backward. With the splash, water went everywhere, wetting Tricia's front.

"Let's get out!" said Bixby, breathing hard.

Tricia heard Kilver's black oaths as he sloshed furiously in the beck.

"Hurry, Meg, slam that door and lock it!" she cried when the three of them had huddled through it. They knocked on the wood above and waited until Mrs. Gunnthorpe bathed them with light when she slid aside the panel.

Tricia told the woman, "We cannot stay down there! Kilver is after us, and he is raging!" The worried woman hurriedly moved aside the bedclothes.

"How can I ever thank you?" Tricia exclaimed to Lord Bixby. She and Meg breathlessly hoisted themselves up with his help through the bed frame. Tricia collapsed against the wall, trying to recover and calm her thumping heart.

"Marry me!" replied Bixby with feeling.

Tricia looked down on him emerging with a cobweb stuck from the crown of his blond hair to his ear, and giggled. She removed the web, stepped aside so he could heave himself up, and remembered why she had gone into the tunnel in the first place. She panicked. "Tell me, Lord Bixby, did you see Rowan down there?"

"Rowan? No. Does he make that cramped avenue a haunt of his?"

"He's missing! We haven't found him on street level so I hoped someone had sent him down there."

"There have come numerous men catapulting into those nether regions—what a slimy place! –but not Rowan. You think this is serious?"

"Deadly serious!"

"Then I say we go above and try from there. But, when things die down, he should come out of hiding, wherever he is."

"I am praying so," said Tricia, thinking uneasily of Kilver and his diabolical mind.

CHAPTER 24

Where There's a Will

The water was crippling; so cold that Rowan's lungs felt constricted. As he stabbed his arms forward one after the other and kicked with all his might, his boots and clothes were heavy and threatened to drag him under. He prayed they would all make it ashore on the waves, for it was a long swim.

The wind touched frigid fingers to the top of his head, so he dove and swam deeper. When he surfaced again, he saw the old man collapsed over his oars, safely on shore. He was a sturdy one, but he had been ill only yesterday.

Earnie, flailing his free arm, turned to swim on his back. He shouted, "Beware those standers, Rowan!"

It was just then that a wave lifted Rowan and carried him, rapidly gliding toward the blessed shore. Turning on his back, he was thankful to ride its force, for he was tiring fast from the debilitating North Sea. The wave carried him delightfully until it rammed him against an underwater obstacle so hard that he yowled. The base of his back crunched the top of a sharp rock, almost knocking the wind out of him.

Thereafter, a numbing sensation afflicted his lower extremities. He tried to kick. The flashes of pain at the base of his spine gave him agony. He forced his arms to pull harder. He revolved and sank under water as the surf pushed him past the huge black stander Earnie had warned him about. He kept his eyes wide to see if more such perfidious rocks lay in wait for him.

The sea was full of light from the setting sun. Surges of minute bubbles, ropes of seaweed, and a chunk of driftwood floated before his stunned eyes. It was quite frightening. What had happened to him?

The water became shallow. When he struck his boot on bottom sand, he tried to stand up. *The pain.*

He fell forward. He resigned himself to pulling with his arms through the wet sand the last few yards. Lacy scallops of surf tried to spit him up onto smooth sand, but he was too heavy. Exhausted, he lodged on his chest as the sparkling foam raced by.

"Mr. Rowan!" Young Earnie staggered toward him after throwing his oars with a clatter toward the cliff wall. "Can you get up?"

He tried, but to his dismay, his lower limbs were so afflicted that he could only drag them along by digging his elbows into the backwash, which gave him but an escaping foundation. "Like a house upon the sand," he said aloud. He shook his head, groaning.

Earnie and his father looked very concerned. They took Rowan between them and hauled him higher up the beach. Old Earnshaw, shading his eyes, looked seaward and cursed himself for a fuzzock, letting his coble go straight for a stander. Although Earnie and Rowan offered words of comfort, the old man shook his head in self-incrimination.

Rowan lay spent, his cheek on dry, silken sand. It looked like spice with dots of slate and flecks of diamonds sparkling in and out of focus. He sighed out his thanks to God and embraced the earth.

"We got to git t' shelter," Earnshaw declared. He pulled off his knee-high fisher boots and poured the water out.

"Here comes someone!" said Earnie suddenly as he drew off Rowan's water-logged boots.

The movement to his hips made Rowan groan. He raised his head and saw his blue gansey on the skipping form of Septimus Flint. "The very man I hope will take us in."

"Not him!" Earnshaw turned and fixed Rowan with a pop-eyed stare.

"Why not?"

He spat, "E's as daft as a skuttle!"

"So? If he helps us warm up, will you not be grateful?"

"There's nowt so queer as t' likes o' him," growled Earnshaw, running a hand through his dripping white hair. They had all lost their caps.

The hermit was soon upon them, his round eyes goggling as he halted his sprint just short of Rowan. "It's *you*, Your Grace? Aye-yi!"

Ignoring Earnshaw's slack jaw of surprise at the ducal title, Rowan smiled up at the little man from his prone position. "Mr. Flint, how provident that you spied us! Meet Mr. Earnshaw of Bay Town and his son, Earnie. It's their coble that cracked up and spewed us out."

"A wreck!" cried Septimus Flint. "I saw it through my spyglass. Survivors, ho! Praise to our Lord!"

Rowan explained with gratitude in his voice, "The Earnshaws saved me from the Press Gang. Then this misfortune overtook their boat. We are avoiding the Bay because the Gang still lurks."

"Aye! Avoid it! Come, Your Grace; you and these Mr. Earnshaws. I shall harbor the survivors!" He did a delighted jig, kicking sand into Rowan's hair.

Old Earnshaw, stooping to heft Rowan under the arms, muttered, "Silly gobbins!"

"But a Good Samaritan, isn't he?" whispered Rowan. He managed to heave himself over, preparatory to rising. "Thank you, Mr. Flint. It would be pure heaven to rid ourselves of these chilling wet garments." When he stood propped between father and son, he buckled at the knees. Pain convulsed his lower half.

The hermit danced around him, crying, "Your trousers are torn and you are bleeding at the back!"

"Well, use tha brain-box," barked Earnshaw. "Doan't jubber there, leaad t' way!"

Septimus Flint scooped up Earnshaw's and Rowan's boots and scampered ahead, looking back only when he had traversed the cliff path beneath his abode to the turning-back point. "Not dead, any of you!" he cried in triumph, lifting an arm to the sky.

Earnshaw eyed Rowan fiercely and said, "Fond as a turnip!"

With great effort, Rowan pulled himself up the

narrow path by his forearms and elbows. What was wrong with his legs? Alarm quivered in his mind. He prayed to God to please let the damage be but temporary. Once in the cave, he tried to stand, but could not maintain it for long.

Nevertheless, Mr. Flint cried joyfully, "Look at His Grace, standing by himself as before."

"Jest what do you mean by 'Is Greace'?" demanded Earnshaw, bewildered by that as well as by the cavern in which they stood, high above the glimmering, twilit sea.

Rowan sank to the floor and reluctantly said, "I hope it won't dampen our friendship, Earnshaw and Earnie, but I must confess that my full name is Lucas Beaufort, Duke of Rowan."

* * *

It stunned the fishermen very much. They sat or reclined near the Duke, who was wrapped about the hips in a wool blanket. Earnshaw cast yet another wary glance at His Grace. Apparently the fisherman could not reconcile himself to the fact that a Peer of the highest rank had hobnobbed with the likes of him and his son. Because of his stupidity, this Duke was now injured. He voiced his deep regret more than once, and kept shaking his head.

Mr. Flint had cheerfully helped them peel off their wet clothes and provided towels, but Earnshaw the elder had not allowed the hermit to tend to Rowan's gashes. He had shouldered the little man out and demanded what he needed, down to the clean rags that he wrapped snugly over the Duke's middle.

Rowan had been given back the use of the blue gansey he had given Mr. Flint when they first met. The wool prickled gently against his skin and warmed him. The breeches he now wore were Mr. Flint's. He ripped them apart enough to get them on him. When Rowan had protested the destruction of the garment, Flint insisted that he could easily sew them up again.

The men's faces glowed in the mellow light of six candles set in a crystal candelabrum. Earnie the younger huddled in a much-too-short coat of the solicitor's, wearing matching knee breeches of black silk. He drank tea from a flowered porcelain cup which Mr. Flint said was his wedding china.

Old Earnshaw was so bulky that nothing the hermit had would fit him. Earnshaw insisted a blanket would do until his clothes dried by the fire on the outside ledge. His white, muscled arms and brown hands stuck out of a red and green tartan blanket.

Septimus Flint was braiding onion stems when Rowan asked, "Do you mind putting us up for the night, Mr. Flint?"

"Not a-tall. Was going to urge you to stay if you made a move otherwise, Your Grace."

Earnshaw cleared his throat in a rumble. "If tha gives me tha second lantern, Ah'll be off."

Septimus Flint said. "Stay please, Mr. Earnshaw. I advise that it is too risky to go back now at high tide. Do not forget the Press Gang! They want men!"

"Press Gang doan't want me."

Such argument went on until Rowan halted them

by saying he would need Earnshaw's help as well as Earnie's in the morning, or how would he ever get back to town? He could hardly move. That settled the matter.

Earnshaw accepted Mr. Flint's tentative offer of a little whisky.

Their gleeful host modestly received Rowan's high praise for the repast he had spread before them. They feasted on fried crabs, roast potatoes, bread, tea, and huge, soft blackberries he had picked on the moor above the cave.

Covering a yawn, Rowan asked, "May I sleep in that back room, there, Mr. Flint?"

The white head nodded enthusiastically. He suggested the fishermen lie in the middle of the cave. With Earnie's help, the solicitor whisked away the dinner things and lifted the plank table out of the way.

"May I have one of those candles?" asked Rowan.

When he was settled with the flame throwing light and shadows on the dozens of rolled documents in their cubbyholes in the wall, Rowan waited. He felt impatient for the others to settle down to sleep.

Tiptoeing near, Mr. Flint's eyes glistened with pleasure as he looked down on the Duke. "I must say you look content. Not a very ducal bed, is it? Hee hee! I am sorry."

"It's top-o-the-trees right now, Mr. Flint. I am exceedingly grateful to you."

"Aw, 'tis naught."

"Where will you sleep, Mr. Flint?"

"I have my bunk in the hollow." He motioned toward the main room. "It has a secret entrance. I couldn't put you in there; the bed's too small for your great length, hee, hee! I've been looking with my spyglass over the sea, and there are no boats. The Navy ship pulled up anchor and sailed south, but they might have men moving by land right over us. I will check on you in the night, Your Grace."

"Please don't. Get your sleep. We'll all be right and tight, thanks to you."

Rowan sat up and watched the skinny leg disappear behind the trunk of dishes. Rowan looked at the intriguing rolls of paper and took one down. It proved to be an old game conviction. He thrust it back and removed another, a sale of land in Raw. He scanned records of payment, deeds to properties, and law suits.

The swishing, crashing sound of the pounding tide filled the cavern as he read on. It was surprising how protected he felt. He knew there were birds also sheltering in the cave entrance, for he had heard their wings beat as they swooped to perch there. They must be friends of Septimus Flint's.

At last, with sore eyes and aching back from his side position, the Duke unrolled a document that said, *Last Will and Testament of Lord Wyndhurst, Leigh Claremont, also known as Leigh Ravenscar.* It was dated 30th January 1810.

Excitedly, Rowan read that the Earl's son, referred to as David (Ravenscar) Claremont, was heir apparent, following his father, to the title of Lord Wyndhurst, *if he wishes to claim it of his Highcourt House, Cavendish Square relations in London . . . All my inheritance, including my merchant ship,*

The White Dove, shall be his.

To Patricia (Ravenscar) Claremont, his daughter, he left a dowry of four thousand pounds and a trust of an equal sum to be paid her quarterly every year of her life. There were generous provisions for his wife, Lucretia, and at the end, a rider that made it clear that, if sole survivor, David or Patricia Claremont would inherit each other's portions. There was no statement which named a guardian.

Rowan lay on his back, exulting. "Thank you, God!" he whispered.

He heard an accidental strum of the lute strings as if someone bumped the instrument. He blew out the flame. He shoved the Will under his blanket and lay still.

He heard Septimus Flint pad toward him with sounds of sniffing. "Your Grace? Did you just snuff your candle?"

"That I did, Mr. Flint."

"Why couldn't you sleep? Are you in terrible pain?"

Rowan's interest in the Will had overridden his pain. He moved his legs and there it was. "It's bearable when I lie still."

"Mm-hm." The hermit sounded skeptical. "I could give you some whisky."

"No, thanks, I don't drink whiskey. Mr. Flint, I need to confess that I have been looking over some of your legal documents, with great interest, I might add."

"Aye-yi! Ye have?"

"Yes, and I found the Claremont Will. Mr. Flint, the Earl of Wyndhurst died. He and his Countess drowned in a coble which was rowing them to his ship, *The White Dove.* I know you will find that painful, but it's the truth. This happened eight months ago. Now their daughter, Patricia, needs help to claim her inheritance. You, Mr. Flint, are the only one who can help her."

"I am? But how can I help the girl?"

Rowan was grateful that he seemed lucid. "You can read her this Will. It will change her life for the good."

Mr. Flint sat down close in the dark. Rowan could just make out the outline of his white hair. "Aye-yi, they are really dead?"

"Yes. Leigh and Lucretia Ravenscar, as they were known in Robin Hood's Bay, are both gone to their eternal reward, and so is their son, David. He was killed in the Peninsular war against Napoleon. Only Tricia is left. She really needs you, Mr. Flint."

The hermit said nothing for some time. He sighed deeply. "Why must everyone die?"

"It is to be hoped that those we love are beginning a better life, never to die again," said Rowan.

"Yes, that's it. Jenny is waiting for me on that beautiful shore. The Countess is waiting to see me, too."

"I am sure she is. Will you help her daughter, Mr. Flint?"

"Where is she? Is she a wee lass without a home? Could I keep her here?"

Rowan smiled. "She is no longer a wee lass, but grew into a young lady while you weren't looking. She even came to visit you the other day. Do you recall?"

"No!"

"The lad with me, whom you said looked like his mother? That was Tricia, Mr. Flint."

"Aye-yi! A young lady? I thought she was David. What a muddle! Why would she not dress as a female?"

"She has had to hide her identity from Lord Kilver."

"Lord Kilver!" This he squawked so loudly that old Earnshaw mumbled and shifted in the other room.

"Shh," admonished the Duke. "Kilver *claims* to be her legal guardian."

An outraged sound huffed from the solicitor. "He most certainly is not!"

"Bravo! That is precisely why we need you. With this Will, you can prove that he is in error, and that the Marquis of Wyndhurst, Leigh's brother, is her nearest male relative."

"Do you know what Lord Kilver would do to me if I were to suggest that he has done something amiss?" rasped Mr. Flint.

"I know. He would try to find a way to put you in gaol at the very least. But I am not asking you to challenge him. I will do that. All I ask is for you to read this Will before Tricia and some witnesses."

"That is a gratifying prospect, Your Grace," declared Septimus Flint. "Yes, yes, we must save the little lass from Kilver. That would make the Countess happy." He leaped up and scurried away.

CHAPTER 25

The Duke's Sacrifice

Tricia held her breath and read with Lady Caro the note which had just arrived in their parlor at The Fisherman's Arms.

> *My Dear Lady Caro,*
> *I just returned to my hotel and have something of import to show you. I hope it will be convenient for all of you to call on me at three o'clock today.*
> *Your humble servant,*
> *Rowan*

"My darling is safe!" screeched Jewel. She had poked her head between theirs to read.

Though her heart swelled with relief, Tricia frowned and queried, "Why did he send a message? It would have been but a few steps to come here in person. Aunt, is it not a bit strange?"

"Rather disquieting, to say the least. Where could he have been last night?"

Lord Bixby walked in as the ladies set aside their luncheon napkins.

Jewel cried, "Tell us instantly how he is!"

Their visitor looked rather pulled. "He's . . . ah,

in quite good spirits, which is astounding under the circumstances. But I came to ask Lady Tricia something." He looked beseechingly at her and said, "Who is the best surgeon in town?"

"Surgeon!" the ladies cried out.

Lady Caro demanded, "What happened to the Duke last night?"

Bixby looked troubled as he twisted his hat in his hand. "I wasn't supposed to tell you, but I might as well. He was grabbed by the Press Gang."

"*No!*" cried Tricia, and Lady Caro clutched her.

Jewel looked aghast and shrieked, "How could they grab *him?* He's a Duke!"

Tricia motioned that they all sit, for Bixby looked white and needed a chair. "He was attacked without warning, knocked out—"

"Rowan knocked *unconscious?*" Tricia put her hand on her heart and felt like she was choking. He had come here for her sake.

"But he kicked a hole in the boat they rowed him in," Bixby went on eagerly, "and that made the two Press Gang men sink. Good for Rowan, eh? He was taken up by some fishermen but, as they avoided the Bay, they wrecked their coble on a stander south of here, and Rowan and those men had to swim for it. That's when Rowan crashed into an unseen stander! He was very lucky to make it to shore with such an injury to his back."

The ladies gasped, their eyes pinned in horror and consternation on Bixby.

"A hermit, he says, led them to his cave high in the cliff side. There they recuperated for the night."

"Oh, in the *cave,*" Tricia sighed. "At least he

wasn't with mice. Is he any better now?"

Bixby, despite his attempt to sound casual, looked grave. "He . . . ah, has to recuperate. Can you come this afternoon?"

The ladies assented as one, but continued in their exclamations, pelting him with questions.

Tricia consulted with Mrs. Gunnthorpe, and wrote the name and direction of the top surgeon in town, a Mr. Newell. This she gave to Lord Bixby, who handed it outside to Stefan, the footman who was waiting to run and summon the man.

"Let Rowan answer the rest of your queries, ladies, please," Lord Bixby said to the other women. "I wasn't there. I was holed up in the tunnel, damp but safe as nun's beads. Unless you count my altercation with Kilver," he added, glancing at Tricia.

She moved toward him and exclaimed from the heart, "Lord Bixby, you were a wonder in the tunnel! A true lifesaver! I owe you a huge debt of gratitude, so thank you, thank you, thank you!" She squeezed his arm.

He smiled and looked gratified. "My absolute pleasure, Lady Tricia." After a moment, he said, "Rowan and I are wondering what he was doing down there."

* * *

"This is one of your new gowns from Madame Yvonne in London that you haven't worn yet," said Sarah as she held the lovely confection up for Tricia to duck into. Tricia was trying to visualize all that Bixby had recounted about Rowan's ordeal, and mechanically put her head and arms into a puff-sleeved pink cotton gown with lacy scallops at the bodice and hem.

How revolting that the Duke had endured such ignominious treatment; that he had been a victim of that chilling, barbarous practice. She would lecture Rowan that he should always wear his coronet, mantle, and surcoat if the trumpeters were not hailing "Duke, Duke!" before him wherever he went. She could just imagine his expression if she said that.

When she and the other ladies filed toward the Bay Hotel at five minutes to three, a stiff wind blew across the water and wavelets surged onto the bricks of Wayfoot.

"Lady Tricia!" cried a feminine voice from King Street. She saw Lady Kilver with her maid, Lizzie, running ahead doing the hailing.

Tricia motioned Lady Jewel on into the hotel, for her cousin did not like to stand with a wind ruining her coiffure. Tricia did not want her to hear whatever Lady Kilver might say anyway. Lady Caro hung back with Tricia and shut the black and white door on Jewel. "Be careful what you say, Tricia," she advised. "I don't trust that Kilver woman."

It seemed odd to see Lady Kilver bundled in a brown pelisse and a tightly tied green bonnet, actually out of the house. "Good afternoon, Lady Tricia," she said. "I need to talk with you. You alone."

Lady Caro gave Tricia a reminding look, nodded pleasantly at Lady Kilver, and went into the hotel.

Tricia led Lady Kilver to a sofa in Mr. Simby's

parlor, which was hung with watercolor paintings of Bay Town and the sea. Lady Kilver twiddled her knitted reticule strings. Finally she pulled them tight and looked up, a light of determination in her squinted eyes. "I know something, Tricia, and I am afraid of it."

Tricia knew that there could be much to fear, living with Kilver. "Do you want to tell me?" she asked, though she did not want to hear about him.

"Yes. It's about your friend, the Duke of Rowan."

"What about him?" Tricia's heart began to thump hard.

"Pultney wants him gone."

Tricia gripped her chair. "Gone from here? Or gone from life?"

"Away from here, that's certain." Lady Kilver's deep-set eyes darted from side to side as she considered the other possibility.

"Why? Because the Duke is helping me search for my father's Will?"

"That's one reason. And he doesn't want to lose you."

Tricia shuddered. "My money, you mean, and my ship?"

"That's it, Tricia."

"Does he dread that the Duke will find proof that he's taking and using what isn't his?"

"Yes. But there's worse." Lady Kilver moved closer to Tricia on the sofa and darted a glance at the closed door. "Pultney looked pleased with himself last night," she whispered significantly. "When I heard that a Duke had gone missing from this hotel, I knew that he put the Press Gang up to it."

Tricia could hardly believe it. "*He* put them up to it?"

"It sounds fantastic, I know, but only yesterday, he said he heard the Press Gang had made a sweep of Whitby and were on their way north. Now why would they come south just hours after that?"

Tricia's pulses beat in her temples. "Yes, he was on his way to Whitby yesterday; to buy a horse, he said."

"He bought no horse."

"You really think he did such a despicable thing? Do you think he told them to nab the Duke of Rowan?" Tricia was on her feet, her eyes so outraged that Lady Kilver shrank back.

Though she looked like a scared rabbit, she said, "I have proof, Tricia. I found the drum in our cellar."

"What drum?"

"The one they always bang when they sight the Press Gang! Pultney hid it in advance, don't you see? That is why it took so long to get rid of those horrible Navy men. Oh, do not say a word to anyone! But I feel it imperative that you know so you can watch over His Grace." She fumbled for her handkerchief and wiped her eyes which had the tears of terror sparkling in them. "I must go now, before I'm missed." She heaved herself to her feet.

Tricia grasped her by her stout arms. "Thank you, Aunt, for telling me. What ghastly news, but I am glad I know it. The Duke is safely back now, thanks to God, but I know nothing about how he is. Would you like to see him?"

"I cannot! Lord Kilver might hear of it."

"Where is he?"

"Off across the moors on horseback toward Fylingstone, he said."

"Do you know why?"

"No. He did say that he would be back to show you your house late this afternoon. He acted like he just heard the Duke was missing. Be careful, Tricia. I cannot bear to think of his forcing you under our roof again. Cling to those Claremonts."

Her aunt did understand. Tricia embraced her.

With Lady Kilver gone, Tricia asked for directions and climbed the stairs shakily to the Duke's room on the second floor. She knocked, and it swung open, for it was ajar.

It was a small whitewashed room with two corner windows. Lord Bixby sat in a chair, his back to the window overlooking the bay. He jumped to his feet. Facing him, sitting up in bed, was Rowan. His handsome face was so dear that Tricia felt like throwing herself upon him and hugging him in glad relief that he was alive. Instead, she went to him, pressed his hand, and asked, "Your Grace, what is this all about?" She gestured over his covered legs.

"Pardon me, Lady Tricia, if I don't rise. It feels better to sit like a statue. This is but the result of Mr. Earnshaw's poor coble crashing against a wicked rock, and my ignorance in not preparing myself for hidden standers." He looked at her regretfully from under his eyebrows.

"It was not Rowan's fault," stipulated Jewel, rising from her chair.

"Oh, but it was," he contradicted her. "Young Earnie shouted me a warning the moment before."

Tricia told him gravely, "You're lucky, Your Grace, to have slipped through the Press Gang's grip."

"That I am." They locked eyes solemnly. She bit her lip as tears formed in her eyes. His gaze turned quizzical.

She moved to the window to turn her face away to the view of the water.

Jewel declared staunchly, "They never could have held him."

Tricia felt compelled to refute such a naïve statement, but the Duke said, "They held me for several hours, unconscious and bound. If the good Lord hadn't seen fit to waken me when He did, it would have been mighty difficult to prove who I was on board that Navy ship. I was dressed like a local."

Bixby nodded. "And I thank God that Tricia had the sense to send me down into the tunnel."

"That was very wise," said the Duke, smiling at Tricia. "Bix, I am sorry now that I sent you that summons from London, and landed you in this."

"I'm not sorry!" Tricia objected. "Lord Bixby fought Kilver on my behalf!" She explained how Lord Bixby had finished her fight with his coach whip.

Rowan looked rigid with disbelief. "Tricia! You met him alone down in that tunnel?"

"A maid and I, yes, but Lord Bixby came running after we screamed for help."

The Duke passed a hand over his forehead with worry, and then brightened. "Good going, Bix!"

Bixby said modestly, "After she had given him *what for* and made him land helpless in the water,

Rowan. I just took over. What a courageous lady our Tricia is!"

Mr. Simby knocked and popped his head in, saying, "Your Grace, Mr. Septimus Flint has arrived, and we stabled your horse. Your footmen will wait outside to escort the man back home."

"Wonderful. Ah, Mr. Flint, I've been expecting you." The Duke put out his hand with a warm welcome.

Lady Caro squeezed into the small room and took the other chair, hastily vacated for her by Bixby. The little man caused eyes to widen around the room. He was dressed in a black coat and antiquated breeches shiny with age, but Tricia thought he looked endearingly dapper. Swinging the bent top hat off his bald crown, he bowed to the Duke in the bed, his white beard touching his shins.

She heard Lady Caro say low to Jewel, "He's Tricia's gentleman friend. Do you think he's too old for me?"

Tricia heard Jewel titter and drawl, "Born in the year of our Lord only knows when."

Tricia frowned at her.

Mr. Flint held a long wooden tube protectively to his chest. He rolled his eyes over the other occupants of the room.

The Duke made introductions to Lady Caro, Lady Jewel, and Lord Bixby. "And here is the person you have come to see: Lady Tricia, the wee lass you said you remember."

She shook his hand warmly. "I am delighted to see you again, Mr. Flint."

"Oh no, I am the one in delight. Aye-yi! You

look like her." His eyes twinkled. "Do you dance?"

Smiling, Tricia replied, "Yes. I even waltz."

Septimus Flint turned to the Duke. "But you cannot dance, Your Grace. Not now, and maybe not ever, eh?" He shook his head in solemn regret.

Jewel slowly clutched the arms of her chair. Her face went white. "Why can he not dance, now or ever?"

The little old man turned to look at her. "Because His Grace's spine is hurt, and his hips and legs troubled him all night."

"But they will soon be well!" cried Jewel, pinning a challenging look on the Duke.

Rowan cleared his throat. "Lady Jewel, please, not to worry. The pain seems to be gone as I sit still. It's better to feel nothing than the pain in most cases, is it not?   I trust I will be feeling sensations again before long." He gestured over his lower half.

Lady Jewel queried in horror, "You can't feel *anything*, Rowan?"

"Not at the moment." Rowan adjusted his sitting position and shook his head. "Do take a seat, Mr. Flint. Bix, if you will move my legs over, he can sit on the end of this bed and spread out his paper. You have something important to read to us, Mr. Flint."

Tricia was so concerned about Rowan's having suffered great pain, and now loss of feeling, that it took her some time to realize what Septimus Flint was reading. She heard her father's name. Bye and bye, she could scarcely believe what the little man was saying. Obviously, this was a different will than the one Kilver had foisted upon her.

She looked Rowan in the eyes. She saw watchful gladness shining there.

Overcome, but not wanting to interrupt Mr. Flint's reading, she mouthed an astounded "Thank you!" to him.

A lump rose in her throat to hear her family names, knowing that her father had written the words with the aid of Septimus Flint years ago. It was a relief to hear about her allowance and her dowry, but when his voice halted, she asked breathlessly, "Does he name a guardian?"

"No, lass."

Lady Caro exclaimed, "That's wonderful!"

Septimus Flint declared, "This means that, by default, ye are to be cared for by the Marquis of Wyndhurst, who is your nearest male relative. Aye-yi, isn't that good? Kilver cannot have anything to do with ye."

Tricia was instantly hugged by Lady Caro, who clapped her hands and kissed her. She then turned to Rowan, wanting to know how he had achieved it all.

While Rowan tried to disclaim, Lord Bixby smiled and congratulated Tricia and then shook Septimus Flint's hand.

Jewel sniffed and said, "It sounds to me like you did it all, Rowan. Well, good, our work here is over. Now we can go home."

The Duke announced, "I will inform Lord Kilver that we have the authentic will. Mr. Flint cannot, of course, be involved in disputing that bogus document that Kilver had Mr. Snipley read to us. It is important that none of us reveal that this good solicitor helped us because we must protect him.

He has done us a magnanimous service, has Mr. Flint. We thank you, Sir!" The Duke reached under his blankets and set a leather purse casually on the hermit's knee.

"Payment?" The little man gaped at it.

Tricia smiled at him. "Don't you usually receive payment for services rendered, Mr. Flint?" She vowed to pay Rowan back for the purse.

"Sometimes. Never so promptly, oh no."

"Mr. Flint," she said suddenly, "you don't plan to live in your present abode through the winter, surely!" She cast a look at the Duke. It was preposterous. The man would freeze to death the first day of frost.

"Yes, Lady Tricia, it has been my retreat since the month of May. That was after my little house on the cliff's edge fell into the sea."

Everyone looked shocked.

"I knew it would tumble one day, so when the clouds looked ominous for a tremendous rain storm a-comin', I removed all my best belongings and moved to the Laurel Inn. I went searching for an abode until I found my cavern." His eyes sparkled proudly. "No legal ties to it by anyone. Since my own property is no longer there, but fallen onto the rocks and washed away with many other houses, my cave is all I have."

"It's a lovely place with an unparalleled view of the sea," said Tricia, "but for the winter months, you will want something warmer. I offer you rooms in my house, Mr. Flint."

"Your house? The property mentioned in this Will?"

"Yes, Soaring Gables."

The Duke looked pleased, winked at Tricia, and locked his fingers together over his waistcoat, watching the hermit make up his mind.

Septimus Flint looked at each person in turn, and then dropped his forehead into his hands. When he lifted his face, the eyes that sought Tricia's were wet and gleaming. "You have always been so kind to me, Countess. I would be happy to live near ye."

Tricia smiled, rose to shake his soft hand, and said, "I am not the Countess, but her daughter, Tricia, Mr. Flint. Thank you for such sweet memories of her. I don't mind if you confuse us now and then. It keeps her alive, in a way, doesn't it?

"Alive! That's it," he agreed, and kissed her hand with deep respect.

The others gathered around Mr. Flint, and everyone accepted steaming teacups handed to them by a maid who pushed in with a loaded tray.

Tricia hunkered down beside Rowan with a plate of iced cakes.

"For me?" His eyes smiled into hers.

She whisked a linen napkin onto his lap and balanced the saucer and cake plate on top of it. "I wish you well, Duke," she said unsteadily.

"What brought that tremor to your voice?" he quizzed under the hubbub of the others' conversations.

Her heart was too full. She must only vocalize one aspect of what she felt. "You have done everything good for me. Now, because of your selflessness, ill fortune has come to you, and you are hurt. It's just not right!"

Where no one else could see, he gripped her

fingers. "Tricia."

Her fingers intertwined with his. Lovingly, she looked at him, and then dropped her eyelids. Jewel had turned their way.

Unseen, Rowan caressed the underside of her wrist and said reassuringly, "Tricia, if I never walk again, this will still have been worth it."

Into Lady Jewel's eyes jumped fiery wrath.

CHAPTER 26

Disquieting Developments

Tricia put her hands on her hips and said, "The bundles I saw through the window are all gone from my bedchamber!"

"What do you make of it?" inquired Lady Caro, looking around the charming room in Soaring Gables which Tricia had occupied before her parents died. The print in the bed curtains and at the windows had small rosebuds on a pale pink background, and the furniture was all beautifully inlaid. It had not the dust that other rooms had, for articles had been stored all over it, and the bedcovers showed impressions.

"Lord Kilver stalled us," Tricia said, "and whisked away whatever he had stored in here."

"I imagine that means he shouldn't have had those bundles in the first place." Lady Caro picked up a wax French doll in a white wig and panniers. "Haven't we gone far enough now that he heard you're absolutely not under his jurisdiction?"

"What do you mean, *far enough?*"

"Tricia, I worry. Let's not antagonize that eel any further. Who knows what he'll do?"

"Are you saying that we must wink at his thievery?"

"Not wink at it precisely, but I fear for you and Rowan if you try to uncover *all* of his sordid doings."

"Come, let's go smile guilelessly at him then." Privately, Tricia huffed. They descended the white staircase to the hall with its raspberry silk walls and arched white doorways.

In the drawing room, Rowan sat in a Bath chair with his hands on the large wheels. Jewel sat at the late Lucretia Ravenscar's escritoire, writing furiously.

Lord and Lady Kilver milled about. Lady Kilver kept worrying her reticule strings as she staunchly studied the watercolor pictures on the walls. They were painted by her sister, Tricia's mother, and featured Bay Town, the heather moors, and the sea. One had Tricia and David as children looking out over the water from the cliff's edge.

The Duke looked pensive, Tricia noted. An hour ago, he had had himself moved up the hill in a sedan chair carried by his four footmen. He called it a ridiculous parade, but he could not walk or even ride his horse.

Rupert had run to deliver the Duke's letter to Lord Kilver's house, informing him of the Will. The Duke had written that, unless Lord Kilver could produce a later version signed authentically and witnessed, he had no foot to stand on. He reminded him that Lady Tricia expected to be let into her house that day, as promised, and he named an hour.

Kilver had been there promptly with the key, his wife with him.

"Find your dolls?" he drawled now, his eyes

snapping.

"Why yes; all but one, that is. Have you seen my infant doll anywhere?"

"Me?" he queried, splaying his thin hand across his chest.

Lady Kilver frowned in concentration. "Pultney, there was a doll that turned up at home. What happened to it?"

Kilver queried, "Would *I* pay attention to such a thing?"

"I'll look for it," Lady Kilver promised Tricia.

As Kilver baited her now, Tricia wondered if he had resigned himself to the fact that she was nevermore to live under his roof, nor be a prisoner under his power. She fervently hoped so. She could not stand the sight of him. Adding to his former sins, he had set the Press Gang on her Duke.

As they all filed out and she locked the front door to Soaring Gables, she had the distinct feeling that he had been tense in her house despite his pose of unconcern. Inspecting all the bedchambers, she had noticed dust in some rooms and not in others. Of course he had stored things there. It was difficult for her to hold her tongue.

As they all walked toward the town in the twilight, Tricia approached Lord and Lady Kilver. Putting her hand safely through her aunt's arm, she asked him, "Where is *The White Dove* now?"

"The ship? I have it in Scarborough," said Kilver. "I keep the business going well. No need to worry that it's stagnating. It has always been a merchant ship, hasn't it? So it shall remain."

She drew a breath of courage. "You will have to

turn it all over to the Marquis of Wyndhurst now."

"Well, well!" snapped Kilver. "We will have to see about that!

* * *

The next morning, Jewel burst into Tricia's room at the inn. "They're here! Get up, get up! Papa and Mama are here."

"They are?" Tricia rose from her pillows and blinked at Jewel's animated face.

"They received my first two letters, and here they are! Lady Caro's talking with them in the parlor. They can't believe we're here in this cramped little town in the middle of nowhere."

Tricia kicked off her covers slowly and murmured, "They are my guardians now."

"If I were you, I should hurry and don a good gown, not some country thing." Jewel arched her brows and left, swishing off in a green batiste frock with sheer sleeves.

Sarah heard her, and was scrambling into her clothes in the dressing room. She stumbled out, cap askew. "What will you wear then, My Lady?"

"The pale blue muslin with the blonde lace. Sarah, I have a new family all of a sudden, but I am not sure if I'll like it."

"You still have Lady Caro, and if I may say so, My Lady, she's the best of the lot."

"She sure is. What are Lady Jewel's parents like?" Tricia asked presently as she toweled her wet face.

"Very fine, to be sure," was all Sarah would say.

Mrs. Gunnthorpe, their landlady, was in a tizzy. Tricia saw the woman's distress as she came dashing out of the kitchen. "Whatever's the matter, Mrs. Gunnthorpe?"

"Lady Tricia, I feel so inadequate! I wonder if Her Ladyship will find anything at all to her liking. Never has my humble inn been so invaded by Nobility, and so many of them," she expounded. The silver didn't match, but it was all the real silver she could scrape together. The scones had baked too brown, but there was no time to make any more.

"Never mind that, your food has been delicious, and you are serving us very well—in many more ways than one," Tricia assured her. "I am so thankful to you."

The woman nodded gratefully, her eyes watered, and she ran to hiss orders at her maid.

Tricia pushed her temple curls in more firmly, hoped her crown switch would stay on, and entered the parlor. There was Jewel, roosting between a French blue bonnet covered in netting and purple plums, and a handsome man in a dark brown coat.

At sight of Tricia, he rose. His elegant brows lifted. Tricia could see where Jewel got her looks. He had dark brown hair streaked with silver. His nose was patrician and his mouth was etched with fine lines. He smiled and exclaimed, "Undoubtedly you are Leigh and Lucretia's daughter!"

"Yes, My Lord. You are my uncle, Lord Wyndhurst. I am glad to know you." She curtseyed.

"Indeed, and I am honored. I hear from Jewel that I am now your guardian. What a piece of news. This is my wife, Lady Wyndhurst."

The sharp-eyed Lady stretched her purple glove to where Tricia had to weave her way behind the Marquis to touch it. "Patricia, is it? How interesting this is."

"It is a pleasure to meet you. I'm called Tricia."

"Mmm," she said, her gray eyes assessing Tricia up and down while her mouth smiled. She wasn't anything to look at, with her sagging cheeks and graying frizz. Her high neckline only emphasized her short neck, and she wore several rings over her gloves. These she presently removed, one by one, and arranged on the center of the table so that she could draw off her gloves in order to eat. Decidedly, Jewel displayed less vulgar taste and manners. She must have learned her air of refinement from her father.

Tricia felt relieved when Lady Caro breezed in. The breakfast proceeded with Jewel doing most of the talking. Her mother inquired loudly, "So you are engaged, in truth, to the Duke of Rowan, dear Jewel?"

"I am!" replied their radiant daughter, who proceeded to take out of her bosom the article which had been her dear Rowan's unique way of asking for her hand. She said he had been too, too shy to venture the proposal in person right away.

Lord Wyndhurst looked puzzled, but Lady Wyndhurst was in alt, reading and exclaiming and showing her husband the clipping though she had read it aloud already. *"Let hopeful maidens weep,* it says. How Jewel's friends must envy her!" She cast Tricia a pointed look, including her in the friends. "Caro, this is phenomenal." She quickly changed her tack. "But Jewel was destined from her bright childhood for the very pinnacles. Haven't we always known it?"

The Marquis cast his dark, quick eyes over his daughter. "Yes, Caro, you have done excellently in our absence. I believe I shall increase your portion."

"Clive, of all the impertinence!" snapped Lady Caro. "Now pay attention to your newest daughter, Lady Tricia. I am prouder of finding her than I am of anything."

He smiled and gave her his immediate attention. "I must hear the whole story bye-and-bye. Jewel wrote a few lines, but your letter told me more, Caro. For now I'll just say welcome, Tricia. You are very welcome in my house."

"Thank you, Uncle." She would wait to tell him he would have her money and house and a ship under his direction until she came of age or married. She hoped he was up to taking it all away from Kilver.

All that must wait, though, for the rest of the meal was a continued celebration. Jewel had summoned her parents at the time Lord Kilver caused Rowan to head north. She sent another plea during the Press Gang threat. But she said nothing about those things now. She obviously wanted to revel in her engaged status without distractions.

As the meal broke up, Tricia whispered to Lady Caro that she needed to go out.

"Where?"

"To see Rowan."

"I'd like to come with you, Tricia. We won't tell the others."

"But won't they descend on him as soon as they can turn?" asked Tricia worriedly. "I need to run over there now."

Lady Caro looked peeved. "Clive and Dorothy are inviting him to the Raven Hall Inn for dinner. That's where they are staying, and taking Jewel with them. Dorothy wants to do it up as grandly as possible, even in these country wilds. She said she heard Rowan can't be jounced by coach yet to London, but she thinks it's fine to jounce him up to the cliff top for dinner. We shall see what he has to say about that. I told her that you and I will stay here for the nonce."

"Yes, let's stay." Tricia squeezed her hand. Did her aunt know how important it was for her to be near the Duke?

* * *

When she saw him in a Bath chair near the two corner windows in his tiny room above the Bay, her heart tugged. He watched the waves and the herring gulls, his profile still.

Tenderly Tricia whispered from the doorway, "Your Grace?"

He turned his head. At sight of her, he flashed a white, happy smile. "Lady Tricia! –and Lady Caro, too. Come in."

"So you are still confined to that chair?" asked Lady Caro.

"Yes, the surgeon was here and said I must ride in this contraption, and not even try to walk."

"For how long?" inquired Lady Caro.

He wore a dark red waistcoat over white shirt

sleeves and a black stock over his collar. He was obviously bound about the hips beneath his black pantaloons. "That remains to be seen. Please don't look so worried. Why such long faces?"

"Why indeed!" Lady Caro presented him with a miniature bouquet of violets she had picked from plants at the inn. "Your engagement is being rejoiced over, Rowan, for your in-laws have arrived."

Rowan blanched. "Arrived? Where?"

"At The Fisherman's Arms. They sit exulting over you just a few steps away. They plan to invite you to something-or-other tonight on the cliff top. I expect you will be welcomed with banners and horns and marriage settlement papers."

He ran a hand through his hair and gave a mirthless laugh. "Yes, I see. Please sit down, ladies."

Lord Bixby strolled in. He hailed them with cheery good mornings, patted Rowan on the back, and plunked onto the bed next to Tricia. While Caro's and Rowan's dialogue centered on Lord and Lady Wyndhurst, Bixby turned a smile on Tricia. "While they're celebrating the union of their families, why don't we take a walk along the beach?"

Tricia, who felt oddly constricted by the subject matter, stood up. "Yes, please. We're going out for a minute, Aunt Caro." Her hope of speaking to Rowan alone was dashed, anyway.

Rowan suspended his conversation. Tricia felt that he did not quite approve of her leaving with Lord Bixby.

Her cheerful escort helped her down the stairs

and drew her hand through his tweed coat sleeve as they descended to the sand at the bottom of Wayfoot.

"Lady Tricia," he said, squinting up at the birds swooping here and there against the cliff face, "I want to thank you for your help in hiding me while that gang rampaged through town."

"I thought you already thanked me. Besides, I did nothing. I am the one who owes you undying gratitude for fighting off Lord Kilver. That truly was a chivalrous deed, Lord Bixby."

"Lady Tricia, please call me Graham. Or just Bixby."

"I couldn't first-name you, My Lord, as we are only acquaintances, but I would like to know your surname." She smiled.

"I am Graham Dashford. I do wish you felt close enough to first-name me, as you put it."

Tricia laughed that off and strolled north, looking up at the cliff top. "Soaring Gables is my house, there, standing alone." It looked dignified with its mellow honey-colored stone and its curvilinear gables gracing the door and its long, arched windows on three floors.

"It looks very nice. I would be pleased to see it."

"I am taking up residence, so come and visit me soon."

"You are?" He looked surprised and a bit chagrined. "When will you move in?"

"As soon as the staff I hire has it ready. Our old and wonderful cook is coming back, and she promised to spread word among our former servants to see if anyone is available. I already have a gardener and a new housekeeper promised.

I'm so happy! People in this town are so loyal, and want to help."

"Do you plan to remain in Robin Hood's Bay, then?" Bixby asked in dismay.

"Perhaps. Lady Caro said she will live with me for awhile."

He protested, "But you should come back to London, Lady Tricia! You are such a darling there! Even Brummell told me to convey his regards to you, which I forgot to do. I know many others are scanning the crowd at every rout and ball for the sight of you. My *dear* Lady Tricia, you cannot bury yourself here at the edge of the world, as stunning as the view may be."

"I doubt that my location in the world makes that much difference."

Lord Bixby took her by the shoulders and looked into her eyes, his blue ones direct. "Madam, your exact location is of intense importance to *me*."

Tricia blinked, smiled, and asked innocently, "Why?"

He eyed her hungrily, gave her a little shake, and said, "Because I want to marry you!"

She thought she had heard him banter something like that in the tunnel. "You do?" She realized with a sinking heart that he meant it.

He was gazing at her with such a lovelorn air that she tried to step away.

"Yes, Tricia, my love!" He lifted his hands to her cheeks.

She pushed them down. "No!" She glanced nervously up at the window of Rowan's room, high in the hotel.

"You're right; I should not get carried away in

public. I'm sorry. But what do you say, Tricia? Could you love me? I absolutely adore you, you know."

She had known he liked her, and she liked him, but this was too much. "What I know of you I do like, Lord Bixby, but I cannot just marry you."

"Why not? Oh, I suppose you feel we need more time."

Tongue-tied, she nodded.

He laughed in sudden gladness and relief. "All right, I'll wait. That will be a worthy pastime: waiting for the most exquisite being in the world."

Tricia felt worse and worse as they walked back to the hotel. She quaked at what she had done with that little nod. Had she given him hope? Of course she had. She wondered, fitfully, if that had been a stupid thing to do.

There was nothing wrong with Lord Bixby. He was good-humored, courageous, good-looking in his sun-tanned, blond, and blue-eyed way, and seemed to possess all manner of virtues. His only fault was that he was not Rowan. All other men paled when held up beside him.

CHAPTER 27

In Love, We Hate Companions

The cheerful melody of the *Brandenburg Concerto No 1* by Bach filled the ballroom of the Raven Hall Inn on the cliff top moor when Tricia entered it. Lady Caro headed for the ladies' retiring room to fix her olive green ball gown, which had a bowknot coming loose.

Tricia halted when she saw the back of Rowan's dark head in his Bath chair. The combination of his stillness, the lilting music, and the scented, flower-filled rooms gave her a helpless feeling. She wanted to be anywhere but here to watch Rowan slip further away from her.

The orchestra conductor saw her blinking her wet eyes. He gave her a gratified look, and continued to lead his musicians with renewed dedication to his moving art.

She could not walk past Rowan, for he might turn and see the remains of her tears. She could never explain, so she fled from his view.

The inner parlor swarmed with guests who flowed into the largest room of the inn. This inn was where King George III had stayed on that historic visit to improve his nerves. Tricia seated herself on a chair hidden from the crowd by a spray of red roses and Queen Anne's Lace. This was Lady Jewel's night in every respect.

Apparently every noble's and gentleman's family in a wide radius had been bidden. That seemed a feat indeed, since Lady Wyndhurst and Jewel had had only three days to plan this betrothal ball. *A ball!* In her sensitive mood, Tricia giggled. Rowan couldn't even dance. Somehow that made this nightmare a peg better.

A trumpet flourish arrested them all. People parted, and as Tricia stood to look, she saw the Marquis of Wyndhurst wheel his future son-in-law to the foot of the staircase facing the steps.

Lady Jewel appeared at the top. That signaled the musicians, who swelled the rafters with the strains of *Toccata and Fugue in D Minor.*

Jewel looked down at Rowan through half-closed eyes, her lips rouged for the occasion. She unfurled her lace fan with a flick and descended. Her gown of white cambric had green ribbons crisscrossing the bodice and a red rose in the middle. She wore a necklace of emeralds, and bracelets over white gloves. Braids were wound around her chignon.

As she reached the bottom step, she smiled widely at Rowan, leaned over, aware of her deep décolletage, and kissed him oh-so-chastely on the forehead.

Tricia groaned.

A young lady nearby heaved a sigh. She took to whispering with her companion. "Can't he ever walk again?"

"Grandfa says likely not because he can't feel anything down below."

Tricia leaned and stared at the girl with dreadful foreboding pounding in her temples. "What did you say?" she asked politely. "Who is your grandfather?"

"He's the surgeon, Mr. Newell. Who are you, Miss?"

"Tricia Claremont." She shook hands with Miss Newell and her friend, a Miss Oglethorpe. "What did Mr. Newell say about the Duke not walking again?"

"He doesn't think he will because he can't feel any sensation in his nerves."

A jolt of shock wracked Tricia's whole being.

Rowan, looking splendid in a black evening coat and blinding white cravat, was smiling shyly as people filed by and congratulated him.

How could he be so brave? It nearly broke her heart to watch him shaking hands and making pleasant remarks.

"Let's join the queue," said Miss Oglethorpe. "I'm so nervous, but I'm dying to meet him. He must be the handsomest Duke in Parliament."

Tricia followed them, knowing it was inevitable that she felicitate the radiant couple. Her fears for the Duke's condition made her light-headed. She breathed deeply and prayed, *Please, dear God, let him recover.*

When she came face to face with Jewel, an embrace was in order.

Jewel hurriedly caught Tricia's lifted arms and said, "Careful! Don't muss me!"

"Best wishes to you, Cousin," said Tricia, sighing inside.

"Yes, thanks!" Jewel skewered Tricia with arch

triumph in her eyes, and then turned a gracious smile on the man who came next.

Tricia turned to see the Duke watching her from his Bath chair. His noble character caused her to feel choked. In a rush, she said, "I wish you well, Your Grace. God bless you and make you well!" She squeezed his hand, and pulled away to flee.

He did not release her. "Tricia?" he inquired, looking concerned.

"My Lord Duke!" she said with a desperate edge to her voice. She yanked away from his grip before he could ask her anything more.

* * *

Twenty minutes later, Tricia slammed the chamber door in The Fisherman's Arms and threw herself onto the bed. She could not stand it. The Duke and Lady Jewel were going to be married! She, herself, would be forced to live near them in the bosom of the Marquis's family. She turned onto her stomach and sobbed.

In her mind, years stretched on to infinity in which she would always see them together. She would have to visit them in that beloved mansion in Park Lane, where she had been his page and confidante. There she would have to watch Jewel kiss her Duke and bask in his kind attentions. "I will *not!*" she cried, and punched her pillow. She would likely even be godmother to one of their children.

Fiercely, she slew the pillow until feathers flew from a hole in the end. She shoved it to the floorboards, where it made a swirling white mess.

Now she understood the meaning of the words she had once read, penned in the previous century by William Walsh: *I can endure my own despair, But not another's hope.* She had thought that idea was utterly mean and selfish, but now it felt true. Jewel preened in her heights of glory—and well she might—for she was about to marry the best man in existence.

Up from the bed Tricia dragged herself. Her head pounded. She poured water into the flowered bowl and lowered her face into it. She did not breathe for a full minute or more. She stood up, threw her head back, and with eyes closed, let the water flow down her neck. She stumbled to the window and wrenched it up. She welcomed the blast of wind, and willed it to freeze her face and with it, her feelings.

Dear God, I cannot bear this, her heart cried.

* * *

Rowan said, as their receiving line concluded, "This ball was certainly a surprise to me, Jewel." He looked around at the forty-odd people he had met, only one other than Bixby whom he knew from London.

"Were you pleased?"

He felt at a loss for words. "I cannot dance, of course, but it's been diverting to watch you and everyone else."

Jewel flashed him a flirtatious smile. "I'm sorry I had to dance so many numbers."

"Not at all. You owed it to everyone who came."

"Too true. But Rowan, when we get back to

London, my parents will give me a real ball, so when can that be? When will you be able to dance with me?"

"If I'm going to recover, I could possibly be up in a fortnight or more. Who knows?"

"Sublime!" Jewel squeezed his arm. "Father, in a fortnight we may have the ball." She went off to dance with her father, who smiled and nodded at Rowan.

The Duke looked at them askance, and then turned to resume words with Lord Bixby. He had periodically come by, asking where Tricia was.

"I said I have not seen her in the past three-quarters of an hour." Rowan had not meant to sound so testy, but he felt even more so.

"I wanted to dance with her, but she is nowhere to be seen," complained his friend, looking agitated. "Nowhere!"

Rowan remembered the suffering face she had tried to hide from him before she yanked her hand out of his grasp and streaked out of the ballroom. He frowned darkly.

"Asked her to marry me," said Bixby, and took a sip from his goblet.

"*What?*" Rowan whirled his head and saw his friend's proud face. "Then she up and disappeared?"

"No, no, no! I asked her the day we walked on the beach."

"You did? What did she say?" Rowan braced himself as he waited for the answer.

"She said . . . hmm, what exactly did she say? Something about liking me and about needing more time . . . or did I say that? Anyway, I mean to ask her again when she knows me better. There's *hope*, Rowan!" He grinned from ear to ear and punched his friend's arm.

"Ow."

"Sorry, old man; I forgot your bruises. I've got plenty myself," he added, kneading his shoulder where Kilver had struck him. "My jaw is healing. How is your head?"

"Pardon?"

"Your head, where the Press Gang hit you. Does it pain you?"

"I have a sizable lump."

Bixby changed his tack as they watched Jewel swirl by, vainglorious smiles for people watching her from the sidelines.

"You've got yourself a beauty there, Rowan. Maybe I've got myself one, too. Aren't we the lucky pair, though? Brummell will be pure envy— bet?"

"I wouldn't put money on his envying the marital state," returned Rowan, "and wouldn't that emotion be impossible to prove?"

He felt Bixby staring at him in perplexity. "Well, I wasn't planning to write it in the betting book at White's."

Rowan told him, "Go dance with my fiancée, will you? Then escort her back here."

"Well . . . sure, if you want me to." Hesitatingly, Bixby dragged himself off.

The Duke, in the interval, hurriedly wheeled his chair toward the door. He had seen a familiar shade of hair as a woman peeked in and withdrew. "Lady Flitcroft!" he called.

Around the corner she posed, patting her hair in

a mirror before coming in. "Oh Lucas! I just had to come."

"What for?"

"To get a glimpse of you." She looked him over thoroughly. "Devastatingly attractive, as ever. But goodness, I heard you were in a Bath chair."

"As you can see," said Rowan curtly. "What brings you to this part of the wilds?"

"I'm visiting my estate, of course."

"What compelled you to leave London during the Little Season?"

She gave a little laugh. "I know what you mean, but I had some little affairs to take care of at home; boring business and such. My husband is no longer here to take care of such things, so I must do it all."

"Ah. Did you come bearing more gifts for me?"

She warmed to him instantly.

He went on, "I'll bet I can hazard a guess at how you came by those little items, such as exotic tobacco. Shall I try? No? Then answer me this," he said, blocking her thoughts of departure with his wheels. "Why did you help Kilver perpetuate his scheme in Hyde Park? How could you use your little girls as decoys and lures?"

She tightened her lips and twirled her string of pearls nervously.

The Duke pressed on. "I'm not sure what you planned to do that night, but I know it had something to do with Lady Tricia, and very likely it was to kidnap her!"

"But, Lucas!" She affected a laugh. "Kilver and I were just on a lark. We would never have hurt the creature."

"Oh, no, Kilver is far too considerate for that!" snapped Rowan. "I want to implant into your minds, both of yours, that you must kiss your designs against Lady Tricia good-bye. She is legally the ward of the Marquis of Wyndhurst. That's him over there."

"I *know* who he is," throbbed Lady Flitcroft, offended. "I know who all noblemen are."

Rowan gave her a censorious glance. "Why do you stay in Kilver's country house? Especially when his wife isn't there? Why was he at yours the last time I left it?"

She cringed under his stare. "When?"

"When I took up his oily hat and he got mine," ground out the Duke.

Lady Flitcroft crossed her arms tightly. "He came later than he expected and begged refuge of my butler, not wanting to wake anyone. I was never more surprised to see him in the morning, and you gone!" she added with a pout.

"It seems you are destined to be hit with surprises."

She looked unsure of what to say next.

Rowan moved his legs slightly and grimaced.

She focused on them. "Are you . . . I mean; is there hope for you to get out of that chair?"

"Well," he said and gave her a straight look, "I may never walk again."

The whites of her eyes enlarged enormously. "*Never?*"

The Duke raised his shoulders in a helpless gesture.

She stared at him. "Why not?"

"I can feel nothing."

Transfixed, she breathed, "Where all?"

"From my waist down."

She was the picture of utter shock followed by dismay.

Jewel, arriving behind his chair in time to catch their last few exchanges, gave a sharp gasp. Pointedly ignoring Lady Flitcroft, she leaned over Rowan and said haltingly, "My dear, did you ask for me?"

"Yes, Jewel. The supper bell chimed." With a penetrating look at the astounded Lady Flitcroft, he discovered her backing slowly out of the hotel.

Unable to help it, he grinned to himself as Bixby arrived and pushed him into the supper room. Rowan felt that one good thing had come of his misfortune: he was rid at last of the amorous Lady Flitcroft.

Jewel asked angrily, "What were you talking to her for?" She flashed an insincere smile at someone and continued walking beside his rolling chair, her hands in fists.

"She came to the ball," said Rowan. "Didn't you invite her?"

"Certainly not!"

"Calm yourself, Jewel. My mission was to challenge her for aiding and abetting Kilver the night they tried to take Tricia during the fireworks."

"Bixby, wheel him there, next to my chair," ordered Jewel. Her words tumbled out in whispered ferocity. "Rowan, you must understand that a woman of my rank and sensibilities cannot abide such a scandalous woman to be noticed by you. Not for any reason in the world. Promise me you will never speak to her again."

Rowan smiled. "Barring civility, I promise."

Jewel's bosom rose and fell in her apparent relief. She directed a self-satisfied look at Lord Bixby as if to say, *See? He'll do anything for me.*

Lord and Lady Wyndhurst entered the dining room, followed by ranks of the highest society who could be ferreted out of Scarborough and Whitby and country estates. Jewel, by way of making conversation, sighed with her cheek on her glove and said, "I do so love parties, don't you, Rowan?"

He gave her a level look and said from the heart, "I hate them."

"You what?" She blinked uncomprehendingly. Then, with a smile for Lord Bixby, she said, "Just now, yes, since you are confined to that chair and cannot dance."

"I detest them at any time."

Unperturbed, Jewel said, "But we will be obliged to have many."

"No, we won't be obliged," the Duke returned, lifting his hand to Mr. Richard who, across the ballroom, was merely passing through the hotel, not one of the party.

Jewel contradicted with a determined smile in place. "You don't know what you're saying, darling. A Duke and Duchess must entertain the whole spectrum of the Peerage, especially the Prince of Wales on occasion. What do you mean, we won't be obliged to give parties? We certainly will. You attend them all the time; I've seen you."

He smiled ironically. "I have gone to scores of them in my day, but only because I had to search out a woman with whom to share my life."

Jewel fixed a bright stare on him.

Bixby hung on every word.

"Now that I've found you," continued Rowan, taking her hand and kissing her gloved knuckles, "I can bow out of that insipid life and go on to more important pursuits."

"Such as what?" Jewel challenged him, a dangerous glitter in her gaze.

He paused, then leaned toward her and said, "Striving to beget heirs." He made the most subtle gesture over his lower half.

Bixby whooped out laughing.

Rowan cocked his head and eyed Jewel suggestively.

Her stare grew enormous. He wondered if she would strike him. She did not. She rose quickly from her chair and stalked out of the room.

Her mother descended on Rowan immediately. "Where did Lady Jewel go?" Rustling in a puce gown, she smiled in an ingratiating manner, one eye on her other guests. Rowan knew that not a whiff of discord was to be borne.

"Out that door, Lady Wyndhurst."

"Didn't look too well," added Bixby, "maybe needed air." Bixby's lips twitched.

Looking stiff and displeased, Lady Wyndhurst went after her daughter. In a few moments they were back, Jewel slipping regally into her place. Her mother cast Rowan a warning look.

Bixby kept trying to catch Rowan's eye in silent camaraderie.

Rowan ignored him as they lifted glasses for the first toast. He wasn't supporting Bixby's hopes and dreams, either, and Bixby better know it.

CHAPTER 28

The Invalid

"I hope this room will please you, Mr. Flint."

"Please me? Aye-yi, Lady Tricia, you find me overwhelmed." Indeed he looked to be. Smiling, he fingered the purple velvet coverlet on the carved bed of cherry wood. "This is better than a chamber in the house. I can come away to my own snug abode when my duties are done. Here is so much room for my work!" He skipped into the adjoining chamber. Boxes of his legal documents were ready for him to sort into the pigeon-holes Tricia had had built for him.

It had frightened Mr. Flint to see the first room she had suggested for him inside the house, for it was too close to other people. She called in carpenters to fix up the rooms above the coach house, and with the second-storey space he was delighted. From his windows, he had a panoramic view of the sea at about the same height as from his cave. Tricia promised to have a balcony built for him, too.

Lady Caro had been given Tricia's mother's room, all gold and ivory and vermillion. Jewel and her parents were still ensconced in the Raven Hall Inn with plans to remain another day before returning to London. Lady Caro had told them she would stay with Tricia.

"For how long?" Jewel asked.

"For as long as it takes for us to settle her inheritance. I believe we have to wait until that ship returns."

Jewel rolled her eyes. "What will you do here in this boring place?"

Lady Caro twinkled. "Oh, chat with the fisher folk and learn to paint seascapes. Perhaps Lady Kilver will teach me to make lace. Oh, and Jewel, there are always the shops."

"There is nothing in those shops! I, for one, cannot wait to get back to London, and Almack's."

"Without your Duke?" asked Lady Caro. "That's right; you can go around and brag. That should buoy you along."

"Aunt!" Jewel had shuddered with wrath.

Caro had just laughed and added, "I know you, Jewel."

Tricia thought about her aunt's jibe concerning the Duke. She knew it rankled with Jewel that he did not leap at the chance to head south with her, but insisted on staying in Bay Town under the care of his Robin Hood's Bay physician, Mr. Newell.

Lord Wyndhurst remonstrated that His Grace should see the court surgeons in London's Harley Street, where he would receive far more professional care.

Rowan shook his head, smiled apologetically, and said it would pain him too much to be moved, or to endure any travel in the state he was in. Collectively, they all realized that he suffered a graver condition than he had let on.

"He must come here, Aunt," Tricia said as the two ladies stood arm-in-arm on the grassy cliff-top gazing at the red-roofed town. Tricia eyed the Bay Hotel in particular.

"Who, Rowan?"

"Yes. He can have the ground floor guest chamber. He cannot stay holed up in that hotel room."

"How compassionate you are, Tricia."

"It's not that. It's the fact that he must have daily care."

"And you wish to give it to him." Lady Caro patted her cheek. "Invite him, by all means."

Tricia flushed and said, "You invite him, Aunt. Please?"

"I can, but I shall have to say that you recommend it, as this is your house."

"Then say, for the good of his recovery."

"For the good of his recovery," echoed Lady Caro, smiling wisely. She went straight in and wrote the letter.

* * *

The next day, as Tricia cut French blue hydrangeas for the hall table, she heard marching feet crunching on her fine gravel drive. She peeked around the side of the house. It was the Duke's four footmen bearing the town's sedan chair into the curve before the front door. Tricia felt a thrill when she saw the Duke's dear face. She tucked her flowers into her basket and tried not to dash too quickly to welcome him.

Lady Caro opened a window of the drawing

room and said, "I'll give the order for cups of tea and those fresh scones I smell."

"Order coffee instead, Aunt. He prefers it."

"Hello, Stefan," Tricia said in a friendly way as the red-haired footman reached to open the front door of the sedan chair.

With downcast eyes, he touched his forelock and said, "Good day, Your Ladyship," and then he reached down to move the Duke's booted legs.

Rowan's eyes lit on Tricia from beneath his hat brim. He comically screwed up his face against the sun, peered about, and quavered, "Is this the home for the derelict?"

Tricia burst out laughing.

He exclaimed in his normal voice, "Unbalanced hermits and unmanned Dukes! Who will it be next? Lepers? Unwed mothers?"

She crossed her arms over her pale yellow gown and said, "I thought you would be more comfortable here than in that tiny room with the spray sheeting your windows."

"Sorry, kind maiden." He took Tricia's hand and kissed it, eyeing her from under his black brows.

She felt so gratified. She watched his footmen carry him to his Bath chair, which she had waiting at the top of the half-circle steps.

Warmly, the Duke said, "Good morning, Mr. Flint."

"Good morning to ye, but it's Flint now, Your Grace."

"Ah. Flint." Rowan was wheeled into the drawing room. Lady Caro swept in, saying, "Rowan, I am thrilled to the gills that you condescended to come. Do we dare to hope you'll stay awhile?"

"I don't know." He smiled at her.

Tricia eyed him.

"Upon what would it depend?" asked Lady Caro, settling herself into a striped pink chair.

"Upon whether there would be enough to do here."

Tricia's mouth fell open.

Rowan gesticulated with his hands. "It might prove rather . . . dull."

"Of all the cheek!" Tricia began, turning a startled eye on her aunt, who was having silent whoops.

Tricia's face flushed.

Rowan grinned at her. "Lady Tricia, I shouldn't roast you when you are so charitable to me. If you find you have extra room for me and my entourage, and truly wish to harbor us, I agree to stay, most gratefully."

"Until when?" inquired Tricia, her embarrassment masked by bluntness.

"Until my limbs can bear my weight enough to carry me away."

"Then where will you go?"

"To marry my love," he replied.

Deflated, Tricia said, "Oh." She excused herself and slipped out to the hall. Squelching her feelings of love which deepened every time she saw him, she called to her new serving maid, "Is coffee ready?"

"No, My Lady," returned Mollie. "They just ground it, but the water hasn't boiled yet."

"Set out the crab rolls with the scones because he might be hungry. Oh, and remember the jam. Help Cook in any way you can. Use the lace-edged napkins."

"Yes, My Lady."

Tricia hastened to find Sarah, who was helping the housekeeper. "Are there towels and soap in the Duke's room? Did the paraffin man come yesterday with new candles? Good. Make sure the Duke has perfectly straight ones in his sconces."

It had been a scramble buying items which were needed in the house, but the maids had scoured the town all morning, and returned laden with baskets and bundles. The house felt almost like a home again, well stocked and aired.

Sarah said, "His Grace's trunk is arrived, but I don't know if I should touch it. Does he have a gentleman's gentleman?"

"Did you notice those four footmen? One of them must be good for the task." Tricia went to ask, "Your Grace, can we unpack your things?"

"Let Stefan do that. He's training for the late Eldred's position."

Tricia giggled. "Wouldn't Eldred go into conniptions if he knew His Eminence would be replaced by a footman?"

"I expect he would." Rowan beckoned her and lowered his voice. "Tell me: how came you to place Septimus Flint, Solicitor, in butler's shoes?"

"Oh, he wanted that post. He declared he would not live here without performing services on a daily basis. I told him he had already done such a wonderful service for me and needn't worry about anything more, but he jumped up and down almost in rage to think that I expected him to accept charity. So I asked him what he would like to do."

"And he proposed to open doors and polish your

silver?"

"Our hermit said he likes to be dignified sometimes." She met Rowan's interested eyes. "Since he retired from his law profession and there weren't many balls to attend, I pointed out that butlers dress to the nines every day. He latched onto that with relish."

Rowan grinned incredulously. "After he ran around naked in his cave and swam in the ocean for exercise?"

"He says he is giving up his childish ways. He quoted from Scripture, you know. I truly think he's better." She tapped her head.

Rowan nodded. "He seems to be on an even keel, thank God. Perhaps he was too much alone." Thoughtfully, he quoted, as if to himself, *"And the Lord God said, It is not good that the man should be alone . . ."*

Lady Caro took it up by saying, "That's where the Lord God said he would make an help meet for him."

"Yes," Rowan agreed. "I am convinced that a man needs one. This is nice," he gestured round the fresh, comfortable room.

As pink and yellow roses waved outside the lace-curtained windows, a kitchen maid carried in a silver tray. Tricia hurried to help her, and, between them, they lowered it to the table in front of Rowan. Lady Caro poured coffee for the three of them.

Tricia sighed with a sense of well-being. It was wonderful to have a man in the house. "I invited everyone here for the evening, My Lord Duke," she said, passing him the plate of golden scones just out of the oven.

"Mmm, these smell good. Who is everyone?" He eyed her askance.

"Lady Jewel, her parents, Lord Bixby, and Lady Kilver."

"Without Lord Kilver?"

"He's out of town. That's why I invited her."

In private, Tricia told Rowan and her aunt about the drum Lady Kilver had found in her cellar. She repeated the suspicions Lady Kilver had voiced about her husband's directing the Press Gang to Rowan in particular.

Her listeners were both stunned.

* * *

Tricia's housewarming party proved a domestic success. After a lovely dinner full of lively conversation, Lord Wyndhurst suggested a walk on the cliff to view the phenomenal bay for the last time.

His wife hung back saying, "But Rowan can't go. I'm sure the ground out there is too rough for his chair."

"Please go, Lady Wyndhurst," Rowan urged. "You must not miss the orange sunset on the waves."

Lady Caro spoke up and encouraged it as a pleasant interlude. "Rowan has seen the view from his hotel for days."

Lady Kilver, timidly following the tonnish Claremonts, found her arm grasped by Lady Caro, who asked if she could learn lace-making from her over the next few days. "You can come here to teach me, and we'll have good treats to eat. Tricia has a very skilled kitchen staff now."

Tricia thought the overture a welcome change, one that had come about after Lady Caro heard how Lady Kilver had demonstrated great courage in striving to preserve the Duke from Lord Kilver's perfidy.

Jewel declared, "I shall stay here with Rowan." She paced the drawing room, making it clear to Tricia that she wanted a *tête-à-tête* with him.

With a glance at the Duke's face in evening light and shadow, Tricia reluctantly went out on Bixby's arm.

Septimus Flint hopped up from his chair in his pantry where he liked to read great tomes with minute spectacles perched on his nose. These he whisked off and opened the door with energetic pleasure.

"No need to remove your spectacles," said Tricia kindly.

"Thank ye, My Lady. Gentleness personified."

Bixby chuckled and guided Tricia down the stone steps, startling two white gulls into flapping away, mewing. She hardly knew what to say to Bixby. She wondered what was transpiring in the drawing room with Jewel and the Duke left together.

"Come see my mother's roses," she said vapidly to Bixby. "It makes me happy that they're blooming."

"Be glad to."

Tricia knew a window of the drawing room was open near the Duke's chair, so she leaned to smell a red-tipped white rose. She asked her escort if he had a knife to cut some. While he searched about his person, she heard Jewel say, "I do not understand why you're staying here, Rowan. It isn't proper."

"I explained that I shouldn't be moved. What's improper about it?"

"Tricia, my unmarried cousin, lives here without parents, and she invited you to stay?"

"Your aunt is the one who invited me. She is firmly in residence in place of parents. The ladies have my recuperation in mind. I don't understand, Lady Jewel, what worries you about this arrangement. I find it very touching. Helpful."

There was a pause. "It's just not the thing for you to stay with other women. Please come back to London where you belong."

"I say," whispered Bixby, cutting a prickly-stemmed bouquet for Tricia as she touched each rose that she wanted. "What's going forward in there?"

She tiptoed out of the rose bed. "Lady Jewel finds it improper for the Duke to stay here," she whispered.

"There's no way he can go now; we all know that. Come, Tricia. Not the thing to eavesdrop."

She felt like eavesdropping all the more, but dragged herself away. Taking the roses Bixby held, she drank in their scent and sighed. She would put these in Rowan's bedchamber.

When she and Bixby had circumnavigated the house, the others stood bathed in pink sunset at the edge of the world, as it seemed. The Marquis was pointing.

Bixby slipped his arm around Tricia's waist.

"Please, Lord Bixby. You must not."

"Couldn't help myself. You look divine, Lady Tricia, with your swooping eyebrows and eyelashes so long and dark. It jellies my insides to gaze on your angel face. You should see how you glow in this golden light."

She softened. "Well, thank you," she said with a little laugh. "A girl does like to hear a compliment, especially if it's meant sincerely."

"You will hear more of them throughout your lifetime if you will but spend it with me, Lady Tricia. I love you!"

Her heart skipped. Not this again. "Yes, so you have told me before."

His round blue eyes looked so hopeful under his pale lashes that it hurt her not to instantly comply.

"I am still thinking," was all she could say.

Why couldn't she just say, *No; leave me alone; you're nice but I don't love you?* Because it would hurt him, that was why. What was she to do about him? She shivered delicately and said she was chilly, so perhaps they could go in.

When they passed into the hall, she heard raised voices from the drawing room. With a wide-eyed look, she pointed Bixby into the library opposite, and told Flint to direct the others in there when they came through the door.

"Aye-yi!" Flint sized up the situation and nodded vigorously.

Tricia ran down the steps to the kitchen, which was directly below the drawing room. She went into the pantry and pulled the door after her. In the dark, she stepped onto a shelf and tugged a lever in the ceiling.

She could hear Jewel saying stridently right

above her, "Why do you oppose me because I want us to get married in St George's Hanover Square? It is where everyone will expect my wedding—a wedding of such importance—to be held!"

"I imagine that's true. People would expect your wedding to take place in that eminent church."

"Dear Rowan, let me set the date and reserve with St George's," she urged.

"No, Jewel, my dear. It's just too much pomp for me. Definitely not my style. I have envisioned an old country church . . ."

"Rowan!" she begged, an angry edge to her voice.

"Jewel, I cannot even get up the steps outside it, nor walk down the aisle."

"Oh! You stubborn man!" Tricia heard footsteps run right over her head, then the vibrating slam of a door.

My! Tricia quietly replaced the ceiling panel. Her father had built many escapes into his house to foil the Press Gang. This opened from a grate in the drawing room floor which was covered by a Persian carpet under the table. No one else in the house knew it existed.

The maids and Cook stared as Tricia fumbled her way out of the pantry and dashed through the kitchen with no explanation. She turned back and said, "I forgot how many black currant preserves we still have from last year."

In the entrance hall, Tricia spied Jewel's hem rounding the top of the stairs, and an odd sound like a sob. Was she in tears? Surely not *Jewel.*

Torn between Rowan and Jewel, she peeked into the drawing room.

He sat in his Bath chair with bent head, his legs

thrust before him.

"Your Grace?"

"Come here, please, Tricia."

She liked his tone. It brought back the days of Patrick.

"Am I a lout?" he asked her.

"Why?"

"Ha, you didn't say no."

"It depends on what you've done."

Heavily he said, "It seems to be my lot in life to go against the wishes of women and upset them terribly."

Tricia brightened. "You've been doing much better at that lately," she commended him. "Bixby told me about Lady Flitcroft at the Raven Hall Inn. I am so glad you sent her running, but he didn't tell me how you achieved that."

His eyes smiled, and he said, "We must be serious for a moment. Do you think that, if I have been too hard-headed with my fiancée, I could ask you a favor?"

"What would that be, Your Grace?"

He put his chin on his hand and looked darkly out the window. "Tell Lady Jewel that I will do anything she wishes."

Tricia stared at him in disbelief. "Dear Duke, I will not! Any respectable man will not do *anything she wishes.* You may deliver such stupid messages yourself!" She made for the door, trembling with outrage.

"Tricia." He cocked his head and studied her. "Come here, if you please," he said softly.

"What for, Your Grace?" She went and looked him steadily in his beautiful eyes.

"Thank you. I needed that confirmation of my instincts." He threw her a challenging look. "Never tell me that you, in Lady Jewel's position, would succumb to the oddest, most contrary notions of your husband-to-be."

"It would depend upon how odd the notions were, and if they were something I could live with. Having one's own way isn't everything. Loving *is!*" She tried to walk out in a composed manner, but wondered if she would make it to the door without giving away her bursting emotions.

She made it to the landing on her way to her own chamber where she meant to powder her nose. She was surprised to see, in Lady Caro's open room, Jewel sitting at the dressing table regarding her reflection. She didn't even move or turn when Tricia entered. As she wondered whether to speak or leave, Jewel looked accusingly at her in the mirror and said, "I've never liked myself."

Tricia could not believe her ears. "What?"

"You heard me. I want to be different. But I can't." Jewel slipped off the stool and crumpled onto the carpet. There she lay, her face resting on her arm. She pounded the carpet. Presently she emitted squelched, angry sobbing.

God help us, Tricia prayed, totally at a loss. What could she do or say? She sank to her knees beside her. "Jewel?"

"What!" she snapped. She rolled to her back and stared coldly at Tricia through wet eyes.

"What can I do to help you?"

"*You* wouldn't help me."

"Why wouldn't I?"

"Because I would never help you," she admitted.

"That doesn't mean *I* wouldn't if you needed something that was in my power to give you."

"Cut line!" Jewel sat up suddenly and her eyes narrowed. "That's right, you are so *good*."

Tricia screeched, "I am not good! And if you don't like yourself or want my help, I'll leave." She added quietly, "But I don't enjoy seeing you downcast."

Jewel lifted her nose and sniffed several times. She resumed her seat at the vanity and riffled through her aunt's bottles and porcelain boxes. Soon she was powdering her face all over.

Tricia took a comb and rewound one of her own pinned-on curls. "If you're not happy, Jewel, there must be a reason."

"The reason is that I want us to be married in St George's, Hanover Square, and have a reception ball with the Prince, and go to Paris for our wedding trip!"

"And Rowan doesn't?"

"No!" With venom, Jewel spat, "Men! What do they know about what's right? Why must they force their narrow-minded views into a Society lady's wedding plans?"

"Why doesn't he want to do all those delightful things?" Tricia inquired.

"Because he doesn't like parties, he says."

Tricia said carefully, "Jewel, have a bit of consideration for him just now. He can't dance, or even walk about to socialize. Can you expect him to like long aisles and sea voyages and Parisian balls, all from the great pain and annoyance of that Bath chair?"

Jewel's eyes flashed. "He said he's *never* liked

balls! He said he only attended them to find a wife.”

"Well, isn't that extremely flattering to you?”

"No! Well perhaps, but he *must* hold grand balls! He has a fabulous ballroom, and he's a Duke!” She tightened her fists and stared, fuming, in the mirror. "I can't be a Duchess without them!”

CHAPTER 29

The Trials of Love

As Mr. Newell, Rowan's physician, departed from Soaring Gables the next morning, Tricia held the page of sketches to her breast. *Will these work?* she wondered. *What if they didn't?* She must not be chicken-hearted, she told herself. It was hope for the Duke she held in her hands.

She entered his sunny sitting room with its dark green and white papered walls, yellow velvet draperies, and curving Sheraton armchairs.

"This is an ideal room for scenic vistas," the Duke remarked, looking up from the writing desk. "Tricia, do you look worried?"

"Possibly, but I have taken heart from what Mr. Newell said."

"What was that?"

She said, "He fears there is a nervous disorder afflicting your lower limbs."

The Duke chuckled. "He does, does he? How sage our man is."

"Yes, and he has a prescription for you." Tricia smiled hopefully.

"Why did he not give it to me, then?"

"He probably hadn't the courage."

"But you do? What on earth does he prescribe?"

Tricia waved her paper. "Exercise."

"Let me see that!"

Tricia, dimpling, whisked the paper out of his reach. "He wants me to supervise a program of movement for your legs. He has been reading in his medical journals, and showed me a 'Sermon on Exercise' by one Benjamin Rush."

"Sermon on Exercise," Rowan scoffed, eying her from under his lowered brows. "Somewhere in the Bible it says that bodily exercise profiteth little."

Tricia consulted her page. "I would have to read that in context because it likely means toward our salvation, don't you think? Mr. Rush says that all exercises calculated to impart health, strength, and elegance to the human body are beneficial."

"Elegance? Now that is what I need." The Duke grinned at her. "That's all very well for those who can do them."

"But listen to this, Your Grace. Rush writes that, of our soldiers who were wounded in North Carolina in the American Revolution, those who marched to catch up with their comrades recovered the use of their legs more quickly than those who were left behind. You see? We must move these ducal limbs even if you can't feel anything."

The Duke chuckled. "I don't think so."

Tricia smiled sweetly up at him as she kneeled at his feet. "Lionel," she directed, "come and show His Grace how the first one is done." She laid on the floor the sketches of a human anatomy with arrows indicating motions of the legs. "Start with this one. Lift each foot separately to a level position, and then let it down. Do so ten times,

Lionel."

The Duke shot her an exasperated glance, but his lips twitched. "What a waste of time."

Tricia urged Lionel on. He raised and lowered the Duke's long legs.

She asked, "Can you feel anything, Your Grace?"

"Vague embarrassment."

There came a knock on the door.

"Come in," she called. She hoped it was Lady Caro to help convince their recalcitrant invalid to cooperate.

Tricia gasped. It was Lord Kilver who strode in. Behind him, Septimus Flint was waving his arms, making it clear that he had tried to stop him.

Kilver scoffed and said, "I see you have Tricia kneeling at your feet, Duke. What servitude does he demand of you, eh, Trish?"

Rowan whipped out, "Watch your tongue, Kilver. I am the guest of two compassionate ladies who believe I should recuperate best here. We are following the doctor's orders."

"What, are you still incapacitated?" He gestured over Rowan's legs, the outline of bandages visible through the buff pantaloons.

Rowan said, "I lost sensation in my limbs. I appreciate your concern," he added with irony.

"Can you feel that?" Kilver bent over and squeezed either side of Rowan's knee.

Tricia expelled, "What impertinence!"

"No sensation at all?" Kilver reiterated, half smiling. "You can't walk, Duke?"

"Not at the moment, no."

Tricia saw what Kilver saw: the vital, handsome Duke sitting immobile but looking as manly and powerful as ever.

"I hear from Lady Flitcroft that you won't cause much of a sensation with the ladies anymore." Kilver's hiccupping laughter grated on Tricia's ears and made her furious.

"Did you come here to lift his spirits? –or to infuriate us all?" she cried.

"Trish, keep out of this. Well, well, it looks like I can even kick you, Duke, and you won't feel a thing." Lord Kilver made to jab his boot at Rowan's shin.

Lionel stood up and faced Kilver, while Tricia dove at the villain with all her might. "No, you won't!" she screeched, pushing him with a vengeance. "Get out of this house!"

Kilver caught her and shook her with intense fury. She recoiled from his touch and screamed. Lionel moved to help her, but the Duke, galvanized, raised himself by his arms to a leaning stance against the desk. Ambushing him from behind, he yanked Kilver off of her.

Kilver whirled in astonishment.

Rowan shoved him with such impact that he landed sideways on the carpet several feet away. "What was the meaning of that?" the Duke challenged him.

Lord Kilver nursed his shoulder with a groping hand. "I ought to call you out," he snarled.

Tricia said, "*You* can't call *him* out! You're only a Baron. Now apologize!"

Kilver, rising to his feet, shot an enraged look at her. "What's that? I see the Duke can stand."

Rowan still leaned against the desk, supported by his hands, watching Kilver through a deadly squint.

Tricia said, "You should be relieved that he can at least prop himself up. It was your doing, and your evil plan that sent the Press Gang into this town! It's your fault that the Duke was taken and hurt, and we all know it!"

Kilver stood paralyzed by her words. Finally he spat, "You should be thrown behind bars, you imaginative little—"

Lionel moved between them, his arms shielding her from him.

"What was your intent?" she pressed. "Answer me that!"

"You like to story-tell and play-act, don't you? You should've tried the stage."

"Kilver!" warned the Duke, his pupils dark as musket balls.

Though her heart thumped, Tricia said boldly, "You said you were off to Whitby to buy a horse, but I suspect that's when you went to catch the Press Gang. You sent them here, and I want to know why!"

Lord Kilver was obviously guilty, but he barked a laugh and directed a scornful look at Rowan. "If you believe her tales, Duke, I assume you'll call me out."

"If you presume that to be provocation for a duel, I gladly disappoint you," said Rowan icily. "Now go!"

Kilver swore and marched out, his boot heels leaving black marks on the newly-polished floor.

She followed to make sure he left. Flint scurried to open the door.

Lord Kilver took the little man by the beard and gave it a sharp tug. "You dirty whiddler!" he spat between his teeth. He snatched the hat Flint held out, and flung the door shut behind him with a shuddering slam.

"Dear Flint!" crooned Tricia. She grasped him by the narrow shoulders and looked sorrowfully into his round, blue eyes so full of bewilderment. "That should never have happened. That brute! Why does he terrorize this town? From now on, keep the door locked, and if you see him coming, do not open it. Will you be all right, Flint? I'll bring you a cup of coffee and some lemon cake covered in lemon curd, if you like."

"Thank ye, Lady Tricia. I would like some." He went slowly into his pantry and picked up his spectacles with a shaky hand. "My Lady," he said, looking at her over the tops of them, "he was sore because he knows I produced the proper Will."

"I am sure you're right. I owe you so much."

"Nay, Lady Tricia, this house for you, and my own rooms in the carriage house, are beyond my wishes. But I thank ye most of all for the love ye've shown to an old man like me. God is so good, full of blessings for us."

Tricia swiped at her eyes and turned to see the Duke being pushed in his chair by Lionel to the windows of the drawing room. She went to the kitchen and ordered the coffee and cake for Mr. Flint.

She felt she should somehow restore tranquility to her home, for the hate that had flared up from Kilver's intrusion had let a bad spirit into the house. She retrieved the sheet of exercise diagrams and went into the drawing room. "Your Grace, there are more of these movements I must show you."

"You're determined on this course of action, are you?" He grinned and shook his head.

"Try to accept that we must do everything we can to circulate your blood. It could help restore your feeling." When he tolerantly looked at her without arguing, she picked up his booted foot and raised it gently to a level line.

"No, Tricia, not you," he protested. "Besides, what good will it do when I can barely feel your actions?"

"You are not to say such things. It's good that you can feel even a little." She looked decisively at Lionel. He must remain her ally. "All the more reason to work on your muscles, Your Grace. Lack of effort will do no good whatsoever. Lionel, lift his left ankle. I'll lift his right one in turn." Lionel did so.

The boot would not budge for her. "Your Grace!" she accused, meeting his eyes and seeing mischief there. "What unpardonable, uncooperative behavior, even for a Duke!"

He laughed.

While he was so relaxed, Tricia lifted his leg.

"What goes on here?" It was Lady Jewel's voice censuring them from the doorway.

"Oh Jewel," said Tricia, rising to her feet, "and Lady Wyndhurst! Good morning. Come in."

Their curious eyes were framed by lavish plum and tan bonnets. It was plain that they wondered what Tricia was doing on the floor, handling the Duke's boot and complaining of his behavior, while he laughed out loud.

"What is all this fun and games?" was the way

Jewel put it, eyeing Tricia menacingly.

"Come in, Ladies, and deliver me from this torture," said Rowan.

Jewel demanded, "What torture?"

"He is supposed to let us exercise him, but he is such a refractory patient," said Tricia, gesturing Lady Wyndhurst into the largest chair. "I fear we will get nowhere. Would you like some coffee?"

"Perhaps. Good morning, Lord Bixby," said Lady Wyndhurst, smiling over Tricia's shoulder.

Tricia turned, and there he was, just arriving with arms outspread as though he were delighted to see them all before him. She felt shy as she went to greet him, knowing that he was waiting for her to fall in love with him. "Lord Bixby, you will help me convince the Duke that he must act in his own best interests."

He smiled at her admiringly, kissed her hand, and strode to eye Rowan with head-shaking censure. "Causing Lady Tricia trouble? She, who ministers to your every need? For shame, Duke."

Again, Jewel challenged Tricia. "What were you doing to him when we came in? Rowan obviously finds it ridiculous. You must take your hands off him at once."

Tricia, feeling mulish, retorted, "It's not good that he won't cooperate." She cast him a hurt look.

He achieved a look of penitence.

Lady Wyndhurst asked, "Where is Lady Caro?" She pulled Tricia by the arm until they stood out in the entrance hall. She whispered, "We must let Jewel have words alone with Rowan. How shall we get Bixby and the footman out?"

"I will call them," said Tricia, wondering at the

need for subterfuge. She turned in the arched doorway and said, "Bix, will you accompany us? Oh, and I need your help, Lionel, if you please."

* * *

Left behind as the door shut, Rowan watched his pacing fiancée with curiosity.

She appeared to deliberate as she fiddled with her sparkling spencer buttons.

"By all means," suggested the Duke, "take that off so I can admire your figure in the lovely frock I suspect you have on under it. If you come here, Jewel, I can help you remove it."

She stiffened. "No, thank you. I cannot stay long because we're off to London tomorrow, and I must see my things packed."

Rowan tipped his head to one side, trying to see the face behind the plum colored bonnet. "I shall see you there, then?"

"Yes." In a preoccupied manner, she picked up a green apple from the table, turned it over, and put it back on the red ones in the bowl. "Rowan?"

Trying to make contact with her hooded eyes, he replied, "Ye-es?"

Her brow knitted. "Did you mean it when you said you won't be married in St George's Hanover Square?"

"Yes, I meant it."

"Why not?" she challenged.

He said slowly, "I sensed a self-righteous attitude abounding there; people patting each other on the backs, so to speak, for their good works. They appear to be more interested in show and display more than anything."

"I say!" Jewel objected, but Rowan lifted his hand so he could continue.

"I cannot go asking God to join me in holy wedlock in a place where sermons are given to please the flesh. I think that's why that church is so popular with the rich. People flock to hear what they like to hear. Jewel, I need the true Word, which speaks to my spirit. I hear and feel that spirit in our church, and there is where I wish to be married. That is the most important thing to me. And, may it please God; it will be to my wife as well." *God in Heaven,* he prayed silently, *I need Thy almighty hand to move in this matter.*

Jewel cried, "I cannot imagine what you think is wrong with the kind of preaching in that elegant church. I think it is much more interesting than what we hear at the one you and I attend. I have to go there with Lady Caro because I must have a chaperone, and she won't go anywhere else."

"It's because she and I like to hear the Truth, which is spoken there, Jewel. It's a great pity that you don't appreciate those rich sermons."

"They get interminably boring to me, and there aren't that many fashionable people who attend; my friends, I mean."

Rowan let his forehead fall to his palm.

She added, "I'm glad Mama is back. Now we can go where we want."

Rowan had stopped listening as his thoughts whirled over her pathetic words.

She was saying, "So, you see, Rowan, I must deliver some news."

The Duke sat back and watched her.

"I think . . ." She snatched a red and white rose out of the vase and pull off petals. "That is, my mother also wants the best for me, and I . . ."

"Jewel, what *is* it?"

"As you will no doubt understand one day, we . . . we must not marry."

He let out a whistle as of surprise.

"Each other, that is," she hastily clarified.

"My word! What have I done? Is it what I've just explained to you?" He leaned forward on his elbows, all attention.

She looked bereft of her calm veneer. Though her eyes moved in fits and starts, her words would not come.

"Jewel! Release whatever words are jumping on your tongue. I am a man; I can take it."

"It has a little to do with your religious fanaticism, but there's more. I have thought about what I want in life, and it came as a great shock the other night to hear that you do not have the same desires at all."

"Which desires do I lack?"

"Social desires! You do not wish to host balls, or take your Duchess out to the European capitols, or make a point of entertaining the Nobility who matter. In fact, you want to do *nothing* that is important to me!"

"Ah," sighed Rowan, "what a contrary nature I have. If I promised you I'd change for you, Jewel, I would likely lie awake nights, chastising myself for promising what I could not deliver." He went on, "This new affliction, as you are already aware, puts paid to any plans I may have formed to become more sociable for your sake. Have I disappointed you so tragically?"

"Yes! Dreadfully!" She whirled to face him, her eyes intense. "To deny me all that you *could* shower me with if you wanted to is disappointing in the extreme! I could not stand to refuse invitations, not use your box at the opera, and not hold dinners for the Royal Dukes and the Prince himself. It would be cruel to shutter me up like a nun, never able to throw open the doors to your grand house in Park Lane—" Her voice broke. "Just go to that serious church all the time and not St George's Hanover Square!"

Rowan squeezed his lashes together, knowing full well that he could never please her, even if he tried. Strains of a symphony began in his heart.

Jewel looked infuriated by his failure to turn all to rights by a word. "So this is where our betrothal must end!" she snapped, and snatched up her reticule.

The Duke, gesturing to his inert legs, quietly asked, "Be totally honest, Lady Jewel. Did this injury play a part in killing your love for me?"

Jewel, hastily striving to mask her guilty look, said, "Your present state is most unfortunate, but it is not the only reason for my decision, as I have told you."

Earnestly Rowan said, as he moved his legs, "You have one mistaken impression. I would not keep you like a nun. I am happy to say that, as of this hour, I only lack feeling from the knees down."

Jewel gasped in outrage.

As she marched out of his sight, the words singing in Rowan's heart were thanks to God on high.

CHAPTER 30

The Agony

Septimus Flint padded into the library across the hall from where Rowan and Jewel had parted.

Tricia put the book of poetry she had been reading aloud into Lady Wyndhurst's hand, and gave Flint her attention. "Yes, Flint?"

"Lady Jewel Claremont is ready to depart," he said, swinging an arm toward the door. "She awaits her mother in the carriage."

Lady Wyndhurst jumped up, tied her bonnet ribbons, and took her leave, thanking Tricia for the coffee and delicious cake.

Tricia wondered why Jewel had not come to say good-bye.

"Bixby, what are you doing today?" asked Lady Caro, spooning more lemon curd onto her cake.

"I came to ask Tricia to take a drive with me. Didn't think I should ask while Lady Wyndhurst was still here, you know."

Tricia told him, "Thanks, but I shouldn't leave just now."

"Why not?"

"I must exercise the Duke."

Bixby snorted. "Sounds like a horse."

"Maybe you can help me convince him that to

follow the doctor's orders may help his recovery."

They filed out of the book-lined room and joined Rowan in the sunny drawing room. Tricia sniffed, and instantly felt that something momentous had happened. He was smoking his pipe. When she saw him, she knew he must have run his hands through his hair numerous times, for some of it stuck roguishly out of place.

Lady Caro broke in on his pensive mood. "What's wrong, Your Grace?"

Rowan put his pipe aside and said, "Lady Caro, may I have your company for a few minutes?"

Tricia and Bixby exchanged glances and made their exit. He asked, "Shall we walk outside?"

Tricia whispered, "I wonder what's wrong."

"Your aunt will discover it."

Flint flung wide the door, and the breeze lifted Tricia's curls. As they passed down the walk, she heard, through the drawing room window, what sounded like a shriek of either laughter or chagrin; she couldn't tell which. Or, it could have been the gulls.

She said suddenly, "Bix, you cannot imagine what Lord Kilver did this morning." She regaled him with the whole horrible scene where he actually meant to kick the Duke, but how Rowan hoisted himself up and threw him across the room after his insults to her.

"I am flummoxed!"

"Is there nothing that can be done, Bix? Peers, just because of their titles, cannot normally be prosecuted. That means obstreperous cads like he is can walk away from any guile, mental or physical, that he inflicts."

"True. Unless another Peer accuses him."

"Do you think you or Rowan would do that? And if you did, what then?"

"We would set up a court of Lords in Westminster Abbey and try the blackguard."

"That should be done. But somehow, I don't think His Grace would do it. He's too kind to act in retaliation for wrong against himself. But you should have seen him show his steel when Kilver grabbed me!"

Bixby looked ecstatic. "Good for Rowan! What did Kilver do?"

"He weaseled out of here, trying to taunt the Duke into calling him out, which the Duke found beneath him to even consider. Kilver was so mad when he left that he pulled Flint's beard!"

"That's despicable. You say Kilver wanted Rowan to call him out? Of all the presumption!"

Lady Caro appeared on the steps outside and beckoned to them. "Leave Rowan to himself for awhile," she told them, looking grave.

"Why?" asked Tricia, staring at her fearfully.

"Jewel has jilted him."

"What?" cried Bixby. "Zounds! Unbelievable."

Tricia's heart took wings all of a sudden and beat hard against her breast. Jewel was *not* to marry Rowan?

Lady Caro motioned for them to accompany her around the house, as the housemaids were setting up to wash the front windows and the footmen the coach. "We must get away from all these servants' ears," she said, passing into the flower garden. Even there, the gardener toiled, carrying an armload of weeds into a wheelbarrow.

They walked to the eastern side of the house where Tricia leaned on the warm stone of the chimney, her hands against it for support. She fought not to betray the joy that kept leaping through her, leaving her breathless. Rowan was truly free of Jewel?

Lady Caro, with one eye observing Tricia from under her parasol, said to Lord Bixby, "Jewel apparently finds Rowan too much his own man. She is a social butterfly and must flit here and there, always in the midst of things."

"And Rowan shies away. I know."

Lady Caro's hazel eyes bored into Bixby with questions. "He could've fooled me. He is always so genial, and he has that charming reserve about him in public. Who would have thought that he really detested rubbing shoulders in the *haut ton?*"

"Not showing it is the mark of a true gentleman," put in Tricia, studying the toes of her shoes. "But don't you think Jewel released him lightning-quick after he became an invalid?" The very idea made her blood boil.

"I'll say," Bixby agreed.

"Between us," stated Lady Caro, "we all know that Rowan asked for Jewel's hand in order to save her face."

"I was astounded when he did it," agreed Bixby. "Now he is relieved of that chivalry. It would have been an exorbitant price to pay: a whole lifetime!"

"Yes," said Lady Caro, "but the absolute most important difference between those two, which would totally have wrecked Rowan's life, is the fact that Jewel does not believe in the same Jesus that Rowan does. And as we do." She looked at them solemnly. "She is so cynical that it would never have worked. I thank God from the bottom of my heart for sparing our Duke, for that would have been a marriage unequally yoked."

"Yes," said Tricia, feeling more relieved than ever. She asked cautiously, "How is the Duke taking it?"

"You will have to ask him, but I can see that he is shaken by it," murmured Lady Caro. "I recall that some time back, he found her to be perfect Duchess material." Lady Caro shook her head in regret as she picked a red rose. "What a good man Jewel has thrown away." She tossed the withered rose aside, scattering the dead petals.

Tricia met the watchful eyes of Lord Bixby. He seemed to be trying to discern her thoughts. She did not want him to see how thoroughly she agreed with her aunt's last statement.

He said, "I need to look in on Rowan despite what you said, Lady Caro. My best friend, after all." He excused himself and hastened across the grass.

Tricia joined her aunt beneath the white parasol. "How is he really?" she asked.

"It's hard to say," she said, taking Tricia against her bosom and patting her back. "I wish I could hold him like this and comfort him. Ahh, if I was but ten years younger, I would give it a good try."

Tricia gave a shaky little laugh.

* * *

After Lord Bixby had seen the Duke, he soberly told Tricia that Rowan was closeted for a rest. "He isn't in the mood for conversation, so why don't you come for a ride in my carriage?"

With an element of reserve, she agreed. "Lady Caro has to come," she said.

He was disappointed, but the three of them were soon bowling along at a fast trot on the windy road north. Tricia failed to concentrate on much that Lord Bixby said to her, which he noticed from the outset. As they passed the ancient St Stephen's Church, he said, "I'll stop rabbiting on, Tricia. I know you're worried about them."

"Them?" repeated Tricia. She felt guilty. "I *am* worried about Jewel's sense of values."

"Why? Do you blame your cousin for backing out of a union with someone who is no longer . . . well, a whole man?"

Tricia quelled him with a disbelieving glare. Lady Caro eyed him, too. "Not a whole man?" cried Tricia. "Just what do you mean by casting such a slur upon him?"

Bixby's face blanched. "Why, I didn't mean anything against my friend, oh no! But his not being able to move as before is all I meant, you know: escort a wife around, and dance, and all that. Heard him tell Lady Flitcroft he can't feel from the waist down. Aw, I shouldn't be telling such things to . . . to ladies. Beg your pardon."

Tricia set her chin at a dangerous tilt. "It's time we returned home." She said the minimum in reply to his pleas for understanding. But at his request for forgiveness, she grasped his hand sincerely and forgave him.

* * *

By the time they reached Soaring Gables again, she had forgiven Lord Bixby with her heart. She chatted to him about her childhood antics, and explained a very silly game she and her brother, David, had played which often went on for days. One would start it by putting a sprig of heather behind the other's ear when they least expected it, and run off. The other had to wear it on his or person and wait for a chance to slip the sprig behind the other's ear, or chase them and hold them still until they could achieve it.

He and Lady Caro laughed.

When his carriage halted before her drawing room windows, he handed her out. While he reached in for his gray top hat, Tricia irrepressibly plucked a snip of purple heather from the ground and tucked it above his ear.

He whirled with a surprised exclamation.

Tricia, with laughing eyes, sprinted off to the back garden. As she rounded the corner, she spied the Duke in the window seat of his allocated bedchamber. She was embarrassed to be seen making such a mad dash, but it was too late to turn prim, for Bixby's running footsteps thumped on the walk. He made straight for her, his eyes full of grinning revenge, twirling the heather menacingly between his fingers.

She gave a little scream and darted for the rose trellises. Why, oh why had she started this stupid game with him? She had only tried to lighten the mood. What must the Duke think of the two of them?

* * *

At the window, the Duke made an impatient sound. His eyes were glued on Tricia as she squealed and laughed, running through the arch of climbing roses, Bixby after her, coattails flapping. What on earth was in his hand? What was he trying to do with it?

Around and around Tricia dashed, her yellow gown flying up at the hem, showing lace and fluff and pretty ankles as she flew over the grass and back onto the stone path, crying, "I'm sorry I started it! This is too daft! No!" she screeched as he caught her.

Rowan's eyes darkened in displeasure as he watched Bixby grasp her firmly around the waist, smile ear to ear, and push her bonnet back off her head. Was he going to kiss her? Rowan kept his eyes ferociously pinned on them. When her hat was down, Bixby lifted some little wispy thing and, though she cringed and rolled her head away from him, he crammed the item onto the top of her ear with no apparent mercy whatsoever.

Tricia shouted as she grabbed it off, "You cheated! It has to stay on your ear. You're in for it now, Bix!"

"I hope so!" he threw back, pushing his hat more firmly on his brow and, looking over his shoulder, grinned like an idiot as he ran away from her past Rowan's window.

Having hastily moved to the other window in his Bath chair, he saw Tricia walk slowly to the back door of the house, picking apart whatever she was holding. She did not follow Bixby, which relieved Rowan more than a little.

His neck felt constricted, so he jerked his cravat off, round and round. It had hit him like a knife in the back when Bixby pierced him with the news that *he* had asked Tricia to marry him. Rowan knew, in that moment as never before, that he himself loved her to distraction. It had been pure agony to be tied to Lady Jewel, and the most monumental reason had been Tricia. He loved her, needed her, and lived for her. Even a glimpse of her trusting, loving face brought sunshine into his soul.

Now, since his harrowing tie to Lady Jewel was severed, he could not stop thanking God. But, as Rowan removed the jet buttons from his shirt, a new agony hit him.

Bixby had told him that Tricia was considering his offer; that she needed time to get to know him better. After what Rowan had just seen between them, his pulses pounded with fear. Had Tricia accepted him? Was that what their merry chase was all about?

The possibility fell like a rock into the pit of Rowan's stomach. That had to be it. She would hardly allow Bixby to grope and grab her in such an abandoned fashion unless they had love and an understanding between them . . . would she?

Rowan ground his teeth and pulled the shirt out of his breeches. He thought of the Hobart ball, where Bixby had made it known he had his eye on Tricia. Lately he had fought Kilver in the tunnel for her, and she had voiced aloud her great appreciation.

Rowan's legs were tingling again, so he moved them heavily, trying to kick his boots off. He felt too clumsy, unable to make his muscles do what he wanted to. In exasperation, he yanked at the bell pull.

While it still swung back and forth, the door opened and Theodore, his footman, plummeted in. "Yes, Your Grace?"

"My boots. Pull the blasted things off, will you?" He recalled, in nostalgic detail, the time Patrick Raven had fallen on her little bottom pulling his boot off, and the fire irons had toppled on top of her. He hadn't even guessed she was a female.

How kind she was. Now she was trying to cure him of this affliction. Oh, to go back in time and be able to cavort with her again, in all her energy and fun, like Bixby was doing today. Rowan felt useless and left out of things. It made him bad tempered.

Even if Bixby were not in Rowan's way, why would Tricia take *him* as a husband? He could not imagine any woman, no matter how sweet or understanding, wanting to link herself for life to a useless man in a Bath chair. Lady Flitcroft and Jewel had made that abundantly clear.

He groaned aloud as the depression settled like a load on his chest.

Theodore asked fearfully, "Is something the matter, Your Grace?"

"Continue," motioned the Duke, flushing in embarrassment. He watched as his second boot came slowly off in Theodore's hand.

Rowan sighed and asked to be helped to his wash basin and then to his bed. He thanked his footman and dropped onto the bed, where he laid his head back onto the pile of half a dozen pillows. They were too high for comfort, so he groped behind him irritably until he got a hold of one. Thinking of Bixby winning his way into Tricia's heart, he threw the pillow past his bedpost with force.

* * *

A heavy *thud* hit her face and knocked her off balance. As the pillow fell to the floor, Tricia reacted. "Your Grace! Why did you attack me like that?"

"Where did you appear from?" he demanded.

She had wondered why he had looked so pained at his window seat, and felt there was something very wrong, so she had come in quietly. It astonished her to see Rowan lying in bed, his night shirt on already, his dark hair tousled against the white pillow pile. Her first glimpse of him had shown an angry-looking face. After hitting her with his rage-driven pillow, he looked appalled.

"Did you hear me coming?" she queried suspiciously.

"No, Tricia, I did not." He rolled onto one elbow, running a harried hand through his hair.

Theodore, who was fighting laughter, picked up Rowan's boots and stowed them in the armoire.

The dejection and furor she had seen in the Duke's face alarmed her. Had Jewel really broken his heart?

When she was playing that vapid heather game with Bixby, Rowan had looked very disturbed through the window. Now this pillow had been hurled at her, powered by strong emotion. Tricia's mind whirled in uneasiness as she picked it up. Is he that broken up by Jewel's jilt?

She forced herself to regard only the outward manifestations of his melancholy. She dropped the pillow near the headboard. "What is this all about?" she asked him lightly.

"Accept my apologies, Lady Tricia," he said, lifting deadly-serious eyes to hers.

She gripped the bedpost and said, "This is not like you, Your Grace, going to bed before dinner. Aren't you hungry?"

"No. Thank you, anyway." He motioned to Theodore. "Bring me my dressing gown. I did not expect a Lady to call."

Tricia stood her ground.

Theodore brought a dark blue silk garment and held it for the Duke to shove his arms into.

Tricia asked, "How are your legs now, Your Grace?"

"Not much good."

Tricia knew she must cheer him up and give him hope.

"I will exercise you a bit now, since I'm here." Though she knew he would protest, she grabbed his ankle and lifted it.

He eyed her guardedly, but she would not look at him. She kept on raising and lowering his leg, then bending it up and down, which worked the knee.

Lionel came in and watched surreptitiously, likely wondering if he should help. Tricia moved to repeat her motion on the Duke's other side. It amazed her that he was not reprimanding her or being recalcitrant.

Though she kept her back toward his face, she grew so curious to see how he was taking her bossy manipulations that she sneaked a look back at him. His agate brown eyes glittered on her from between slits of black lashes as he lay against his carved headboard. She could not read his expression, but she wondered if he winced.

"Is this bringing about any sensations at all?" she inquired softly.

"Yes," he said in a rather choked voice.

"Really? Like what?"

"Pins and needles! Ow!"

"Hallelujah!" she cried.

"No, no, don't go off into jubilation. It's only a little ways down—yowch!" He kicked her, and she fell back into Lionel, who was passing behind her, or she could have hit the floor.

"That was not done on purpose!" Rowan said with a grimace, pulling his leg back into line with an effort. "My muscles took a mind of their own."

Rather shaken, she could hardly watch his discomfort. "I do hope this means that you're getting better, Your Grace." She told Lionel and Theodore to rub his legs vigorously. She went down to the kitchen and ordered him a dinner tray to be served in his room.

She stayed away from the ground floor until dinner was announced. Lord Bixby was to stay and partake with Lady Caro and herself. Tricia had sent in a little message with the Duke's food tray, saying she hoped he would change his mind and join them all in the dining room at seven o'clock.

Sarah came in with a warm satin ribbon she had just pressed for Tricia. She took a folded paper from her apron pocket and said, "Here's a letter for you, My Lady."

Tricia took it, and saw her Duke's black writing on the creamy paper. Her spirits took little wings, and she read:

> *Dear Lady Tricia,*
> *I am sorry for hitting you with one of the pillows you so generously provided for my weary head. Please excuse me from your dinner table this evening, but do come by at supper time and bring me any scraps of news I may not have heard.*
> *Thank you for your kind efforts on my behalf. You are a woman in a million. I appreciate you more than you know.*
> *Your devoted servant,*
> *Rowan*

She thought how very nice it was to hear that he appreciated her. She would happily go in to see him at supper time. She reread the letter. He wanted news. What could she tell him? Did this mean he was lonely?

Sarah said, "The Duke's footmen are all prowling around the servant's hall with nothing to do. His Grace sent them all out and locked his door."

Tricia stared in perplexity. "How did he do that?"

"Had them put him in his Bath chair and turned the key after them."

Tricia thought about Lady Jewel's rejection of Rowan as a husband that morning, and sighed, "I imagine he has had a terrible day—several days!—and his nerves and body need rest more than anything."

* * *

After dinner, as the sun sank onto the moor with a glorious red blush, it filled the dining room with light that touched Tricia's curls with a red-gold gloss. Lord Bixby had left reluctantly after she refused to continue their sport with the heather.

As soon as Flint saw him out, Tricia beckoned Lady Caro and shamelessly proposed that they have second portions of pudding.

Lady Caro laid down her fork. "This crundle pudding is out of this world, and that sweet whipped cream—mmm! My, but you are a beauty, my girl. That mouth is so touching, but why does it droop at the corners?"

Tricia blinked to attention. "Aunt Caro," she said, "I wonder what we should do about the Duke."

"Do about him?"

Tricia fingered her lace neck ruff and said, "Consider His Grace's woes: Lord Kilver schemed to have him kidnapped and hurt, Jewel coerced him into an engagement, then crushed his pride in this public jilt. I have to make him exercise, and the tingling it causes seems excruciating. He has nothing to make him happy."

Lady Caro sighed and considered. Her expression brightened. "We can cheer him up. Perhaps a musical evening or a card party?"

"Aunt, he does not like parties."

"Oh, true. What does he like?"

"Horses, which he cannot ride now? I don't know. Reading books? He relishes adventure and challenges," she said with conviction, "and he likes to laugh. But I don't know how to afford him any hilarity in his present state."

"Nor I. What you can do is provide him with newspapers, books, and any anecdotes you have to tell about your day. Talk about Flint, the servants, anything quirky or stupid that occurs around here." Lady Caro rose with renewed energy and said, "I'll ask him to play at chequers with me beneath the rose trellis tomorrow. That should get him out and give him something to occupy his mind."

Tricia chuckled. "Best of luck with that stimulating entertainment. I'll try to move his limbs again after your game brings him to bounding good spirits. You must let him win, Aunt."

"I'll try my best to be fascinating company," added Lady Caro, touching her coiffure flirtatiously, "but Tricia," she said seriously, "I believe you are the only one who can spark him into good humor."

* * *

Tricia bade her good-night, and went to Rowan's room at supper time, which was eleven-thirty by the clock in the drawing room. She carried a bouquet of white roses arranged in Queen Anne's lace.

"For me?" he asked, flashing a shy smile at her from the armchair, where he sat with his feet propped on a footstool. He received them from her, grasped her hand, and kissed it.

Tricia blushed. It was lovely to feel his lips on her skin. "Yes, but I wish I could do more to bring some joy into your life, Your Grace." She felt like hugging him. She remembered what Lady Caro had said, that if she were but ten years younger . . . Tricia couldn't bring herself to do it.

Rowan smelled a white rose deeply and set the vase on the nearby table. "You do that just by walking in. Tell me," he added brusquely, "do you have any news to impart?"

She sank to a chair and wondered at the challenging tilt of his head. Why were his eyes suddenly boring into hers? "What would you like to hear about?"

"Anything of import that may have happened in your life."

Tricia blinked. "Why, nothing, except that Lady Caro and I got rid of Lord Bixby right after dinner by not inviting him to stay. Then we tore back to the table and gobbled up more crundle pudding." She put her chin in her hand and dimpled. "Do you want some more? Or a little soup and herring toast for supper?"

Rowan watched her with full attention, his dark eyes really staring at her. He blinked, heard what she had asked, and said, "No, thank you. That pudding was so good that I had two helpings after dinner."

When she smiled, he relaxed back and smiled, too, apparently feeling much better. So Caro was right; any chirpy conversation did cheer him up.

He said, out of the blue, after the clock had ticked a few times, "So you haven't accepted any offers of marriage or anything while I've been holed up in here?"

Her eyes riveted to him in puzzling inquiry. He

was examining the plaster ceiling design.

"No!" she said, "and that was a ludicrous question."

"You know, that's a truly beautiful pattern!" he remarked enthusiastically, craning his head around to see its complete circumference.

CHAPTER 31

Exercises in Exasperation

The next morning, when Tricia appeared in the doorway to the dining room wearing a gown of light sea green, Rowan smiled appreciatively. She was so slender and lovely. She moved with a grace she probably didn't even know she possessed. How opposite she was to the London ladies, who he heard spent months learning how to move from a drawing room to a dining room, and gesturing in the proper way.

Lady Caro said, "Shall we play at chequers after breakfast, Rowan?"

He touched his napkin to his curving lips and said, "That would be something frolicsome to do."

Tricia giggled and said, "We know you will soon be at *point non plus* staying here, so please tell us what would entertain you, and we will bring it about."

Lady Caro inserted, "Even if we have to play Nine Men's Morris with you around the clock."

Tricia added, "Or hire Morris Men to dance for you with their sticks and bells."

The Duke sipped his coffee, grinned, and said, "I can hardly absorb all this graciousness. However, if this does not seriously upset your plans, ladies, I would enjoy a drive along the coast. In fact, I've ordered my coach, and was on the verge of inviting two beauties to accompany me."

"I would love it of all things!" exclaimed Lady Caro. "Tricia?"

"Yes, a lovely idea. But first, Your Grace," she said, taking a seat with her plate of eggs and ham from the sideboard, "we will go through a few motions of your limbs." The smile she gave him was a flash of spring, but there was iron behind it.

Rowan moaned dramatically.

As she turned wide eyes on him, he lifted a hand. "I think that is a commendable plan: martyrdom first, with earned rewards to follow. I feel myself back at Eton."

* * *

In the drawing room, standing before her open Bible on a stand, Tricia placed her hand on her heart. "Stefan," she said as he walked by the arched doorway, "please call all the servants in here. I have forgotten the most important part of running a household."

"My Lady? They are all to drop whatever they're doing?"

"Yes, please."

When Mr. Flint and the new housekeeper, Mrs. Chandler, along with Sarah, Rowan's footmen, Cook and her helpers, Mollie and the gardener had assembled, Tricia crossed the hall to the dining room. She saw that the Duke and Lady Caro looked curious about the commotion. "We're to have morning prayers," Tricia told them.

"Why, how commendable," said Lady Caro.

"No, Aunt, it's needful. Will you join us?"

The Duke, beginning to push his wheels, said, "Yes, of course."

The servants were all ranged as far back against the furniture as possible, hands folded. The maids looked sidewise at the handsome Duke as he rolled in.

Tricia went to Flint and said low, "Can you lead us in prayer? We want to pray for the Duke's recovery."

"Aye, Lady Tricia," he replied, his face serene. "We all want that." He stepped forward, closed his eyes, and bowed his head.

After moments of silence, the servants began to drop to their knees. Tricia lowered herself to a hassock, and even Lady Caro descended to the carpet, her sprigged gown billowed about her.

Septimus Flint began in a soft voice; his hands twined together, "Dear Heavenly Father, we desire to thank Thee for our manifold blessings, especially our salvation through Christ our Lord. We beg Thy Divine goodness and mercy in healing His Grace the Duke of Rowan. May we all serve him, and these benevolent ladies, to the best of our abilities. Give us of Thy strength and wisdom to overcome any evil that may assail us. Protect us all. In the name of the Father, and of the Son, and of the Holy Ghost. Amen."

"Amen's" echoed around the room.

The Duke remained with his head down and his hands clasped. By his attitude, Tricia knew that he was moved. He turned to Septimus Flint and said, "Thank you." Straightaway, he wheeled himself out of the room.

Tricia told Flint that they would make morning prayers a part of each day, and asked him to set a time. Then she invited Rowan outdoors for his dreaded exercise program. The air and the change of scene, at least, should do him good.

She asked Rupert and Theodore to roll up a carpet and carry it to where the view of the Bay was best. She donned a cape of tan which covered her frock, and followed Stefan as he energetically pushed the Duke across the uneven flags.

Mollie came running. Out of breath, she told Tricia, "My Lady! Cook is upset about something, and has sent you this note."

Standing in the warm sunshine, Tricia read,

> *Your Ladyship,*
> *I don't understand it, but someone has been in the storage cellar, moving my crates of molasses and other stuffs to where they are not convenient. All the servants deny doing it, and so do His Grace's footmen. I believe them.*
>
>> *Your devoted*
> > *Cook*

Tricia saw Rowan being assisted from his Bath chair to the carpet on the turf by his four footmen. She wondered about the letter in her hand. Had Kilver sneaked into her house with his key and done the moving? The possibility gave her real alarm.

"Will you fly away with me, Lady Tricia?" called Rowan as he lay on the Persian carpet eyeing the wide blue sky and white clouds above. "Where, pray tell, could this take us?"

Tricia took one look at his eyes brimming with adventure, and smiled. His spirits seemed so much better today. He held out his arms as if he expected her to run and topple into them. She laughed.

The footmen fought to hide their grins, but unsuccessfully.

Adopting a rigid composure, Tricia directed, "Take off his boots, please, Theodore."

"O-ho!" Rowan protested. "Shall I let her undress me here, where the clouds and the gulls and all creation can see? Perhaps the sun would do me good."

"Yes, Your Grace," quipped Rupert, and they all laughed.

Tricia's snap of the prescription papers served to jolt Rowan out of his daydreams. She consulted the drawings and said, "Stefan and Lionel, push on the balls of his feet, while you, Your Grace, give them good resistance."

Tricia spied her aunt at the upstairs window in high gig, with Tricia's spyglass trained on them.

The Duke said, giving in with a grin when he saw Lady Caro spying, "Dash it if you and Mr. Newell don't render me ridiculous." He extended his legs, stiff as ramrods. Before long, the footmen were pushing him off the carpet until his head was in the grass.

Tricia could not stem her laughter. "Not that hard, you men. Oh dear, pull him back and begin again."

"Lady Tricia," said the Duke with a savage look

from between his black lashes, "what have I done to deserve this rack?"

Biting back a smile, she raised her chin. "Now bend his knees one at a time up to his chest. Ready?"

Before the Duke could so much as protest, Lionel and Stefan were folding the ducal limbs, touching his knees to his waistcoat very gently, for Tricia had warned that his injuries must be coddled.

Rowan sighed and gave up. "Oh, if Brummell could see me now! And wouldn't Alvanley just double over?"

"Now work his feet," said his task mistress, pleased with their progress.

"What does Your Ladyship mean?" asked Stefan.

"I shall have to show you, I suppose."

Rowan rose to support himself with his elbows. He admonished her, "A Lady should not do such things without a gentleman's by-your-leave."

"Then give me leave," she retorted, dimpling. She knelt on her cape before him and reminded him sweetly, "You won't feel a thing." To Stefan she said, "Be so good as to prop his calf upon your knee. Lionel, take the other side."

Amidst quips from Rowan and adroit maneuvering by the footmen, Tricia grasped one of Rowan's white-stockinged feet. Summoning a no-nonsense attitude, she massaged the manly foot with her thumbs. In fascination, the servants watched their master thus commandeered.

Rowan said in an odd voice, "I think truly, this job should be done by a footman."

Everybody roared with laughter.

When Tricia reached the middle of his arch, his

foot flew up, cutting Stefan in the chin, knocking his teeth together. The Duke rolled over on his side, forcefully trying to pull his spasmodic leg into line.

Stefan nursed a bloodied tongue.

"My word!" Tricia exhaled in wonder. "I do believe this massage is good for you, Duke. Every time you exert yourself, or your blood otherwise starts moving faster, your muscles react. Isn't that a wonderful sign?"

He subsided into stillness. "Extremely heartening," he returned from the level of the carpet. "Can we forego whatever else you had planned for this session?"

"Yes, Your Grace, until tomorrow. You have done very well." She gave him an appreciative smile for his compliance. How grand he looked, lying there, the grass waving beyond his dark hair. His expression melted from exasperation to softness as he looked up at her.

Tricia felt a rush of longing that she and this Duke could forever be together, even as now, through fun or danger, exasperation or understanding. She wished fervently for his love so she could freely show him hers.

* * *

When Rowan's horses trotted friskily along the road to Whitby, Tricia sat in the coach next to Lady Caro and opposite their ducal escort. Although her feminine heart sighed over his charming presence, she increasingly admired his resilience in coping with his tragedies. That he had been cast into despair over Jewel's jilt did not cause Tricia to hold it against him. A Duke's ego must, at times, be a fragile thing and a heavy burden to bear. After all, the higher you were, the further you could fall.

Jewel and her parents had called just as the spasm concluded Rowan's carpet ordeal. They were all seated in the drawing room when Tricia and the Duke entered with the footmen en masse, all of them flushed with outdoorsy vigor and smelling of sea air.

Lady Jewel, attired in a tomato red traveling costume with a tan bonnet, ran her eyes over Rowan and then Tricia. Her expression did not match her well-modulated greeting, for she looked disdainful. "We are here to say good-bye."

Rowan insisted on accompanying them to their carriage, and rose slightly by means of his arms from his Bath chair to bow his head over Jewel's and her mother's hands. He sank back onto the seat to shake hands with His Lordship.

"We shall see you in London, hopefully in fine fettle, Duke," said Lord Wyndhurst, his eyes not quite resting on the prime specimen of manhood who was lost to him as a son-in-law.

"We'll meet at White's before long," Rowan agreed.

No one had pressed the question of when Tricia might arrive in London. She suspected that Lady Wyndhurst was not overly thrilled with the prospect of tagging her new niece along to drawing rooms when she had Jewel to continue launching before the noses of the *haut ton* and its marriage market. Tricia wondered what reception poor

Jewel would find in West End mansions now. It was almost unheard-of for a lady to jilt a personage as important as the Duke of Rowan.

Tricia was mightily relieved to have Jewel and her parents gone. It was such a blessed feeling to remain in her home with the Duke and Lady Caro and Flint, and also Sarah, the London maid whom Lady Caro insisted on keeping.

Wheeling on the high road north, Rowan, watching the sea, said, "Let's halt. That looks like old Earnshaw." He rapped his walking stick on the roof. "Yes, that's young Earnie waving his cap."

The coach slowed nicely and pulled off the road to let a fish cart go by. Stefan opened the door to the sounds of rushing surf and mewing gulls and gusting wind. The Duke pulled on the edges of the door to heft himself out. Lionel and Stefan aided him to move with his arms on their shoulders.

Rowan called, "Ladies, will you join me in a stroll?"

Lady Caro smiled at Tricia. "This is good for him."

Watching his well-shaped legs moving stoically one before the other, Tricia agreed. Arm–in-arm with Lady Caro, she said cheerfully, "This is the kind of thing he likes."

Down below, on the blue-green sea, was a bright canary yellow coble. Mr. Earnshaw and his son were lowering the sails and beaching it. Rowan looked bent on descending the slope to meet them, so Tricia fastened her bonnet ribbons tighter and gripped Lady Caro's arm to support her over the heather.

"What do you suppose we're doing?" Lady Caro

asked, her eyes interested.

"Enjoying a diversion. The Duke is one for spontaneous jaunts, and the Earnshaws have become his friends since they fished him out of the Bay."

The foaming sea swirled, but Earnshaw stood in his tossing coble and hollered, "Nah then, Yer Greace, what about it?" He gestured to the new craft in which he balanced.

"A spanking fine vessel," shouted the Duke, nodding. "Did you paint it yourself?"

"Aye."

"I ought to come try it out," yelled the Duke.

"Nay, tha'll get clarted wi' mucky mud."

Young Earnie jumped with a splash out of the boat onto the beach. Soon he was vaulting up the bank toward them. Upon the level, he raised his cap to the Duke and put a wind-flapping paper into his hand. "Here's from m' father."

That made Tricia realize that Rowan had deliberately arranged this meeting.

"And how's the bump on your crown, Your Grace?"

"Quite subsided, I believe."

He unfolded his paper while the footmen looked away at the sea birds landing nearby. When the paper had received his study, Rowan tucked it into his coat pocket and indicated that Stefan should give the young man something.

At the sight of money, Earnie backed away and warded it off with gimlet eyes. "No, thank you, Your Grace! You've done too much already. Much obliged for the coble. It's a skimmer, the best we've had. I admired it in the boat shop for the last month. Didn't ever think it would be ours!"

The Duke smiled. "That's good to hear."

Tricia and Lady Caro lifted their eyebrows at each other.

Earnie called, "Good day, Your Grace. We'll see you . . . you know when."

"Yes. Good day. Would you ladies care to stop at an inn for refreshment?" he called, approaching with his arms heavily over his footmen. "I would like to continue north a ways."

An adventurous spirit infused Tricia and her aunt, so they gladly accepted. They waved at the Earnshaw men pulling on their oars. Tricia dared not commend the Duke for his gift of a new coble, but privately she applauded him.

Rowan did not wish to stop in Whitby, but would rather seek out a little inn with a grand view of the North Sea, he said. Shepperton skirted the town the best he could, and steered them up a winding road past a collection of cottages, workshops, and a lime-burning kiln. He pulled in the horses in front of the Mulgrave Castle Inn.

When they entered, they were curiously assessed by the proprietress. She was all attention, watching Rowan half-carried in by two of his footmen. She curtseyed in awe, introduced herself as Jane Bell, and asked what Milord desired.

Tricia had heard that notorious name in connection with smugglers. She was a coarse sort of woman, with her voice as low as a man's.

Rowan treated Mistress Bell with as much respect as any lady at the Hobart ball. His footmen steered him to the corner table which was partly screened off, making it the area for "gentry," as Jane Bell called it. The Duke, who was far above gentry, genially ordered cider, coffee, and whatever else Mistress Bell would serve each of them from their voiced preferences.

Tricia was shocked to see him motion the woman closer. He checked that the other guests weren't listening, and said, "I'm with Kilver. The vessel's been sighted this morning off Bay Town."

Jane Bell alerted at that, and gave Rowan a look of understanding. "What kind of tea was that, Milord?" she queried loudly.

"Black or green will do," said Rowan.

Tricia wondered how he dared to pass on such false information, pretending to be allied with Kilver.

Rowan motioned for Lionel and Stefan to come to him. They awaited their refreshments with Shepperton at the bar, but moved immediately. The Duke said, "I will take a walk outside while Mistress Bell makes the coffee and tea. Will you excuse me, Ladies?"

"Certainly," said Lady Caro, watching him move away with assistance. "He is such a restless man; he just cannot sit still long. That this injury had to happen to him is truly a shame."

Tricia watched them descend a series of steps on the slope and follow the retaining wall as it curved away. Rowan's hat could be seen turning back and forth as he found something to catch his interest along the wall.

"Aunt, will you excuse me? I want to go see what he's doing."

"You're leaving me here? All right, I can see you need the activity, too. Go. I'll drink tea. But don't,

I pray, be above five minutes."

"I won't." Tricia let herself out through the creaking door.

The Duke stood in the shade of the wall, with only Lionel to lean on. Tricia passed Stefan and asked, "What are you doing?"

"I am keeping watch, My Lady."

"Can you tell me what for?"

Suddenly Stefan's voice grew hard. "For chaps like that who come snooping. The Duke wants no one around while he snoops himself."

Tricia turned and saw a fat man leave Jane Bell at the inn door and come plying his walking stick toward them. "I'll go tell the Duke," she told Stefan, "while you go engage *that* in conversation."

Tricia hurried around the curving wall. The Duke was reaching for something in the wall. "What is it, Tricia?"

"An old man is coming. He was talking with Jane Bell."

The Duke pushed, something scraped, and Tricia saw a rectangular stone halfway out of the wall. Lionel quickly replaced it, making it look undisturbed.

"A hiding place?" she whispered to Rowan.

"Yes," he said, looking satisfied. "Come, Tricia, sit here by me. Tell me about your childhood by the sea," he suggested so the approaching man would not suspect that they had been doing anything but talking.

They assumed a lazy, conversational manner. Tricia described playing in the Bay sand. Once, she had spent hours constructing the Whitby church high enough on a pile to make some of the

199 curving steps which led up to it.

The man lifted his hat as he shuffled by them, and continued on his way.

"How did you know those stones came out?" Tricia whispered when he was well out of earshot.

"Earnshaw told me. Earnie brought me a drawing of where this place was to be found. Lionel could spot exactly which stones were loose because his father is a stonemason."

Tricia smiled appreciatively at Lionel. She whispered to the Duke, "Was it true what you told Jane Bell? Was a ship truly sighted?"

"Oh, yes. Earnshaw thinks the hull and sails that appeared on the horizon an hour ago belong to *The White Dove*." He touched her hand as he said, "It's your ship, Tricia. We cannot let Kilver keep it."

Tricia's heart began to thump. She feared that her Duke would get hurt again if he interfered with Kilver. Noting his determined profile, she prayed to God to protect him in whatever he did.

"I don't know who that man was," Rowan murmured as he leaned onto Lionel and then Stefan, "but he was curious about us. Let's make tracks. Better yet, no tracks." He winked at Tricia.

She let out a long, dreamy breath. He had the power to slay her with a look.

CHAPTER 32

Secrets Concealed

Sitting with the Duke at a table outdoors beneath her rose trellis, Tricia asked him, "Why did you tell Jane Bell that you were with Kilver? And why did you let *her* know that the ship came in?"

The leaves waved behind the Duke's head as he lowered his coffee cup and said, "Earnie is going to watch what happens now that I have given her that information. The Earnshaws have it figured out that the Mulgrave Castle Inn is a signal station, and Jane Bell works with the smugglers. They hide booty in that wall we looked at."

Tricia threw a crumb of her scone to a bright-eyed robin and said, "I must alert Mr. Richard from the Customs Office. He and his men must watch for contraband from my ship. Oh Rowan, because it belongs to me, I could land in grave trouble!"

"We must point Customs Officers in Kilver's direction."

"What good would that do? Everyone fears him."

"I'll tip them off to watch his movements. The Customs men will then check the ship's bill of cargo against what is actually on board."

Tricia cocked an eyebrow. "But smugglers

always lift their goods first. Then they allow the Customs Officer on board to inspect a much lighter load."

"I am sure that happens, but the sitters should be watching for cobles that try to slip shoreward in the night hours. We must catch Kilver at it. Tricia, will you be so good as to help me to my chair?"

She smiled, glad for the chance. "It is the least I can do."

"What, sweet Lady, is that supposed to mean?" She enjoyed the way he directed questions at her with that assessing sparkle. For a shy gentleman, he looked very spirited.

"The least I can do is to help you physically when you are bending over backward to help me with my dilemmas. How could I possibly fare in this situation alone?"

Rowan looked at her sternly and declared, "No young lady, least of all an heiress to a ship used fraudulently, should face illegal doings alone. I do wish Lord Wyndhurst had stayed," he mused. "I could have used his help." He hefted himself to his feet, grasping the table and the rose trellis, and moved until his boots were positioned evenly beneath him to hold his weight.

Tricia approached him, impressed. "It seems that you have progressed a great deal, Duke. Can you lean on me a little? We can make it there together." Sarah came running from the house in her apron, but Tricia frowned at the helpful maid, who backed off. She grasped him tightly around the ribcage, and in her mind, she made it an embrace.

"Thank you," he murmured after he plunked into his Bath chair. "You are too good to me." Before she could deny it, he wheeled himself away toward the garden door, where Theodore waited with a makeshift ramp up the steps.

* * *

For the next hour, Tricia wondered about *The White Dove*. She would go crazy dwelling on possibilities, so she went to find Lady Caro. She asked her, "Shall we go in and visit the Duke? I should ask him to do some more exercises. I actually think they're helping!"

"By all means," said her aunt. "I almost split laughing watching your last attempts. What you got him to do, Tricia, I could hardly believe."

Tricia knocked on his chamber door, a bouquet of pink roses in her hand.

Lady Caro sniffed them appreciatively. "Thank you for mine," she said. "The yellow ones are so sunny beside my bed."

The door opened at last. Rupert lifted his finger to his lips.

"Is the Duke asleep?" Tricia asked in a whisper.

"Almost, Your Ladyship."

"So early? Is he not feeling well?"

"No, Your Ladyship."

"What is the matter?"

Rupert was about to speak when Lady Caro pressed, "Is it his spine?"

"I imagine so, Your Ladyship."

"Let us know when he wakes up. We'll hold dinner back for him if necessary. Supper, too." Tricia put the vase of roses in his hands. "Place these beside his bed, please."

"With pleasure, My Lady," said the large-nosed Rupert, sniffing them.

"He suffers more than he lets on," said Lady Caro as they retreated to the entrance hall.

"I'm sending for Mr. Newell."

"Yes, do," urged Lady Caro, starting up the white staircase. "Lord Bixby is to come for dinner. I wonder if Rowan will be up to joining us."

Tricia, in her room giving orders to Sarah, decided to go for Mr. Newell herself. Pulling on white wool gloves and a blue pelisse and bonnet, she looked out the window at clouds of fog which had shrouded the Bay in the last half hour. She caught a glimpse of someone moving near the carriage house. A horse with a low-capped rider appeared as a ghostly outline cantering in the near distance. The swishing dark tail melted away as the mists swirled. Who was that rider? She felt afraid, but he had gone. She hurried to Flint's pantry and called his name.

The little man poked his head out, spectacles tipping off his small nose.

Tricia caught them.

"Aye-yi! Lady Tricia, how may I serve ye?"

"Who has been here just now?" she asked while she noted that the lock on the front door was still secured.

"No callers all afternoon. Only the fish woman at the back door at two of the clock, My Lady."

"Flint, I saw a rider behind the carriage house a minute ago. Did you see him ride by?"

"Aye-yi, did somebody approach and I failed to see? I keep watch for Lord Kilver. I keep both doors fastened, Lady Tricia." He looked bewildered.

"That's all right; you cannot stand with your eye to the window all day long, Flint." Tricia took him with her to do a hurried check of the carriage house and environs. They found no one, and heard nothing but the birds and the crash of the waves far below.

She set out for Bay Town on foot, taking Sarah with her, both of them bundled against the moisture permeating the air. Was her father's beautiful ship really out there enfolded by that gray shroud? She felt a need to hasten. She warned Sarah to watch her step as they sped down the cobbled streets.

The surgeon was just returning to his home, looking weary as he dismounted from his horse in Chapel Street. "Good evening, Lady Tricia."

"Mr. Newell, after you stop and eat something, will you please go up and see the Duke? He made some good progress with sensation and moving his legs a little, but I believe his condition is worse, for he is down in bed already."

"Yes, Your Ladyship, I'll come."

Tricia described her efforts with his prescribed exercises. "He has done some each day with my supervision, but he doesn't relish them at all. His muscles sometimes go into spasms."

"They do? Why, that's a very good sign!" said Mr. Newell, his face lighting up. "That is usually the first indication of some hope of nerves returning to a little function. I will run the Duke through the motions myself while I'm there, and I will stress the need for continuance."

Feeling happy at such encouraging words, Tricia

made her way to the Customs House.

"Mr. Richard, please," she said to the skinny young clerk with long hair who bent over a sheaf of papers at the counter.

"Eh? He's in with the Captain now; cannot be disturbed."

"The Captain of which vessel?"

Evasively he said, "The one off shore."

"The White Dove?"

The clerk hesitated.

Tricia smiled and told him, "I am on the Customs' side, so never fear, you can tell me. I will wait here to see Mr. Richard."

He pointed to two chairs where she and Sarah could wait.

Tricia saw, through the bubbled glass in the door, that Mr. Richard was indeed speaking to a Captain, for the man with his back toward her sported epaulettes on his coat.

She rapped on the window, turned the door knob, and slipped in despite the scrambling of the clerk behind her.

"Mr. Richard," she said to the surprised men rising, "I am here to meet the Captain of my ship." She smiled at the Customs Officer and then turned to the stranger. "Do you command *The White Dove,* Captain?"

The man bowed his fair head. "I do, Ma'am." He was a watchful, serious young man with sun-tanned skin and a straight bearing.

"This is Captain Trevellyan, Your Ladyship," said Mr. Richard. "Captain, this is the late Leigh Ravenscar's daughter, Lady Tricia Claremont."

The Captain looked bewildered, and hastily

bowed to her.

Politely, Tricia said, "Captain Trevellyan, have you see Lord Kilver yet?"

"No, Your Ladyship, I expected to meet him later. Tomorrow."

"Then you have no knowledge of my existence, I presume?"

"That's right, Your Ladyship. With all due respect, I believe you to be mistaken, for Lord Kilver owns *The White Dove*."

"I am not mistaken, Captain. He should never have told you the ship belongs to him. It does not. From now on, you are not to deal with him anymore, not even in regard to the cargo he ordered, and which you have delivered here. Do you understand?"

"No, I certainly do not."

"Captain Trevellyan," cut in Mr. Richard, "the ship is hers. Kilver has been doing with *The White Dove* as he wishes, but a Will was read the other day that proves the vessel belongs to Lady Tricia, here. The whole town knows it. Lady Tricia, we're about to check the goods."

"Wonderful. I will come with you." What a lucky inkling had brought her here.

Captain Trevellyan looked at her askance as he fastened a row of gold buttons on his coat. "The sea air is cold, Your Ladyship, and the dinghy quite small."

"I am dressed warmly enough, Captain, thank you." Tricia took the arm Mr. Richard offered her, and they walked in business-like silence down through the street to the boats.

Two French sailors eyed Tricia and Sarah with

appreciative brown eyes. Captain Trevellyan told them to ready themselves to row him and his guests to the ship.

Mr. Richard, with bills of cargo in a satchel, stopped to talk privately with one of his sitters. Tricia knew he was alerting them that he and she were going to check the ship's cargo. The sitter handed Mr. Richard one of his pistols.

Her attention turned to the sight of Mrs. Willoughby's stout form huffing and puffing her way up the sand to Wayfoot. Tricia went to greet the woman she had known all her life, and whose daughter, Mollie, now worked for her as a kitchen maid. "What's new with you, Mrs. Willoughby?"

"Oh, nothin' much, Beany—I mean, pardon me— My Lady! Got to get home and see if my bread's risen so I can bring it to the bake shop."

At this time of the evening? The woman seemed to be moving heavily. As she caught at the stone wall for support, she missed, and the bulge of her hip shifted. Tricia sensed something very odd, so she decided to collide with the woman while pretending to catch her. When she did so, Mrs. Willoughby lost her footing on the stone steps and fell into the sand.

"Oh, dear!" cried Tricia loudly. "Look here, Mr. Richard, I need your help."

Mrs. Willoughby gave an angry gasp and a red-faced heave, but could not manage to get to her feet.

Mr. Richard hurried to assist. Before the woman could cover her legs with her skirt, Tricia pointed. Her stockings bulged unnaturally.

Mr. Richard said, "Mrs. Willoughby, I demand, in

the name of the King, that you hand over what it is that you conceal in those stockings."

"Mr. Richard!" she quivered. "What are ye talkin' of?" she sputtered as she rolled to the side. He hefted her to her feet.

Behind her back, Tricia pointed at the woman's skirt, suspiciously wide at the hips.

Mr. Richard called over his shoulder, "Captain, there will be a slight delay." Brooking no refusal, he added, "Do not board that ship without us."

He took the blustering Mrs. Willoughby by the arm and marched her to his office. There he asked that Sarah strip Mrs. Willoughby of all that her voluminous gown concealed. He turned his back.

To Sarah's goggling eyes, unused to smuggling practices, the sight of three pig bladders full of rum tied around the woman's waist caused her mouth to drop open. Tricia's, too. When those had been hefted onto Mr. Richard's desk, Tricia had to tell the mother of her maid to pull down her stockings.

With tears spurting out of her eyes, Mrs. Willoughby untied her garters and rolled down the wool hose. Tricia and Sarah stared in fascination. Around the woman's calves was wound beautiful lace, layers and layers of it.

"Oh my! Unwind that lace, please, Sarah," Tricia directed. Gently she asked the flustered woman, "Have you anything else?"

Mrs. Willoughby jutted her chin stubbornly.

"I would hate to subject you to a more thorough search than this," said Tricia with a necessary edge to her voice. "Please understand that *The White Dove* belongs to me, and it is imperative that you show me everything you have that has come off my ship. I must pay customs for it."

"That vessel belongs to *you*, Beany?" The woman gaped at her.

"Yes. And my inheritance has been illegally used to finance the whole cargo, I am sure. But it shall not be a smuggling ship ever again, beginning now."

The woman gave a wail and dropped her face to her hands. "How could I do such against the daughter of Leigh and Lucretia Ravenscar? I didna know, truly I didna!"

"Who put you up to this?"

"You know who," was all she would say. She, too, was afraid to name him aloud.

"Lord Kilver?"

The woman looked scared but said nothing. She sniffed wetly for awhile, then dug into her bosom and pulled out several ropes of brown, which she clattered onto the desk. "That's all I have. There's much more to come in the cobles, though."

Mr. Richard examined the plunder. He lifted the brown rope and said, "Tobacco. How clever. It could well have been overlooked with all the hemp rope on that ship. My, my, what a lot of expensive-looking lace."

"Was it on the bill of lading, Mr. Richard?"

He shook his head. "No lace listed. No tobacco, either. Rum was, but I suspect the quantities were much diminished. Mrs. Willoughby, you are to stay here in custody until I return." He directed his clerk to secure and watch her.

Down at the Dock, the sailors waited, gripping the dinghy's bowline.

"Where is your Captain?" demanded Mr. Richard.

"Monsieur call him to l'hotel," said one of the sailors, motioning toward the Bay Hotel.

With Tricia in his wake, Mr. Richard strode in and asked Mr. Simby to point him to the Captain's whereabouts. He was with a man in a private parlor, Mr. Simby informed them.

Tricia heard her name called, and turned in the doorway to find Lord Bixby vaulting up the steps from the street. "I've just come from your house," he reported, his eyes a-light, "but Rowan wouldn't see me. Your aunt's in fidgets over him as well as over you. She said I'm to find you and escort you home for dinner. The surgeon arrived as I left. How *is* Rowan?"

"We'll know after Mr. Newell's report. Bix, I can't go home *now*. Can you help us here? We have intercepted contraband!"

She told him excitedly about the Captain whom Mr. Richard would confront about the cargo when they boarded the ship. "Will you follow whomever Captain Trevellyan is meeting, and find out where the person goes? Oh, I wish Rowan was up and about! This is such a crucial moment. I am sure that contraband is being rowed from my ship to Kilver's coffers by the boatload!"

Bixby was instantly motivated, and agreed to spy. "Lady Tricia, I'll do anything you ask."

She dashed off a fervent note to the Duke to tell him she was off to the ship and with whom. She added, *If you can set someone to watch through Flint's spyglass for any signs of movement on water or land, and send reports by your footmen to the Customs House, you will do me a great favor. In haste, Tricia.* On the outside, she printed: *For the Duke: Urgent! Open*

Immediately, and dispatched it by Mr. Simby's messenger boy.

Tricia's ride in the dinghy over the dark water proved a chilling experience. The damp fog hung over the surface and hid the narrow shapes of pointed houses and chimneys on the shore. Each dip of the oars swirled the sea into murky motion. It smelled of wet wood, fish, and tar.

"We all realize, Captain," said Mr. Richard as the dinghy at last pulled alongside the anchored ship, "that you have been sailing under Lord Kilver's orders. This is not to happen any longer, so I strongly advise you to make a clean breast of all that is on this vessel."

"Aye, Sir," said the Captain, looking stressed. Tricia saw that he did not know whom to believe or where his allegiance should lie. Now here he was, in the presence of a Customs Officer and a slip of a girl who claimed to own the ship he had sailed in and out of European ports for two months.

Tricia gazed up at the familiar hull with its three masts disappearing into the fog. As they were about to board, she saw a faintly yellow coble between the rolling mist and the water.

Mr. Richard, halfway up the ship's ladder, indicated he must hurry after the Captain to keep him in sight. Tricia waved him on, for she wanted to see who approached. She told her French seamen to row her toward the small craft while she held up a lantern.

It held Mr. Earnshaw and his son, Earnie, as she had hoped it did. Behind them, wearing a visor cap of black sealskin and a dark gansey, sat Rowan.

Tricia stared at him, first in perplexity and then

in delight. "How did you arrive so soon? I just dispatched my letter to you!"

"What letter? Tricia, why are *you* here in such perilous waters?"

"I am inspecting *The White Dove*. This Captain doesn't know whom to believe, Kilver's minions or me. This is a wonder that you're here, but what prompted you to come?"

When the boats were side by side, the Duke leaned over, grasped Tricia's arms, and said into the space between her bonnet and her ear, "We thought to pose as smuggling help to see if any goods would be given us to spirit away. But now that you've acknowledged us, I wonder if they'll believe us."

Looking into his lively eyes gleaming on her, she whispered, "I'm sorry! I've spoiled it. Oh Rowan," she tugged him back as the boats would have parted, "we caught one smuggler already, and we know others are out, but the Customs Men are prowling. See their lights?" Several appeared intermittently through the lifting fog.

"Right."

"Lord Bixby is keeping a suspicious man in his sights," she continued, "so I hope he fares well. What I must do is keep Kilver from filching any of these goods, but *how*, Rowan?"

He said, "Go aboard and look over your ship. We will figure something out." He smiled. "Use the courage that you have in abundance."

Her heart swelled. The boats parted.

So he had slipped out of her house by the aid of those Earnshaws, and left Lady Caro and the staff believing he was in bed, the rascal! How had he done it?

She and Sarah climbed with some difficulty up a rope ladder to the wooden deck of the vessel, peopled with sailors. They were moving to and fro in great activity, hefting casks and bales from below decks and piling them near the rails. Tricia realized that the task of accounting for everything against the Captain's declaration list was a formidable one.

Captain Trevellyan led her and Mr. Richard down a companionway which took them past horn-windowed lanterns flickering in narrow passages. He knocked on a door and hailed two shipmates to accompany them.

Mr. Richard opened his case, which contained a pen and ink, and marked his list as they checked a hold full of rum. The sailors moved aside casks of brandy, bottles of champagne, and bales of silk for Mr. Richard and the Captain to verify.

"What is that?" asked Mr. Richard, pointing.

"Those are the apples listed, thirty boxes," explained Captain Trevellyan. The top box was opened, and they saw rows of red apples. Mr. Richard made them open each box and he checked them off, some green apples, some yellow.

So it progressed, through storeroom after storeroom. In one of the deepest holds, Mr. Richard pointed out ropes of tobacco hanging with extra docking line. Triumphantly he emerged, smiling at Tricia. "It was provident that you caught on to Mrs. Willoughby. That is how I detected all this tobacco. Thank you very much."

Tricia noted that the young Captain glanced at her, and looked more haggard than ever.

"Captain Trevellyan," she said, "for anything that is found in excess, write it down carefully on your list, and you will be free of blame as far as I am concerned. Lord Kilver has no longer any legal power over me or my inheritance. That includes this ship and everything on it. The Marquis of Wyndhurst will oversee it all."

The man looked dubious, so she added, "The Duke of Rowan is in Robin Hood's Bay at the moment. He will likely press charges against Lord Kilver. Do you understand the ramifications?"

"I believe I understand what you have said, Your Ladyship, but I would appreciate verification."

"You have it from me," threw in Mr. Richard, raising his hand as he scanned his list for sixty bales of raw silk. "You have only sixteen listed, Captain."

Thereafter, Trevellyan gave up trying to protect himself. He admitted that Lord Kilver had financed the whole operation, and he felt accountable for delivering the goods to him.

"If you do," Mr. Richard replied, "I'll cheerfully clap you in irons in the name of the King. Better follow the advice of your generous benefactress, whose money Lord Kilver used to finance this. You may leave His Lordship to the Lords."

* * *

When the sailors rowed Tricia ashore around midnight, she was tired but exultant. Gazing up at the ship's bow, she longed for her parents. The figurehead was a white winged dove but with a woman's head, a beautiful likeness of her mother. This was the ship her father had had built in the

Whitby shipyard.

Tricia had accompanied him on countless jaunts to see how the work progressed, and her mother often joined them. How shocked they would be that their pride and joy had been used with intention to outfox the King's Revenue Men. She must do everything necessary to clear up this shambles.

The French sailors escorted her and Sarah home, holding lanterns to light their way. Tricia shivered, and felt her weariness as her front door came into sight.

Flint was still up, peering through the window. "Aye-yi! I feared you had drowned, My Lady! Praise be to God, you are safe! I opened your letter to the Duke, for he was not to be disturbed for any reason. That's what Rupert said. I reckoned the letter should be read. I took my spyglass and put it to my eye up in the carriage house."

"Yes, Flint? Did you see anything?"

"It was foggy, but finally it lifted, so I kept watch. Sure thing, I saw three fisher cobles set out from Point Ness. What were they were doing out there at that time of night, Lady Tricia? Were they out for some running o' goods? I sent a letter to the Customs Office, as you said to do if we saw anything amiss. That quick Rupert ran it there. Ten minutes ago, I saw the Customs cutters go after them. They shot their firearms. Aye-yi! I hope they caught the runners, Lady Tricia." His rounded forehead deepened in its furrows and his eyes were enormous with concern.

"Thank you, Flint! You showed such presence of mind! Thank you for opening my letter and acting on it." Tricia hugged the little man, who blissfully laid his white mane on her shoulder.

To verify her suspicions, she asked, "Did you say the Duke is not to be disturbed?"

"Correct, My Lady."

"What explanation were you given?"

"That is all Rupert told me."

"When did the Duke come in?"

"Come in, My Lady? He never left." Flint looked befuddled.

Tricia wondered if the little man mixed up his days and hours. Or could Rowan have slipped out of the house unseen? Perhaps he left when Flint was looking through the spyglass in the carriage house. Otherwise, he could not go unnoticed with his cavalcade of footmen assisting him everywhere.

"Has anyone called since I went out?"

"Lord Bixby came, and Lady Kilver, too. Neither of them wanted to stay. Lady Caro dined alone. She is worried about you, My Lady. Go to her at once. Not good to live in fear."

"I agree."

"Here is a message from Cook. She went to bed after waiting two hours for you. I advised her to write her business, but as she cannot put pen to paper of her own accord, I wrote it for her as I did the last time."

"Very good, Flint. You are a boon to us all."

Tricia read by the girandole on the landing.

Your Ladyship,
The storeroom has been trussed up again. Worse this time. No servants admit anything.

In truth,
Cook

"Is that you, Tricia?" called Lady Caro, the light from her candle illuminating her concerned face. She padded down the steps in her night rail and lace-edged cap, her auburn curls hanging to her shoulders.

Tricia ran up to meet her, grasping her hands. "I hope you aren't upset that I've been gone. I've been on my father's ship!" she said excitedly. "We got the Captain to declare everything. The ship is bursting with merchandise from other lands. We caught Mrs. Willoughby smuggling lace and tobacco with pig bladders full of rum under her skirt! And the Customs men are firing at the runners!"

Lady Caro threw up her hands. "Goodness! What a town this is! London is but a peaceful pasture to it. My dear, what cold hands. Come, you are wind-blown as can be. How did your curls ever stay on?"

Tricia laughed. "Are they still on? That's a relief."

Lady Caro said, as they reached Tricia's chamber, "Would you believe it? That stubborn Duke wouldn't even admit the surgeon when he arrived!"

"He wouldn't?" Tricia smiled. "I know why. He wasn't here. Did you see him leave?"

"Leave? He's been holed up in his bedchamber all afternoon and evening."

"No, he hasn't. I saw him in Earnshaw's coble."

"I do not understand. Rupert said—"

"Rupert was left behind to make everyone think

Rowan was in his room," said Tricia. She picked up her candlestick. "We will confront him with his subterfuge later, but now I'm going down to check on this cellar business. Something strange is going on. Read this letter."

"I questioned the servants about that already," said Lady Caro. "Everyone looked afraid, but none sounded guilty."

"I must investigate."

"I'm coming with you," said Lady Caro.

As soon as they unlocked the door to the storeroom under the kitchen, cold air wafted at them. Tricia saw a door close at the far end. She grabbed her aunt's arm. "Did you see that? A man was there!"

Lady Caro stood transfixed, her candle illuminating her worried face. "We must be very cautious."

Tricia, on the other hand, felt emboldened from the events of the evening. As she moved bravely between wooden boxes, her flounce caught on one of the crates. When she pulled it loose, the cover clattered off. Inside were rows of red apples just as she had seen on the ship. "A-ha, isn't this curious! My cellar is, indeed, a smuggler's storehouse, Aunt!"

She hurried to the door in the far shadows. Before she touched it, it flung open, and in plunged someone bearing a large bundle. One end was ripped, and Tricia saw the sheen of silk. The bundle lowered, and the man rising with his lantern was Lord Kilver.

"No!" she cried involuntarily.

He whirled, his eyes glittering in horrified

surprise upon her. "What are you doing here?"

"What are *you* doing here? You can't smuggle goods into my house!" she cried.

"*Your* house? Can't I? Nay, nay, I'm your guardian, so it's mine."

She took one look at his determined eyes and ran.

Dodging stacked crates, he chased her, yelling, "You think you own this place? You're not even of age! I'm going to put some sense into you once and for all!"

As she hurried fearfully around stacks of goods, she snatched two of the apples to hand, and threw one at his head. It hit him with a hard *crack*. He grabbed his forehead and swore.

"*Good*, Tricia!" cried Lady Caro. "Come quick! We can lock him in if you hurry!"

Kilver was not downed by any means. His eyes glinted evilly as he lunged after Tricia. She threw the other wooden apple at close range. It knocked him on the nose, but he climbed over a box, wrenched away her candlestick, and had her in a vise-like grip before she could squeak or run.

"You meddler!" he expelled, spitting into her ear. "I bet I have *you* to thank for all my troubles!" He shook her, and pushed her against the wall and spat, "I'll get you once and for all!"

Tricia, wild-eyed, grappled and struck him repeatedly for all she was worth.

Lady Caro stumbled through the barrels, her leaping candle flame lighting Kilver's bulging neck veins. The grip he had on Tricia's gown cut the neckline into her skin as he shook her, but the well-made garment would not rip.

"Stop that!" screeched Lady Caro, kicking at his rump with woefully soft slippers. "Help! *Help!*" she shrieked over her shoulder. "Servants!"

Kilver shoved her away, barking, "Begone, woman! Hush up, or your turn's coming. You high and mighty ladies will taste what crossing me has earned you!" He tripped Tricia with his boot, and she fell among the stores.

She added her shouts to Lady Caro's, and kicked him viciously so that he couldn't get near her.

Lady Caro scurried in the background, her light casting shadows to jump.

Tricia heard a crackle. She saw a flare of light. Suddenly Kilver jerked back and looked wildly around. The man's hair was on fire! As it flared up, he looked like the very Devil. He swiped madly at his head, screeching diabolically, but to no avail. The fire flickered higher and higher, snapping along his oily hair like the fireworks in Hyde Park. It was the most fearful sight Tricia had ever seen.

She backed away like lightning from the ghoulish furor in his eyes.

"Come, Tricia! Away!" shouted Lady Caro with a terrified edge to her voice.

Kilver, desperately gyrating, grabbed at Tricia's gown and buried his flaming hair into it, screeching in agony and batting the material over his head.

Tricia drew up her legs in fright. "My flounce is on fire!"

Lady Caro grabbed Tricia, pushed her over, and ripped at the ties down her back. "Get out of this dress—quick! Pull your arms out."

Kilver, with the fire now lessening on his charred scalp, beat out the flames from the gown and from his pantaloons, and let flow a string of invectives.

Air flowed into the room suddenly and a shape moved at the open door.

Tricia gasped. "Run, Aunt! Someone else is here." She looked back as they fumbled toward the kitchen door. "Stop, Aunt! It's Rowan!

Kilver shot a hand into his coat and pulled out a pistol. Before Tricia could cry out in warning, a report nearly split their eardrums.

"No!" she heard herself scream over and over. "Rowan! Rowan!" Smoke burned her eyes.

The Duke stood with a gun in his hand, his eyes pinned on Kilver.

Kilver looked helplessly at his right hand in which his pistol loosened from his bloody fingers and clattered to the stone floor.

"Tricia! Did he harm you?" The Duke's words were soft and deadly in the aftermath of the reverberating shot.

"Yes! He always harms me!" she cried, watching Kilver. "Take his gun away!"

Kilver inched toward it, reaching with his left hand while his right hand bled in spurts.

Rowan dived full-length and slammed away Kilver's gun until it ricocheted off the back wall.

Lady Caro ran, knocking things over, and scooped it up. "Is it loaded?" she asked and pointed the barrel at Kilver.

His eyes were wild and he didn't reply.

She said, "I'll test it, then." Boldly, she cocked it at him.

"No! Don't! Of course it's loaded!" he yelled.

"Oh, Duke," he hooted, "I thought you said you couldn't walk. So how is it you're here and on your feet, shooting at me?"

"I am a great deal better, thanks to God and Lady Tricia's ministrations. Now, Lady Caro, you may follow this demon with that weapon ready in your hand. Tricia, please open that door and call Rupert in."

With a thrill of energy she sprang to pull the iron ring in the door. The smell of earth pervaded the tunnel. Rupert appeared at her call, and hastily tied Kilver's wrists behind his back with one of the silk bale cords as Rowan instructed.

"Get your hands off me!" Kilver spat over his shoulder, fighting to get away, but Rupert continued to drag him by the underarms despite his skinny-legged kicks. "Lionel!" Rupert called as they approached a stout door.

It opened and Lionel appeared.

"Help me with this blackguard." Whereupon both footmen secured the snarling Kilver with relish.

Rowan asked, "Are the Customs Men in sight?"

Lionel replied, "They just arrived, Your Grace. I'm glad you caught this!"

"Customs Men!" Kilver mocked. "How did you get them here?"

The Duke said, "I've been busy. You expected you had the 'all clear' in this town, since I was stuck in my Bath chair, didn't you?"

Kilver's voice shook with rage as he snapped, "You can't do anything to me, Rowan! I'm a Baron!"

Lionel cheerfully shoved him along the tunnel.

Rowan said, "Your crimes are so many and so serious that you will be stopped, Lord Kilver. You will be tried in Westminster Abbey by a host of Peers. Until then, you will lodge in the Tower of London. It is all arranged."

Kilver gave a mighty lunge of his body, trying to free himself, but the two footmen held him.

Tricia, carrying a lantern behind them, was worried about Rowan's legs. What command he held over them under these dire circumstances. It truly was phenomenal.

"Stefan, are you there?" Rowan called as they entered the cellar of the carriage house. It was chock-full of casks and crates.

"Yes, Your Grace." Stefan plunged out of the shadows.

"What about Theodore?"

"Here, Your Grace." He promptly appeared from another tunnel which let in a draught of sea air.

"Alert them now," directed Rowan.

The Preventative Men were hallooed by Theodore. They trooped up a track in the cliff side, apparently having climbed from their boats on the shore.

The Bay Magistrate, with two of his men, responded to Rowan's tattoo on the ceiling. They hastily clumped down the steps from the carriage house, with Flint, wide-eyed, in their wake.

How, wondered Tricia, had Rowan gotten all of these forces assembled in time? Her heart swelled with admiration and monumental gratitude. She stood in Lady Caro's embrace, shivering in her chemise. She stared as if through a daze at Lord Kilver, his head a charred field of different lengths of singed hair or horrid flame-red patches of none.

"Oh, my loving Aunt!" she whispered. "You were brilliant! However did you think to set his hair on fire? It saved me!"

"Oh dear Tricia, I got the hair-burning idea from Jewel."

CHAPTER 33

The Horseman

Tricia woke early the next morning to the loud mewling of the sea gulls. She sat up and stretched her arms toward her lace canopy. She stopped suddenly, for she caught sight of something through one of her long windows. A dark horse cantered past the climbing roses. She had only a glimpse of the horse's tail before it dropped out of sight at the cliff's edge.

"There he is again!" She scrambled out of bed. Without waking Sarah, she threw on a sprigged wrapper and hastened downstairs. She almost bumped into Stefan coming around the corner from the Duke's rooms.

"I must see him!" she said.

"You cannot go in there just now, My Lady. Terribly sorry."

"Why can't I?"

"Because . . . because it's not proper, Your Ladyship," he replied, looking at her attire.

Tricia hugged her frilly wrapper over her nightgown more modestly and said, "I *will* go in."

* * *

Rowan lifted a hand in greeting to Lord Bixby. He beckoned him to the table he occupied in the corner of the Bay Hotel's dining room just as he was tucking into a heap of eggs and a salmon steak. "Right on time," he said. "What did you find out from Lady Flitcroft's steward, Bix?"

"Can I swig some of that blackberry juice? I'm ravenous."

"Surely." Rowan passed him the crystal decanter, emptied his water goblet into a violet plant on the table, and passed the glass to Bixby. "I'll order you breakfast. Tell me: where have you been since the wee hours? You have too much dirt on your breeches to have slept."

Bixby quenched his thirst with a long drink. He smiled and related excitedly, "After you told me what occurred in Tricia's cellar, I rode over to Fylingstone, that estate of Kilver's. Since Kilver was carted off to the Tower of London, I thought I could check on what he's been doing at Fylingstone lately. Lady Flitcroft's spineless steward was jumping into a dogcart when I galloped into the drive, so I grabbed him and put out his lights." Bixby grinned proudly.

Rowan applauded. "You are a game one."

"Then I stormed the place, showing my dagger to the porter. He finally agreed to let me see where Kilver kept his ledgers because I told him his master was never coming back, but that Lady Kilver was, so he better not think of looting the place. I found a new shipment of wine in the cellars, and ropes of tobacco galore. That's all that reached Fylingstone so far. I wrote it all down and delivered the list to the Customs Office. They sure are a-buzz over there."

"Excellent!"

"Oh, and I left Kilver's ledgers with Flint. He was shedding tears and ranting about what happened to Lady Tricia last night when Kilver attacked her. How horrible! I'm so thankful you were there in time to save her."

Rowan said, "Thanks to God for that! But prime work on your part in tracking down Lady Flitcroft's smuggling role with Kilver. Lady Tricia will appreciate all your cleverness and quick action." Rowan wondered if her gratitude would take the same form toward Bixby as her embrace and tender words to himself last night. He sincerely hoped not. He could still see her luminous eyes sparkling with tears when she kissed his cheek, saying, "Rowan, you were wonderful! I will thank you all my life."

"That's one beautiful ship, by the way," Bixby was saying, thinking he was following Rowan's unseeing gaze. *The White Dove* lay at anchor on a gleaming blue sea, her dark hull graced by a white figurehead.

Rowan murmured, "It isn't every young Lady who finds herself heiress to such an item."

"Or to all that went with it," said Bixby wryly.

"Tricia has been through a great deal."

"She sure held up well."

The Duke lifted the dome off a dish and served Bixby a baked apple smelling of cinnamon. "What are you planning to do now, Bix? Back to London soon, I expect?"

His friend flushed and looked uncomfortable. "I don't rightly know when I'm going back."

Rowan lifted his brows a fraction and said, "I may see you before I leave, or I may not. Stay well, and accept my gratitude for all your help, Bix."

Bixby's head bowed and he said, "It's nothing. You know we would both do anything for Tricia."

* * *

Rowan's bed was empty.

"I *knew* it!" squeaked Tricia.

Stefan had the grace to look abashed.

"I do not appreciate being fobbed off, and will tolerate it no longer, Stefan! As mistress of this house, I request that you keep me honestly informed when I ask you direct questions."

"Yes, My Lady. But His Grace, who I work for," he emphasized, "told us last week that whenever he left by the hidden panel in the floor, we were to say he was not to be disturbed."

"Last week was last week! The danger is over now, and the reason he did that was to keep Kilver from knowing he was out and about. I'm sure the Duke does not mean for you to keep telling *me* fibs."

"I suppose not, My Lady, but I'll have to ask him."

Tricia gave a long-suffering sigh. "Where is he now? The truth!"

"Out. Meeting Lord Bixby at the Bay Hotel, Your Ladyship."

"I see. Thank you. And Stefan," she said, shutting the Duke's sitting room door so they could talk alone, "will you please tell me why you have been so dour toward me these past weeks? All the other footmen show better attitudes and answer me pleasantly. What is the trouble with you?"

His pale eyelashes flickered and his eyes did not meet hers.

"Please. I want to know."

"Your Ladyship, it's just that when you were a page and I jeered at you and wrestled you, and all that unspeakable stuff, I had no idea you weren't a lad."

"Well, good. That means my disguise worked."

Stefan eyed her with chagrin. "I beg to differ with you, My Lady. It wasn't good, because I thought you were a very good, honest boy, and I was a little envious of how the Duke took such a liking to you and all. You took the shine off of us footmen. I wanted to squash you; to put you in your place."

"Really?" said Tricia.

"Your Ladyship, I don't think it was right for you to cavort with us like that, pretending you were of our class when you are so far above us. That was hard to countenance after we found out."

"So that's it." Tricia eyed him up and down in his casual Robin Hood's Bay attire of tweed coat, fawn breeches, and knee boots. "That's what's been bothering you?"

"Yes, My Lady. Will you forgive me for all I did against you? The butter? And barging in on you in your . . . bath?" He flushed all the way to his neck. "I don't know how you put up with me."

* * *

When Tricia had dressed for the day, she skimmed down the staircase and told Flint she would take a jaunt on the cliff, for it was a glorious, cloudless day with delicious air to breathe.

"Aye-yi! My Lady is going out alone? Mustn't go! Not alone!"

She assured him that she would only go a short distance, not even past her property. "Since Lord Kilver is in shackles and probably close to the Tower of London by now, I feel safe."

"My Lady," called the housekeeper, striding purposefully toward her. Something weighted down her apron, which she held up at the corners.

"What do you have there, Mrs. Chandler?"

"Cook wants Your Ladyship to see what was down in that storeroom. I have never heard of such a thing in my life." She indicated the shiny red apples.

Tricia took one and examined the realistically-painted wood. "I knew these weren't real as soon as I threw one at Lord Kilver. What are they for?"

"One cracked, Your Ladyship. Maybe from your throwing it at the blackguard. There, it's that top one. I think you will want to examine it."

Tricia pulled pieces out of the splintered apple. Bits of wood sprinkled out. When she had a hole, she smelled the aromatic contents and handed the apple to Flint, who was nearly skipping in suspense.

"It's tea!" he declared, his eyes revolving as he savored the mouth-watering scent. "Exceedingly fine tea!"

"What sophisticated deception is practiced in these smuggling runs!" Tricia exclaimed, "Thank you, Chandler." She told her to muster her servants as well as Rowan's, and make it their priority to record all the contraband. She would not go into her cellar to check the goods herself. She wanted to stay away until it was whitewashed and fixed with sconces and shelves for Cook's pickles and fruit preserves. Then, perhaps, when it looked like a bright and different place, the memories would fade.

Last night seemed like a nightmare, not reality at all, for today there were veils of cloud lace in the high blue sky. Kittiwakes called from the grass at the cliff's edge. The lines of wash barely twitched down in Robin Hood's Bay, and the multicolored cobles winked across the glistening blue sea. With the morning sun on her face, Tricia clasped her hands, and her heart opened in thanks to God for saving her from so many evils.

At the edge of the cliff, she descended a narrow path. Pressed into the soil were the horseshoe prints she was looking for. She followed them down onto the ledge paralleling the ocean which dropped away dizzyingly beneath. It reminded her of her descent with Rowan from Flint's cave, although this one was wider and safer.

The path led her to a dug-out tunnel, which was concealed from below by bushes with wilted leaves. Someone had obviously erected them to hide the man-made opening in the cliff side. This was where all those goods had been passed into her cellars. Kilver must have had the tunnel dug while he kept her house locked up.

No more would he control her! He had been trundled off in a tightly-guarded coach which the Magistrate had waiting at Rowan's orders. The Magistrate said Kilver lashed out at them all and declared it was Nadine Vavasour, Lady Flitcroft, who had got him into the smuggling operation, and that it was all her fault.

Rowan had laughed out loud, along with other men.

Paused before the tunnel entrance, Tricia shaded her eyes and studied her ship, lying at anchor so prominently in the Bay. She could see movement aboard her, and cobles in tandem unloading her goods. She felt great enthusiasm for the new project before her. To learn where goods were being purchased and sold—now that Napoleon was confined to St Helena and ships dared to sail to the shores of France—would prove enlightening. Could she someday take a voyage? Why not?

Who could she take with her? The fun of being with Isidore Hobart came to mind, but such a plan was unlikely to be approved by Isidore's protective mother. Lady Caro would possibly like to be Tricia's partner in adventure, but would that satisfy? Her aunt was a dear, and Tricia loved her, but the figure who loomed before her mind's eye was the Duke.

She sighed. Wouldn't it be heavenly to walk the rich planks of that deck arm-in-arm with him? –to sit across from His Grace in the elegance of that richly decorated dining room, partaking of fresh delicacies from the sea? And to occupy that stateroom of gleaming teak with the massive bed which only lacked cascades of romantic mosquito netting to diffuse the candlelight . . .

Here she had to close the door on the Duke lying in the bed just as he had lain at the inn in Huntingdon when she had worked the pain out of his back muscles.

A black horse galloped along the wet sand from Bay Town toward the base of the dizzying cliff which she had just descended about a third of the way. A dark Bay Town cap and coat, black pantaloons, and black boots were all she could make out of the rider from her vantage point. She watched tufts of sand rise from the hoofs until the rider urged the horse to the base of the cliff path. It was a steep climb in some places, and when they reached a jutting outcrop, the horse stumbled and a large clod of the cliff went tumbling down, rolling with increasing speed.

The man stopped the horse and slipped back over the tail, for the track was too narrow to dismount from the side. He spoke, and the animal's ears pricked. He slapped his mount on the flank and the horse charged up the path straight toward Tricia.

Watching its powerful muscles and wild eyes, she was thankful she had a place to duck into: the tunnel entrance. The laboring animal vaulted by her, warm and sweating, four feet kicking dirt all over her pink gown as it passed her.

The black cap brim hid the man's face as he walked up the path.

She stared intently, hardly breathing as she waited.

He hummed and looked up at the sky. It was the Duke!

He remained unaware of her. Fascinated, she watched him smile to himself as he strode up the slope with nothing odd about his gait whatsoever.

She must get to the bottom of this. She shook out her gown and stepped into the path to meet him.

He halted in surprise. "Tricia!" His white smile flashed and his eyes sparkled, making him so handsome that her knees threatened to give way.

Nevertheless she placed her hands on her hips and called, "Duke! Are you walking?"

He paused at speaking range. "Why, yes."

"How is it possible?"

He laughed low. "Happiness has cured me."

"I cannot believe you."

"Attribute it to the exercise, then. Either way, I have you to thank. After God, of course, who did it all through you. You see before you a man bursting with thanks."

Tricia backed against the wall of the cliff and gazed up at him, for he now stood before her, shading her from the sun.

She wanted to be here alone with him, and yet she dared not be. She felt dizzy because her Duke stood so near, gazing down into her eyes. She breathed, "Could it truly have been the exercise? You didn't do enough of them."

"I did more on my own in the privacy of my room," he admitted with a smile. "Lots more; ask my long-suffering footmen."

"Good for them! Good for you, I mean."

He went on, "But your care for my affliction was all I needed. Your touches, both physical and of the heart, pulled me out of my inability to feel."

Knowing she ventured into deep waters, she asked, "To feel what, Your Grace?"

He grasped her to him by her waist, then his arms gathered her about the shoulders, then her face felt his touch. "Love. I love you! Oh, Tricia!"

He kissed what was nearest: her forehead.

While her mind reeled in pleasure and her heart soared with love, he undid the ribbon under her chin and pushed the bonnet off her head.

As she watched his eyes glow into hers with that love he spoke of, she whispered from a bursting heart, "Oh, how *much* I love you, dear Duke!"

"You do?" He took in that declaration for an instant, beamed all over his face, and then kissed her.

Tricia let her love for him pour forth in all its beauty, pain, and pleasure. She sighed as they parted for breath. "Rowan! Do you really love me that much?"

"Oh, much more!" he assured her, and kissed her again.

CHAPTER 34

A Time for Lace

"Come here, Tricia, quick!" said the Duke suddenly that afternoon. "Bixby's coming up the walk." Rowan reached for her hand and pulled her onto his lap.

"Coward," teased Lady Caro, eyeing the Duke. Her lips had been curved in great satisfaction for hours.

Rowan laughed softly. "Perhaps you think so, Lady Caro, but in truth, I shall save him the pain of asking her again."

Tricia enfolded her fingers lovingly with Rowan's and wondered how Lord Bixby would take this.

Her Duke tightened his arms around her in a way that sent her heart somersaulting.

Lady Caro examined the lace that Lionel had delivered. "Tricia, look. We should use this for your wedding clothes. I am sure it is *Point d' Argentan*, possibly even from Louis XIV's reign! This is the most exquisite stuff I've ever seen."

"I stashed some fine lace in my library in London," remarked Rowan, then dropped his voice to a whisper, "except that it's Bixby's, and he may not like it used on Tricia's trousseau since she's marrying me." He composed his roguish look as

Flint announced their friend.

Lord Bixby lifted his quizzing glass and stared, London style, at Tricia cradled in the arms of the Duke. He blanched white for an instant.

She rose and went to grasp his hand. "Bix, we're so glad to see you."

Rowan asked, "Will you do something for me, my friend?"

As Bixby stood woefully bereft of words, the Duke went on. "I would like you to be my Best Man. You are, you know—the best friend a man could possibly have. Lady Tricia and I are planning a wedding."

"Oh. I see." Bixby shot a forlorn look at Tricia.

Lady Caro inserted, "We wish them very happy, don't we?"

"Yes." Bixby looked beside himself as he rose from kissing Tricia's hand. He shook hands with Rowan, squared his jaw bravely, and said, "I'll be honored to stand by you."

Tricia, feeling choked, said, "Dear Bixby, you are my friend, too, aren't you? I couldn't bear it any other way."

"You know how I feel about you, Tricia. That will never change. Well, actually, it must. Yes, yes, we'll be friends, too." He flashed a smile over her, took up his crop, bowed to Lady Caro, and made a quick exit.

They heard Flint bid His Lordship a good afternoon.

Rowan whistled and met Tricia's troubled gaze.

"Nothing to fret over," said Lady Caro. "There was bound to be an epidemic of love-sickness as soon as you let Tricia out of that page's uniform.

When you get to London, you will have more shattered gentlemen to face. Tricia, I am quite sure you did not lead him to believe you would marry him, did you? You would not have had an exciting marriage. I turned down all the gentlemen who wanted to marry me because they were too dull."

"Oh Aunt, I don't know if I led him on or not. I told him I liked him, but that his proposal took me very much by surprise. And the second time I told him I was still thinking."

Rowan gave a short laugh. "If a woman told me she only liked me, and was still thinking after my second proposal, I would see the light."

"What about Jewel?" Lady Caro asked, piercing the Duke with a most inquisitive stare.

"We never discussed love, or even like."

"Ah yes, you felt compelled to rescue her from ruin. I was grateful to you in our hour of crisis, but Rowan, how could you face such an enormous sacrifice?" Lady Caro marveled.

The Duke took Tricia's hand in his and drew her to the long window where the white roses danced in the breeze. She watched his dark eyes soften as he answered Lady Caro's question. "I could not face it, Lady Caro. Not with Tricia lodged so firmly in my heart."

Tricia's lips parted in wonder as she gazed at his dignified profile. Lodged in his heart?

"I prayed to God for some way of release. He let me crash against the solid rock, you might say, and the result was what ultimately drove Jewel away."

Lady Caro sighed dramatically.

Tricia felt her hand lifted slowly to Rowan's lips. She lifted her other to his thick hair, and her heart melted to think that this wonderful man would really be hers, all hers, in four weeks.

Lady Caro said, "True love is *so* inspiring. Perhaps I should give myself a chance with the newest batch of widowers in town."

As they laughed and encouraged her, she said thoughtfully, "But that's my Jewel, sticking up for her vanity as always. That girl will get what she wants in the end: a body in trousers with showy carriages and an opera box. But what's in his head and in his heart may not be to her liking, poor vapid thing. I shall have to take her under my wing. Her mother is useless."

"Please do, Aunt," urged Tricia.

How would Jewel feel now, with the future stretching before her of visits to the ducal mansion in Park Lane, to witness the lovers there? Tricia could hardly believe the scenario in her daydreams had reversed so magnificently. She told herself never to exult over Jewel's miserable loss.

"Excuse me, My Lady," said Theodore, the footman, from the doorway. "Would this be the doll you were looking for?" He presented Tricia with a well-worn baby doll in a white gown and frilled cap framing its porcelain face. It looked sadly in need of care.

"Yes, this is mine. Wherever did you find it?"

"Lady Kilver just delivered it, My Lady. She said she found it in the study at Fylingstone."

"Lady Kilver was here? This was at Fylingstone?"

"Yes, My Lady, but she would not come out of her carriage."

Lady Caro said, "Likely she dares not come for mortification over all that her husband has done against you."

Tricia murmured, "Poor Aunt Kilver. Let's visit her tomorrow and tell her our news, Rowan." Suddenly, she said in dismay, "Oh look, my doll's head has been broken off, and glued back on."

Rowan took the doll and examined the crack. "Hmm. Lionel, have those boxes been delivered from Earnshaw yet?"

"What boxes?" asked Tricia curiously.

"I had Earnshaw and Earnie take a look at the Mulgrave Castle Inn to check if Jane Bell had received any goods from *The White Dove*. Earnie reported that they found the cache behind the stone wall stashed with contraband. The first box was infant dolls, he said, and he didn't know why they were so important to hide."

"Really!" Tricia said, musing.

Stefan carried in a wooden crate which he set on the tea table. When the cover was pried off, a sweet scent rose into the room. There were scores of porcelain-headed baby dolls in rows, dressed in cheap muslin gowns.

Tricia gave one to her aunt, one to Rowan, and examined one herself.

Rowan asked, "Have you your scissors by you, Lady Caro?" With them in hand, he carefully snipped the threads holding a head to a cloth body. From within the head, he pulled out cotton lint, and they heard something clink. He peered inside the neck and shook the doll's head over Tricia's lap. A half-dozen tiny glass bottles fell onto her blue gown.

Lady Caro gasped and drew near. They exclaimed over the dainty stoppers and the labels that said *Parfum Vanille Lavande.*

Tricia uncorked one and waved it languidly under their noses. "What a lovely combination: vanilla and lavender! Mmmm!"

Lady Caro murmured, "Costly, I suspect. Do you suppose all of these dolls' heads contain this much perfume?"

"We shall declare it, but what will we do with all of it?" Tricia asked Rowan.

"Keep as many as you like," he said, "and give the rest as bridesmaids' gifts. If there are too many for you to save, you could give some to the ladies at our wedding reception in London." He winked at Lady Caro.

"Wedding reception in *London?*" With a probing stare at his charming grin, Tricia said, dimpling, "Dear Duke, we need to talk."

* * *

They took his traveling coach to the moors, with only Stefan on the perch and Shepperton on the box.

Tricia sighed and said, "The freedom of being betrothed! No chaperone."

"Yes, what bliss." He gathered her closer by her waist, and she snuggled her arm around his neck.

"Oh, Rowan, where did you go on that black horse? I saw you in the mist once and wondered who the horseman could be."

"I went to spy on Kilver. I had Mr. Richard alert the Customs Men with our plan. Earnshaw recruited from amongst the fisher folk and the Magistrate's crew. Our aim was to catch Kilver in the act so we could turn him in. No one in this town dared to touch him otherwise."

"They all followed your lead? Rowan, you are so good for this place. Aren't you glad you're a Duke?"

He squinted at her between his black lashes.

When she squeaked in mock fright, he grasped her to him and said against her ear, "You and your *Duke, Duke!* Just wait until you discover what being a *Duchess! Duchess!* is all about." He pulled her face to his and kissed her.

Tricia wanted to float on the waves of love that the ducal lips evoked, and she did so for an interval. Finally she opened her heavy eyelids. She put her hands on his broad shoulders to keep him from kissing her more. "What about that lovely horse? You sent him off running. Isn't he lost on the moors by now?"

"He's mine," said the Duke. "I had him brought over from my estate in Lancashire. He's clever, and already knows the way to the stable at the Bay Hotel." He caressed her cheek. "They have plentiful nosebags there."

Tricia twined her hands around his neck. "What estate?"

"One I have near Burnley, where I keep nice horses and good dogs."

"I love nice horses and good dogs. What else is there?"

"Oh, a house at the end of an avenue of trees, good tenants, and sheep to keep the park clipped close."

"My dear Duke, it sounds ideal and . . . secluded." Tricia, realizing the longing she had conveyed, buried her face into her beloved's shirt front.

There was a smile in his voice as he asked, "Would you like me to take you there?"

"Yes, please. When we're married." Tricia could hardly believe she had all of these prospects ahead of her.

"Where would you like to be married?"

"Not in London, if you don't mind?"

"No St George's Hanover Square?"

She eyed him and shook her head slowly.

Rowan grinned and suggested, "If you want the wedding near Soaring Gables, we could consider the church you constructed in the sand as a child, the one with over a hundred steps. Is the truth spoken there?"

"Oh yes. How nice that you, too, should think of Whitby church. For some time, I have thought it would be the most romantic thing imaginable to ascend those 199 steps in a bridal gown. Now I see it as a grand arrival for a Duke." She poked him and added, "With maidens emerging from the ruined Abbey nearby to shower you with bracken and heather."

"But couldn't I watch from the top as you ascend the steps with your lace veil trailing for miles behind you?"

"We do have a lot of lace."

"I will be ready to come and pick you up halfway, and carry you to the top, where you will marry me."

Smiling irrepressibly, she added with deep satisfaction, "Now you can traverse those steps after all. But won't you want to have your London friends, like Beau Brummell, at our wedding?"

Rowan said, "I will be pleased as punch to inform

Beau Brummell that his protégée waltzed out of his proprietary arms and into mine for good, but I don't feel a need to have him at the wedding."

Suddenly looking concerned, Rowan asked, "Were you cut by any ladies after the Hobart ball?"

"Yes, I felt a little persecution, but Isidore and her mother were friendly in the following days. Not to worry, Rowan, for when I am yours, everyone will receive me. Whether you admit it or not, you are the darling of Society. You *were*, I mean." She grinned and added, "Since wealthy Dukes are only good for hooking into marriage, you are now worthless." She smiled gloriously and whispered, "But worth more than the world to me."

"Why, thank you. That reception in London, which Lady Caro insists on giving us, is unavoidable, I suppose?" he murmured into her curl.

"Reception?" She looked up, not daring to move her lips any closer to his, though the temptation was great. "I suppose we could survive one reception for her sake. We'll be married, and can face the dizzying throngs together."

"That's how I feel, Tricia. It will be a pleasure I never dreamed of to show them the beautiful woman who is marrying me. After that, we won't have to go much amongst people unless we choose to. We can live here sometimes, and at my two country houses in spring and summer, and in London when Parliament convenes in November. With your ship for diversion, we'll have a lot to keep us occupied. What do you think of these ideas?"

She could stand it no longer. She squeezed him

round the neck and kissed him what she intended to be a quick one on the lips. But, as the wheels left the road and pulled off into the heather and halted, Rowan had become so attached to the kissing idea that he only halted when they heard a knock on the window.

Tricia sprang dizzily away.

Stefan opened the coach door. "Your Grace wanted to walk?"

They stepped down to the purple moor. When they had gained the privacy of distance, Rowan said, "Tricia, I must confess that I have something I am ashamed of."

"Whatever could it be?"

"Having my footmen deny you access to my rooms, making you assume I was asleep was deceptive, I know." He captured her hands in his. "I'm sorry."

"You were wise to keep Kilver thinking you were stuck there, Rowan, so I understand. But how did you leave to go roaming without being seen by Flint or anyone?"

"My dear, there's a stairwell down from the corner under the armoire in my room, didn't you know? I'm sure Kilver did. I believe he came in to use that staircase to prepare the cellar and tunnels for the arrival of the ship that day. He was undoubtedly furious to find me lodged in that room with the armoire solidly over his trap door. That's one reason he itched to kick me. He came to the cellar one night and barricaded the door at the bottom with crates of molasses so I couldn't get through that way myself. I sent my footmen to move them."

"So that's who messed up Cook's pantry?"

"I was especially concerned that he would try to weasel into your chamber that way. Stefan or Lionel have slept at the end of your corridor armed with pistols every night."

"They have?" Astonishment and gratitude swelled her heart. She walked toward Stefan and said, "I am touched by your nightly vigils, Stefan. Thank you! I shall never forget your good care of me."

Stefan bowed to her, and turned to leave them alone, his shoulders at a proud tilt.

Rowan said, "He doesn't know it, but tomorrow he receives his promotion to the exalted position of valet with a hefty increase in wages."

"I'm glad," she said as they walked arm-in-arm toward the cliff's edge. "I was so frightened when you went missing that day after you kissed me on our way to Flint's cave. I was so mixed up between the glory of that stolen moment of love, and later that day, to the terror of possibly losing you to the Press Gang." She shuddered. "You have been so selfless in attaining all that is good for me. How can I ever deserve you? I can only take you, my darling Duke, as a gift from God."

Rowan pulled her to him and held her cheek against his beating heart. "You are my gift."

Tricia pointed south. Off Robin Hood's Bay, they could see *The White Dove*. She asked, "Do you mind taking her over? There's no sense in the Marquis dipping his oar in if he signs my dowry and everything over to you, is there? My question is: do you want a ship on your hands?"

Rowan shaded his eyes as he squinted out to sea.

"How can I say this? Since this morning when you agreed to marry me, I've harbored many dreams."

She slipped her fingers through his. "What kind of dreams?"

"I am hoping that you and I can make a tour of European capitols. You know, start with Paris, that city of romance, and sail on from port to romantic port."

"Oh yes," breathed Tricia, bright-eyed. "But how will Lady Jewel stand to hear it?"

Rowan grinned sidelong at her. "My lips are sealed. Will you sneak away on some morning tide with me, hmm? Take a magic carpet ride over the waves with me?"

"Smuggle me away, you mean? If only you knew how I long for such illicit doings!" She hugged him and thought of living with His Grace the Duke of Rowan on the ship.

"What is it, Tricia? What brought that special gleam to your eyes?"

She hesitated.

"You're my confidante, remember?"

"Yes. Could we, perhaps, drape the bed in the stateroom with white netting?" She added hastily, "If we sail to warmer climes, we won't want to be bothered by pests." She shot him a dancing look.

The Duke laughed. He pulled her under his cape with one hand and lifted her face with the other. What she saw in his eyes promised an exciting world that had nothing to do with ships or ports.

"Tricia, you may *wear* that netting if you wish. No need to blush, my angel," he added, smiling as he watched her long lashes dip, "for no pests will bother us. I'll put a new lock on the door."

Tricia's imagination soared.

"I, too, have a wish," he added. "I long for a repeat performance of something I cannot forget. It was the best night of my life."

Her heart thumped. "What night was that?"

"When you gave me that expert back rub. Might I have another . . . someday?"

She giggled. "When we are married in four weeks, it will be my pleasure to give you an encore."

His face lit in anticipation. "Four weeks? That's forever. Let's be married tomorrow."

"Rowan, I can only marvel at you," said Tricia, distracting him from that line of thought, for it was a well-known fact that, by law, they needed three weeks of Marriage Banns called in church before they could wed.

"What are you marveling at now?" he asked, taking her hand and merrily leading her to the coach that stood in silhouette against the pink sky.

"I'm marveling over the joys you have given me, and all the striving you have done to save me, Rowan. I am no longer afraid of anything!"

She glowed with love as her admiring Duke smiled into her eyes. She breathed, "You could only have done those things because you have a hero's heart."

The End

Mellyora Ashley

Thank You from the Author

My dear Reader,

Thank you for reading this book! I loved writing A HERO'S HEART, and hope you had an invigorating adventure with Tricia and the Duke.

If you enjoyed the book, I am delighted! I would be so grateful if you, my reader, could help me in any of these ways:

1. **Tell your friends** about the book.
2. **Post a review** on your book store's website.
3. **Ask your library to order it.**
4. **Buy FORBIDDEN ARABELLE,** or any of my other books.
5. **Visit https://mellyoraashley.com to sign up** on my contact page for email announcements of my next books.

I appreciate your support so much!
Your Kindred Spirit,

Mellyora Ashley

Scan this QR code to visit Author's website: mellyoraashley.com

BONUS: Read on for a preview of

FORBIDDEN ARABELLE

Georgian Sister Series, Book 1

London, 1752

CHAPTER 1

A Coach Full of Men

"Do you know who *I am?*" Lady Bastwicke demanded, her close-set eyes snapping in fury.

The stolid coachman, wrapped to the eyes in a snow-encrusted scarf, merely stared defiance at her, dangerously uninterested in who she was.

Lady Bastwicke enunciated as though explaining to an idiot, "*I* am the Viscountess Bastwicke! You must take me to London, and this young lady with me."

Arabelle, warming her hands at the inn's

fireplace, marveled at her mother's aggressiveness. Could she really force a stranger to do her bidding by such means?

The coachman eyed the Viscountess from under his crop of grey eyebrows and declared, "I cannot do it, Madam."

Lady Bastwicke shoved a chair noisily over the floorboards and hissed, "What insubordination! Obey your betters, and open up two spots in that coach at once!"

Arabelle lifted her fur muff to her face, hiding her chagrin. Her mother could have asked this coachman gently for the favor of a ride. How would she ever gain his cooperation in this abrasive manner? After all, he was not one of her servants to command.

The man drank deeply from a tankard, and slammed it onto the refectory table. "I told you, Madam, that I have three gentlemen, a tailor, and no extra seats!"

Undeterred, Lady Bastwicke put her beak of a nose to the frosty window, eyed the situation outside, and whirled to point at him before he escaped. "That commodious vehicle holds more than four persons, surely! Why do you even consider taking those people—a tailor, you say!—if not us?"

"In this blizzard, few stages dare to run," he threw back. "A military man must return to Woolwich according to his Captain's orders so I put myself at his service, seeing I have three teams of horses between here and London. But other folk, especially women," he spat, eyeing the grandiose specimen before him, "should stay put!"

Lady Bastwicke exploded, "I am not folk! Or a mere woman! I am a Viscountess, man! My outriders tried and failed to dislodge my own coach from a snow bank. You stay and listen to me! It is already past midday, and the snow falls thicker than ever. I demand seats in your coach for myself and my daughter. She is already nineteen, and must—I repeat must—enter London Society this week, do you hear? There is nothing else to be done!"

The coachman snorted and cast the Viscountess a thoroughly disgusted look. "Enter Society! Not in my coach!" he growled, and took his last bites of bread and Cheddar.

Lady Bastwicke, yanking on her orange kid gloves, told Arabelle icily, "Let us be off." To the man, she said, "I already ordered my outriders to put my trunks in your boot."

At that, he turned menacing and threw his muffler across his neck, flinging chunks of ice over her. "Then I shall order my guard to toss them into a snow bank!" he roared into her face. He stomped across the uneven planks of the common room, making them vibrate, and plunged out the arched door into the white world. The door slammed and shuddered behind him.

Arabelle hurried to her quivering mother, whose small green eyes spat fire as she furiously swiped melted snow from her chin.

"Listen, Madam." Arabelle was forming a daring idea. "I shall go and ask the soldier who hired the coach if he is willing to accommodate us. If he is, what objection can the coachman then have? He will make a higher profit, if he can squeeze us in."

Lady Bastwicke pushed Arabelle to the door with sudden determination. "Go! Ask, of all things! Be forceful. After all, if you had not insisted on breaking our trip to see your useless Aunt Claracilla, we would not be in this fix."

Arabelle winced. "Yes, Mother."

"You've forgotten already. Call me Madam, not Mother."

This, Arabelle had discerned, was to keep the public thinking, whenever possible, that the Viscountess was not old enough to have such a grown daughter. "Yes, Madam. If I do not return, please follow me."

Lady Bastwicke grabbed her arm again, painfully. "Make sure you do not introduce yourself to any men in that coach. We are far above them, and do not forget it. No talking to that military chap beyond asking for space, mind."

"No, Madam."

Out in the quiet world, Arabelle took a deep breath of frosty air. The gold letters on the wine-red *Aynscombe Stage* were nearly covered by the fluffy snow that had fallen during the change of horses. Two wheelers were already in the tracks of the former team, with ostlers hooking their traces. A red-nosed groom held the four collared Percherons that snuffed out puffs of air, their dark manes and tails vivid in the whirling whiteness. Lanterns cast iridescent orbs of light at each corner of the coach with its snow-banked wheel spokes. Arabelle could not see through the steamed windows, but she hoped that the occupants would be more civil than their driver.

The coach door creaked open. Arabelle saw a

gentleman's head emerge. He had sleek, white hair pulled back into a queue at the nape of his well-shaped head. When he turned, she saw a smooth forehead and black brows that marked a dramatic contrast to his white hair. He looked to be in his mid-to upper twenties. Arabelle had never seen such an arresting man, so handsome, vital, and fit. One of Boucher's paintings, which she had admired at a Canterbury exhibition, came close to portraying such a paragon, but this one lived. His midnight blue coat accentuated his wide shoulders and swung past shiny boots as he kicked down the steps. He placed a black three-cornered hat on his head as he spoke to the guard.

That individual held a silver horn. He cupped a hand to his mouth and bellowed, "Coach!" It was the signal for passengers to board.

The moment had come for Arabelle to address the man before her. Surely he was the military personage for whom the coachman ventured forth in such a snowfall. The grandeur of the man's confident bearing made her heart thump. What could she say? She had not envisioned begging for space from a man with such an air of command.

Her mother's words thrummed through her head: *There is nothing else to be done!*

He bent to reenter the vehicle. Soon he would be gone. And there went her mother's outriders, trotting away through the falling snow to deal with the Bastwicke carriage, deeply stuck in a snowdrift.

"Sir?" called Arabelle, hurrying toward the *Aynscombe Stage* despite her qualms.

The man placed a white gauntlet on the doorframe and ducked back out. What a way he had of cocking his head as he searched the whirling snow for who had spoken.

"Sir," she repeated, "would you possibly—" Drawing near, she met his interested look and felt so awestruck that she lost her train of thought.

"Would I possibly . . . what, my beauty?" his voice caressed her.

With astonished pleasure, she asked, "Would you have room in your coach, Sir, for two stranded ladies? We need . . . that is, we would like to reach London tonight." She felt a prick of guilt, for tonight signaled a theatre party that her mother simply had to attend. Arabelle's eyes nevertheless played over his sculpted face with hope.

For a moment he gave her no reply, just looked at her as though drinking her in.

Arabelle gave him a little curtsey. When a horse snorted, she looked up into the man's black-lashed eyes. Was that a twinkle lurking in their blue depths?

"Yes, Miss," he said with feeling. "We certainly have room for *you.*"

She blushed, and felt a dangerous thrill in accepting his offer.

The coach door next to them flew open and slammed against the body, knocking snow down like a waterfall. Within the vehicle, three men's noses turned, and fascinated eyes regarded her.

* * *

The enrapturing of Simon Laurence was quick, and unlike anything he had ever imagined. This dark-haired beauty made him want to know her in every sense of the word. How did she do it? He gazed at her. By the power of a lively, appealing spirit that peeped at him from behind long lashes and a tender blush—that was how. Was she the desired dream that he so badly needed, hovering here before him in the ethereal whiteness? Surely so, for her hazel eyes seemed too fixed upon him in sweet curiosity to be real. But glorious reality hit him sharply in the leg as he backed into the iron coach step.

"Let me enter first and help you up," he said with an elated timbre to his voice.

She glanced toward the inn over her shoulder, and then flashed him a dazzling smile. "Thank you, Sir; you are a most benevolent man. It surprises me to receive such help from a stranger."

Instantly, he wanted to help her more. What incredible fortune had brought this cheer-producing beauty to his hired coach on this unlikely day? "As I said, you are infinitely welcome." He viewed the curves of her face, framed by a burgundy hood with a dark fur lining. The seductive power of her eyebrows alone was enough to cause men to drop what they were doing to appreciate. What, he wondered with racing pulse, did the rest of her form look like beneath the sweep of burgundy cloak?

As soon as she put her trusting hands into his, he felt himself flooded with the need to sing the song, *I have found her! I have found her! The woman my heart doth crave.* But he kept it to himself. He fought to ignore the sick accusation that pierced like a dagger to his midsection. *You already have someone,* it thrust home brutally.

He steadied her on the step. Her slender fingers in pink gloves tightened around his, making him proud that he could protect her from slipping, at least. A pink silk skirt appeared as her cloak parted. He saw one shapely high-heeled pink patten over a matching shoe, and caught a glimpse of her slim ankle in a pink stocking. A swirling gust of snowflakes blew her hood back from her long, dark hair, revealing her graceful neck.

She smiled her thanks at him. Simon's heart did a drum roll as the lantern light glistened on her lips.

The other three men had scrambled aside or half to their feet in the confines of the interior, trying to make space for the dark-browed beauty with the enquiring eyes. They fell to their seats like dominoes as she passed through the doorway. The cool smell of snow came with her, sifting like sugar off the folds of her burgundy cloak. A sprinkling fell onto Simon's glossy boots, and he felt the thrill of privilege.

"Do join us, Mademoiselle," said Sir Pomeroy Chancet, seated inside, his throaty voice throbbing with delight. In his early thirties, the Baronet was full of zest as he exclaimed, "What a glorious treat!"

Simon winced at that gentleman's overt reception, then said, "Sir Pomeroy, why not let the lady face forward?" He gestured that Sir Pomeroy should vacate his place and sit opposite her.

The obtuse Baronet, however, whisked his purple gauntlets off the seat, twitched his rump sidewise, and with an elegant gesture and an acquired French accent, said, "Of course she shall face forward. A window seat, Mademoiselle? 'Tis the most scenic side of the Maidstone-London Road." His red lips grinned widely as he patted the place he had hastily contrived for her next to himself. She sank into it with a grateful smile.

Simon, resuming his former spot on the backward seat opposite her, heard his brother, Radford, clear his throat in curiosity. The other two men looked from her to him and back. Simon veiled his eyes to hide the fact that he wanted to sit next to her as well as they did. As he watched her dipping dark lashes, on which snowflakes lingered, he realized that across from her was by far the best place to be. It would be a rare treat to feast his eyes on her for even a mile.

To think that God had made such a beautiful woman! And all he could do was delight in her presence for the space of a journey.

To buy FORBIDDEN ARABELLE, please visit:
https://mellyoraashley.com

Glossary

These terms were used in the Regency period, and are found in this book.

Barouche-Landau – An expensive four-wheeled carriage drawn by two horses, with two collapsible hoods, one for the front-facing passengers and one for the rear-facing passengers. A smaller version of a landau.

Beaver – A top hat originally made of the beaver's under fur.

Frieze coat – A plain coat in a coarse woolen fabric.

Gansey — A wool sweater for fishermen who required a warm, hard wearing, comfortable garment that resisted sea spray. Coastal towns created identifying ganseys based on their original patterns. They were more complex the farther north the garment spread, with the most complex evolving in Scottish fishing villages.

Haut ton – Exclusive high society.

Little Season – A period of the winter traditionally adopted by the upper echelons of society for a series of fashionable events, especially in London. The most important time was called the Season.

About the Author

Mellyora Ashley enjoyed her job as an executive secretary, but as a few years passed, she longed to finish her romantic novel. Her husband urged her to stay at home, raise their sons, and write. Her first book, A LADY IN DISGUISE, was published by Zebra Kensington in New York.

Besides writing books, she is a playwright, director, and an award-winning costume designer for theater and opera. She was the editor of a monthly Christian publication, and taught a college class called "Write to Delight."

Mellyora enjoys traveling abroad, where she thrills to see the realism of her book research. Visiting and exploring with her friends in many countries, she finds inspiration and stunning locations for her Regency and historical novels.

Mellyora Ashley

This is one of her favorite verses:

> *Whatsoever things are true,*
> *whatsoever things are honest,*
> *whatsoever things are just,*
> *whatsoever things are pure,*
> *whatsoever things are lovely,*
> *whatsoever things are of good report;*
> *if there be any virtue, and*
> *if there be any praise,*
> *think on these things.*
>
> *Philippians 4:8*